DEEP
IN THE
HEART

DEEP IN THE HEART

A Novel

GILBERT MORRIS

DOUBLEDAY LARGE PRINT HOME LIBRARY EDITION

INTEGRITY®

P U B L I S H E R S

Nashville

This Large Print Edition, prepared especially for Doubleday Large Print Home Library, contains the complete, unabridged text of the original Publisher's Edition.

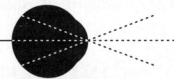

This Large Print Book carries the
Seal of Approval of N.A.V.H.

DEDICATION

To Johnnie, a beloved wife—from Gilbert, a devoted husband.

Almost fifty-five years ago I stood at the altar of a small church and watched a young woman with dark hair and dark eyes come down the aisle—and she was beautiful.

She gave me her hand and I took it, and have never let it go.

The hair is more beautiful than ever, though it's silver now. The eyes are still fresh and sparkling, and she is more beautiful in my eyes now than she was at that moment so long ago.

Thank you for more than half a century of love and joy and faithfulness. Most things in this world change rapidly and are lost; but you are the same as you were when we joined hands and hearts.

The old Book says of the daughters of Job, "And in all the land were no women found so fair as the daughters of Job." In my heart I always read that verse a little differently: "And in all the land was no woman found so fair as my beloved wife, Johnnie."

DEDICATION

To Johnnie, a beloved wife—from Gilbert, a devoted husband.

Almost fifty-five years ago I stood at the altar of a small church and watched a young woman with dark hair and dark eyes come down the aisle—and she was beautiful.

She gave me her hand and I took it, and have never let it go.

The hair is more beautiful than ever, though it's silver now. The eyes are still fresh and sparkling, and she is more beautiful in my eyes now than she was at that moment so long ago.

Thank you for more than half a century of love and joy and faithfulness. Most things in this world change rapidly and are lost; but you are the same as you were when we joined hands and hearts.

The old Book says of the daughters of Job, "And in all the land were no women found so fair as the daughters of Job." In my heart I always read that verse a little differently: "And in all the land was no woman found so fair as my beloved wife, Johnnie."

PART ONE:

ARKANSAS TERRITORY
March-July 1831

CHAPTER
ONE

A stiff March wind from the Midwest swept down through Missouri before dropping over the lip of Arkansas's Ouachita Mountains into the river. Each night, transparent layers of ice crusted the serpentine river but melted during the day as the pale sun reached its zenith. Now at midafternoon a gunpowder gray sky hung over the land, and the hoarse barking of a dog broke the utter stillness of the woods.

A fat gray possum scurried along the riverbank, headed for a large chinquapin oak. But mortality caught up with him as a huge red hound dashed out of the woods and, without breaking stride, opened his enormous jaws and clamped them on the possum's neck. One quick shake of the dog's head, and the neck broke with a distinct snap. The dog dropped the limp body and sat down, his jaws open, his pink tongue lolling out as he panted.

Two boys emerged from the woods, and the shorter one yelped, "Look at that, Brodie! Ol' Anthony Wayne done caught our dinnerfor us!"

The taller of the two did not speak but came and stood beside the dog and the dead possum. At fourteen, Brodie Hardin stood an inch over six feet and was as lean as an oak sapling. His auburn hair poked out from under his limp black felt hat, and his light green eyes glowed with pleasure as he leaned down, roughly caressing the dog's head. "You done good, Anthony Wayne—real good!" He stood for a moment, watching as the smaller boy nudged at the possum's fat carcass with his toe, then shook his head. "It's gonna be a pain to carry this varmint to the house, Clinton. He must weigh at least twenty-five pounds."

A stubborn expression settled on Clinton

CHAPTER
ONE

A stiff March wind from the Midwest swept down through Missouri before dropping over the lip of Arkansas's Ouachita Mountains into the river. Each night, transparent layers of ice crusted the serpentine river but melted during the day as the pale sun reached its zenith. Now at midafternoon a gunpowder gray sky hung over the land, and the hoarse barking of a dog broke the utter stillness of the woods.

A fat gray possum scurried along the riverbank, headed for a large chinquapin oak. But mortality caught up with him as a huge red hound dashed out of the woods and, without breaking stride, opened his enormous jaws and clamped them on the possum's neck. One quick shake of the dog's head, and the neck broke with a distinct snap. The dog dropped the limp body and sat down, his jaws open, his pink tongue lolling out as he panted.

Two boys emerged from the woods, and the shorter one yelped, "Look at that, Brodie! Ol' Anthony Wayne done caught our dinnerfor us!"

The taller of the two did not speak but came and stood beside the dog and the dead possum. At fourteen, Brodie Hardin stood an inch over six feet and was as lean as an oak sapling. His auburn hair poked out from under his limp black felt hat, and his light green eyes glowed with pleasure as he leaned down, roughly caressing the dog's head. "You done good, Anthony Wayne—real good!" He stood for a moment, watching as the smaller boy nudged at the possum's fat carcass with his toe, then shook his head. "It's gonna be a pain to carry this varmint to the house, Clinton. He must weigh at least twenty-five pounds."

A stubborn expression settled on Clinton

Hardin's face. He was ten years old, stocky and strong with brown hair, brown eyes, and a stubborn cast to his lips. "You carry him, Brodie, and I'll take the gun. Maybe we'll get lucky and see a deer."

"Shucks, you couldn't hit a deer if I tied him down!"

"Could too!"

Clinton continued to squabble with his older brother, but finally Brodie groaned, "Clinton, you'd argue with a rock. We'll tie this here possum's feet together and put a stick between them and tote him home like that, but I'm carryin' the gun."

Ignoring Clinton's protests, Brodie selected a sapling and, with some effort, cut it down with his pocketknife. After trimming off the branches and tying the possum's feet with string from his pocket, he centered the animal on the pole and nodded. "I'll go in front in case some more game comes along."

"No, I'm going in front!"

"All right, just get moving." The two lifted their catch, with Brodie carefully pointing the double-barreled shotgun at the ground as they walked along. He was silent, but Clinton, never at a loss for words, commented on what a sorry hunting trip it had been. Brodie inwardly agreed, for he had hoped for a deer or even a coon. He hated the taste of possum, but at least it was better than going back empty-handed.

Within twenty minutes Clinton was already complaining about the sapling cutting into his shoulder. Brodie ignored him for as long as he could, then said impatiently, "All right, I'm tired of listening to you yap! You'd talk the legs off a stove! I'll tote the durn old possum by myself." Dropping his end of the stick, he stepped back, allowing the possum to slide off. He'd thrown the animal over his left shoulder, keeping his right free for the shotgun, when he heard a sharp buzzing sound.

"Snake, Brodie!" Clinton yelled.

Brodie's flesh seemed to turn to stone, but his mind was racing. He heard the rattle on his right. Jumping to the left, he frantically tried to aim his shotgun in the direction of the buzzing. As he fell to one side, he caught a glimpse of a gray blur—a movement so fast his eyes could scarcely take it in. He felt a bump against his right shoe, and fear coursed through him from his toes to the top of his head.

The snake was enormous! It stretched out a full six feet, and Brodie's heart skipped a beat at the sight of the large triangular head and the rapid flickering of the forked tongue. The rattler started to draw back into a coil, and Brodie fell down full-length, fumbling to find the trigger. His hands seemed to have no more life in them than the shotgun he held. He willed the gun to sweep around, but it moved so slowly he wanted to cry out. Finally, as the snake coiled itself tight, Brodie thumbed the hammer back, making a sharp click in the air. As the snake's head started to rise for the strike, Brodie pulled the trigger. The gun roared and reared up, the recoil pointing it up at the sky.

The sound filled his head, and he was momentarily stunned, not knowing if he had hit the snake or missed it.

"You got him, Brodie—you got him! You got the ol' scudder!"

Brodie sat up carefully, light-headed from the effort, and stared at the body of the snake thrashing around wildly. Anthony Wayne barked frantically, circling the writhing reptile.

"You shot his whole head plumb off!"

Clinton exclaimed. He grabbed up the sapling they'd used to carry the possum and poked the snake with it, yelling like a wild Indian. Slowly Brodie got to his feet. His legs were unsteady, and for a moment he thought he was going to throw up. Mastering himself, he walked over and stared down at the headless, twitching creature.

"Look at 'im! The biggest 'un I ever seen!" Clinton yelled. "Let's count them rattles."

Brodie's stomach lurched at the sight of the large rattler head lying several feet away on the ground, a mangled mess. He waited, unable to speak, then after a moment said, "Well, let's take him home, Clinton."

"We'll skin him and hang his old hide up over the door."

"Reckon as how we'll do more'n that. We'll have him for supper."

Clinton whirled and stared at Brodie, his eyes wide with disbelief. "We ain't neither eatin' no snake!"

"Yes, we are. I heard Pa say one time that snake was good eatin'."

"It's a sin to eat a snake! The Bible, it says so!"

Clinton had been baptized by a traveling Baptist evangelist the previous summer.

Since that time he had considered himself the spiritual leader of the Hardin family. He had, in fact, become quite unbearable, and Brodie threw up his hands in a gesture of helplessness. "A sin to eat a snake? The Bible don't say that!"

"You don't know nothin' about the Bible, Brodie," Clinton pronounced dogmatically. His face grew stubborn, and he added, "It was an ol' snake that got us into all this here misery and trouble we're in right now." Thinking for a moment, he added, "A blamed old snake and that woman Eve. It was her and that snake that did it all!"

"You keep your mouth shut, Clinton," Brodie said sharply. "Now help me load that possum back on the stick! We'll tie this snake on too, 'cause we're gonna eat both of these critters, no matter what you might have to say about it."

For the rest of the journey home, Clinton mouthed dark prophecies about the fate of those who ate snake flesh. Brodie gritted his teeth and said nothing, except once when he groaned, "I wish you hadn't ever gotten baptized, Clinton. You used to be a pretty nice fellow, but that baptizing ruined you for shore!"

★ ★ ★

"You get back there and take your turn, Tarleton!"

Jerusalem Hardin sat on a three-legged stool, her hands busy milking a nanny goat. She reached over and thumped the nanny's kid on the nose, pushing it away from its mother's teats, then laughed as the little billy goat squealed. "You'll get your turn when I'm through here." Turning back, she continued to aim the stream of rich milk into the tin pail. She had jokingly named the nanny Esther, for she had always thought the name was beautiful, while this particular goat was singularly ugly. Esther had the most evil-looking eyes Jerusalem had ever seen, and her coat was a mismatched conglomeration of dirty gray and reddish ochre. But for all her hideous looks, Esther was easy to milk, content throughout the process to nibble greedily at the forage Jerusalem had thrown out for her.

An insistent cry caught the woman's attention, and she turned to her own baby, who was lying flat on her back kicking her hands and feet. "Why, Mary Aidan, you look like a turtle on its back that can't flip over."

Jerusalem squirted a few drops of the rich milk into her left hand, then using the fingers of her right, applied the warm liquid to the infant's lips. The baby began vigorously sucking her mother's fingers. "I swan, Mary Aidan, you're a caution! You like this nanny's milk better than you do mine." She patted the baby on the stomach and ignored her cries as she continued to milk the goat. She had drawn off all she dared, leaving enough for the billy goat, named Tarleton after a British officer in the Revolutionary War. Her grandfather had often spoken of Sir Tarleton as the most hated man in the British army, and he thought it made a fitting moniker for the already cantankerous little goat. He had also named the hound Mad Anthony Wayne after another of his notorious commanders in the Revolution.

Stepping back with the pail of milk held securely in her right hand, Jerusalem turned to retrieve her baby, and at once Tarleton butted his way in and began feeding. In one deft motion she swept up Mary Aidan, threw her onto her left shoulder, and left the barn. The cold March wind bit through her thin linsey-woolsey dress, and she made her way quickly across the chicken yard.

A black-and-white-speckled rooster with a ragged comb shot out from the group of hens and made for her feet, pecking sharply at her ankles. Jerusalem kicked him, sending him fluttering away. "You'd better pick up some manners, Judas, or one of these days I'll cut off your head and eat you!" Her daughter had named the annoying animal Judas, and Jerusalem had hated him for years. Yet he had filled the chicken yard with his progeny and had managed to evade foxes, skunks, hawks, and other predators. Her eyes ran over the chickens. She knew each one of them by name, for her twelve-year-old daughter, Moriah, had named them all. Some of them had odd names, biblical names, such as Jemima and Sheba. Other names, such as Shushi and Beetle, simply came out of Moriah's active brain.

The house she approached was a common dogtrot cabin, consisting of two large rooms separated by a covered passageway. It was made of walnut logs and covered with cedar shakes. Jerusalem knew every inch of the cabin and had chinked the gaps between the logs three times in the twelve years since Jake had built it.

She stepped into what all of them called

the big room. Her glance went at once to her grandfather, Josiah, who was sitting in front of the fire, his head bobbing and his eyes closed. Jerusalem took pleasure at the sight, as she did almost every time she entered the cabin with its smooth wooden floor. For three years she had lived on a dirt floor, with Jake promising her constantly that he would put in a real one when he had time. He had gotten as far as ordering the rough lumber from the sawmill. But in the end, it had been Jerusalem who had hired Abe Simmons, the black carpenter, to come plane it and sand it until it was as smooth as glass.

She moved past the room's sparse furnishings—a table, two chairs, and several stools. She passed by the ladder to the loft, where the children slept at night, and noticed how quiet the house was this afternoon with the boys out hunting. Laying Mary Aidan on her stomach in a wooden cradle, she stood for a moment watching the baby's arms and legs kick. "You'd better learn how to crawl pretty soon," she said sternly and then smiled, a smile her husband used to adore. She was not beautiful, though most people thought so, due to the liveliness of her expression. When she was courting Jake, he had told her, "You can say more with your eyes, Jerusalem Ann, than most women can say with their mouths."

Jerusalem opened the cabinet over the table and removed the lid from a glass jar. She poured the goat's milk into it, capped it, and stared at it, then shook her head. "I wish I hadn't lost them two nannies," she murmured. The wolves had taken them during the winter, and the cow had gone dry, so Esther's milk was all they had. She knew she had to get another cow or more goats somehow.

Jerusalem Ann Hardin was a methodical woman; she'd had to be to raise six children and do the demanding work of the farm. Jake had been gone for almost a year and a half trapping furs, except for one short visit last summer, so most of the planning and work fell on her. She would keep a mental checklist of all the things she had to do, ticking things off one by one as she accomplished them.

For a time she stood there in front of the larder, studying their meager store of food— two jars of blackberry preserves, one of plum, two of figs. Some flour and meal, but not enough of either to feed her family for long. She reached out and touched the sack of potatoes and shook her head. *Not enough.* She thought then of the smokehouse, which had been raided by foxes that ruined much of the meat they had put up. Little was left by the end of the winter—just a little salt meat, a hard end of ham, and a few other remnants. For a moment she stood there adding to her mental list of things to do. She knew that during the coming months before winter returned, she needed to raise a garden, fill the smokehouse with fresh meat, store potatoes, and gather herbs and hang them from the ceiling to dry. It all seemed overwhelming, but then the vein of humor that lay in her caused her to smile again, and a small dimple appeared on her cheek. "Lord, I don't reckon as how I have to fret. We've never missed a meal yet." Then she chuckled and said, "'Course, we did have to *postpone* a few!"

She worked quietly preparing what little food she had for the evening meal. Hearing her grandfather coughing, she looked over at him. He straightened up and blinked his eyes. Walking over to him, she reached out her hand and stroked his hair. A sense of relief washed through her as he looked up at her with recognition. *It's one of his good days. He knows me.* She patted his cheek and said, "How are you feeling, Granddad?"

"I feel fine." Josiah Mitchell did not get up but reached out and touched Jerusalem's hip, as if to reassure himself. "Where're the boys?"

"Gone hunting."

"I orter o' gone with 'em."

"Maybe tomorrow. How about some tea?"

"Sounds good, granddaughter."

Jerusalem hung the kettle in the fireplace that dominated one end of the room, and as soon as the water was boiling, she made sassafras tea. She poured two mugs full, handed him one, then pulled up a chair and sat across from him.

Josiah held his tea for a moment, looking down into it as if it contained some mystery, then slowly raised it to his lips. He was eighty-three years old and had fought in George Washington's army during the Revolutionary War. His skin was darkened by the sun, for he had lived out-of-doors all his life. After the Revolution he had gone to the mountains and trapped furs. Later he had worked as a riverboat man on the Missouri River for a number of years. All of his life's pursuits had been harsh, and most of the men he had lived and worked with were now dead. His old hands were unsteady and covered with liver spots. His face sagged, but Jerusalem could remember when it was strong and had few wrinkles. His eyes, however, were still bright—at least on his good days. For the past two years, he had been troubled by a strange affliction. Jerusalem did not know what to call it. At times he would cease to speak, or if he did, his remarks had nothing to do with reality. The spells used to last only a few minutes, but lately they had been getting longer.

"I recollect once when I was in Daniel Morgan's command. We overrun a lobster-back camp. The Redcoats was havin' tea. We kilt most of 'em, and the rest run off." He sipped the tea, and his lips turned themselves upward in a smile. "We all had some of that tea, and I remember I sat myself down right on the body of an officer in a fancy uniform. Old Morgan laughed at me and said I didn't have much taste in furniture. That's been a long time ago, granddaughter, but I still remember that shore was good tea."

Jerusalem had never tired of her grandfather's stories of the Revolution, or of his time in the mountains. He had been a strong man in his day and was one of the few completely honest men she'd ever known. She sat for a time listening as he spoke, then finally she heard a sound from the bedroom and got to her feet. "I'll be back, Granddad."

She moved quickly through the door to the bedroom and went to the cedar bed that dominated the room. Her mother, Jewel, was coughing, and blood had spattered the front of her nightgown. Jerusalem reached down and pulled her mother into a sitting position. She grabbed a cloth off of the table next to the bed, dipped it into the basin, and began to wipe her mother's face. "Now, Ma, you stop that coughin'. Here, have a sip of water."

She held her mother upright until color came back into the thin, drawn face. Jewel Mitchell Satterfield had been a strong woman until a year ago, and then she had begun complaining of a pain in her stomach. At first it had not seemed too serious, but now the pain was constant and increasing. "Do you feel like getting up, Ma?"

"I . . . I think I might, daughter."

Ten minutes later, after getting her mother cleaned up, Jerusalem helped her through the door to a chair at the table. Josiah looked up at her and said, "How're you feelin', Jewel?"

"I don't complain none."

"You never do," Josiah said. He came over and put his hand on his daughter's shoulder and stroked it for a moment. He had lost his wife thirteen years ago, and Jewel was his only living child. He stared at her with an unreadable expression, then moved back to his chair.

Right then the front door slammed, and Jerusalem turned to see Moriah come in grasping a small coon to her chest. At the age of twelve she had her mother's dark red hair, but her eyes were brown like her father's. She had a bright, alert expression and nodded at her mother. "Ma, I'm teaching Charlie some tricks."

"You put that coon down, Moriah, and boil your grandma some eggs. Two of them."

"Yes, ma'am." Moriah put the coon down

in a box, and the little fellow immediately reared up on his hind legs and peeked over the edge. He looked like a masked bandit with his bright eyes.

"When that coon gets big enough, he'll be good eatin'," Josiah said mischievously.

"You ain't eatin' my coon, Grandpa!"

"I don't reckon I will, nor any of them other varmints you take to raise."

As Moriah walked over to the larder to get two eggs to boil, Jerusalem went back into the bedroom, removed the soiled bedcovers, and put on fresh ones. She carried the dirty linens out to the dogtrot, where she stuffed them into a large wooden box, then went back into the big room. She sat at the table talking to her mother until Moriah set a small plate with two soft-boiled eggs in front of the sick woman. "You try to eat all of this, Mama," Jerusalem said.

Josiah shuffled across the room and sat down beside his daughter. He reached out awkwardly and ran his hand over her hair. He was a big, gentle man, despite all the violence and grief he had seen throughout his life. The look on his face seemed to say that he knew more hard times were ahead for him.

"Here come the boys," Moriah exclaimed. She ran to the front window and looked out, then yelped, "They got somethin'! Why . . . it's a huge *snake,* Ma!" she cried out. "And a fat ol' possum!"

"A snake and a possum? Well, there's supper, at least," Jerusalem said. Her eyes twinkled as she looked at her grandfather. "Will you have snake or possum tonight?"

"I've et both, granddaughter. They ain't neither one bad eatin'."

Jerusalem went outside, and for the next few minutes was subjected to Clinton's loud protests. "We'll all go straight to the pit if we eat that ol' snake, Ma! It's in the Bible!"

"Clinton, stop being foolish. Your religion is gettin' a little bit aggravatin'. There's nothin' wrong with eatin' anything God has made."

Clinton started to argue, but at a stern look from his mother, he shut his mouth.

Jerusalem put her arm around her older son. "You two did fine, Brodie." *He's the gentlest of all of us,* she thought. *I don't know how he'll make it in the world if he don't toughen up a little.*

Meanwhile, Clinton simply could not be

still. "We'll all go to perdition if we eat that snake."

"Hush your mouth!" Jerusalem said quietly. "You go clean that possum now, and I'll clean the snake myself. And if you don't want to eat it, then don't."

Clinton sat at the table bolt upright, displeasure written across his face. His mouth was drawn into a tight line as he stared at the large bowl containing the stew that made up the main dish for supper. Jerusalem had bowed her head and asked the blessing, and when she looked up, she saw Clinton's angry expression. "If your religion forbids you to eat it, then don't eat it, Clinton," she said and winked at Brodie, who sat across from her.

"That's right, Clinton," Brodie said, keeping a straight face. "I don't think you oughta."

Jerusalem filled the plates from the deep bowl for everyone at the table except Clinton. She said sweetly, "You can have biscuits, Clinton, and maybe some blackberry preserves."

Josiah Mitchell had watched the exchange with a slight smile. "I purely admire a man who stands up for his religion, Clinton," he said solemnly. "I surely do!"

Clinton stared around the table and saw that everyone was trying to contain their smiles. He suddenly picked up his bowl and stuck it out toward Jerusalem. "All right, I'll eat the ol' snake. And when we all wind up in the fires of judgment, I'll be reminding you all of this."

Everyone at the table laughed, and Mary Aidan, who was sitting in Moriah's lap, kicked and crowed.

"You sure know how to mix up a tasty stew, granddaughter," Josiah said, taking a bite. "I declare, I believe you could make somethin' good out of a skunk!"

"Well, we have Brodie to thank for this," Jerusalem said.

"It wasn't him," Clinton snapped. "It was Anthony Wayne that done caught that ol' possum, and it was an accident that Brodie shot the snake."

"It was not. I aimed to blow his head off and I did!"

After dinner there was still enough daylight left for the older children to go out and play for a while. Jerusalem saw her grand-father go off to the other room of the house where he slept, and then she put her mother back into bed. "You take a rest now," she said. "You ate good tonight. You'll feel bet-ter tomorrow."

"Thank you, daughter."

Jerusalem went to check on Mary Aidan, who was sleeping soundly and sucking on her fist from time to time, then turned and left the cabin to gather eggs. There were none, and then she remembered that Moriah had brought them all in earlier in the day. Hearing the sound of horse hooves, she looked up and saw a buggy pulled by a pair of matched bays. Narrowing her eyes, she recognized Ryland Rusk, the vice-president of Planters Bank in Arkadelphia, the town six miles away. She watched as he got out of the buggy and tied the lines. Suddenly, she felt a sharp pain in her leg, and looking down, she saw the black rooster Judas. Without a wasted motion, she leaned forward, grabbed him by the neck, swung him around three times, and with a swift twist, wrung his neck. The headless body hit the ground, rolled over, then got up and began running around. "You're an active chicken now," she muttered, "but you won't be for long." She then turned to face Rusk, whose face registered his shock at the sight.

"Well," he said, grinning, "I see you're having chicken for supper."

"Good evening, Mr. Rusk."

"Miz Hardin, good to see you." Rusk was a big, brusque man, well over six feet. He had an ample paunch, which he tried to cover up with good tailoring. His face was florid, and he had a pair of small eyes and a prominent nose. He took off his hat and ran his hand over his hair, which was plastered down with Macassar oil.

"I was on my way to the McAdams' place, and I thought I might stop by here so we could talk a little about your loan."

"I see. Well, come inside, Mr. Rusk."

"Oh, come now," Rusk said with a smile. "You can call me Ryland."

Jerusalem did not answer. She went inside but did not offer the man a seat. He was a notorious womanizer, and his poor wife was helpless to defend herself from his disgraceful treatment. She was a plain, frail woman, and the four children all took after their father, so she was bullied by all of them.

Rusk waited for an invitation to sit down, but when she remained silent, he cleared his throat and said, "It was a right hard winter for you, I suppose, Jerusalem."

For a moment Jerusalem considered telling him that she was Mrs. Hardin but instead said, "Yes, it was."

Rusk moved so close to her that she could smell his shaving lotion. "Your husband's been gone nearly a year and a half. A healthy woman like you must miss having a man around."

"I manage," she said, backing up as far as she could.

Her reply was blunt, but Rusk went on. "Well, I suppose we may as well face up to it. Your bank note is coming due in two weeks."

"I'm aware of that, Mr. Rusk."

"You know, it sure would be a shame for you to lose this place." Rusk waited for her to comment, and when she did not, he said, "That's what'll happen, you know, Jerusalem, if the note's not paid. When Jake borrowed that money, we made that clear to him."

Jake Hardin had mortgaged their property to buy a fancy racehorse. He had not mentioned it to Jerusalem until after he'd bought the animal, and they'd had a terrible quarrel about it. She tried to persuade him to sell the horse and pay the loan back right away, but Jake had dreams of making it big at the racetrack and took him off to Little Rock to race him. Unfortunately, the animal evidently had a weak heart, for during the second race, he dropped dead. Jake had left for the mountains immediately afterward, barely pausing long enough to say, "I'll go trap enough furs to pay off the loan, Jerusalem Ann." That had been almost a year and a half ago, and there had been no word from him whatsoever.

"I'd like to ask you to extend the loan until my husband gets back. He's trapping furs. I'm sure he'll be back soon with the money to pay you."

"Well, that wouldn't be real good procedure, so maybe we could work something out . . . just the two of us."

Jerusalem stood still, her heart racing under Rusk's unnerving stare. She had met the man before, and each time he had held her hand too long when greeting her and had squeezed her upper arm whenever he got the chance. When he stepped forward and tried to put his arm around her now, she pushed him away and said, "There's nothing here for you, Rusk."

The banker's ruddy face grew even more flushed. He started to grab her, but something in the woman's steady gaze stopped him, and he said stiffly, "Well, I guess the bank will just have to follow its own procedures—unless you change your mind."

"I won't be changing my mind. Good day, sir."

Jerusalem watched as the big man shoved his way out the door, anger in every line of his body. He jumped into the buggy, slashed at the horses with his whip, and tore off with the team in a dead run.

Jerusalem released her breath and congratulated herself on not losing her temper. She walked slowly out of the house and down a path until she reached a small graveyard surrounded by a freshly painted white picket fence. There were only three graves in it—the old and sunken grave of her father, Mark Satterfield, and two newer ones that were still mounded up. She walked over to the newer gravestones, knelt down, and ran her fingers over the carved names. *Robert "Bobby" Hardin*, 1826-1830, and *Hartsell Lee Hardin, 1828-1830.* For a long time she sat there touching the cold stone, thinking, *Only a year since I buried my boys—and it seems like a lifetime!*

Finally, she stood up and stared up at the darkening sky. "Lord, I'm just nigh about played out. I've got to ask you for a little help. I got plenty upset with you when you took my boys. I didn't speak to you for a long time, but I been thinkin' about it—you let me keep my other children. Maybe those two would have gone wrong and shamed me, but it hurt me somethin' terrible to lose them. Reckon it always will." She went back and touched the stone again. "I don't see how I can go on, Lord, so I guess I'll just have to ask you to take my hand." She turned abruptly and walked away.

CHAPTER
TWO

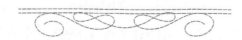

"Whoa up there, Abishag—there's a good girl!"

Jerusalem paused for a moment after bringing the blue-nosed mule to a halt in front of the Planters Bank. She was fond of the animal—quite a beauty for a mule—and named her Abishag, after the beautiful young Shunammite girl in the Bible who had served King David in his old age. Abishag was an anomaly as a mule, being sweet-tempered, and Jerusalem had no trouble hitching her to a buggy. Her other mule, Samson, was huge and had the temperament of a rattlesnake. Jake had been able to handle him through the liberal use of a club, but none of the other members of the family could do a great deal with him. Even as Jerusalem sat in front of the bank thinking, she wondered how she was going to get Samson and Abishag hitched together as a team to do the spring plowing. But that was the least of her problems right then, for if she didn't find a way to work something out with Ryland Rusk, there'd be no spring planting.

Sighing, she got out of the buggy, walked around to the other side, and picked up Mary Aidan, who was wrapped securely in a thick blanket. Jerusalem pulled the blanket back and smiled at the baby. At the age of six months, Mary Aidan had learned the art of charming her mother, grinning at her toothlessly. "You are a darling, Mary Aidan Hardin," Jerusalem whispered and touched her daughter's smooth pink cheek.

Putting the baby over her shoulder, she turned and let her eyes run down the streets of Arkadelphia for a moment. The sullen March weather had plagued the land and given the town the look of a slatternly woman just waking up.

"'Tis the ugliest town I ever saw, and

that's saying a lot," Jerusalem muttered, then walked quickly toward the bank. The wind whipped bits of paper and trash along the street. A few people were stirring, but they all seemed paralyzed by the unusually cold March winds.

Stepping through the door of the Planters Bank, Jerusalem took in the scene at a glance. Toward the back of the building, a counter five feet high with a brass network framed the tellers' windows. She was surprised to see at least a dozen people there waiting, some of whom she knew. She got at the end of the line, and a tall, rawboned woman turned around and greeted her with a smile.

"Hello, Jerusalem. We missed you'uns at church Sunday."

"Baby was ailing, Martha. Did I miss anything?"

"The preacher made a mess of it. He preached on election—or tried to. I swan, Jerusalem, only the Lord knows where he gets them crazy ideas of his! I reckon we got what we deserved for lettin' a Yankee who kin read Greek come down here and pastor our church."

The two women talked for a moment, and

then Jerusalem saw Alvin Carstairs, the president of the bank, come out of his office. "Excuse me, Martha. I need to talk to Mr. Carstairs."

Jerusalem was aware that Ryland Rusk had been watching her ever since she had entered the bank. He was seated at his desk talking with a roughly dressed farmer, but his eyes were fixed on her. Jerusalem had to pass by his desk to reach Mr. Carstairs.

"Hello, Jerusalem," Rusk said as she walked by.

She gave him a spare nod, then went to stand before the president. "Mr. Carstairs, I need to speak with you."

Carstairs was sixty-four years old, a slight man with a weak chin. He wore a beard to cover it, but the scraggly growth only served to emphasize the flaw. He was a nervous man, and his hands fluttered over his vest as he nodded to Jerusalem. He took out his watch and looked at it, then said, "Why, yes, Mrs. Hardin. What is it?"

"I wanted to talk to you about our loan."

"Oh, you'll have to talk to Mr. Rusk about that."

"I'd rather talk with you if you don't mind."

"I'm sorry, but I let him handle all small loans. You understand. I'm sure something can be worked out."

At the banker's haughty tone, one of Jerusalem's "moods" came over her. Jake had first called them that, and the rest of the family had learned to recognize them. Her grandfather called them "fits," and they amused him no end. As a rule Jerusalem was a straightforward woman with control over her emotions, but from time to time something would rise up within her, and she would hear herself saying words she had no intention of speaking. More than once it had gotten her into serious difficulty. Even as a young girl this trait had been evident to her family, and her parents had tried to curb the habit. It came upon her now as she thought of Rusk's brazen advances toward her the day before. She raised her voice so that everyone in the bank could hear plainly and said, "Mr. Rusk has already offered to help me with my loan. Yesterday he stopped by and said that if I would show him some affection, he'd give me an extension." The anger in Jerusalem's voice left no doubt in anyone's mind as to what she was referring to.

A silence as profound as that of an ancient tomb buried in the sands of Egypt reigned over the room. Every individual in the bank sat or stood as if frozen, every eye fixed on the tableau playing out before them.

The first sound was a strangled gasp from Ryland Rusk, whose face had turned crimson. He got up from his desk, knocking over an ink bottle in his haste. He ignored the black mess spreading over all his papers and took two steps toward Jerusalem. "That's . . . that's not the truth!"

Jerusalem turned to face him, holding her baby close. She met his eyes and was disgusted by what she saw there. "You're a little man, Ryland Rusk, a bully and a liar." Knowing that Rusk was hoping to become the new bank president upon Alvin Carstairs's impending retirement, she inwardly gloated at the damage she hoped she was bringing to his reputation. With her back straight, she walked right past Rusk until she got to the door. Then she turned, her green eyes glowing with the anger that burned within her. "When my husband comes back, I'm sure you can expect a visit from him, and it won't be a pleasant one."

She whirled on her heel and swept out the door.

The color left Rusk's face as he scanned the room, seeing every eye fixed on him. "That . . . that woman is *unsound*! Why . . . this is absurd. There's something wrong with her mind."

Martha Grimsley's robust voice rang out. "There ain't nothin' wrong with Jerusalem Ann Hardin's mind, Rusk."

Desperately, Rusk retorted, "She . . . she's running scared. Why, she tried everything she could think of to get me to extend that loan."

Another one of the customers standing in line, a thickset man wearing a black alpaca coat and a fawn-colored hat pushed back on his head, had been watching Rusk. He turned and aimed a mouthful of amber tobacco juice at the brass spittoon, then wiped his lips with the back of his sleeve and said in a clear, piercing voice, "If I was you, Rusk, I'd arrange to be out of town when Big Jake comes back."

Ryland Rusk stared at the man, and his voice turned squeaky. "I tell you, there's nothin' to what that woman says!"

Rusk looked around at all the people who

were staring at him, and an awkward silence greeted him. At that moment he knew he had made a grievous mistake. He knew Big Jake Hardin's reputation as a fighter and a brawler, and fervently wished he had never laid eyes on Jerusalem Hardin!

Moriah Hardin grabbed a young cattail and pulled it out of the mud along the river's edge. She broke off the muddy base and tossed the stalk alongside others she had stacked on the bank. The Ouachita River was higher than usual, so she had to wade out a ways in order to add to her stock.

"I hate pullin' these old cattails, Brodie. Ain't we got enough yet?" The thin girl looked over toward Brodie with her plaintive brown eyes and whined, "I wanted to go hunting this morning with Grandpa."

"We gotta have these cattails. We need 'em to eat."

"I ain't no cow to eat stuff like that."

Brodie smiled at his sister. He was very fond of her and said, "You like 'em pretty good when they're cooked into one of Mama's good stews."

"Just because I like to eat 'em doesn't mean I like to gather them," she said.

Cattails had become a staple of the Hardin family diet during the recent hard times. Every part of the plant was edible, from the roots all the way up to the green spikes. Peeled and boiled, they served as a vegetable. They could be pickled for salads, and the young shoots were a fair substitute for poke sallet. Jerusalem had even learned how to grind the roots into a flour that could be used like cornmeal. She had taught Moriah how to cut up the whole sprout, roll the pieces in cattail flour, then add salt and pepper and fry them.

As the youngsters continued with their task, Moriah's bad humor did not abate. She kept complaining about getting all muddy until finally Brodie came up behind her, threw his arms around her, and picked her up. "I'll just throw you in the river," he threatened. "Maybe it'll wash some of the orneryness out of you."

Pinioned by Brodie's strong young arms, Moriah struggled to get free. "You let me down!" she cried.

"No, I think you need to be baptized." He laughed, then added, "You see what a nice fellow Clinton's been since he's been baptized."

"He's been meaner than a snake ever since he got religion! Now, you lemme down!" Moriah demanded.

"Here you go." Brodie pretended he was about to heave her into the river.

"If you throw me in," Moriah screamed, "I'll catch you asleep snoring with your mouth open and drop a worm in it!"

Brodie laughed. "You would too, wouldn't you?" He put her down, pinched her cheek, and said, "Come on, I guess we got enough cattails to make a load."

The two gathered up the cattails into two cotton sacks. They had made a good haul. As they turned to plod homeward along the road that ran parallel to the river, Moriah calmed down and began to talk seriously. Brodie was more of a listener than a talker, and the young girl had become accustomed to sharing her problems with him.

"Brodie, there's somethin' wrong with me."

"There's nothin' wrong with you."

"Yes, there is. Look at me. I'm skinny as a snake."

Brodie glanced at Moriah in her thin cotton dress. She was indeed slender. She had begun shooting up but not filling out, and now she was as awkward as a young colt.

"Martha Grimshaw is just the same age as me, and she's already gettin' a bosom and I ain't. What if I never do?"

Brodie was amused at his sister. "Don't worry. You're only twelve. Some girls don't get their figures until they're fourteen or fifteen. You'll get everything you need when you get older."

"But what iffen I don't?"

"You'll be as purty as Ma when you get your growth."

Moriah considered this for a time and shook her head. "Ain't got no more shape than a skinny ol' rake handle!"

Brodie was carrying his sack over his left shoulder. He reached out and put his arm around her. "You're going to be prettier than a pair of green shoes with red strings."

Moriah flashed him a beautiful smile. Her coloring was something to see, with skin as clear as could be and red hair that caught the sun and had golden gleams in it. The two walked along, but Moriah was not through with telling her problems. She had the habit of going down a list with Brodie of all the things that troubled her. "I'm afeared we're gonna lose our farm, Brodie."

"We ain't gonna lose it."

"We are, too, iffen we don't pay that bill. I shore wish Pa would come back."

Brodie did not answer, for he was worried as well, although he tried to cover it. Their father had been gone for almost a year and a half now, and the last time he had returned from his travels, he had stayed no more than a month. It seemed it had become Jake Hardin's habit to leave for extended periods and come back just long enough to give his wife another baby. It had not always been like this. Brodie could remember when his pa stayed around most of the time. He used to take Brodie hunting and fishing, and had spent a lot of time with him. He had worked on the farm, too, apparently contented. But now Brodie had trouble remembering what his pa looked like.

"Pa'll come back, and we'll pay off that loan."

Moriah looked at him, fear reflected in her eyes. "Grandpa is losing his mind, ain't he, Brodie?"

Brodie could not speak for a moment.

Though he didn't want to think about it, they were all aware that something terrible was happening to the old man. Whenever Brodie needed advice about anything, he had always looked to his great-grandfather, especially during recent years with his father gone so much. For as long as Brodie could remember, his greatgrandfather Josiah had had a sharp, keen mind, but lately it seemed to leave him at times. The periods were getting longer and longer when he was not himself. "I reckon he ain't right."

"It seems like everythin' bad's happenin'. Why is that, Brodie?"

"I don't know, sis. I just don't know. But we'll make it through all right. You'll see."

Brodie continued to encourage Moriah as they walked along. When they reached a bend in the river, they looked up and saw two mules carrying four riders.

"It's them old Brattons," Moriah muttered. "They ain't worth dried spit."

Indeed, the Brattons were considered a lower order among the civilized folks of the Ouachita River basin. They made their living mostly by making corn whiskey and selling it, but rumor had it they were involved in other illegal activities such as stealing, and there was suspicion of even worse things.

Brodie grew tense, for the Brattons were bad news. "Give 'em the road, Moriah," he said.

The two hugged the side of the road, but instead of passing them, Luke Bratton pulled up the nose of his mule and turned to face his sister, saying, "Lookee what we got here, Ellie. Some fine, upstandin' citizens."

Ellie Bratton was seventeen. Her face was not entirely clean, as was usual, but that did not detract from her good looks. "Why, that's Brodie Hardin! Gettin' to be a real man, ain't you, now? You better come callin' on me someday pretty soon."

The three Bratton boys looked exactly alike. They all had muddy brown eyes and roughly cut black hair, and were dressed in a motley assortment of overalls, pants, and denim shirts. They were large for their size, the largest being Duke, who sat with his brother Horace on the other mule. Duke was holding a jug balanced on the back of the mule. He grinned and said, "You need more man than that, Ellie."

Luke hopped off the mule and stood there looking at Brodie and Moriah. All three of them had been drinking, and he said, "Gimme that jug, Duke. These two look thirsty." Duke laughed crudely and surrendered the jug.

"Shore, let 'em liquor up a bit. It'll make 'em look happier."

Luke came over and said, "Here, Brodie, take a belt of this."

"Don't reckon I'd care for any."

The Brattons all had volatile tempers, and at Brodie's refusal to have a drink, Luke Bratton's eyes grew hard. "Too good to drink with me, I reckon."

"No, I just don't wanna drink."

"All right, then. We'll let missy here try it. Here, what's yore name, missy?"

"None of your business," Moriah snapped. "And I don't want none of your old rotgut neither."

All the Brattons laughed, and Horace, the middle brother, said, "She got the best of you there, Luke. Come on. Let's git to town. We're wasting our time here."

Luke, however, was angry. "You're gonna take a drink of this, girl!" He reached out and grabbed Moriah by the back of the neck and lifted the jug to her lips.

At once Brodie stepped forward and tore his hand away. "Leave her alone, Luke."

"Well, lookee here," Luke said. "From what I hear, your womenfolks ain't all that high-tone anyhow. I hear your ma's been real obligin' to that banker just to get her loan renewed."

Brodie broke out in a cold sweat as he faced the burly Bratton boy. He was fully as tall as Luke, but all of the Brattons were broad and muscular, and Brodie felt like a sapling by comparison. But he did not even think about that. His arm flew up almost of its own will and caught Luke Bratton squarely in the mouth. Sturdy as he was, Bratton stumbled backward, and blood spurted out between his thick lips. Advancing toward Brodie, he snarled, "Hardin, I'm gonna teach you a thing or two. First I'm gonna bust you up real good, and then I'm gonna bash your teeth out so you'll have snags! When I'm done with you, you'll walk astraddle when you try to get home."

"You leave him alone!" Moriah shouted. She stepped beside Brodie and tried to put herself between them, but like lightning, the two older Brattons jumped off their mules, and Horace grabbed her and held her back.

"Let me hold that jug," Duke said, grabbing it out of his brother's hands. "We don't want nothin' to happen to that." Then stepping back, he said, "Now bust him up, Luke."

Brodie knew he had absolutely no chance against the brawny Luke. Nevertheless, he flung himself against him, throwing one or two blows that had no effect. And then a solid punch from Luke caught him high in the temple, and the world seemed to whirl around him. Brilliant flashing lights, red and yellow and green, exploded, and he did not even feel it when he hit the ground.

Moriah fought against the grip that Horace Bratton kept on her, screaming and kicking, but he merely cuffed her on the side of the head and said, "You be still, girl. That brother of yourn needs to learn hisself a lesson."

Moriah tried not to watch as Brodie staggered up, over and over, to strike feebly at Luke, who merely laughed and knocked him down again. Finally she began to cry, "Please, let him alone!"

"He ain't had enough yet," Luke said.

Ellie spoke up in Brodie's defense. "I guess that's about enough, Luke."

"You keep out of this, Ellie. You're too tenderhearted."

Moriah's eyes were dim with tears. She felt helpless as she watched Brodie slowly try to get to his feet. And each time, Luke pounded him again with his fists, bloody now from the mess he had made of Brodie's face.

"I reckon that'll be sufficient."

Everyone turned at once, for no one had heard the horse approach, nor had they heard the man dismount and come up behind them. Luke blinked his eyes and stared, his mind still preoccupied with the beating he was doling out.

"What'd you say?"

"I said that'll be sufficient."

The speaker was not a big man, and he was slender of frame. He was wearing buckskin pants, a fringed jacket, and moccasins instead of boots. He had an odd-looking fur cap on his head. He had the lightest blue eyes Moriah had ever seen, but they appeared sleepy as he looked casually over the group.

"Butt out of here," Luke said, sneering at the stranger.

"Be mighty happy to, son, but I guess you've had fun enough with that boy."

Luke took a step toward the man and looked down at him. He cursed, then said, "This ain't none of your put-in."

"I said leave that boy alone."

Luke Bratton was a tough sixteen-year-old. He had beaten up grown men many times, and he feared no one. He opened his mouth to speak again, but something in the stranger's expression brought him to a halt. He took a step backward and quickly ran his eyes over the man. He saw no sign of a knife or a gun. Glancing back at the man's horse, he saw two rifles with the barrels sticking up from their case.

Duke stepped forward now, scowling. The man's back was to him, and he had not yet seen his face. He yelled, "This ain't none of your put-in! Get on your way!"

The man turned and studied Duke. His voice was summer-soft as he said, "I guess, old son, you'd better be on *your* way."

No one had challenged Duke Bratton in a long time, and the man standing before him looked almost frail next to his own bulk. Duke had beaten men until they had nearly died, broken their ribs, and had reputedly gouged out a man's eye in a drunken brawl in another town. Now he was seething. He hated to be crossed. Pulling back his light denim jacket, he exposed a heavy pistol stuck inside his belt. "Git on your way, mister, 'fore I stomp you!"

Moriah could not believe what she saw next. The buckskin-clad man simply reached out, in no apparent hurry it seemed to Moriah, plucked the pistol out of Duke's belt, lifted it almost casually, and brought it down on his head. The thick, thumping sound was much like that of a hammer striking a watermelon.

The man kept his gaze on Duke, who stayed upright, even though his eyes began to roll up so that the whites were visible.

"Duke, are you hurt?" Ellie asked.

Bratton made no answer. He slowly turned and took two steps. As he walked, his knees grew rubbery, and he went down slowly, a section at a time. His knees hit first, and then his entire upper body fell forward. He made no attempt to protect his face, which struck the hard dirt.

"You kilt him!" Ellie cried.

"Maybe not," the man said, his voice casual. He walked over to Duke's prone body and stared at it, then said pleasantly, "I reckon he won't be botherin' you anymore today." Turning to Moriah, he said, "You ready to go, missy?"

"Shore nuff am!" Moriah had been released by Horace, and she ran toward her rescuer.

"How about you, partner?" the stranger said to Brodie.

Brodie's vision was clearing now. His face was all bloody, and he ran his hand across it. "I'm ready."

"Come along, then."

He turned to the rest of the Brattons, who were staring at him openmouthed. The young woman had jumped off the mule, run to her brother, and turned him over. He was breathing, but his eyes were still rolled upward. She felt his head and said, "You done busted his skull!"

The man seemed not to have heard. He held the revolver, looked at it carefully, and then said, "I'm lookin' for the Hardin place."

"That's us! I'm Moriah Hardin." She stared at the man and asked, "Who are you?"

"My name's Clay Taliferro. Well, life's full of coincidences. Maybe you'd be willin' to take me to your place. I've got a letter for your ma."

"From Pa?" Brodie said weakly, still dizzy from the beating.

"Yep, sure enough." Taliferro turned and faced the Brattons. "You tell him if he don't die, he can have his pistol back anytime. I reckon I'll be stayin' in these parts awhile. If he wants it back, all he has to do is come apologize to Miss Hardin here for usin' vile language in her presence." He gave the two Bratton boys his steady attention, then said in his soft voice, "If you two are feelin' frisky—why, go ahead and jump."

Brodie stared at the Brattons and saw that both of them stood absolutely still. Taliferro grinned at them, then turned away, nonchalant as anything. Brodie, still trembling from the beating, accompanied Taliferro back to his fine bay, and then the man turned to him and said, "I bet you're Brodie."

"That's right."

"Your pa has told me all about you. Here, you get on this horse and ride. Me and Miss Moriah, we'll walk alongside for a time." He picked up the two sacks of cattails and asked, "What d'ya do with these here cattails?"

"Our ma shore knows how to cook them up for a meal," Moriah said.

"Does she, now?" Clay replied, but thought, *They sure must be going through hard times to have to eat cattails.*

Brodie hung on to the saddlehorn and glanced back to see the three Brattons glaring at the man. He looked down and saw that Clay Taliferro was completely untroubled. He felt strange, as if something had come into his life he had been looking for. "Do you really know my pa?" he asked, looking down at the tanned face of the newcomer.

"Why shore as a cat's got climbin' gear I do!"

As the three of them moved away, Horace spat in the dirt and cursed. "I'll get him. You see if I don't!"

Ellie laughed harshly. "Why didn't you take that pistol away from him when he give you the chance?" She turned her head to one side and said thoughtfully, "I reckon a real tough man has come to this here territory, boys!"

★ ★ ★

Jerusalem was busy cleaning up the cabin, taking advantage of the quiet while her mother slept and her grandfather was out fishing. Her peace was broken when she heard Clinton cry out, "Somebody's comin', Ma! I ain't never seen him afore."

Jerusalem put down her cleaning rag, walked to the door, and stepped outside. She took in the fine bay with Brodie sitting in the saddle and Moriah walking alongside the stranger dressed in buckskin. She did not say anything, but she let out a little gasp when she saw Brodie's bloodied face. Moriah broke away from her conversation with the man and came running toward her.

"Ma, this is Clay. He's a friend of Pa's."

Jerusalem studied the man as he came forward and pulled his hat off. "Howdy, ma'am. I'm Clay Taliferro. Friend of your husband's."

Jerusalem saw that he was not a handsome man but had a strong, masculine appearance. He had a wide mouth, high cheekbones, and his hair was tawny and tied by a short piece of leather behind his neck.

"I'm glad to know you, Mr. Taliferro."

"I reckon Clay's all the handle I need. I'm right proud to meet you, ma'am. Jake's told me all about you. I feel like I know the whole family already."

Moriah interrupted the exchange, spilling over in her excitement to tell her mother what had happened. "Them old Brattons stopped us on the road, and Luke Bratton, he said somethin' bad about you, so him and Brodie got into a fight, and Luke was—"

"Hold on, Moriah," her mother chastised her. "You can tell me about it when we've taken care of our guest . . . and it looks like your brother could use some attention." Turning to Clay, she said, "Please come inside. Clinton, go turn Mr. Taliferro's horse into the corral. And give him some feed."

"I expect he'd appreciate that, ma'am."

Jerusalem turned and led them all into the house. After inviting their guest to be seated, she told Moriah to go fetch some water, then said to her son, "Sit down, Brodie. Let me wash your face."

"Oh, I can do it, Ma. I ain't hurt bad."

Jerusalem looked at the puffy eyes and said, "We need to get some cool water on those, or you won't be able to see out of them." When Moriah returned with a bucket of water and handed it to her mother, Jerusalem insisted Brodie sit down, then, taking a clean cloth, applied the water to his wounds.

As she cleaned up his face, she listened to Moriah finish her story in rapid-fire fashion, ending with, ". . . and then when Duke horned in, Clay here, he just pulled that gun Duke always carries and whacked him over the head with it! Old Duke went down like an acorn falling off a tree."

Clay was watching the girl with a slight smile. "Well, he used vile language in front of your daughter. I purely can't abide vile language, ma'am."

Nodding, Jerusalem said, "It's almost noon. I know you must be hungry. I'll fix something."

"That's right kind of you, ma'am. I could use a bite," Clay Taliferro said. "It's been a mighty long ride to get here."

Jerusalem had warmed up the snake and possum stew, but had eaten none herself. She was sitting across from Taliferro, who had told them about how he had met her husband, Jake, and how the two of them had become partners in the fur trade, trapping in the headwaters of the Missouri high in the Montana Rockies with a Frenchman named Henry Saint-Cyr.

"We done right well, ma'am," he said, taking a sip of the sassafras tea. "We got snowed in the last part of September, and then we left, but a few days out, Jake stepped in a bear trap."

"Stepped in a bear trap! How did he do that?" Clinton demanded, his eyes big.

"Some fool set it and hid it, and Jake stepped into it. Them things is mighty powerful."

"Was he hurt bad?" Moriah asked.

"Broke his leg. Me and Henry set it, but he was gonna be laid up for a while."

"You left him at Fort Laramie?" Jerusalem asked.

"Yes, ma'am, I did. Jake wasn't able to make the trip. He asked me to bring you this letter and this cash money to take care of things."

Jerusalem took the leather pouch that Clay extended toward her. She opened it and found a dirty half sheet of paper. She

read it silently and then lifted her eyes and looked around. "Your pa says he misses you something fierce, and he hopes to see you soon." She turned to the man in buckskins, who sat slouched back in the chair, studying him and wondering what sort of man he was. "Why didn't Jake come home again last year before the winter started?"

The question seemed to embarrass their guest. "Why, I don't rightly know, ma'am. We didn't do too well the first year. Maybe he wanted to get more furs."

The answer did not please Jerusalem, but she did not comment. "He spelled your name here—but I can't make it out. It looks like T-a-l-i-f-e-r-r-o, but you said your name was Tolliver."

"That's the way you say my name, Miz Hardin, just like it was *Tolliver.* I wish it *was* spelled right, but I reckon my ancestors was pretty poor spellers."

"Why don't you change the way you spell it?" Moriah asked.

"Oh, I'm used to it now. Gives me somethin' to talk about."

"How'd you lose the tip off your finger?"

"Bear bit it off."

"Why did you—?"

"Moriah, hush! Don't pester Clay with your questions." Jerusalem smiled at Clay. "We're in debt to you for bringing the letter—and the money."

"Why, I owe Jake a lot. Me and him got along fine."

"When will Pa be comin' home?" Brodie asked quickly.

"I can't rightly say. It depends on that leg pretty much."

Somehow Jerusalem knew that Clay Taliferro was not telling all that he knew about her husband, but she did not want to pry, especially in front of the children.

She was holding the baby, and now she said, "Moriah, you go change this baby and put her down for a nap." She stood up, handing the baby to Moriah, then extended her free hand toward their guest. Clay was surprised, but he blinked and took it gingerly.

"We thank you for your trouble. You'll stay for supper, won't you?"

"I ain't in no hurry to go no place, ma'am."

"We'd be happy if you'd stay the night with us. You can sleep in my grandfather's room. We've got a spare bed in there."

"That's shore kindly of you, ma'am. I'd be mighty obliged."

"Clinton, please show Mr. Taliferro where he can sleep and put his things."

Jerusalem waited until the room was cleared, except for Brodie, who was standing by the fireplace. She went over to Brodie and looked up at him. There was a special bond between these two. He was by far the most intelligent, and the most sensitive, of her children. She often feared for him, knowing he was growing up fast and would soon be entering a rough world on his own. Her heart ached for him because times had been hard since his father had been gone so long. Now she put her hand gently on his battered face. "So you got whipped."

"Real bad, Ma. But I'll stomp him when I get bigger."

"What'd he say about me?"

Brodie dropped his head. "Oh, nothin' much, Ma."

"Brodie, don't lie to me. Don't *ever* lie. No lie is ever as good as the truth. Now, what'd he say?" She listened when he told her, and thenshe put her arms around him. He was half a head taller than she now, and she felt his thinness but knew that his strength would develop in the years to come. She looked up into his face. "Always stick up for your family, Brodie, even if you take a beating for it."

"I will, Ma." He hesitated, then said, "Is there enough money to pay the bank off?"

Jerusalem had already counted the money in the pouch. She took a deep breath and said, "Enough to hold them off for a time—and then we'll see."

CHAPTER
THREE

"Ma, this here baby ain't no girl child! She's a plumb ol' *fountain!*"

"You just change the diaper, Moriah, without any comment." A slanting ray of pale sunlight came in through the window, illuminating Moriah and the baby. Moriah expertly changed the diaper, then shoved the baby into a flannel nightgown as if she were shoving a piglet into a sack. Picking up her little sister, Moriah held her high in the air and jostled her until Mary Aidan began to giggle. "Go on and giggle. We're gonna have a second flood if you keep wettin' so much—and we ain't got no ark neither."

"Let me have her," Jerusalem said. "I want to feed her before she starts hollerin'."

Moriah handed the baby over to her mother, who sat down and began to nurse her. "You better go out and gather some eggs. I hope they keep on layin' like they have been."

"Ma, did you know I told Clay about that old Rusk and what he done to you?"

Jerusalem stroked Mary Aidan's silky red hair and said, "And who told *you* about all that?"

"Oh, shoot, *everybody* knows that, Ma!" Moriah said airily. "You know how it is in Arkadelphia. Everybody knows everybody else's business."

"Now, you shouldn't be tellin' Mr. Taliferro things like that, and you shouldn't call him Clay."

"He told me to, Ma. And he told Brodie and Clinton the same thing."

Jerusalem rocked slowly back and forth, stroking Mary Aidan's hair and thinking about the three days that had transpired since Clay Taliferro had arrived. He certainly had made himself at home and talked freely about Jake—except for those things Jerusalem desired most to know about her husband. Something about the whole story of Jake's failure to come home for nearly a year and a half, except for one short visit, did not ring true in Jerusalem's mind. Though she was by now used to her husband's wanderings, his behavior was still not acceptable to her. Her musings were interrupted by Clinton, who came running in and yelling.

"Clay's back, and he done brung a big, fat deer, Ma!"

"Well, that's good. We can use some fresh meat."

"I'm gonna go out and help him dress it out," Clinton said importantly. "He said I could use that big ol' knife of his."

"I'm going, too, Ma," Moriah said.

Jerusalem nodded as she continued to rock the baby. When Mary Aidan was satisfied and had dropped off to sleep, Jerusalem gently laid the baby down in the cradle. She turned and walked outside to the dogtrot, stepped down, and walked over to the skinning tree. Clay was standing in front of the fat doe he had strung up by the hind legs and turned to face her when he heard her footsteps.

"Good morning, Jerusalem Ann," he said

cheerfully. He had not shaved, and his tawny, straggly beard had a hint of red in it. "Brought in supper."

"That's good, Clay."

"I'm just fixin' to let Clinton here do a little of the work, if that's all right with you."

"He needs to learn."

Clay looked down at his buckskin shirt for a moment and then shook his head. "This is going to be kind of messy. I think I'll save a little wear and tear on my shirt, if you'll pardon me, ma'am." Before she could reply, he pulled his shirt off over his head.

For a moment Jerusalem was taken aback by the sight of his bare chest. Her first impression of him had been that he was skinny, but now she could see that she had misjudged him. Clay did not have the heavy, bulky muscles her husband had, but there was not an ounce of spare flesh on him. His arms writhed with lean muscles whenever he moved. His stomach was flat and marked with small squares of solid muscle, and there was a hint of speed and quickness about him. He reminded her of the mountain lion she had shot once that was trying to take one of her cows. Taliferro possessed the same grace and strength she had seen in that animal.

"Golly, Clay, what done that to you?" Moriah asked.

Clay turned and looked down at his chest. A huge scar started just below his left shoulder and ran all the way down to his right hip, marring the symmetry of his lithe form. "That? Why, I got that little scratch from a fellow by the name of Jim Bowie."

"You was in a knife fight?" Moriah said, her eyes fixed on the scar.

"Yep, and this here was the knife that done it." Clay pulled a huge knife with a twelve-inch blade out of its sheath and held it up. It glinted in the morning sunlight, and Clay shook his head. "I took it off of Jim and gave him something to remember me by. It was quite a fracas."

"What were you fighting about?" Jerusalem asked.

"Oh, I disremember."

"I'll bet it was over some woman, wasn't it, Clay?" Moriah demanded.

Clay suddenly laughed and reached out and tousled Moriah's hair. "You're too smart, young lady. Now, let's get this here deer cut up. Here, Clinton, you take this knife and slice this doe right down along here."

"This here girl child's got a right pretty name—Mary Aidan. How do you spell Aidan?"

"A-i-d-a-n," Jerusalem said. "It was my grandmother's name. It's Irish."

Clay was holding Mary Aidan on his lap, tickling her chin and grinning, when she giggled at him. "She's gonna be spellin' that name for people all of her life—just like me."

Old Josiah was sitting at the end of the table. It was one of his good days. His eyes were bright, and he spoke up, saying, "How come you know so much about babies? You handle that there young'un like you knowed about 'em."

"Oh, I know all about babies and women," Clay said, nodding with assurance. "I got me a foolproof system that makes 'em all love me to death."

"I'd like to hear it," Jerusalem said, staring at him oddly.

"Well," Clay shrugged, "you handle babies and women just alike. You give 'em everything they want when they want it, and they'll hush."

Jerusalem laughed aloud. She had a beautiful laugh that came from deep inside, and her eyes lit up. "That's the most foolish thing I ever heard in my life, but I like it."

"Why, it's foolproof if you think about it. When Mary Aidan here gets hungry she hollers, and as soon as you feed her, she's got what she wants, so she hushes."

Jerusalem was amused. "I feel sorry for your wife."

Clay lifted his eyebrows in surprise. "Sorry? Why, what woman wouldn't want to be treated like that. Wouldn't you?"

"No, it'd be like being married to a bowl of mush."

"Well, I'd like it," Moriah said. "When I grow up you can marry me, Clay."

"Why, I might do that, honey. But likely not. In another couple of years, there'll be so many young bucks around here chasin' after you, you won't be able to count 'em— and I'll be too old to chase ya."

He turned to Josiah and asked, "Did you ever see General Washington, Josiah?"

"Many a time in all weathers."

Clay shook his head in wonder. "I reckon it seems to me like seein' the Lord Himself."

Clinton spoke up loudly, "That there is idolatry, Clay. You go to perdition for sayin' things like that. Why, you might as well bow down to a graven image!"

Clay winked at Jerusalem, then said, "Well, pardon me, Clinton. I didn't mean to offend your religious sensibilities. What'd he look like, Josiah? George Washington, that is."

"A big man, big all over. But it was more than size. He could make men do jest about anything, Clay." Josiah Mitchell sat loosely in his chair, his mind going back to a time long ago. They all waited for him to say more, for he was like a living history book. Finally, he smiled and said, "I had a drink with him once."

"You drank with General Washington!" Clay exclaimed. He leaned forward, his eyes alive with interest. "How'd that come about?"

"It was that one winter at Valley Forge. We was a lean bunch of scarecrows, I'll tell ya. Half of us didn't even have shoes. We had to wrap our feet in rags. I'd got me a jug from somewhere, some kind of rotgut whiskey. We'd been eatin' shoe leather almost, and the general he come by. He stopped and looked down at us. He didn't say nothin', but I seen somethin' in his eyes, and finally I said, 'Have a drink, General.'"

"What'd he say, Grandpa?" Jerusalem whispered.

"He said, 'No thank ye,' and that made me mad. I said, 'You too good to drink with us, are ya?'"

"You said that to General Washington!" Brodie exclaimed. "Wasn't you scared?"

"What could he do—shoot me? He needed men for his army too much for that. Besides, by that time none of us keered much. No, he got off his horse and came over and took that jug away from me and took a big swig, then handed it back to me without sayin' a word."

"Did you say anything?" Clinton asked.

"Shore did. I looked at him, and it was the only time I remember tears in my eyes. He done that to men, somehow. I said, 'Now, General, I'll fight for you until the last drop of my blood!'"

A silence went around the table, and they all looked at Josiah Mitchell. Then suddenly the old man fell silent, and the spark of memory faded from his eyes. Clay said, "What happened after that?"

But Jerusalem saw that he was slipping into one of his memory lapses, and wherever it was that her grandfather went during those times, his mind had left behind those at the table. "He's through talkin' for a while, Clay." The children all looked away from the old man, and Jerusalem said quickly, "I'm going into town to make the loan payment at the bank."

"Maybe I could go along with you," Clay said. "I need a few things."

"All right. Brodie, you go hitch up Abishag to the buggy while I get ready."

"Can I go too, Ma?" Moriah began to beg.

"No, you can't," she said.

Both Brodie and Clinton asked also but received a flat denial. All of them knew that when their mother said no in a certain way, she meant it.

As they passed by the small farms that closely surrounded Arkadelphia, Jerusalem remarked, "We're going to be behind on our plowing."

Clay looked out at a farmer who was plowing with a span of big mules. "I reckon so," he said. He slapped the reins on Abishag's back and said, "She's mighty small for heavy plowin'."

"Yes, we had to sell our best mule to make it through the winter. Now all we got left is Abishag and that monster Samson."

"He's a good-lookin' mule—big and strong."

"He's mean as Satan himself. He bit Jake one time right in the small of the back. Jake had turned his back on him just for a minute. I thought Jake would beat him to death, but Samson is hardheaded. Brodie can't hitch him up at all. Maybe we can find some good mules. We need a good one."

"Maybe I can have a little talk with Samson."

"You know how to plow?"

"I looked at the hind end of a mule every day of my life, it seems like, until I was fifteen. Then I quit."

Jerusalem turned and stared at Clay. She was a blunt woman at times and asked what had been on her mind ever since Clay had arrived. "Are you married, Clay?"

"No."

The answer was curt, but Jerusalem Hardin was a persistent woman. "Have you ever been married?" She waited for him to answer, and he paused for so long that she said sharply, "It's a simple question, Clay." Clay turned to stare at her, and she saw something in his face she had not seen before.

"I had an Indian woman, but we only got married by her tribe's customs. Not white man's ways."

"Where is she?"

"Dead."

From the finality with which he answered and the look on his face, it was as if he had hung up a No Trespassing sign, and at once she changed the subject. "Well, here we are. What are you going to do?"

"I'll let you out at the bank, and then I'll tie up somewhere."

"It's right over there on the corner," Jerusalem said, pointing to a building.

Clay pulled up in front of the bank, but there was no room to park the buggy. It was a busy Saturday afternoon, and the town was more crowded than usual.

"I shouldn't be too long," she said. "I need to go to the general store. You can eckon I spoke hastily. You'll have to accept ny apology."

"All right. I accept your apology. Come along, Mr. Taliferro."

As soon as they stepped outside, Jerusalem began to laugh.

"What in the world are you laughing at, Jerusalem?" Clay's voice was normal again.

"I never saw a man so scared, Clay. He was shaking. Did you see that?"

Clay grinned. "I reckon he was a mite agitated."

"He was sure he was gonna be scalped."

"Maybe he'll mind his manners a bit more from now on. Come on, let's go get our things."

The two went to Mason's General Store, and Jerusalem used some of the money Jake had sent to buy staples. After she had given the store owner the money, she saw Clay perusing the men's clothing.

He looked up and said, "I'll reckon I'll go buy a few clothes and get my hair cut."

"I have some other things to do. I'll meet you out at the buggy at three o'clock."

"Sounds about right."

★   ★   ★

help me get some things and get what you need for yourself."

"All right, Jerusalem Ann."

Jerusalem got out of the buggy, carefully holding Mary Aidan. She walked into the bank, and her eyes took in Rusk, who was standing beside the row of cages talking to one of the clerks. When he turned and saw her, she could not help noticing the look of shock on his face. She had not seen him since the other day when she had made it clear to all at the bank that their banker lacked noble intentions when it came to married women. *Serves him right,* Jerusalem thought, *for the way he acted.*

He looked around and then came to her and said, "Well . . . hello, Jerusalem."

"I've come to make a payment on the note."

Disappointment flared in Rusk's eyes. "Oh, so you've got it, have you!"

"I wouldn't be here if I didn't."

"All right. Come over to my desk. I'll take care of it myself."

Jerusalem stepped over to the desk but did not sit down. "Just make out a receipt," she said. She reached into the leather bag

Clay had brought the money in, took the bills out, and counted some of them.

Rusk stared at the note, looked up, and said, "Where'd you get this cash?"

"I held up a bank," she said straight-faced, thoroughly enjoying the fact that for once she had the upper hand.

Rusk flushed, and his eyes went small with anger. He snatched up a pen, jabbed it in the ink, and wrote out a receipt. Jerusalem took it, but at that instant she saw Rusk's eyes open wide. She turned around to see that Clay had entered. She had not seen any of his weapons except for the two rifles he had brought, but now he had a cartridge belt, and a huge pistol hung from his left side. She had already noticed that he was left-handed. The huge bowie knife he carried was in a sheath stuck into his belt. She was used to seeing armed men, but there was something sinister about Clay as he stopped and looked across the room. He was looking, she saw, at Rusk, not at her.

Clay slowly walked over to the desk, not taking his eyes off of Rusk. "Is your business finished, Miz Hardin?"

"Yes, it is. I'm ready." She turned but Clay did not move.

When Rusk stood up abruptly, Cla to look up into the banker's face. E Jerusalem it was as if Rusk had shru don't reckon we've—"

"I'm a friend of Jake Hardin, Rusk."

Clay's voice was different from any Jerusalem had heard come out of hi had a steely timbre in it. He usually s with a soft, lilting voice, pleasant and a able, but now he spoke with all the h ness and keenness of the knife that hur his side.

Rusk tried to speak but could not see find the words.

"Jake's not here to take care of his f ily—but I am."

The same silence that had fallen over tellers and the customers when Jerusal had accused Rusk on her previous visit n seemed to fall again. One clerk had his p raised to sign a paper, and he held it the as if frozen in place.

Rusk suddenly said in a high-pitch voice, "Look, there's been some kind of . of misunderstanding here. Miss Hardin,

Jerusalem had finished earlier and waited until three o'clock, but Clay had not appeared. She had nursed Mary Aidan, who had gone to sleep, and put her down in the seat of the buggy, wrapped in a blanket. She got out and walked back and forth, looking up and down the street. Finally, after twenty minutes, her eyes fell on the saloon. An idea came to her, and she picked up Mary Aidan and walked across the street, dodging a heavy-laden freight wagon pulled by four struggling mules. She stepped up on the boardwalk and went to the swinging doors, hesitated a moment, then stepped inside.

It was dark inside the saloon, which was lit by oil lamps, and at first she couldn't see very well. Her eyes ran around the room, and then she halted as she spotted Clay at a table talking to a black-haired woman in a scanty, low-cut dress. He did not see her until she walked across to him and said in a spare voice, "Let's go, Clay."

Clay had a glass of whiskey in his hand, and he turned so quickly that some of it spilled out over his hand. He set it down and said, "Why—" He could not seem to finish the sentence.

"Is this your wife, honey?" the black-haired girl sitting in front of him asked.

"No," Clay said quickly.

"She must be your mama, then."

The other customers in the saloon laughed, and Clay got to his feet, his face red.

"I reckon I'm ready," he said.

"Come back, honey, when your mama says it's all right," the girl said, laughing.

Clay followed Jerusalem outside and walked silently across the street. He helped her into the wagon, then climbed in and picked up the reins. He turned to her and said, "Jerusalem Ann, it ain't fittin' for you to go into a place like that."

Jerusalem did not answer. She was staring at Clay and said, "You don't look like yourself."

Indeed, Clay Taliferro didn't look like himself. The buckskins he had worn to town were gone, and he was wearing a pair of gray trousers, a white shirt, and a colorful vest. A string tie fell over his chest, and a pair of fine black boots shone on his feet. His hair had been cut, and the beard had been shaved off, leaving his skin glowing. He had, she saw, a wedge-shaped face and looked ten years younger without the beard and the shaggy hair. "You smell wonderful," she said dryly.

"That was the barber. He put some cologne on me." Clay's face was set in a frown.

Jerusalem suddenly began to laugh. "I bet your mama never came in and dragged you out of a saloon before."

"No, nor my wife neither," Clay said, but suddenly he turned to her and grinned. "You pull a man up short, Jerusalem Ann Hardin. You purely do!"

At breakfast the next morning, Jerusalem discovered that Clay had bought not only a set of fine clothes, which he told her she could bury him in if it came to that, but work clothes, heavy jeans, a blue denim shirt, and heavy-duty brogans.

"We're gonna do some plowin' this mornin', boy," Clay said to Brodie as they ate.

"Oh, shoot, I hate plowin'."

"So do I, partner. I ran away from Tennessee when I was fifteen so I wouldn't have to look at the back end of a mule, but you know"—he winked at Jerusalem— "somehow I miss it. I've been longin' to be lookin' at a mule's hind end for quite a few years now. Maybe I can get the plowin' caught up."

"You don't have to do that, Clay," Jerusalem said quickly. "I know you hate it."

"Didn't you hear me? I been missin' it."

"Can't nobody plow with that old Samson," Clinton scowled. "He's one mean ol' mule."

"You think he's mean?" Clay said. "Well, boy, you ain't seen mean yet. I'm the one who's mean. Come on and let me give you a lesson in how to make friends with a mule."

The whole family traipsed out, and Moriah whispered, "Ma, he's liable to get hurt. You know how mean old Samson is. Pa couldn't hardly handle him, and Samson is a lot bigger than Clay."

Jerusalem did not answer. She had her eyes fixed on the two mules in the corral.

"Brodie, you bring Abishag out here. That's gonna be your mule. That nice old Samson, he'll be mine."

The whole family was nervous.

"He's dangerous at both ends, Clay," Brodie warned. "He'll bite you, or he'll kick your brains out if you give him a chance."

"Oh, this mule's just been misunderstood. He probably had a hard time when he was a baby, but I'm gonna make friends with him."

Jerusalem stared as Clay walked up to the big mule. Samson was a huge animal, and the whites of his eyes showed as Taliferro approached him. She was caught unprepared for the suddenness of it, for as soon as Clay was within striking distance the big mule's head shot up, his lips spread, and his big teeth looked enormous. She could not follow the movement of Clay's hands, they were so fast. He gripped the mule's lower lip with his left hand and ran the other hand into his upper lip. She saw the big mule rear up and try to strike at Clay, but somehow Clay was lifted off the ground. She saw him twist and pull at the mule's lips, at the same time avoiding the slashing hooves. Samson brayed as if a mountain lion had bit him, and Jerusalem saw blood flowing over Clay's hand. Samson tried to back away and flung his head. Clay's feet left the ground again, but his hands were clamped in a death grip on Samson's lower lip. The blood was down over his elbows now and spattering his face.

"He's gonna kill Clay, Ma!" Moriah cried out.

But Samson suddenly began to whinny in a strange, high-pitched sound. Clay's feet came to the ground, and he held the mule down and seemed to relax his grip. "We're gonna be friends, Samson. Just depends on you how soon." Clay released one hand and wiped the blood off on his shirt. He did not take his eyes off the mule. He held his head close to the ear of the mule and began speaking softly.

Jerusalem and the children watched as if hypnotized as Clay finally released the mule's big lip. Samson's eyes were white and rolling, and he was trembling all over. Clay walked over to the trough, washed the blood off his hands, and came back and said, "Get me some grease, Brodie. Samson's got a sore lip and a sore nose."

As Brodie ran into the barn to get the grease, Clay walked back to Samson. The mule made another attempt to bite him, and Clay simply clamped down on his lip and nose again, and Samson screamed but began trembling worse than ever.

When Brodie brought out the grease, Clay applied it to the mule's lips and nose. Samson trembled as if he were in a high wind, and Clay turned to say, "He'll try it again a few times, partner." He looked over at Jerusalem, who was squeezing Mary Aidan too hard, making her squeal.

"Mules are like women, Brodie," he said loudly. "You gotta be firm."

Jerusalem suddenly smiled. "You tried this method on many women, Clay?"

Clay grinned. "Yep, on two that I can remember. One of 'em shot me in the leg and the other one stabbed me with a hatpin."

"Stabbed ya with a hatpin!" Moriah said, her eyes big. "Where'd you get stabbed?"

Clay winked at her and said, "It wouldn't be proper for me to say, honey."

Jerusalem stared at Clay, a glint in her eyes. "You know more about mules than you do about women, Clay Taliferro."

Clay stared at her. "Don't bet on that, Jerusalem Ann."

An hour later Brodie was walking along behind Abishag. He passed by his mother, who was standing at the edge of the field. He stopped the mule and said, "I've never seen nothin' like that, Ma!"

"I never did either—and neither did Samson."

"Ma, do you think he'll stay around?"

Jerusalem looked at Clay, who was walking along singing some sortof foolish song behind Samson. The big, powerful mule pulled the plow through the rich earth as if it were nothing. She studied him for a moment and then smiled. "I reckon he will, Brodie."

CHAPTER
FOUR

The knifelike pain came so suddenly it took her breath away. Sometimes it would gnaw at her steadily for hours or even days. There were good times when she could smile and move around, but when it hurt like this, she could only struggle to keep from crying out and disturbing others.

As Jewel Satterfield lay in her bed holding her stomach and compressing her lips, a bar of pale sunlight shone through the window to her right. She watched the tiny dust motes dancing in the beam and forced herself to think of pleasant moments in her life, anything other than the white-hot pain that tortured her without mercy.

For months now this room had been her prison, but Jewel knew it would not hold her much longer. One day soon she would step out into the blazing light of God's glory. For her, heaven was as real as the logs that bound the walls of the room, as real as the sunlight that touched her face with warmth and made her blink and turn away from its brilliance. Her faith in heaven had always been strong, even when she was a small girl. Now fifty years of thinking about it, reading about it in the Bible, and listening to sermons had created in her heart a deep assurance that all her suffering was only temporary.

Hearing a door open, Jewel quickly moved her hands, ignoring the pain. She smiled at Jerusalem as she entered the room. "Good morning, daughter."

"Good morning, Ma. I'm going to clean you up and feed you a good breakfast today."

Jewel wanted nothing more than to stay in bed, but she knew she would make the effort for Jerusalem's sake. "All right, daughter. I hate to be such a bother."

Jerusalem merely smiled and began to bathe her mother's face from a basin of warm water she had brought in. Jewel knew she was searching for signs that would indicate how good or bad a day her mother was having. Hiding the pain had become a game to Jewel, but it was difficult because Jerusalem was a discerning woman. She always had been, and now as Jewel submitted to her daughter's ministrations, she kept her face from revealing the excruciating pain that went on within. Instead, she asked about the family and kept Jerusalem occupied with her questions.

Finally, after she had slipped on a clean nightgown and a worn, thin robe, Jewel got out of bed, aided by Jerusalem's strong hands. She tried to keep herself straight, but the strength even to stand had left her long ago. She glanced down at her frail body, which seemed to be that of another woman. In her mind she still had the strong frame she had been blessed with throughout most of her life, but now she saw nothing but a wasted form. She was shocked to realize how frail she had become.

"Here, sit down, Ma. I got some fresh

mush on the stove. It oughta set good on your stomach."

Jewel sat down in the chair. She had so little padding left that it was painful, but she let none of her suffering show. When Jerusalem set the bowl of steaming mush in front of her, she smiled. "That looks good, daughter."

"Try some of this here fresh milk. And I got a little sugar left too."

With no appetite at all, but a desire to please Jerusalem, Jewel added a few spoonfuls of goat's milk and half a spoonful of sugar. She noticed the thinness of her fingers and of her arm but stirred the mush and then bowed her head and said, "Lord, we thank You for this food and for every blessing. Be with our family, in Jesus' name. Amen."

"Amen," said Jerusalem. She had made herself a cup of strong black coffee and sat down to drink it as her mother ate. "Mary Aidan's asleep for a change."

"I'll be glad when she gets those teeth cut."

"So will I, Ma. It makes her so fussy."

"Where are the young'uns?"

"Outside with Clay doin' somethin'."

"They do cling to that man, don't they?"

"They miss their pa. Young'uns like a man to do things with."

Jewel looked up quickly. It was unusual for Jerusalem to speak ill of Jake, and even this was not a direct criticism. "I reckon you're right," she said. "I wish Jake would come home."

Jerusalem lifted her cup and took a sip, then gazed out the window. She could see the cotton fields ripening, the plants having burst through the earth, reaching for the warm rays of the sun. She got up, walked to the window, and stood there for a moment. Finally, she shook her head and took her seat again. "I don't know when Jake will be back."

Jewel stirred the mush and took a small bite of it. "Clay's done wonders the last four months."

"Yes, he has—and he's hated every minute of it. At least the plowin'."

"He never said nothin', did he?"

"No. He's made a game out of it." Jerusalem sipped her coffee again. "It's odd how a man can make a place perk up. All the fences are straight now and repaired. That barn was fallin' over, but now it's all braced. We've had plenty of meat on the table. It seems all he has to do is walk into the woods and some critter just falls down in front of him, beggin' to be et. He made that crop, just him and Brodie. I don't know what would have happened if he hadn't come, Ma."

Jewel hesitated, then said cautiously, "He does like his pleasure."

Indeed, both women were quite aware that as hard as Clay Taliferro worked, there were times he would take off early and stay away all night. He would come in with his eyes red-rimmed and his speech slurred. No one ever questioned him about this except Moriah and, at times, Clinton. Once Clinton had blurted out, "Clay goes over to them ol' saloons to see them scarlet women! I told him he's goin' straight to perdition if he don't quit that!"

Jerusalem had said sharply, "That's none of your business, Clinton! You keep your oar out of it."

As the two women sat talking, Jewel said softly, "I've been praying for the Lord to touch Clay—show him the errors of his ways and bring 'im back to a straight an' narrow path."

"He needs it," Jerusalem said, shaking

her head. "But it's not for me to judge. Can't you eat some more of that mush, Ma?"

"I think I'd just like to sit in the rocker out on the porch."

"All right. I'll take you out there for some fresh air." Jerusalem carefully led her mother out to the porch and helped ease her into the rocking chair.

"This is mighty fine, daughter. You go on about your work now. I'll be fine here."

"I'll bring you some tea."

As Jewel gently rocked and waited for her tea, she saw Clay coming up from the river in the wagon. All three of the older children were with him, and they were singing a song. As they got closer, she was able to make it out:

Where, oh, where is dear little Nellie?
Where, oh, where is dear little Nellie?
Where, oh, where is dear little Nellie?
Way down yonder in the pawpaw
    patch.

Jerusalem could hear Clay's clear voice sing the verse, then the children joined in on the chorus.

She's pickin' up pawpaws, puttin' 'em
in her pocket.
Pickin' up pawpaws, puttin 'em in her
pocket.
Pickin' up pawpaws, puttin 'em in her
pocket.
Way down yonder in the pawpaw
patch.

As the wagon drew up to the cabin, the singing stopped, and the children all leaped out. Clay climbed out slowly and walked over to the porch. From the scowl on his face, Jewel could tell he was dissatisfied about something.

"I'm sick and tired of haulin' water from that doggone river," Clay said as he got out of the wagon.

"If we had a spring," Clinton piped up, "we wouldn't have to haul water all the time."

"Yes, and if a toady frog had wings, he wouldn't bump his rear," Clay snorted.

Jerusalem had brought Jewel's tea and paused as Clay walked up to the porch. "I know it's worrisome," Jerusalem said, "but we've gotta have water."

"Well, I've half a mind to do somethin' about it."

Jerusalem said calmly, "I've been tired of haulin' it for twelve years, Clay. You've only been haulin' it for four months."

Clay took off his straw hat and stared at Jerusalem almost angrily. "Well, I don't intend to put up with it anymore."

"What are you going to do about it, Clay?" Moriah chimed in.

"I'm gonna dig a well. That's what I'm gonna do."

All three children stared at him. "Ma's been after Pa to dig a well ever since I can remember," Brodie said.

"Well, then it's high time the thing was dug! Before I leave here, I'll see a well so nobody don't have to haul water all the way from that river."

Ever since he had been at the Hardin farm, Clay had been dropping veiled hints that he would leave. He would say, "Before I leave this place, I'd better straighten up that barn." He'd throw himself into the work of bracing the barn back into an upright position, but then he would stay, apparently forgetting his threat. When he had first said he was going to leave, the youngsters had become agitated, but he had said it so often by now, no one paid much attention anymore.

As Clay began to carry water into the house and pour it into a big barrel in the corner, Moriah whispered, "Ma, you don't think he'll really leave, do you?"

"He's not left yet."

At the same time she remembered that whenever Clay made one of these threats, he would go to town after finishing his chore and come back red-eyed. Twice he had returned with the marks of a fight on his face. And he usually came back reeking of cheap perfume, but Jerusalem would ignore this.

Clay came out of the house and said, "We gotta have us a water diviner."

"I ain't never believed in findin' water with a wand," Jerusalem scoffed. "If'n you're gonna dig a well, just dig it someplace handylike."

"That's just like you, Jerusalem. You never give no thought to nothin'. Might go straight down to China or hit bedrock. No, sir, you gotta go about this in a scientific manner."

"Scientific! You call those water witches

scientific? They're all frauds," Jerusalem declared.

The argument soon became so heated that the children were a bit alarmed. It was a familiar scene, however, for Jerusalem and Clay often had different opinions, and neither of them hesitated to state their minds bluntly.

"I said I was going to dig this well, Jerusalem, and I aim to do it—before I leave here. But I ain't diggin' no dry well. Don't you know any water diviners around here?"

Moriah piped up, "Ellie Bratton's a water diviner."

"She is?" Clay said. "Why, she never told me that."

"Well, she is. She found the well for the Williamsons," Moriah said, "and two or three others I can think of."

Clay jammed his hat on his head. "Why, then, I'm goin' over and gettin' her right now." Saying no more, he jumped in the wagon and headed out, keeping the mules at a fast gait.

"What'd you have to tell him that for, Moriah?" Jerusalem scolded.

"Because it's so."

"You ain't got no sense at all, Moriah,"

Clinton said. "Ellie's a scarlet woman, and she's draggin' Clay right down to the pit! That's what them bad women do." Then he broke into a favorite quotation from Proverbs 7: "'For she hath cast down many wounded: yea, many strong men have been slain by her. Her house is the way to hell, going down to the chambers of death.'" He glared at Moriah. "That's what the Bible says. She's tryin' to ruin Clay, that's what!"

Usually, Jerusalem found Clinton's Scripture quoting tiresome, but this time she fixed her eyes on him and said, "I think you got that right, Clinton." Then she shook her head. "Now, you children get on about your business. You've got chores to do. If you don't, I'll find you some."

As the youngsters scattered, Jerusalem turned to her mother and saw that she looked pale. "Are you tired yet?"

"I think I'll just sit here awhile longer."

"I'll go inside, but you call if you need me."

Jerusalem went inside, and for the next hour, she stayed busy but could not help thinking about Clay and Ellie. *Clay knows how to tame mules, but he don't know as much about women as he thinks he does.*

Finally, her grandfather came in, and she saw that it was not a bad day for him. "Hello, Grandpa. You're late for breakfast."

"I can eat anything, granddaughter."

Jerusalem fixed a quick breakfast for her grandfather and then sat down with him. As they talked she realized how much she cared for him, but she could tell he was troubled about something. His eyes kept going to the open door where his daughter was sitting on the porch. He turned and looked at her, his eyes filled with sorrow.

"We're goin' to lose her, Jerusalem."

Jerusalem had kept up a front before the children concerning her mother's health, but she saw the truth in her grandfather's eyes. "Yes, we are."

"I wisht it wuz me. Why hain't it me, Jerusalem?"

Josiah's words came so softly that Jerusalem hardly heard them. "I don't know, Grandpa."

Obviously, the question had been eating at the old man for some time. He sat there toying with his cup of coffee and said, "Why did we lose your pa when he was such a young, strong man? Why Mark and not me?"

"I just don't know why." Jerusalem reached over and held his hand, still strong for his age, and he returned her grip.

"I wisht it wuz me," he said again faintly. Then without another word, he got up and walked outside. He stopped beside his daughter, put his hand gently on her head, and murmured a few words before walking away.

Jerusalem felt the weight of all the past years suddenly settle on her. Jake's constant wanderings and absence had been a heavy burden to bear. Every day that she woke up alone, she felt the love she once had for him growing dimmer. He had not proved to be the man she had thought he was. She remembered the days of their courtship, days when she saw nothing but his manly strength. When they were first married and Brodie was born, she was happy and loved him with a fierce love. But that had all changed now. As he began staying away for longer and longer periods of time, she tried desperately to think of how to keep him at home. But in the end she felt like a complete failure for her inability to make him want to stay with his family. Her thoughts gathered in her mind like an ominous dark thundercloud, and only when she heard her mother call her name faintly did she shake them off and go outside. "Are you ready to lie down, Ma?"

"I reckon I am."

Jerusalem helped her mother out of the chair and guided her back to the bed. Slipping her out of her robe, she helped her lie down. The room was so hot she did not need to pull up the covers. Jerusalem sat down, and taking her mother's hand, she stayed there with her for a long time. She knew her mother was in terrible pain and was using all of her strength to keep from crying out. Jerusalem sat there, admiring the indomitable spirit she saw in her mother, as a tear slowly crept down her cheek.

Jewel turned to face her. The disease had eaten away her flesh, and the beauty she once had was now gone. But in its place a divine glow radiated from her eyes. When she spoke, it was to mention for the first time what lay ahead of her. "I wish I didn't have to leave you, Jerusalem—but my time's close."

Jerusalem's throat tightened, and her eyes brimmed with tears. "Is . . . is there anything you want, Ma? Anything at all that I can get you?" The dying woman's eyes closed, and she swallowed convulsively. Her voice was so low that Jerusalem had to lean forward to hear her.

"Just one thing, and I can't have it."

"What is it, Ma?"

Jerusalem waited, but her mother refused to speak. "What is it? Please tell me. I'll get it for you if I can."

"If . . . if I could just see Julie—"

The words came faintly, but when her mother opened her eyes, Jerusalem saw a longing so powerful and strong it made her catch her breath.

"I'd be happy to go if I could just see her once. I know she ain't livin' right, but I'd love to see her. I purely would."

Jerusalem could not speak for the tightness in her throat, and she saw her mother's eyes close and knew that mercifully she had dropped off into a fitful sleep. She sat there holding her mother's wasted hand, then finally lifted it and held it against her teary cheek. She did not move, but her mother's words seemed to echo in her mind, and she knew she had to do something. She began to think of how she could carry out her mother's last wish.

★   ★   ★

"It's Clay, Ma, and he's brought Ellie Bratton with him," Brodie said.

Jerusalem was cutting up a chicken, but she put down the knife, rinsed her hands off in the pan, and wiped her hands on her apron. She came outside and stood there as Clay pulled the wagon up. He had not returned the day before.

As he got out of the wagon, he took one covert look at Jerusalem and said quickly, "Ellie couldn't come yesterday, so I waited."

Jerusalem turned her eyes to Ellie, who had jumped out of the wagon. She was wearing a tight, threadbare dress that was way too revealing for any decent woman. She had bold eyes and smiled crookedly at Jerusalem.

"Hello, Miz Hardin. I've come to find water for you."

Clinton and Moriah, along with Brodie, had gathered, and all three were staring at Clay. Usually he was cheerful and smiling, but now he had a hangdog look about him, and he said again, "I just couldn't get back, Jerusalem."

"I know what you been doin' with that

scarlet woman—" Clinton began loudly. He opened his mouth to say more, but Jerusalem cut him off.

"You bite your tongue, Clinton!" She stared at Clay in a way that brooked no contradiction. Without turning her head, she said, "Brodie, take Ellie back home."

"Wait a minute!" Ellie said, her face turning red. "I come to find water."

"Get back in that wagon, Ellie Bratton. Brodie, you mind what I say."

Brodie jumped into the wagon, and Ellie, throwing an angry look at Jerusalem, climbed in. She turned her head and cursed as they left the yard.

Clay could not seem to find anything to do with his hands. He finally faced Jerusalem and said defiantly, "I needed her to find water so I could dig that well."

Jerusalem ignored him and said, "Moriah, you go take care of Mary Aidan. Clinton, you go down and pick those beans. They're about ready. Clay, you come with me."

For a moment, Clay considered going back into town, but when he saw the set of her shoulders, he knew he had better follow. She led him to the small cemetery and motioned toward the little bench.

"Sit down, Clay." When he did, she sat down beside him.

Clay shifted uneasily and glanced at her out of the corner of his eye and then started to speak. "I reckon I can dig the well anywhere you say, Jerusalem."

Jerusalem did not speak for a time. She was looking at the tombstones, and the silence became so palpable that Clay could not keep still. He shifted as if he would jump up and run away.

Finally, Jerusalem turned and said, "It's none of my business, Clay. You're a man, and men won't rest until they make a fool of themselves with women like that."

Clay sat silently, unable to think of a single thing to say and wishing he had a good excuse to leave. She turned and faced him squarely. He was startled at the intensity of her expression and cleared his throat. "Listen, Jerusalem, I can—"

"Shush up, Clay, and listen to me. All the time you've been here, I've never thanked you for all you've done for us. I didn't know how. I know you felt like you owed it to Jake to help his family, and maybe you did. I guess there's some things between men that a woman just cain't understand."

Jerusalem reached out and took Clay's hand, holding it in both of hers. A startled expression crossed his face, but she did not give him time to speak. "I thank you now, Clay, for plowin' with those orn'ry mules when you hated every minute of it. I thank you for puttin' food on the table for all of us. I thank you for plantin' that cotton in the ground, and I thank you for spendin' time with my children."

Clay Taliferro felt the strength and warmth of her hands, holding his tightly. Jerusalem's eyes, which had always seemed so cool and frank, now had a warmth he had not noticed before. Her green eyes seemed to have no bottom to them, and he could not help but notice the self-possessed curve of her mouth. A summer darkness lay over her skin, and where her dress fell away from her throat, he noted the smooth ivory shading of her skin. She had never looked so attractive to him, and he nervously lifted his eyes back again to her face.

"When Mary Aidan had diphtheria, Clay, you were the one who sat up all night with me for so long." She tightened her grip, squeezing his hand so hard he had to tighten his own hand to meet it. "I couldn't

say what I felt, Clay," she whispered, "because I knew I'd do what I'm doing right now."

Clay saw the tears in her eyes then and muttered, "Why, Jerusalem Ann, I was right proud to do it."

"I know it, but I had to say it out loud. Wait, now, don't you move." Jerusalem got up, walked to the gate of the small fence that enclosed the cemetery, and stood for what seemed like a long time. After a moment, she wiped her eyes with her apron and came back and sat down beside him. She looked at the ground, her shoulders rounded as if they bore some heavy burden. "I've always hated to ask favors, Clay, and I especially hate to ask you. You've done so much already."

"Why, shoot, you just ask it, Jerusalem. What is it?"

"You've heard about my sister Julie?"

"I just know that you have one. The kids have mentioned her a couple of times."

"Ma wants to see her before she dies."

Clay started. It was the first time death had been mentioned, although he was as aware as the others that Jewel Satterfield could not live long. "Where is she?"

"She's at Fort Smith." Jerusalem turned. "Will you go get her and bring her here?"

"Why, certainly I will!"

Jerusalem's eyes held him. "You may have to make her come, Clay."

"*Make* her come? Why—"

"Julie is twenty-five now, but she started going wild by the time she was in her teens. She ran away when she was fifteen, and she's led a hard life since then. She's working in saloons now, and . . . well, you know what that means."

Clay listened as Jerusalem spoke of her sister, not missing the pain in her voice. When she was finished, he said with as much confidence as he could muster, "Why, I'll be proud to do it, Jerusalem."

"Clay . . . it'll be harder than diggin' a well."

"I'll leave tomorrow." He got to his feet, and she rose with him. He hesitated, then said, "You mean actually *make* her come back? That could get a man in trouble."

"I know it, Clay. I hate to ask."

Clay smiled crookedly. He put out his hand and squeezed Jerusalem's arm. "Why, shucks, Jerusalem, I'll bring that scamp back! I'll turn on my charm. She'll come along like a cat following her mama."

Jerusalem smiled briefly. "You don't know Julie."

"I don't know her, but I promise to bring her back."

Jerusalem put her hand on Clay's chest right over his heart. Her eyes were like diamonds, and she whispered, "God be with you, Clay."

CHAPTER
FIVE

~~~~~~~~~~

Shore is a tired-lookin' town. Ain't worth doodly squat."

Clay eased his horse to a halt in front of the livery stable and glanced up and down the street with a critical eye. The main street pretty much defined the town, and the saloons outnumbered all the other businesses at least two to one. All the buildings were wooden. One or two had a coat of fresh paint, some had only the remembrance, and some had never known even one coating but stood silvery gray in the twilight. Slipping off the bay, Clay lifted the Hawkin down and held it loosely in his left hand. He led the horse toward the barn that bore the sign *Williams Livery Stable* and was met by a short, lean individual whose left cheek was stuffed with tobacco.

"Hep you, mister?"

"Need to put my stock up." Clay handed over the reins of his bay and the sorrel to the hostler, who nodded.

"I'm Burt. You want me to grain 'em?"

"Yeah, and rub 'em down good too. I'll pay extra," Clay said as he pulled the bedroll from behind the saddle and threw it over his shoulder.

"Shore 'nough. Fine-lookin' animals. Come fer?"

"Not too far—and yet pretty far too."

The hostler grinned. "If you want to put up, it'll have to be at the Elite Hotel. Only hotel in town."

"Food any good?"

"You can manage to keep it down, I 'spect."

"Did you ever hear of a woman named Julie Satterfield?"

Burt spat an amber stream on the ground, scratched his whiskers, and shook his head. "Nope." That seemed to be the extent of the conversation, for he turned and led the horses into the dark interior of the barn.

The abruptness of it caught Clay off guard. Turning, he starting moving down the street. He discovered that the Elite Hotel was a two-story building almost in the center of town. He entered and found himself inside a foyer with a set of steps to his right and a door to the side that led to some sort of parlor. Through the door at the back, he could see a restaurant of sorts.

A beefy man with a steel hook for a right hand nodded and said, "Lookin' for a room?"

"Yep."

"That'll be two dollars in advance."

"Can a fella get somethin' to eat?"

"Right on in there," the clerk said, nodding. "Tell Hallie I said to cook you up a steak or whatever she's got. Your room is upstairs. Second door on the left."

"I'm obliged."

"Just git in?"

"Yep." Clay half turned, then halted. "Ever hear of a woman named Julie Satterfield? I'm lookin' for her."

"Nobody by that name I know of."

Clay nodded and went upstairs. He was

tired from the trip, and although the room was no more inviting than most of its kind, he found the bed fairly comfortable. He stripped off his clothes, washed as besthe could with the tepid water in the pitcher, then shaved carefully. When he finished, he unrolled the bedroll, put on his best clothes, and brushed his hair. For a moment, he stood there staring at the pistol. Normally, he would have slipped it into the pocket in his vest, but he wrapped it back up in the bedroll and shoved it under the bed. Leaving the room, he went downstairs and entered the restaurant and took a seat. A tall, raw-boned woman approached him.

"You wanna eat?"

"Yes'm, I'm pretty hungry."

"Got chicken or steak or fish for a dollar."

"I'll have the steak, rare."

"I got some green beans just pulled fresh."

"Give me some of those and any other vegetable you can find in there—and some milk if you've got it."

The woman disappeared through a door into the kitchen, and Clay sat back. It was early yet for supper, and only three customers were there, a couple to his far left and a young man in the corner wearing a suit. The young fellow glanced at him and then stared back at his heaping plate of food. Clay waited for his meal to come, relaxing as best he could after his quick, hard ride. He had brought the extra horse to spell the animals now and then, and also for the woman—if he found her. Now that he was here, he wasn't sure what to do next.

A few minutes later, the woman returned with a plate heaped with green beans and a large steak. She set the plate and glass of milk down, then turned to leave. "Excuse me, ma'am," Jake said. "I'm lookin' for a young woman named Julie Satterfield."

The woman studied him carefully, then said, "What you want with her?"

"She's my cousin."

"Nobody by that name in this town I know of, but then she might be in one of them saloons. I don't go in them places."

"Thank you, ma'am."

Clay ate the meal, left money on the table to cover the tab and a tip, and walked out of the hotel. His eyes ran over the town. It would be getting dark soon, and the five saloons he saw would be open. Until then he would just ask around to see if anyone knew Julie Satterfield.

For the next two hours he made his way from the general store to the barber shop, where he stopped to get his hair cut. He tried to be tactful about asking about Julie, but no one had ever heard of her, and he learned nothing of her whereabouts.

Finally, the sun began to dip below the horizon, and the saloon lights began to go on. One by one he began visiting them. He bought a drink in the first one and finally worked his way through three of the remaining four. By that time he was feeling the effect of the liquor he felt forced to buy in order to ask his questions. Two of the saloons had women available for hire, and he had asked his question but got no response except, "What do ya want with her when you got me, honey?"

He entered the last saloon called the Arkansas Diamond. He wandered in and saw a table with some men playing poker. Walking over, he said, "Mind iffen I sit in on a few hands?"

"Have yerself a sit, mister. We'll take your money, just as well," said the dealer, a short man with a pockmarked face and a thin, black mustache.

After losing a few dollars, Clay turned to the dealer and said, "Ever heard of a lady by the name of Julie Satterfield."

"Never heard of her. She a fancy woman?"

"Not real sure," Clay said. "I'm lookin' at the request of her family."

"There ain't no fancy women named that here in Fort Smith or anywhere close around that I know of."

Clay nodded his thanks, threw his hand of cards in the middle of the table, and said, "I guess my three kings takes this hand." Gathering the few dollars he had won, he got up and left. As he walked down the street toward his hotel, he wondered why no one had ever heard of Julie. When he got back to his room, he sat on the bed for a time and looked out the window. Finally he undressed and lay down. "I reckon," he murmured, "I just have to go back and tell Jerusalem her sister's moved on somewhere else."

★ ★ ★

"You movin' on?" The hostler named Burt looked the worse for wear. He shook his head and said, "A man my age ort to know better than to drink a quart of whiskey in one night, but a man hates to admit he's gettin' old."

Clay grinned. "You're okay. You're still vertical. More than I can say for some of my mornings after."

"I grained them horses. Fine animals you got there, mister."

"I guess I'll move out. What do I owe you?"

"A dollar and a half."

He took the money Clay gave him and blinked. "You ort to hang around. You might enjoy the trial."

"Trial?"

"Yep," Burt said. "Might get to see a woman hang."

"Not my style," Clay said.

"Well, plenty of ugly women gets hanged, but Marie Jones . . . she's a real looker. She's got that red hair and green eyes—it's enough to make any man weak in the knees."

Clay instantly stopped and turned. He had started to move toward the horses, but he asked cautiously, "Red hair and green eyes, eh? What'd she do?"

"Why, she kilt her man is what she done. She's a fancy lady. Shot him right in the belly with a thirty-two."

"Killed him, eh?" Clay asked.

"No, he ain't dead yet, but he likely will be. Anyway, the judge is waitin' for him to die so he can try Marie for murder instead of somethin' else."

"Who'd she shoot?"

"She didn't show no sense about who she shot. She shot Bart Hunter. He's the son of the attorney general of Missouri. If his son dies, she'll git hanged all right! Old Man Hunter is real hard on crim'nals. He ain't about to let anybody get by with shootin' his only son. She'll hang if he dies, or if the feller does live, she'll spend ten years in the pen for the shootin'."

Clay said at once, "Reckon I'll get me some breakfast before I leave town. Maybe I'll stay over."

"You better. That'd be some sight to see that pretty red hair go under a hangman's noose."

Clay had noted the sheriff's office the previous afternoon as he had ridden into town.

He walked right in and found the sheriff sitting in a chair tilted back with his head against the wall. "Howdy, Sheriff, I'm John Williams."

"I'm Sheriff Speck—Harold Speck. What can I do for you?"

"I'd like to visit your prisoner."

"Which one? We got five."

"Marie Jones is the one I'd like to see."

Sheriff Speck brought his chair down and put his hands on his desk. He was a mild-eyed individual with a round face and a drooping walrus mustache of an indeterminate yellowish color. He brushed it back constantly as if it were a fly bothering him. "What do you want to see her for?"

"Well, she's a relative of mine, Sheriff. My cousin."

"That's too bad. Marie is in a mess, and she ain't gonna get out of it neither."

"You mind if I talk to her?"

"Be all right with me. She ain't had no visitors. I'll take you up to her. I'll have to lock you in, though."

Clay followed the sheriff up a set of creaky stairs, at the top of which were four cells, all but one occupied by rough-looking men. "Ain't got no women cells. Had to make do with blankets to give her a little privacy."

One of the cells at the end was covered by blankets, and Sheriff Speck said, "Marie, you got a visitor." There was no answer, and Speck shrugged his shoulders. "She ain't very hospitable, Williams." He unlocked the door, and Clay took off his hat and stepped through, pushing the blanket back. "Just holler when you want out. I can hear you downstairs."

A barred window to Clay's right admitted the morning sunlight. It fell full on a woman sitting on a cot with a shucked mattress. The only other furniture in the cell was a table containing a pitcher of water and a basin, and over in the corner a bucket.

"Who are you and what do you want?"

Clay studied the woman for a moment. There was no doubt in his mind that he had found Julie Satterfield.

He moved closer, and the woman straightened up, her eyes glinting. She had the same red hair and green eyes as Jerusalem Hardin. She was wearing a dance-hall-style dress, low-cut and the worse for wear. "Julie, I've come to get you out of here."

The woman's eyes opened. She cursed and said, "Who are you? What kind of lie are you telling?"

Clay lowered his voice to a whisper, for the other prisoners were calling out ribald remarks. Clay moved forward and whispered, "Your ma is dyin'. She wants to see you before her time comes."

Something changed in the woman's face. Her lips twisted, and she stared at Clay. "It won't do her no good to see me. I don't know why she wants to."

"I don't know either. Do you want to go or not? I can't make you go, but I'll take you if you will."

"You must be crazy. They're gonna hang me."

"Will you go?"

"You can't get me out of here, I tell you."

"That's my problem."

"Okay. I got nothin' to lose. If I stay here, I'll be hanging from a noose a'fore long. I'll go if you can get me out of here."

Clay stared at her. "All right." He stood up and called out to the sheriff, who came back quickly. When he stepped outside, the sheriff stared at him.

"That didn't take long."

"Nope. I'm gonna get her a good lawyer. Who's the best in town?"

"Thad Mullins, but he's out of town right now. It won't do much good."

Clay followed him downstairs and said, "I'm gonna get a lawyer, and I want to come back and see my cousin. How long will you be here?"

"We don't have no visitors after nine o'clock."

"Well, it may take longer than that. If I'm a little late, I'd appreciate you lettin' me in."

"I got a man sick," Sheriff Speck said. "I'll have to stay until midnight. The night man is George; he comes on later. He wouldn't let you in, though. He's too scared. He won't even answer the door."

"I'll be here before midnight. Thanks, Sheriff."

Clay walked out of the sheriff's office and slowly moved down the street. He glanced up and saw Julie Satterfield staring at him out of the window. She did not speak or move a muscle but was watching him intently. He turned and ambled away and went back to the hotel. He had breakfast and sat for a long time thinking as he con-

sumed cup after cup of the black, scalding coffee.

Night had come, but Clay had left town late in the afternoon. He had bought a stock of supplies from the general store, had loaded them on the two horses, and given the stablehand an extra dollar for leaving them longer.

The moon was high overhead, round, and as he waited for midnight, he could see the pockmarks on the silver disk. "Looks like somebody has been takin' pot shots at you," he murmured.

Clay had no watch, but he was a good judge of time. When he rode back into town, all the lights were out except in the saloons. He could hear the raucous laughter and the tinny piano music, which suited him fine. He moved back into the alley behind the jail, tied the two horses, and then went silently up the alley toward the front of the building, where he stood silently. There were no streetlights, and only one of the saloons directly across from the jail shed a few yellow beams out of the double doorway. Finally, he saw a man coming across the street toward the sheriff's office. Clay did not move out of the shadows, but when the man approached the door, knocked, and said, "Sheriff, it's me, George," Clay moved quickly out. He pulled the pistol from the holster at his side, and his moccasins made no sound. He came up directly behind the man as the door opened. Instantly, Clay gave George a tremendous shove. George let out a cry, "Hey—!" and went crashing into the sheriff. They both fell flat as Clay stepped inside and shut the door. The two men were scrambling up, but when the sheriff lifted his head, he found himself look-ing into the muzzle of Clay's pistol.

"Take it easy, Sheriff."

"Don't shoot," Sheriff Speck said. "What do you want, Williams?"

"I'm gonna have to relieve you of one of your prisoners."

Speck stared at him. "Marie?"

"That's right."

Clay had carefully thought all this out. Keeping his pistol trained on the two men, he reached out, and pulled the sheriff's pis-tol out of the holster. The other man was not armed. "You two move on in. I'm gonna have to tie you up."

"Don't shoot," George said. "Please don't shoot."

"Nobody's gonna get shot if you do what I say. Just turn around."

Clay swiftly tied the hands of both men and then their feet. "Sorry, but I'm gonna have to gag you. If you started hollerin', it might not be too good."

"I promise I won't holler," George said quickly.

"I'd like to take your word, but not this time." Clay had brought two neckerchiefs, and he gagged both men, not tying them too tightly, but securely enough.

He then tied them together at the ankle and put another rope around their neck. "Just don't struggle, and you won't strangle each other," he said.

He went to the sheriff's desk and saw the peg behind with the cell keys, plucked up the ring, and went up the stairs. A single burning lantern cast a ghostly light into the cells. The prisoners were all asleep, and he went down to the end of the cells and whispered, "Julie!" as he unlocked the door. As he swung it back, the woman came out.

"Take off your shoes," he said. She obeyed, and the two moved silently down the hall and descended the stairs. Clay unloaded the sheriff's pistol, put it on the desk, and said, "Let's go."

He opened the door and looked up and down the street. When he was sure no one was around, he stepped outside, motioned for Julie to follow, then shut the door. He took her arm and led her down the dark alley to where he had tied the horses, then turned and said, "We'll ride out nice and easy."

He moved to help the woman, but she swung into the saddle, her short skirt pulled almost to her thighs, but she said not a word.

Clay had surveyed the town and knew the best route to leave town without raising any suspicion. He led her down a side street on which were scattered a few houses and a few small businesses. As soon as they were out of town, he said, "I'd like to speed it up. Can you hang on?"

"Shore can."

Clay rode hard for the next five hours headed south. Just as the sun began coming up, he saw a line of trees he knew marked a river. He pulled off the road and found a thick stand of trees where he could hide the horses. "We'll stay here till it gets dark. I don't want to be seen." Clay dismounted and unsaddled both horses. When he finished tying them with enough free rein so that they could graze, he said, "As soon as daylight comes, we'll risk a little fire."

"Why are you doing this? Who are you?" Julie Satterfield demanded, looking him square in the eye.

She was taller than her sister, Clay noticed, lacking only a couple of inches of his own height. "I promised your sister and mother I'd bring you back. I aim to do it." Then he turned and went to gather some branches to build a small fire. When he came back, he nodded toward the pack on the ground and said, "There's bacon and a frying pan and some eggs in that pack if you want to dig 'em out."

Thirty minutes later the two of them sat eating out of tin pans. When the sun finally rose above the horizon, casting its first rays of dawn, she asked, "Are we going to stay here all day?"

"Yep. We'll travel hard at night and hole up during the day so nobody sees you. I don't want to leave with anybody seein' you. Does anybody know your real name?"

"No."

"Why'd you change your name to Marie Jones?"

"I didn't want to shame my family."

Julie Satterfield finished her breakfast, drank the coffee, and then stared at Clay, who was sitting against a tree. She came over to him and knelt down, saying, "I guess I owe you somethin'. I've only got one way to pay ya."

Clay blinked with surprise and then laughed. "I don't remember ever turnin' down whiskey or a good-lookin' woman, but I reckon there's a first time for everything."

Julie did not move for a moment. She seemed to find something amusing about being refused. "What are you—some kind of a preacher?"

"Nope. I promised your sister I'd bring you back. Somehow I don't think she'd like it if I did any more than that."

Julie laughed then, and in that instant Clay knew that even if her physical likeness to her sister had not given her away, the laugh would have. She had the same deep, hearty laugh that seemed to bubble out of Jerusalem.

She stood up and said, "What's your name?"

"Clay Taliferro."

"Well, Clay Taliferro, you missed your chance with me. It'll be a cold day before you get another one."

Clay shrugged and said, "Maybe not. Things change. I brought you some clothes in that saddlebag over there."

Julie turned, went to the bedroll, and opened the thongs. She pulled out a brown dress and a bonnet and a pair of ugly black shoes. The sight of them amused her again. She began changing, making no attempt to hide. She glanced back at Taliferro, pleased that he was watching her.

"You sorry you passed up your chance?"

Clay shook his head. "I never waste time thinkin' about what might have been. You'd better get some sleep. We're gonna ride hard tonight."

CHAPTER
SIX

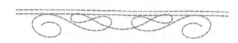

As Brodie walked toward the garden, he heard a solid clumping sound to his right. Taking a quick look, he saw that Anthony Wayne had grasped a fence post in the middle and was trying to bring it to the house. The huge dog brought up all sorts of things to the house, making a mess, but now he had bitten off a chore too big for him. He had the pole grasped in his powerful jaws, but the opening of the corral was only two feet wide and the post was three. Brodie watched with resignation as Anthony Wayne made a run for it and the ends of the post crashed into the uprights. The impact was so great that the dog fell back on his haunches and sat there staring at the opening, a puzzled look in his eye. He got up, backed off, and tried again, but this time with no more success.

Brodie walked over to the dog and said, "Gimme that fence post, Anthony Wayne. You ain't got no more sense than a dead possum!" He tossed the post outside the corral, then watched as Anthony Wayne picked it up and trotted to the house, carrying it as easily as if it were a toothpick. "You're one stupid dog wearing yourself out with something that can't be done."

As Brodie reached the edge of the garden to hoe the beans, he was vaguely dissatisfied. He was taken aback when he saw his great-grandfather sitting in the middle of one of the rows. Whenever Grandpa Josiah "went away," he felt afraid. He could not understand it, but then neither could anyone else. When he got closer, however, Josiah looked up smiling, and Brodie saw with relief that his eyes were clear.

"Come and sit down, boy. You can learn somethin' here."

"What is it, Grandpa?" Brodie sat and

looked at the ground where Josiah was pointing.

"Look at that there ant, Brodie."

Brodie stared at an ant that was trying to move a dead beetle several times larger than itself. The ant was evidently moving toward its home, wherever that was, but a stick had fallen across its way. Now it heaved and pulled and struggled futilely to get the dead beetle across.

"I've been watchin' that scudder nigh on to half an hour," Josiah mused, "and he ain't got the job done yet."

Relieved that his grandfather's mind was clear, Brodie watched the ant and finally said, "You know he ain't got no more sense than Anthony Wayne. That dumb dog was tryin' to walk through the gate of the corral with a big old post in his mouth. I guess he'd be there still if I hadn't helped him get through."

Josiah picked up a tiny twig and stirred the dead body of the beetle. The ant became agitated but refused to give up. "Why don't you just give up?" Josiah said. "Ants is funny things, ain't they, Brodie?" He removed the stick, and the ant continued its progress, shoving the beetle along. "Now, I reckon you think you done that all by your-self, don't you?"

"I don't believe ants think, Grandpa."

Josiah's eyes twinkled. "Wal, some *peo-ple* don't think, Brodie. Reckon you found that out already."

"I don't think myself a heap of the time."

Josiah Mitchell reached out and laid his hand on Brodie's knee. He squeezed it and shook his head. "That ain't right," he said quietly. "As a matter of fact, you're the brightest of all of us. I seen it in you when you was just a yonker beginnin' to talk and move around. I seen you was a thinker even then. Why, many's a day I come on you when you was just sittin' and a-lookin' off into space, and I kept wonderin', what in the world is that young'un thinkin' about? Wor-ried me for a spell, for thinkin' messes some people up, but it ain't so with you."

Brodie was shocked by his great-grand-father's words of praise. He had never said anything like this to him before. Now he stared at the old man and said, "Why, I just think like everybody else, Grandpa."

"No, you don't. You're different, boy." Suddenly he lifted his head. "Hear that?" he said.

Brodie listened hard. He knew his great-grandfather, despite his age, had the best hearing on the place. "I don't hear nothin'."

"Somebody's comin'," Josiah said, getting to his feet slowly.

Brodie sprang up and turned, for he too now heard the sound of hoof beats. "It is somebody! You got the most bodacious hearin' I ever knowed of, Grandpa."

"Helped me keep my scalp a few times years ago. My eyes ain't what they was back then, though. Who be it, Brodie?"

Brodie stared hard and said, "It's Clay, and there's some woman with him."

"Reckon we'd better go welcome 'em, then."

Clay had ridden off over two weeks ago, and neither Brodie nor his mother had given any of the children, or even Josiah, a hint of where he was going. Brodie wasn't so sure he'd come back, thinking he might ride off for good just like his pa did, but Jerusalem had insisted, "He'll be back."

As Brodie and Josiah made their way back toward the cabin, Brodie saw the door open, and his mother came out carrying Mary Aidan, closely followed by Clinton and Moriah. His eyes then turned toward

Clay, who slipped off his horse easily. Clay winked at him and turned to speak to Jerusalem.

"Well, we're back."

Brodie was watching the woman, then when he recognized her, he cried out, "Aunt Julie!"

Julie hurried over to him and grabbed him by the shoulders. She was a tall woman, but she had to look up to his lean six-foot height. "Why, you tall, handsome thing you!" she cried out, her eyes sparkling. "I bet all the girls are lined up to get at you. Give me a kiss." She pulled Brodie's head down, kissed him soundly, and then laughed. "Why, you're blushin'. I like to see a man who can blush. It means he might amount to somethin'."

Brodie had missed his aunt Julie. He knew she had a wild streak in her, but before she left she had paid him more attention than anyone. Now he saw her go to Clinton, who was staring at her.

Clinton remembered her as well, but as soon as she hugged him, he said, "I'm a Baptist now, Aunt Julie."

"Well, I love you anyway, Clinton. Don't let

it get the best of you. And is this Moriah? My, if you ain't a pretty thing!"

Brodie watched as his aunt turned back to his mother. Something passed between them, and the merriment fled from Aunt Julie's face. Brodie saw her grow sober.

Finally, after an awkward silence, Julie said quietly, "Hello, sister."

"I'm glad to see you, Julie." Jerusalem stepped forward and embraced her sister.

Brodie saw that Julie was very stiff with her.

When Julie stepped back, she said, "How's Ma?"

"She's waiting for you. Come on in."

Julie turned then to say, "Thank you, Clay."

"It wasn't nothin'."

"Yes, it was." Julie nodded firmly, then turned and followed her sister into the house.

Jerusalem, despite herself, was shocked at her churning emotions. For a long time, she had tried to put Julie out of her mind, well aware that her sister was leading a careless and immoral life. But the sight of her had stirred old memories, and now, stopping before the door, she said, "Ma's

been keepin' herself alive in the hopes of seeing you."

"Ain't there no hope, Jerusalem?"

"No, she's going home. Go on in, now."

Jerusalem opened the door and stepped aside. She watched as Julie hesitated and then went in. As she glanced over at the bed, Jerusalem saw a look of joy spread across her mother's face. Her whole face lit up.

"Julie—my baby!" she cried out and held up her arms.

Julie quickly went and bent over the bed, embracing her mother. Jerusalem felt her eyes grow dim, and she stepped back and closed the door. This was not her time, but she could hear Julie speaking in a broken tone as she moved away from the door. She went back outside and said, "Moriah, go change this baby's diaper. She's soppin' wet." She moved over toward Clay, who was talking to Brodie and Clinton. He turned to face her, and she studied his tanned face. His eyes were half shut with a sleepy expression, but this was customary with him except in times of stress. "Was it any trouble to find her, Clay?"

"Oh, it wasn't particularly bad."

Jerusalem had learned something about this man, and she met his eyes, saying, "Except for Brodie here, you're the worst liar I ever ran across, Clay Taliferro."

"Well . . . I admit, it was a mite tricky."

"You boys go on. I want to talk to Clay alone."

"Oh, Ma, we want to hear too!" Clinton protested.

"You mind me, Clinton. You and Brodie go on."

As both boys turned away disappointed, she said, "Come on over and set with me." She led Clay to the cemetery, which was the most private place to talk. She sat down, and when he sat down beside her, she said, "Now, tell me all of it." She listened intently as Clay told her how Julie was accused of attempted murder and how he had rescued her from the jail. When he had finished, Jerusalem glanced toward the north. It was almost as if she were trying to imagine all that had happened in the days that Clay was gone. "So," she said quietly, "if that man dies, she'll be hanged."

"They'd have to catch her first. And since we rested during the day and traveled

at night, I don't think anyone followed us. Maybe he'll pull through. She just picked the wrong man to shoot, that's all." Clay nodded sagely, adding, "It ain't wrong to shoot some people. Julie ain't had enough experience shootin' folks. She picked the wrong one, but she'll know better next time."

Jerusalem said nothing but had her face turned away. Clay reached out, pulled her around, and saw the sorrow in her eyes. "It'll be all right," he said. "That man probably won't die, and if he does, they don't know who she is. She was usin' another name there. It's gonna turn out all right."

Jerusalem Hardin stared into Clay's eyes, then turned and leaned forward, staring down at the ground. She did not speak for a long time, and when she did, her voice was faint. "I don't much believe in happy endings, Clay."

The next day Jerusalem hardly saw Julie at all. Her sister spent most of the day at her mother's bedside caring for her. Somehow the excruciating pain Jewel had suffered

with for so long seemed to have miraculously gone away. She was fading, however,
and everyone saw it. Julie had been very
quiet most of the day, but there were times
when Jerusalem could hear her mother talking, and once she thought she heard Julie
crying. Some of that time Jewel was asleep,
and when Julie was not at her mother's
side, she had taken long walks alone,
spurning everyone's attempts to try to talk
to her. Even when Jerusalem tried to coax
her to join the rest of them for dinner, Julie
had declined and gone to bed early.

The next morning when Jerusalem went
into her mother's room with breakfast, she
found her mother already awake and waiting for her. Jerusalem was startled at the
look she saw on her face. The pain had not
come back, and Jewel Satterfield's face
shone with a peace and assurance that
nothing here could explain.

"Daughter, it's time for me to go home.
The Lord has answered my prayer and allowed me to see Julie one last time. Please
call the family."

Jerusalem set the tray down and went
and knelt by the bed, tears running down
her cheeks as she embraced her mother's

frail form. After a moment, she quickly went and called the family together.

Jewel remained awake and alert as the whole family crowded into the tiny bedroom. Her voice was clear, as were her eyes, which glowed like sapphires. She spoke in a sleepy tone, naming each one of them and telling them she loved them. Finally, she said, "Clay, come closer. I want to whisper."

Jerusalem had watched this with surprise. Her mother whispered for a long time into Clay's ear, and she could make out none of it. Finally, she saw Clay nod, and when he turned back, she saw a stiff expression on his face. Afterward, he would never tell her what her mother had said to him. "It was right personal, Jerusalem Ann" was all he would say.

The last person to speak with Jewel was Josiah. He had stood along the wall listening as she spoke to the others, and finally she said, "Pa, come here." He went over and took her hand, and she said, "I am goin' to Mama now. I'll tell her that you'll be along soon."

After this she closed her eyes and went to sleep. She never woke up again, and it was impossible for Jerusalem or for anyone else to tell the exact moment when she finally reached the heaven she had longed for all her life.

The last of the funeral crowd had gone now. The new grave in the small cemetery was filled in, and Julie glanced at it. She was sitting on the front porch with Jerusalem, and Clay was out in the corral working with the mules. The two women watched as Brodie came up to Clay. The boy was at least three inches taller than Clay but skinny as a rail. "Brodie needs to gain weight," Julie said.

"He will. He's going to be a strong man."

Julie suddenly turned and said, "I'm leaving, Jerusalem, but I'm glad you sent Clay to get me."

"It gave Ma what she wanted. I'm glad you came."

"I'll be goin' pretty soon."

Jerusalem said, "You wait here, Julie. I got somethin' to show you." She moved into the house, and when she returned, she had a folded newspaper in her hand. "I picked this up yesterday in town."

Julie took the paper and saw that a small article had been circled. She read it quickly.

The search is on for a young woman who shot, perhaps fatally, the son of the Attorney General of Missouri. The shooting took place in Fort Smith, Arkansas, and authorities are seeking a young woman named Marie Jones. She is twenty-five years old with red hair and green eyes. Contact the Attorney General's Office in Missouri. A three thousand dollar reward is offered for information leading to her capture.

Julie read the article, then looked up. "I've got to get away from here."

"I expect you're right. This is too close to Fort Smith. How come they call you by that name?"

"I didn't want to use my real name." Julie turned and said, "I didn't want to shame our family."

"Did anybody there know your real name?"

"No, I don't reckon so."

Jerusalem said, "You stay here. I've been thinkin' about something." She got up and said, "I need to pray about it a little bit more."

"You sound like Ma," Julie said. "What is it?"

"I'll tell you later."

Julie never asked Jerusalem what she was thinking, but after five days she found out.

Jerusalem waited until everyone had come in to eat supper, and after the meal she looked at them and said, "I've got something important to tell you." Everyone's eyes went to her, and she said, "We're leavin' this place." A silence fell on the group, and Jerusalem spoke with determination. Her eyes went to Clay. "I want you to take us to where Jake is, Clay. It's the last favor I'll ask. Take us to Wyoming."

Everyone stared at Jerusalem, and it was Clay who burst out, "Why, you can't do that, Jerusalem. You don't have no idea how much trouble it is to get to the mountains."

"I've already sold this place—at least I've made an agreement. Papers will be signed next week. I've been without my husband long enough. We're goin' to find your pa, children, and we're goin' to live with him."

Julie spoke up, "You don't have to do this for my sake. I'll get by."

"You can't stay here. You've got to get away, and I reckon there won't be no sheriff goin' out to the mountains," Jerusalem said firmly. "Besides, I'm tired of bein' half a wife. If Jake don't want me, all he's got to do is say so."

His mother's statement shocked Clinton, who said loudly, "But, Ma, the Bible says a man and a wife are one flesh. That's what it says. You can't go against the Bible."

"I'm not, but your pa may be, Clinton."

For the next ten minutes Jerusalem stood there answering all their questions, and finally she said stubbornly, "It's all settled. We're going. Clay, will you take us?"

Clay cleared his throat, and Jerusalem stared at him. "What's wrong with you, Clay? You're the worst man at hidin' his feelin's I ever saw. I hope you don't play poker with that kind of face."

"Well, the truth is, Jerusalem, Jake ain't exactly in the mountains where you think."

"Not *exactly* there? What does *exactly* mean?"

Clay's expression was harried. "Well, just before I left, Jake told me he had decided to open a new business. Him and me heard from an old partner of ours named Gordon Lebonne. Gordon said a fellow called Stephen Austin got a big land grant from the Mexican government down in Texas territory. Told us to come on down. Said he had the land we'd need for nearly nothing. Well, Jake said he was goin' to Texas and start himself a big ranch. I didn't listen too good to the details, but he said as soon as his leg was fit to travel, he was goin' there and findin' Gordon."

"Why didn't you tell me this before?" Jerusalem asked.

Everyone at the table saw that Clay was embarrassed.

"He told you not to tell me, didn't he?" she said, shaking her head.

"I reckon he didn't want to worry you until it was all settled."

"All right. Clay, there's more to this than you're sayin', but we've all got our secrets." Jerusalem drew herself up. "I'm going to Texas with these children and with Julie."

"Jerusalem," Clay said with some agitation, "you don't know what you're talkin' about. You don't have no idea how hard that trail is. Lots of folks get killed on the road to Texas. You'll get some of your family killed on a crazy trip like this."

"That's my problem and not yours, Clay."

"Well, I won't do it! It don't make no sense."

"All right, you can leave then, Clay, with thanks for all you've done."

Everyone held their breath, and Clay's face grew red. "All right," he blurted out. "Good-bye!" He jumped up and walked out.

Brodie at once said, "Ma, you don't want to run him off like that."

"I'm tired of tryin' to make men do what they ought to do. We're going to Texas, and we can do it without Clay Taliferro!"

The next week was a flurry of activity. The papers were to be signed on Friday, and every day there were plenty of preparations to be done. Brodie tried hard to persuade his mother to let him go beg Clay to come along, but she said firmly, "You can't make a man do what he don't want to do, Brodie."

On Wednesday Brodie went to town to

buy supplies for the long trip. When he finished that task, he knew he had to make
one more try. He walked down the street to
the saloon where Clay was prone to celebrate and found him seated at a table with
a half-empty bottle of whiskey before him.
"Hello, Clay."

When Clay looked up, his eyes were
blurry and red. "What'cha doin' here, boy?"

"I got to talk to you, Clay."

"Go on and talk—but it won't do you no
good."

Brodie sat down nervously on the chair
and tried to think of how to put the matter.
Finally he said, "Clay, please go with us to
Texas. I'm afraid Ma will get hurt—or Moriah
or Clinton."

"It's a fool thing your ma is thinkin' of
doin', and I won't have no part of it. You're
right about one thing, though. Somebody's
goin' to get killed. All you have to do is meet
a couple of Comanches, and *all* of you will
get killed."

This was a different Clay Taliferro from the
one Brodie knew. He was unshaven, and his
speech wasn't clear. He drank steadily but
nothing changed. No matter what Brodie
said, he stubbornly shook his head.

"Get out of here, boy. I don't want to talk to you no more. You and that crazy Hardin bunch will be massacred. Now git!"

"All right, Clay. I guess this is good-bye, then."

"Good-bye, and don't pester me no more!" he said as he tried to pour more whiskey into his glass and missed.

Brodie was silent for the rest of the day, speaking only when spoken to. Later that night, Jerusalem came to him and said quietly, "What's eatin' on you, son?"

"I went to talk to Clay today when I went for supplies."

"Didn't do any good, did it?"

"No. He said we're all gonna get killed gettin' to Texas."

"We might be, but we're gonna find your pa, and we got to get your aunt Julie out of here. Besides, I'm sick of this place."

Brodie was shocked. This was the only home he had ever known. "But, Ma, this is our home!"

"It's a place where your pa decided he wasn't as married to me as I was to him.

The only thing I'll hate leavin' is my two boys out in that cemetery. Now, Brodie, you've got to be the man. You understand me?"

"But, Ma, I ain't able."

"You've got to be able, son. Maybe we can hire a guide, but you're the man of the family now."

Brodie swallowed hard. "I'll try, Ma. I'll try real hard."

The wagons were all loaded, and the sun was just peeping over the hills. Jerusalem had fixed the last breakfast in the house, washed the dishes, and had cleaned the house out for the new owner, who would move in later in the day.

They all left the house, and Jerusalem looked over the downcast faces of her children. "You're a sad-lookin' bunch," she said. "I've seen more cheerful faces at funerals."

"Ma, do we have to go?" Moriah whined.

"Yes, we have to go. We're gonna find your pa, and that's all there is to it."

Brodie spoke up. "Well, I guess we'd better go, then." He tried to speak with authority, but his voice was unsteady. Fear had been with him ever since his mother had told him that he was the man now. He knew he was unfit for such a thing, and now he swallowed hard and tried to smile. "It's gonna be a good day."

"Look, there comes Clay!" Moriah cried out.

Everyone turned to see Clay riding up on his bay. He was wearing his buckskins and leading his second horse loaded down with gear. He was dirty, unkempt, and when he pulled his horse up, he ignored them all except Jerusalem.

Brodie watched as the two stared at each other. Neither of them spoke, and finally Clay said, "Howdy, Jerusalem. You ready to go to Texas?"

Jerusalem Ann Hardin smiled then, a free and easy and happy smile, and for some reason she began laughing deep down in her throat. Then he heard Julie laughing the same kind of laugh. The two women looked so much alike! Jerusalem was older and showed more signs of wear but was still a strong woman.

Brodie watched as Clay slipped off his

horse and, going to the other animal, pulled out one of the Hawkin rifles. He came over to Brodie and held it out. "Here, this is yours, Brodie. Try not to shoot me, will ya? It'd be just my luck."

Brodie's throat grew thick. "You mean it's actually mine?"

"Yep, it's yours."

Julie walked over and stood before Clay. She was almost as tall as he was, and now she grabbed his buckskin shirt. "Well," she said, "maybe I oughta give you a second chance, Clay. Somethin' I ain't never given to any other man." She loosed her grip on his shirt, locked her hands behind his head, and pulled him forward. She kissed him and hung on, and Clay held on to her in return.

Jerusalem watched them with a peculiar light in her eyes and a tight line around her lips. Then when Julie stepped back, Jerusalem said, "Well, if all that lovin' is out of the way, we're ready." She came over and put her hand on Clay's cheek. Everyone grew quiet, and then she said, "Take us to Texas, Clay."

PART TWO:

EL CAMINO REAL

July—September 1831

PART TWO:

EL CAMINO REAL

July—September 1831

PART TWO

PLANNING
YEAR

July–September 1991

CHAPTER
SEVEN

The two heavily loaded wagons rumbled along a narrow, winding road that wound through the dense first-growth timber. The trees stood in disorganized ranks like a regiment at ease, casting their afternoon shadows in long lines across the road. For the most part, they blocked the sunlight so that tattered shadows fell upon the faces of both Jerusalem and Julie as they sat on the seat of the second wagon. Julie had balanced Mary Aidan on her knees, but she began to whimper and cry. As always, she thrashed around wildly, slapping her arms up and down and kicking her feet.

"Here, you take the lines and let me have her, Julie," Jerusalem said. "She's hungry."

Julie shook her head. "She's a wild one when she gets that way." Handing the baby over, she took the lines and lifted her head toward the sky and tried to gauge the time. "These mules are pretty tired," she remarked, glancing over to watch the baby as she nursed. "It's a good thing Clay made you buy better stock than those you had."

"He didn't *make* me do anything," Jerusalem said curtly.

"It sure looked like it." Julie grinned as she remembered the enormous argument her sister and Clay had over buying new mules.

Jerusalem had piled the two wagons high with furniture, tools, food, clothing—everything they would hold. When Clay saw them, he had told her bluntly, "Two mules apiece couldn't haul everything you've got in them wagons, Jerusalem. We'll have to buy us a couple of extra ones."

Jerusalem had put up a stiff fight, but Clay had dug in his heels and refused to have anything to do with the trip without buying more mules. "We wouldn't get five miles out of town before they'd quit on us. We really need to buy at least six more."

Julie and the whole family had witnessed the clash of wills, and at one point it seemed likely that Clay would simply walk away. Julie had whispered to Jerusalem, "You'd better not get his back up this time. He'll walk off and leave us, and then what will we do?"

"No, he won't, Julie," Jerusalem had said with an odd look on her face. "He won't be going anywhere except with us."

In the end the two had compromised, and Clay had gone into town to buy six fine new mules.

"Why'd you make such a fuss about buyin' a few mules? You got plenty of money since you sold the place. How much did you get for it?"

"None of your business, Julie, but we'll need every penny of it. I'm not coming back here anytime soon, and I'm takin' all my things with me."

The wagon rumbled on, and for a time the two women were silent. Finally, Jerusalem handed the baby back and said, "Here, let me drive these mules now." She took the lines and hesitated, then said, "I know everybody thinks I'm stingy, Julie. We got a good price for the place, mostly because of what Clay did to put it in shape, but I've got to have enough money to buy another place when we get there."

Julie looked at her sister and raised one eyebrow. "But Jake's already bought a place. Isn't that what Clay told you?"

"Maybe so, but—" She didn't finish the sentence, and finally she shook her head. "Jake's given me reason to look out for myself. He hasn't shown much evidence of being any good at that."

Julie did not answer, but she nodded her head imperceptibly. "That's a good idea you've got there. You hang on to it." She held the baby on her lap and toyed with Mary Aidan's hair, pushing her rosy cheeks in. They rode on for a while in comfortable silence, then Julie spoke up. "You know, when Clay sprung me from that jail that first night out I tried to pay him for his trouble."

"Pay him? You offered him money?"

"I didn't have any money, Jerusalem." She laughed deep in her throat, then said, "I offered him somethin' worth more than money." She looked over expecting an argument from Jerusalem, but her sister did not respond. "He turned me down. First time that ever happened." She waited for Jerusalem to comment, and when she did not, she went on, "He said he was doin' it for you."

Jerusalem then turned and looked directly at her. "Leave him be, Julie."

"Why should I? Do you want him?"

"Don't be foolish! I've already got a husband."

"No, you ain't. You've got a man who don't care one whit for you. Jake ran off and left you every chance he got. You can call him *husband* if you want to, but I'd say take what you can get."

Jerusalem did not respond to her criticism, saying instead, "Look, Clay's stoppin' up ahead. It seems like we're makin' camp early."

Clay had pulled off in a small clearing sheltered by tall walnut trees. Jerusalem pulled her team in behind the lead wagon, then got down stiffly and stretched her sore muscles. She reached up to Julie, saying, "Let me have Mary Aidan." She took the infant, then walked over to where Clay was standing beside Brodie. "Why are we stopping so early?"

"Because it's time to stop," Clay said stiffly. He was obviously still a bit put out with Jerusalem over their altercation about the mules. He turned to the boys and said, "You boys take that firewood we brung. I want an early supper tonight before it gets dark."

Jerusalem watched Clay steadily but made no answer. She walked over and handed the baby to Moriah. "You change her diaper. I'll get the makin's for supper. Clinton, you milk the goat."

"Come on, get your rifle, Brodie," Clay said. "We'll see if we can bring somethin' down before dark for supper."

The two left, and Jerusalem began organizing the meal, getting out the pots and pans from the side box on the wagon while Julie started the fire. Moriah changed the baby and laid her down on a blanket, then went over to help Julie fix the fire. She glanced curiously at Jerusalem and said, "What's Ma so mad about?"

"I teased her and it made her mad."

"Teased her about what?"

"About men. What else would a woman tease about?"

"Are you a bad woman, Aunt Julie?" Moriah asked.

"You bet!"

Moriah looked up at Julie, who had

turned to face her, and said, "I don't care. I like you a lot anyway."

Julie suddenly reached forward and hugged her niece. "I'm a bad one, but I want you to be a good one. All right?"

"I don't know. I'll have to see."

Brodie took aim, held the gun as steady as he could, and pulled the trigger. The recoil slammed against his shoulder, and he peered through the black smoke, saying, "Did I hit it, Clay?"

"Close enough, boy. If it was a man, you would have got him. Now, let's see you load her up again."

Brodie began the process of reloading the Hawkin. He was glad he was so tall, for it meant setting the butt of the long rifle on the ground and inserting powder, shot, and a wad down the muzzle, then pounding them down with a ramrod. He shoved the ramrod back in place, slipped his hand in his pocket, and inserted the percussion cap. "I got her ready!" he said.

"You're pretty fast. That's good," Clay said. His humor had improved, and he watched as Brodie sent several more shots against the blaze he had made on a target a hundred yards away. "The trouble with these rifle guns is you only get one shot. If there's a Comanche runnin' at you and you miss him, you ain't got time to reload before he gets to you. I wish somebody would invent a rifle that'd shoot a hundred times."

"Well, you got your pistol."

Clay pulled the pistol out and said, "Yep, it'll shoot six times, so I can kill six Comanches, but they got to be pretty close."

As always, Brodie soaked up every word Clay said. Brodie's great-grandfather had taught him the basics of shooting, for he had been a mountain man and knew guns.

Brodie fell silent, and Clay glanced over at him. "You look like you swallowed a porcupine. What's the matter?"

"Aw, shucks, Clay, I'm worried."

"Worried about what?"

"About this here trip. Lots of bad things could happen."

"Don't be thinkin' about all that."

"But we'll be goin' through Indian lands."

"Sure will. As a matter of fact, we're in 'em right now. Of course, Cherokees ain't likely to give us no kind of trouble, but you take them Comanches. They're a troublesome lot." He smiled and punched Brodie on the shoulder. " Well, if a Comanche kilt you, he couldn't kill you but once, could he?"

Clay's ribbing helped to relieve Brodie's fears, and it drove his own bad humor away, causing him to laugh. "Well, once would be a-plenty. You know, I ain't a Christian like Clinton. I'd go straight to hell if I died."

"Me too."

"Don't it scare you, Clay, to think of dyin'?"

"Some. I try not to think on it regular."

"You think you'll ever be saved?"

"Sure hope so." He lifted his rifle and fired a shot, then shook his head. "Mostly, I'd hate to die in my condition because of Curly Bill Prentice."

"Who was he?"

"He was a feller I had to partner with for a while—the worst fella I ever got hooked up with. Mean as a rattlesnake. Never gave a man a decent answer."

"What does he have to do with you dyin'?"

"Well, he took a Pawnee arrow in his liver, and he went out cussin' God and me. I couldn't stand Curly Bill even on a two-week canoe trip! Think how much worse it'd be to have to put up with him in the pit as a permanent thing." Clay had a mind that hopped from one subject to another without warning, which made him hard for Brodie to follow. "Clinton told me about gettin' converted in that Baptist meeting. What held you back?"

Brodie stared at the ground and muttered, "That preacher tried to scare everybody into gettin' saved. I didn't like that. If I get saved, it won't be because I'm skeered into it."

"Sounds like good theology to me. Come on, let's get back before it gets dark. Don't look like we're gonna have fresh meat tonight."

Moriah was helping her great-grandfather put the bedrolls for the men and the boys under the wagons. Jerusalem and Mary Aidan would sleep in one wagon, and Julie and Moriah in the other, but the men would sleep on the ground.

As always, Moriah asked questions

steadily as they worked. "Grandpa, how'd you happen to marry up with Grandma?"

"Why, I had to fight for her. Lots of fellers wanted to marry her. I had to whip a whole string of 'em."

"Well, nobody will ever want to fight for me."

"What makes you say that, sweetheart?" Josiah reached out and turned the girl around. He put his hand under her chin and smiled down at her.

"I'm too skinny. Clinton says I look like a rake handle. I ain't got no shape at all."

"Pay him no mind. In a few years you can take your pick."

"So you still miss her? Grandma, I mean."

"Every day of my life, girl! But I'll see her pretty soon."

Moriah leaned down and straightened up one of the blanket rolls. They had put oil-cloth under the blankets and kept another out in case it rained. "You mean you'll see her in heaven?"

Josiah reached out and took Moriah by the waist and lifted her up in the air. He was still a strong man in spite of his eighty-three years. He laughed and then hugged her. "Why shore in heaven! You don't think I'm aimin' to the other place, do you? She was the best Christian I ever knowed, Moriah. Took her nigh onto thirty years to get me converted, but she done it. She prayed for me every single day until I saw the truth of it all. And I'm forever grateful."

"I'm glad. I'm gonna get converted myself someday, but it may be a long time." Without breaking the rhythm of her speech, she said, "Grandpa, where do you go when you go out of your mind like you do?"

The old man scratched his chin thoughtfully. "I can't say. It bothers me considerable. I hope I don't do nothin' shameful."

Moriah reached out and took his hand. "Are you gonna die, Grandpa?"

"We all are, sweetheart. Every one of us. The death rate's a hundred percent."

The smell of wood smoke and frying meat laced the thin night air, and everyone filled up on fried ham, red-eye gravy, and day-old biscuits.

"I brought my sourdough starter with me," Jerusalem said as she dipped a biscuit in the red-eye gravy and gave Mary Aidan just a taste of it. "We'll eat good with what we brought out of the smokehouse."

She hesitated, then shook her head. "I forgot. There was a little honey left. Moriah, it's in that jar in the wooden box right under the seat. You go get it, please."

Moriah jumped up and came around and poured honey carefully on the biscuits that everyone held out for her. When it was almost gone, Clinton protested that he wasn't getting a fair share. He grabbed at the jar, and he and Moriah struggled over it.

"I thought you was a Christian!" Moriah yelled.

"I am, but that don't mean I can't have my fair share."

"Does too! You're not supposed to be selfish none."

"It ain't bein' selfish to want my honey—now give it to me!"

"That's quite enough," Jerusalem shouted. "Christian or not, you two had better share like civilized human beings, or neither of you's gettin' any."

While the children settled their squabble more quietly, Jerusalem rose, walked over to the wagon, and came back with a small jar and handed it to Clay. "Here, Clay, I brought you some apple butter. Since the honey's about gone, you might like this with your biscuit."

She looked at Clay, who took the jar but with the same stubborn expression he'd worn since their earlier disagreement.

"I admit I was rough on you about buying the mules. I know I'm hard to get along with at times. Maybe this will make up for it."

Suddenly Clay laughed, and the stern look on his face cleared. "Oh, you wasn't too bad, Jerusalem. I been skinned plenty worse."

"By a woman?"

"Of course by a woman. Why, I shot a feller once who lit into me like you did!"

Jerusalem hesitated, then when he had slathered a thick layer of apple butter on the biscuit, she reached out and took it from him. She took a bite and nodded, "That's good. There's plenty more."

She stood there for a moment staring out into the darkness. When she didn't say anything, Clay looked up and saw a strange look on her face. "What's the matter?" he asked.

"Maybe that's why Jake ran away—because I was too hard on him."

Clay looked uncomfortable. "Oh, I don't reckon so. That's just his way."

The others were not listening to the conversation, and Jerusalem lowered her voice. "He hasn't been true to me with women, has he, Clay?" She immediately saw Clay's lips tighten and shook her head. "You wouldn't say even if he had," she said, then turned and walked away.

Clay looked at the biscuit in his hand. He ate it thoughtfully, then closed his eyes and leaned forward toward the fire.

The cry of a night bird broke into Julie's dream, and she lunged and awoke, gasping as if she had run a long distance. Moriah, sleeping beside her, said something in her sleep and turned over.

Julie sat up, threw the blanket back, and crawled out of the back of the wagon. Her legs were unsteady, and when she passed her hand over her face, it was wet with cold sweat.

A gentle breeze stirred the sweet and pungent odors of the wood, but she turned to look at the glowing coals and the yellow flames breaking the darkness of the night. Clay was sitting there cross-legged staring into it, and she walked toward him.

He looked up at her and asked, "What's the matter?"

"I had a bad dream." Sitting down beside Clay, she leaned against him, pulled her knees up, and encircled them with her arms. They sat in silence staring into the dancing flames for a moment, then she straightened up and said, "I guess I'm all right now."

The firelight illuminated Clay's face, casting dark shadows in his eye sockets and highlighting his cheekbones. "What'd you dream about?"

"I dreamed I was chasing someone—a woman."

"Why was you chasin' her?"

"I don't know, but I just knew that I had to catch her. And I ran as hard as I could, but I couldn't catch up with her—and then finally I did." The memory of the dream came back, and a shiver ran through Julie's body. She put her head down on his chest and clung to him. She turned her face around. "And . . . and she had my face, Clay. It was *me*."

"Well, it was just a dream. They don't mean anything."

"Why, you were telling Moriah yesterday about how Indians get all kinds of meanings out of their dreams!"

"They think they mean something, but I don't."

"I think they do."

Julie made no move to leave. She knew from past experience that she had stirred him. She looked up at him and put her hands behind his neck. "You change your mind, Clay?"

"About what?"

"I made you an offer when you busted me out of jail. You turned me down. I don't give a man a second chance, as a rule—but I reckon I'd make an exception in your case."

Clay did not move, even though he was very aware of Julie pressing against him. He was aware of the crackling of the fire and the smell of Julie's hair, and finally he said, "I don't reckon so."

Julie straightened up immediately. She brushed her hair back and stared at him with anger. "You don't want me. Is somethin' wrong with you?"

"Plenty."

"I mean, don't you like women?"

"I've liked a few."

"Then why don't you take what I'm offering?"

Clay carefully reached out, picked up a stick, and touched the end of it to the small yellow tongue of flame. It caught, and he held it up in front of his eyes, staring at it as if it had some sort of answer. Finally, he shook his head and tossed it into the fire. He turned to face Julie and said, "I don't know. It's got something to do with—I don't like love used to pay for things. It's like saying, 'If you'll do this for me, I'll give you that.'"

Julie was utterly still. She was staring at him with her eyes wide open, and finally she said, "You make too much of what goes on between a man and a woman."

Clay did not answer, but the moment had passed. Julie rose then and looked down at him. "You know, a woman always wants what she can't have. Be on your guard, Clay. I'll get you sooner or later." She reached out, leaned over, and put her hand on his cheek. "A man always has his weak moments—and I'll find yours."

Clay did not move until Julie went back

and got into the wagon. Then he took a deep breath, held it, and expelled it forcefully. He shook his head, then got up and walked over to the second wagon. Clinton was rolled up in his bedroll, and he did not stir when Clay pulled the blanket back and lay down. He reached out cautiously and touched the bottom of the wagon where Jerusalem and Mary Aidan were asleep. He was startled when Jerusalem's voice came softly, "Good night, Clay."

Suddenly, Clay Taliferro was glad that he was under the wagon, for he knew his face was red. *She's heard everything that fool sister of hers said!* he thought. Aloud he whispered just loud enough so that she might hear him, "Women who listen to other people's talk might hear somethin' they don't need to hear." He waited for her to respond, but she did not. He lay there trying to go to sleep but could not, knowing that Julie's words would stay with him for a long time. A wolf howled somewhere off in the distance, and he turned his head and listened until the sound died away. Then he rolled over and closed his eyes.

CHAPTER
EIGHT

The next day they broke camp early and rode hard again all day. Late in the afternoon, Clay pulled the wagon off the road and stopped beside a small river. A large flock of blackbirds rose up from an adjoining field of corn, wheeled, and flew away into the gathering darkness. As soon he could, Clinton jumped out of the wagon, trotted up, and said, "We ain't gonna stay in here beside this old river, are we, Clay?"

"Yes, we are." Clay was bored with sitting on a wagon all day and glared down at Clinton. "You don't do nothin' but complain, Clinton. When you get to heaven, I reckon you'll find something there to complain about too." Clay jumped off the wagon and started unhitching the mules. He noted that Brodie, who had driven the other wagon for a good part of the day, had pulled up behind him. "Get them mules unhitched, you boys!" Clay called out.

"Why are we stoppin' beside this river? There's a town up there. Can't you see it?" Clinton demanded.

"You hush, Clinton. I need me a bite of catfish. We're gonna catch 'em out of that river and fry 'em up for supper."

Josiah had ridden up on Clay's bay, and now he patted the animal on the neck and said, "That sounds real good. Nothin' like fresh catfish." He straightened up in the saddle and peered down the road. "Looks like we got company." He stepped off the horse and stood there watching as a man came weaving unsteadily down the middle of the road. "Look likes he's so drunk he don't care no more than Claude Harris's mule."

"Who was Claude Harris, and what was wrong with his mule?" Clinton demanded.

"Never you mind, boy! It's just an old sayin'."

As the others got down from the wagons, Clay caught a glimpse of Julie, who was grinning at him. She winked but said nothing, and he turned hastily away. He called out, "Hello. Can you tell us where we might be?"

Their visitor was a tall, lanky man of indeterminate years, somewhere between forty and sixty. He had not shaved in several days, and the front of his shirt was filthy, where he had, no doubt, thrown up. One eye was closed almost shut. He stared at them for a moment, then said, "You're in Louisiana. Ain't you got no sense a'tall? Don't even know where you are?"

"What's the name of that town?" Clay asked pleasantly.

"It's the devil's headquarters no matter what the name is."

Julie laughed aloud. "Sounds like my kind of place. Looks like you've had about all the enjoyment of it you can stand."

The man stared at her for a moment, then without another word staggered off down the road, weaving from side to side.

Clinton called out, "You keep on drinkin' that liquor and goin' into them saloons, you gonna wind up in the pit!"

The man did not turn his head, but they heard him curse and say, "Shut up!"

"I don't think he's a Baptist, Clinton," Clay said, grinning.

"He don't smell like one."

"Depends on which ones you been smellin'," Julie said.

"Me and the boys are goin' fishin'," Clay announced. "I'm partial to a bit of fresh catfish." He looked at Jerusalem, expecting an argument, but she only smiled.

"That would go down right well, Clay," Jerusalem said. "Bring 'em in as soon as you catch 'em. We'll be waitin' to fry 'em up."

"Look, Ma, we caught enough fish for everybody!" Clinton said.

Jerusalem rose to meet them as they came out of the darkness. She smiled as Clinton held up a fish so big it took both hands. "Look at this, Ma, ain't he a sockdologer!"

"My, did you catch that fish, Clinton?"

"I pulled him in, but Brodie had to help me. I could have done it by myself, though."

"Here, let's skin this here fish," Clay said. "Nail him up to that tree, Brodie."

As Brodie found a hammer and nails and proceeded to nail the fish up to the tree, Clay went to the coffeepot on the fire, picked up a tin cup, poured it full. He drank it off without stopping, and Josiah shook his head. "I swan, Clay, I believe you could drink that coffee straight out of the pot."

"Ain't such a thing as a cup of coffee too hot."

"Julie's gone," Jerusalem commented.

Clay bent over to fill the cup again, but at Jerusalem's words, he straightened up. "What do you mean *gone*?"

"She went into town."

At once Clinton piped up. "I bet she went to a saloon. That's what she did. She'll be drinkin' demon rum. You watch and see if-fen I'm right."

"Hush up, Clinton!" Clay said sharply. He turned to face Jerusalem squarely.

The two did not speak, and as Brodie watched them, he saw something pass between them. He had discovered that his mother and Clay seemed to be able to communicate without words. Sometimes just one look from Jerusalem would cause

Clay to be glum for hours. On the other hand, sometimes Clay would make a remark with a certain glint in his eyes that would put his mother in a happy frame of mind, bringing out a deep laugh, when Brodie could see nothing funny.

"I reckon you want me to go after her."

"Well, we're not leavin' her here, Clay," she said, her hands on her hips.

"Just let her come back by herself," Clay said grumpily.

"No, you go get her."

Again the two exchanged looks, and Clay, without another word, went to the wagon. He pulled out his gun belt and strapped it on. He already had a bowie knife in the sheath on his left side. "All right. I'll go fetch her back. You cook the fish." He started to turn, but Jerusalem's voice caught him.

"Take Brodie with you."

Brodie brightened up at once, and he moved over to stand beside Clay. Clay shook his head. "He don't need to be in that kind of a place that I expect she's in. It wouldn't be fittin'."

"Take him," Jerusalem said shortly.

Clay gave his shoulders a shaking and

then said sharply, "All right, let's go, Brodie!"

Brodie fell in beside Clay, but no word was spoken as they headed toward the town. Darkness was falling now, and some bats fluttered overhead. Finally, Clay said, "A Cheyenne squaw's got judgment, I think."

The remark made no sense at all to Brodie, who was puzzled for a time and hurried to keep up with Clay. "What's that about Cheyenne squaws?"

"They got more judgment, I think, than other women. Now, you take your ma. You think she's got good judgment, but she's just like all the rest of 'em. They ain't no reason to a woman, Brodie. They go on emotions—not like us men. We go on hard facts."

Clay's reasoning did not make sense to Brodie, who had found out that it was exactly the opposite, at least as far as Clay and his ma were concerned. *She* was the one who went on facts, and Clay was the one who was likely to fly off the handle just because he felt like it. "I don't know what you mean. I think Ma's pretty smart."

"Why, they ain't smart at all!" Clay protested. "They poke things."

"Poke things? What are you talkin' about?"

"Did you ever see a woman pick a tomato? She pokes at it."

"That's to see if it's ripe."

"Well, maybe so, but they poke at other things too. Like a man. They poke at a man just like they poke at cantaloupes."

Brodie listened to Clay closely, but to him Clay Taliferro was a strange mixture of wisdom and what seemed like pure foolishness. He didn't understand a bit of what Clay meant by his remarks on women and did not interrupt him until they reached town.

The town itself was small, with one main street. Lanterns burned brightly over two or three of the businesses and a couple of saloons.

"I never knew a town perched on the bank of a river that was worth dried spit," Clay muttered. Two men were strolling along, and Clay said, "Howdy. Can you tell me where the nearest sin parlor is?"

One of the men laughed and turned to

point. "Right over there, mister. The Silver Moon."

The other, a short chunky man with a round head and a tall, peaked hat that made him look comical, said, "Watch out for the bartender in there. His name's George."

"I'll watch out for him," Clay promised. "Come on, boy."

The Silver Moon, Brodie saw, was nothing more than a framed building with two windows flanking the one door. The door stood wide open, and the sound of a tinny piano came out along with plenty of ribald laughter. As soon as he stepped inside, he almost choked on the smell of sweat, tobacco smoke, and raw alcohol. But he didn't let that bother him. He had never been in a saloon before and avidly took it in. There were more than a dozen men and three women. He expected a bar, but there was none— only a table with some bottles and jugs on it and a bunch of glasses. A bulky man stood behind the table staring at them. A poker game was going on at one table, and one of the women was standing beside the piano trying to sing to the music. She was mumbling the words and from time to time would giggle and take another drink from the glass on top of the upright piano.

"Why, hello there, boys. Come on over and join us," she said, winking at Clay.

Brodie looked over and saw Julie seated at a table with a black-haired man who wore a white shirt and a string tie. A deck of cards was lying on the table, and Julie had a half-full glass in front of her.

Everyone seemingly had turned to look at them, or so Brodie felt. He followed Clay as he ambled over and sat down in an empty chair. "Good evenin', Julie."

"Who are you?" the black-haired man said.

"Why, this here is Clay Taliferro, and this is my nephew Brodie." Wicked humor glinted in Julie's eyes, and she smiled and waved her hand. "Clay here is my keeper. My sister pays him to keep me from havin' any fun."

Laughter broke out around the room, and Julie waved toward the man beside her. "This is Clyde. He knows how to have fun, don't you, Clyde?" She leaned over and put her hand on the gambler's arm.

"I sure do, honey, and we don't need no preachers in here if that's what you are."

"Oh, I ain't no preacher. We left him back in the camp. His name's Clinton. He wouldn't be seen in a sinful place like this."

Clyde suddenly laughed. He had a thin face and a thin black moustache. His clothes were a little on the foppish side, but he had a thick chest and a breadth to his shoulders that spoke of a powerful frame.

"You better go back and tell Jerusalem that I ain't comin' back until I've had my share of fun, Clay."

Clay took off his hat and put it down on the floor beside him carefully. "Maybe I'd like a bit of fun myself," he said.

"Now you're talkin'!" Julie said. "George, bring another bottle over here and a couple of glasses."

Brodie was shocked when Julie took the bottle, poured a glass full for Clay and about an inch and a half for him.

She handed it to him and said, "Did you ever drink whiskey, Brodie?"

"No, I never did."

"Well, it's time you started. Swallow that."

Brodie looked at Clay, expecting a protest, but Clay shrugged and drank his own whiskey down.

"That's pretty poor whiskey," he said.

"I reckon if it's good enough for us, it's good enough for you," Clyde said.

His eyes bored into Clay, but Clay did not seem to notice. Brodie didn't want to be made fun of, so he tipped the glass back and swallowed the amber-looking liquid. Within seconds he felt as if he had swallowed a red-hot poker. His eyes watered, and he began to cough.

Julie laughed and came over and slapped him on the back. She looked over at Clay and said, "I expected you to have a fit when I offered him a drink."

Clay suddenly smiled at her. "I'm in the mood to have some fun."

"You a gamblin' man?" Clyde asked with a thin smile.

"As far as poker or fightin' or women are concerned, I can't be surpassed, exceeded, whipped, or outdone," Clay said loudly for all to hear. "So, deal the cards, Clyde, and I'll show you where the bear sat in the buckwheat."

Clyde laughed and began to deal the cards. There were two other men in the game, and Brodie watched with interest as they made their bets on each hand. He did not even know how to play poker, and the science of it was beyond him. He was surprised to find more whiskey in his glass. When he looked at Julie, she smiled and winked at him. He drank it down and put his attention back on the card game.

As the evening wore on, Brodie slowly began to realize that his body seemed to be going numb—especially his lips. They wouldn't move right when he tried to talk. From time to time Julie would come and give him a squeeze, and he would find more whiskey in his glass.

After a time everything seemed funny. He laughed when Clay raked in a hand and laughed when Julie poured more whiskey in his glass. Amused at seeing her nephew like that, she said, "You've laughed more, Brodie, tonight than I've ever seen you. I'm proud to see it."

Afterward, he remembered only bits and pieces of what happened. He remembered dancing with a woman who had on a low-cut dress. Some people were laughing at him, he knew, but that was funny, and so he joined in and laughed at himself.

Finally, he heard the gambler called Clyde raise his voice and begin cursing. Then he heard Clay say, "I don't tolerate foul language in the presence of ladies."

After that he remembered very little except the sound of breaking furniture, and that he had thrown himself into what appeared to be a fight. Something struck him on the head, and he remembered falling but never remembered hitting the floor.

Jerusalem heard the sound of stumbling footsteps and a voice raised in a querulous fashion. Josiah had slipped out of this world into some private one and simply leaned against the wagon wheel staring out into the darkness. Clinton had gone to sleep, and Moriah was sitting down behind Jerusalem asking questions. She had gotten down to the subject she always brought up, "Why did Pa leave us, Ma? Don't he like us?"

Jerusalem knew she didn't have an answer that would satisfy her daughter. Now she stood up and said, "They're comin' back." Just to be on the safe side, she handed Mary Aidan to Moriah and picked up the shotgun leaning against the tree. As the figures came out of the darkness, weaving their way into the corona of light from the fire, she put the gun back and waited.

Clay came first with Brodie draped over his shoulder. When he moved to one side, Jerusalem saw Julie behind him. Her hair was down in her face, and her eyes were wild.

Clay's shirt was covered with blood. His nose had bled, and he had a wicked cut over his left eyebrow that was still bleeding.

He brought himself to a halt, swayed, and glared at Jerusalem.

"Well," he said in a royal tone, "I reckon you think I've been drinkin'."

"Haven't you?"

"I ain't touched a drop."

"Here. Bring Brodie over here and sit him up by this tree," Jerusalem demanded.

Clay opened his mouth to argue but then obeyed. Julie helped him put Brodie down, and Jerusalem saw that his mouth was cut and he had a puffy eye. "I'll have to clean him up."

Jerusalem quickly went to get some rags and a bucket of water. She was aware that Julie was watching her, but she didn't say a word to her. She came back and began to wipe the blood from Brodie's face. He woke up and stared at her with glassy eyes.

"I feel awful sick, Ma," he slurred.

Julie came over to him, saying, "Come on, Brodie." She hauled him to his feet and barely got him outside the circle of the campfire when the sound of his vomiting broke the silence of the night.

Jerusalem walked over to Clay and, reaching up, turned his face around. "That cut over your eyebrow has got to be stitched. Go sit down while I get my needle and thread."

Clay made his way to the tree, turned around, and leaned up against it. He slumped down until he was sitting. Jerusalem came back with a small box. She set it down and then picked up the wet cloth and wrung it out and began to wipe the blood from his face.

"Jerusalem?"

"Yes, what is it?"

"I have so been drinkin'. I don't care what anybody says. I been drinkin'."

"You brought them back, Clay. That's the important thing. Now, this is gonna hurt." She sewed up the wound quickly and effi- ciently as if it were a patch on an old shirt, then took her scissors and clipped off the ends of the thread. "Now, go to bed."

Clay tried to get up and fell over on his side. Reaching down, Jerusalem got him upright and led him to the wagon. He got on his hands and knees and crawled under, falling on his bedroll. When Jerusalem went back to the fire, Clinton said, "Ma, Brodie is drunk. They all three are."

"Go to bed, Clinton."

Clinton started to argue as he always did, then seeing the look on his mother's face, he turned and left. He started toward the bed, but Jerusalem said, "You stay with your grandfather. I don't want him wandering off. You better tie a rope to his hand and tie the other end to yours."

Jerusalem began to gather up her equipment, but Julie came over and stood before her. She pushed the hair back out of her face, and her lips were drawn into a tight line. "I expect you'd like it if I left you."

"No, I don't want that."

"I'll do it again. I'm tellin' you."

"I expect you will."

"I ain't fit to be around Brodie and the kids."

Jerusalem was holding the sewing kit in

her hand. She looked at Julie and said, "You're our kin, Julie. Now go to bed."

Julie stared at her sister for a moment and then without another word turned and made her way to the bed in the wagon. Jerusalem and Moriah heard her crawling in, and then Moriah said, "I thought you'd be mad at them, Ma."

"Brodie's my son," Jerusalem said evenly. "Julie is my sister, and Clay's my friend. No matter what they do, nothing can change that."

Moriah chewed her lower lip and then looked up at her mother. "You mean if I turn out to be a bad woman, you'll still like me?"

Jerusalem put her free arm around the girl and looked down at her. "I will, Moriah—for always, no matter *what*."

CHAPTER
NINE

For two days after the Silver Moon incident, not much conversation went on among the travelers. Mary Aidan actually was the most cheerful and vociferous of all of them. She kept crying and laughing just as if nothing had happened. Julie was quiet, but she showed no sign of remorse for her behavior nor for allowing Brodie to get drunk. But Clay found it more comfortable to ride his big bay horse out in front rather than drive one of the wagons.

Brodie asked him once why he was saying so little and keeping his distance. Clay closed his eyes and shook his head. "Well, boy, it's better to walk soft around your ma for a time after you've made a plumb fool of yourself."

By the time Saturday came, everyone seemed to be on better terms. No one had brought up what had happened at the Silver Moon. Jerusalem knew she had to talk to Brodie, who sat in silence beside her in the wagon, but she decided to wait for an appropriate time. Since the mules had strained to pull the loaded wagons all morning, Clay stopped them long enough to switch teams and water them, since the road wasn't far from the river.

Jerusalem had taken the reins to spell Brodie for a while. They hadn't gone far when she saw an enormous pothole in the road. She tried to pull the reins to the right and swerve the mules around it, but it was too late. The front left wheel dropped down into the pothole with a thud and collapsed as the iron rim popped off. When Clay came over and looked at it, he shook his head. "It'll take a wheelwright to fix that." He looked back and said, "We'd best camp here and get that wheel off. I'll have to take it back to town and get it fixed."

It was late in the afternoon, and the town

they had passed through was only two miles back. To no one's surprise, Jerusalem said, "I'll go with you."

Clay gave her an odd look but shrugged. "That's your say-so," he muttered.

By the time they rode back into town and found the wheelwright, it was getting dark. To Clay's dismay the man said he couldn't fix it until Monday because he didn't work on the Sabbath day. Clay lifted one eyebrow and said, "I didn't know folks from Louisiana kept the Sabbath."

"Usually we ain't too particular about it, but the whole town is right in the middle of a camp meeting. Y'all ought to come."

When they got back to camp, Jerusalem got off her horse and went over to take Mary Aidan, who was squalling and wiggling in Brodie's arms. "That baby's hungry," she said as she climbed into the wagon to nurse her and quiet her down. When she got Mary Aidan settled, she came back and said, "There's a camp meeting going on. Service is tonight and tomorrow. We'll all go."

"I won't go. Not me," Julie said abruptly. "You can count me out."

"We better eat now because it might be late when we come back."

Julie didn't go, but everyone else did, including Clay, which surprised Jerusalem. Clinton wanted to know if the preacher was a Baptist preacher, and when Jerusalem told him it didn't matter, he stared at her with a hard expression. "'Course it matters. It might be some stodgy old Episcopalians."

"Episcopalians don't have camp meetings, Clinton. They have too much dignity. Don't be foolish," Jerusalem had returned.

"I didn't know there was this many religious folk in all of Louisiana," Clay said as he looked around at the crowd that had gathered for the camp meeting. He was sitting on one of the benches in the brush arbor holding Mary Aidan in his lap, standing her up and letting her stroke his face.

Jerusalem glanced around at the crowd and said, "It's a passel of folks," she said. "You want me to hold the baby for a while?"

"She's doin' right well where she is. She sure don't look like Jake, does she? That's a blessing."

Jerusalem smiled. "I'm glad you're not

sullied up anymore after what happened in town at the Silver Moon."

Clay knew she wasn't happy about his getting everyone drunk, especially Brodie, and chose to ignore her comment. He knew the least said at the moment, the better.

He had a way, Jerusalem noticed, of going deaf when his personal faults were ever mentioned. She smiled and thought how odd it was and said, "Strange how that child takes to you."

"Females always take to me, but this one's especially got good taste. She beats hens a-pacin', don't she?"

At that moment a short, chubby man with a red face stood up and began to welcome everyone to the meeting. He was the "songheister," as Clay called him, and lined the hymns out they would be singing for the meeting. He would speak one or two lines of the hymn, those gathered would sing them, and then he would give out a couple more lines. He had a piercing voice like a trumpet. Since there weren't enough seats to go around, the crowd simply surrounded him.

The evangelist was a fine-looking man of forty, tall, strong, and deep-chested, with a pair of light blue eyes that hit with the force of a musket ball. He preached for an hour and a half with no apparent loss of volume. When he ended with an invitation to sinners to come and find salvation, at least twenty people went down, many of them crying. Every time one of them "pressed through," shouts of joy went up.

When the service was just about over, Clinton, who was seated down the row from Clay, got up and came to stand before him. "You need to go down and get saved, Clay."

"You reckon I'm that bad a sinner?"

"Yes, you are. Gettin' drunk every chance you get and carryin' on with bad women is just what God wants to save you from. Come on. I'll go with you."

Clay simply laughed. "It's not my time, Clinton."

Clinton shook his head and said, "If you get kilt, you'll be sorry."

"That's enough of that," Jerusalem said sharply. "I reckon we can go now."

Brodie was angry with Clinton, for all he seemed to do was criticize everyone. "Shut up, Clinton."

"Don't tell me to shut up!"

Brodie snapped back, and Clinton lost his

temper and hit Brodie in the chest. Before he knew it, Brodie had hauled off and socked him a good one in the face, giving Clinton a bloody nose. Jerusalem stepped in and separated them, and Clinton threatened, "I'll whip you tomorrow—see if I don't!"

They left the campgrounds, and Jerusalem told Brodie to drive for her. Brodie was carrying Mary Aidan, who was sound asleep. He waited until his mother got into the wagon, handed the baby up, and then climbed up and took the lines. He said nothing for a long time. Overhead, the stars sparkled like tiny diamonds on a velvet cloth, and the moon shone full and silver. After they had ridden for a few moments, Jerusalem said, "How come you're so quiet, son?"

"I guess I was thinkin' about what Clinton said to Clay. I'm a sinner, too, Ma."

"Then why didn't you listen to the preacher and let Jesus save you?"

"I don't know. I just couldn't make myself go down. I never have figured it out. You're a Christian, ain't you?"

"Yes, I am," Jerusalem said quietly.

"Why ain't you never been baptized, then? It bothers Clinton a lot."

Jerusalem reached over with her left arm and put it around Brodie's shoulders. She hugged him tight, and he looked at her with surprise. She smiled and the moonlight was kind to her face. She looked very young to Brodie at that moment, and she smiled at him in a way that made him feel warm inside.

"You're a good boy, Brodie. You're the brightest of all my children. Of all the family, really." She kept her arm around him and looked down at the baby's face. Mary Aidan was fast asleep in the crook of her right arm.

Brodie thought she was through and couldn't understand what she was trying to say. Finally she spoke, and her voice was quieter than usual. "I called on the Lord a long time ago when I was just a girl, and something happened to me. I don't know why I didn't join the church. I just didn't. And then when I lost my boys, I got mad at God. I wouldn't speak to Him until about a year ago. Then I began reading my Bible again and trying to pray. At times I feel far from God. But, Brodie, I know one thing. I love Jesus. He was a real man. I read the parts over and over again where He was good to women and how He picked up little children

and held them. That always makes me a little bit teary. So, I guess I've had a few dis-
appointments in my life, but Jesus never
disappoints me. I expect I'll decide some
day what kind of a church I want to belong
to. So far most of 'em have been a big disappointment to me. I reckon I'm too hard to
please."

Jerusalem squeezed Brodie and shook
her head, then said, "I'll be glad when we
find your pa."

Brodie knew that the conversation about
religion was over as they pulled back into
camp. He had never heard his mother
speak so openly about her faith in God before. As he got ready to turn in for the night,
he began to think on what she had said
about Jesus. He looked around to make
sure nobody saw him, and then pulled out a
Bible his mother kept wrapped in a cloth in
their wagon and started to read, looking for
what it was about Jesus that held his
mother so captive.

Jerusalem went over to where Clinton
was lying and saw that he was awake.
"Clinton, you shouldn't have hit Brodie."

"Well, he didn't need to tell me to shut
up!"

Jerusalem spoke softly for a time, stroking Clinton's hair, and finally she said, "You ought to forgive your brother."

Clinton knew how he had reacted was wrong, but sometimes he just got plumb fed up with his older brother. He mumbled, "All right, Ma, I'll forgive him."

"That's my good Baptist boy!"

"I'll forgive him *now,* but if I don't die tonight, I'll shore whip him tomorrow!"

Jerusalem could not keep back the laughter. She grabbed Clinton and hugged him, saying, "Your religion needs fixing, Clinton, but you're a good boy!"

August had come now, and the days were hot and the nights warm. The animals were getting tired, and so was everyone on the journey. Clay was riding his bay twenty yards in the lead. He began to sing, the words floating back to Julie and Jerusalem, who were riding in the lead wagon:

I found a rose in New Orleans,
Sweetest flower I'd ever seen.

Coal black hair and sparkling eyes
And rosy lips for telling lies.

Clay had a good baritone voice and sang
the chorus with sorrow and great feeling:

Deep in the heart!
O deep in the heart!
Naught can be lost
That's deep in the heart!

Once I held her in my arms,
She swore we'd never part,
But now I only hold her charms
Way down deep in the heart!

All flowers may fade
Their fragrance depart—
But my New Orleans maid
Will ever be deep in my heart.

He sang the final chorus, then Julie called
out to him, "Hey, Clay, come here." He
turned his horse and waited until they drew
the wagon alongside of him. "Who was this
shady lady from New Orleans you're carrying on about?" Julie asked.

Clay shoved his hat back and stared at

her. "You ain't got no respect for a broken heart, girl!"

"Tell us about her," Jerusalem said, smiling. "You should have told us you were suffering from a broken heart. We'd have been more careful of your feelings."

"You two don't know what it's like having your heart busted all up," Clay announced. "Women, they don't feel things as deep as men do."

"Clay Taliferro, I can't believe you said that!" Jerusalem said.

Clay stared at the two, then said, "That New Orleans rose was a *real* woman! You can't hardly ever find them no more. Women just ain't got it *here*!" He put his hand over his heart, gave them what he considered a soulful look, then turned his horse and galloped off.

"I don't think he's sufferin' too much," Julie laughed. "He just wants us to think he's a ladies' man with a broken heart."

"Maybe he is," Jerusalem said, watching as he rode on ahead, a cloud of dust rising after him.

"Clay? Don't you believe it! He's tough as leather."

Jerusalem didn't answer, and for fifteen

minutes the two were silent. Finally, Jerusalem said, "I wonder what she was like?"

"What who was like?"

"That girl who betrayed Clay in New Orleans."

Julie stared with disgust at Jerusalem. "Don't ever believe what a man tells you. They're all liars where women are concerned. He was probably the one who left *her*!"

It came as a relief one day when they stopped for noon break to eat a cold lunch and Clay pointed ahead and said, "I reckon we'll be pullin' into another town pretty soon."

"What town is that?" Julie asked.

"Well, I don't know what they call it. There's two of 'em by the same name. Some call it *NAK-atush*, which is the way the French say it, but other people call it Nako-DO-shus. That's Spanish style, I reckon."

"What happens when we get there?" Brodie asked.

"We turn west and head down what they call the El Camino Real."

"What does that mean?" Moriah demanded.

"Means 'the royal road.' It goes most of the way through Texas, I guess. But pretty soon—" Clay broke off and pulled up beside a grove of trees, placing his hand on the revolver at his side. "There comes somebody, and he ain't out for no pleasure walk."

Jerusalem turned to see a man come reeling out of the woods. He was alone, and his face was scratched. He fell as he started toward them.

"That fellow's hurt," Josiah said. "We'd better see to him."

As Clay and Jerusalem rushed forward toward the man, she noticed that Clay's eyes were searching the woods. When they got to the man, he had risen to his feet, and he was trying to catch his breath. He was a short man dressed in a suit of some kind that had been ripped by the briars in the bushes.

"What's wrong, fella?" Clay said.

"Indians! They're killing them! You . . . you've got to help them!"

Clay straightened up, and his face grew hard. "Where abouts?"

"Back there along the river. Give me a gun. I've got to go help 'em. They're torturing them. Can't you hear their screams?"

At that instant Jerusalem saw a new side to Clay Taliferro. His eyes suddenly had a hard gleam in them.

He whirled quickly and yelled, "Get all the guns!" He grabbed his rifle and tossed the other Hawkin to Brodie, then said, "Get a shotgun, Clinton. Josiah, you got your rifle?"

"Shore have." Josiah was looking into the man's face and said, "How many of them was there?"

"Not many. Only eight or ten, but they're killing the professor."

Clay looked at Jerusalem and said, "You women stay here." Then turning back to the man, he said, "Show us where they are."

Jerusalem came to stand before Clay and said, "You have to go?"

"Yes."

"Then take care of my boys, Clay."

"I'll do the best I can."

★　★　★

Brodie was more scared than he had ever been in his life. He had no trouble keeping up with Clay, who led the way. When he glanced across at Clinton, he saw his brother's face was pale. Brodie wondered if he could kill a man, even an Indian, but the tale the newcomer, whose name was James Langley, had told them had chilled him to the bone. When Clay asked him how many were in the party, he had said, "There was five of us—me, the professor, two drivers, and a guide."

"How'd you get away?"

"I'd gone down to the river for water, and I heard the devils screamin'. I started back toward our camp, but I saw 'em kill the guide, and they had caught the others. We've got to get back, or they'll torture them."

"I expect that's right," Clay said grimly. He kept up a hard pace, as fast as Langley could go.

Finally Langley, gasping for breath again, said, "They're right over that rise there in a clearing."

"Everybody keep quiet and spread out," Clay said. "We'll see what it's like before we do anything."

Brodie took his place in the line as they advanced slowly through the thick undergrowth. The briars scratched his face, but he brushed them aside. Josiah was on his left and Clinton on his right, and they all reached the tree line at about the same time. "Look at them Indians," Josiah said. "They got those poor fellers staked out."

Brodie took one look and grew sick. Two of the men had been stripped naked and were stretched out, tied to stakes in the ground. Some of the Indians were gathered around laughing and cutting at them with knives. Past them, a tall man, also stripped naked, had been tied and hung from his ankles. The Indians had started a fire under him. Two of them were going around cutting him with knives, shouting and screaming.

Brodie felt his stomach turn over and closed his eyes to shut out the sight, and then he heard Clay say, "All right. Here's what we'll do. They won't be expecting us. They're occupied and won't be suspecting anything. Here, take my rifle, Josiah."

Clay handed his Hawkin to Josiah and pulled out his pistol. "I'll get as close as I can and make a rush at 'em. I got six shots here. As soon as you hear the first one, start shooting. Your shotguns won't reach that far, Clinton, so wait until you come in closer. Josiah, you'll have two shots. Brodie, you'll have one."

Brodie noticed that Clay's skin was stretched tight across his face, but otherwise he appeared calm. "Clay, you ain't goin' in alone," Brodie whispered.

"They won't be payin' any attention to me. They're havin' too much fun with their dirty business. Watch now and don't miss. Make every shot count."

Brodie watched as Clay stepped out of the tree line and then started running toward the clearing. Brodie had never seen a man as fast as Clay Taliferro. Clay had raced with him and some young men who had gathered at the farm one day. Clay had simply run off and left them in the dust. Now, as he ran toward the men held captive, he was as swift as a deer.

"Get ready, boy!" Josiah said hoarsely as he took aim. He already had one of the Hawkins up, the other one leaned ready against the tree. "As soon as they see him and you get a clear shot, shoot 'em. Don't try for the head. Right through the belly's a good place."

Brodie lifted the Hawkin and balanced it against a low-growing limb. As he took aim with the now-steady gun, the Indians jumped into focus as if he had looked through a telescope. The two men who were staked out had been screaming, and now, even as Brodie watched, two of the Indians raised their tomahawks and with a dull thud cut off their screams abruptly.

One of the Indians looked up and saw Clay running toward them. He let out a shrill scream and raced to meet Clay. An explosion jolted Brodie as Josiah fired his weapon. The shot caught the Indian in the throat. He fell to the ground, kicked once, and then was still. At that same moment, Clay began shooting. Indians fell with every shot.

Brodie saw one Indian over to Clay's right who still had his bloody tomahawk in his hand. When he turned and started for Clay, Brodie pulled the trigger without hesitation. Black smoke billowed out, and the Indian fell forward with a bullet right in the chest. Josiah fired the other Hawkin, then yelled, "Come on!" He came out of the woods, and the others followed him.

When they got to the clearing, however,

the echoes of Clay's last shot were fading. The Indians lay in sprawled positions, and without hesitation, Clay pulled out his knife and said, "Cut that fellow down while I hold him, Brodie."

Brodie had to shimmy up the tree to the first limb and slash at the rawhide thong that tied the man's feet. Clay caught him as he fell, and the man called Langley came over, his face white as paste, and said, "Are you all right, Professor?"

They all crowded around the man, who was bleeding freely from half a dozen cuts. He was a long-faced man with long arms and legs like a spider. His fingers were longer than anyone's Brodie had ever seen. He had canary yellow hair and a pale complexion. The eyes opened, and the man's lips began to move. He looked up at Clay, and then around at the dead Indians, and a smile pulled the corners of his wide mouth upward. "I say, old chap—good show."

"He's all right, Langley. Breathed a little smoke. Brodie, you and Clinton tear back to camp and tell them we're all right. They'll be worried somethin' fierce about you," Clay said.

"You want me to bring 'em here?"

"No, I don't want them to see all this. Bring a couple mules back. We'll get these fellows back to camp."

The Englishman was struggling to sit up. He coughed and said, "I say, how did you find us?"

"Your man Langley told us."

The Englishman's eyes went to Langley, who was kneeling beside him. "I'll have to give you a raise." He started to say something else but fell backward in a faint.

"He'll be all right," Clay said. "Luckily, they'd only just started on him."

"Them other fellers are dead."

"Some of them Indians ain't dead," Josiah remarked. "They're still a-twitchin'."

Clay rose and plucked his bowie knife from his belt. "They will be soon," he said calmly.

Jerusalem had dressed the cuts on the Englishman's body, and the servant Langley had seen to it that fresh clothing was provided. The professor was sitting now with his back against one of the wagon wheels drinking liquor from a bottle that Langley had brought.

"I thank you, ma'am. You're a fine doctor."

"You lost a lot of blood," Jerusalem said as she gathered up the strips of cloth left over from making bandages.

"Well, this will build more blood," the Englishman said. He drank from the bottle and then said, "I haven't introduced myself. My name's Fergus St. John Nightingale—the Third. You met my servant James here."

"What are you doing in these parts, Professor?" Jerusalem asked.

"Oh, a little study, don't you see. I'm writing a book on aboriginal races."

"What's that?" Julie asked. She had helped Jerusalem staunch the flow of blood and then bandaged him up.

"Savages," Nightingale said.

"Any particular kind?" Clay asked. Langley had brought back two bottles, and now Clay tilted one and sipped it. "What is this?"

"It's champagne," Langley said.

"Makes my nose tickle."

"See if it'll make mine tickle," Julie said. She reached over and took the bottle, tilted it, and drank deeply. "Not much to it, is there?"

Nightingale said cheerfully, "Well, it is a bit frothy, but what can you expect from the French? I'm writing a book on savages. I started in Africa. We had quite a time there, didn't we, James?"

"Yes, sir, we did indeed."

"Will you have something to eat?" Jerusalem asked.

"A bit later perhaps." He looked up at Clay. "I say, old boy, were those Comanches? I'm particularly interested in studying the Comanches."

"No, if they had been Comanches, we'd all be dead. Those were San Carlos Apaches. Don't know what they were doin' this far east. Comanches pretty well wiped them out around here. Run 'em out a long time ago."

"Where were you headed?" Josiah asked.

"We're going to Texas. I understand the Comanches are there."

Clay suddenly laughed. "You're the only man I ever heard of who went lookin' for Comanches. Most people spend most of their time tryin' to run away from them."

"I see I was a bit ill advised."

Nightingale's eyes were the brightest blue that Jerusalem had ever seen. "Will you be going back to England now that you lost your men?" Jerusalem asked.

"Oh no. I didn't actually know those fellows. They were recommended and not particularly handy. I think the guide was lost most of the time."

"We'll have to bury them," Clay said.

"We're going down right through Texas," Jerusalem said. "At least that's our plan. Perhaps you ought to come along with us for a time at least."

"Thank you, madam. That's most kind. I believe I will take advantage of your offer." He tilted the bottle up again and said, "Beastly drinking champagne out of a bottle. James, see if you can find a goblet, will you? Drinking from a bottle—hardly civilized, wot?"

CHAPTER
TEN

The grave was as deep as Brodie's chest, which meant that Clinton could barely see over it. Clay had put the two of them to the task of digging the grave for the three men who had been slain. They had been working hard for the better part of an hour, and Clinton had done nothing but complain since they began. Now Brodie threw a shovel full of dirt up over the edge and turned to stare at his brother.

"Clinton, I'm sick and tired of listenin' to you argue about everything all the time." Brodie looked over at the three corpses, each wrapped in a separate blanket, and shook his head. "Them fellas done set their buckets down, and that's all there is to it! And it's our job to bury them."

"I don't care! It ain't right to bury folks one on top of another like pancakes in a stack!" Clinton gripped his shovel, but he shoved his jaw forward as he always did when he was engaged in an argument—which was most of the time. "I don't think Clay's got any feelin's a'tall. He sure ain't showing any respect for the dead."

"He's tryin' to save us the trouble of diggin' three graves. What difference does it make?"

"Difference! Why, Brodie, you ain't got no more sense than a stubborn mule! When the resurrection comes, how are them fellas gonna get out of here all stacked up like that?"

Brodie shook his head wearily. It was the sort of foolish argument that Clinton loved, but he himself despised. He began throwing the dirt out again, trying to ignore Clinton's hairbrained theological arguments. As he worked, he wondered what Clay and Josiah had done with the bodies of the Indians. They had left camp early the next day, telling the boys to be bring shovels in an hour to the spot where they had fought the Indians. By the time the boys had gotten there, the bodies of the Indians were all gone. Clay had simply said, "Dig one grave right there. Make it deep enough for all three of 'em."

Clinton had looked around and blurted out, "Where are them dead Indians?"

"I put 'em where the dogs won't bite 'em. Now, get to diggin'. Brodie, if that sorry brother of yours don't hold his end up diggin' that grave, slap him with his shovel."

After another ten minutes, Brodie said, "I reckon that's about deep enough." He had to give Clinton a boost out of the grave. Then he scrambled out and brushed the dirt off the front of his clothes. It gave him a queasy feeling to look at the three blanket-covered forms. He had seen the awful things that the Indians had done to them. He had even had a bad nightmare about it, and now he looked quickly away. "Clay didn't say whether to put 'em in or not."

"I ain't touchin' 'em!" Clinton said, backing away from the grave.

"Well, I don't reckon I will either. I guess Clay and Grandpa can take care of that."

At that moment Clay rode up on his bay,

followed by Josiah on one of the mules named Jemima. They got off, and Clay came over and looked down into the hole. "That'll have to do, boys, I reckon. We got to hurry. The womenfolks are comin' to have the funeral."

Clay looked at Brodie's face and then at Clinton. "You boys go wash up and change clothes. When you get that done bring the wagons up here. We'll be movin' out right after the funeral."

Brodie turned, and Clay said, "Take the horse and the mule."

The boys got on and headed back to camp. As soon as they got there, Jerusalem had them wash up and put on clean clothes. Then they all moved out to have the funeral before continuing on their journey. The professor rode in one of the wagons beside Julie. She was wearing one of her good dresses, Brodie noticed, and the professor was dressed in what looked like a new suit. He had on a white shirt, a pair of blue trousers, shiny black boots but no coat. *I reckon he's too sore to put much more on. The way he's cut up, I'm surprised he's wearing anything at all.* Brodie had been shocked at the way the women had treated him when Clay brought him back to the wagons. The poor man hardly had anything on, yet Jerusalem and Julie had treated him with both compassion and dignity as they cared for his wounds. Clinton had been even more shocked, for his strict view of religion caused him to be extremely modest, even around his brother.

Brodie noticed that the professor was lively enough and kept up an animated discussion with Julie. More than once, he heard Julie's deep laugh at something the professor had said. Sitting beside his mother, he said, "It looks like Julie is enjoyin' herself."

"She's got a new man to make eyes at," Jerusalem said.

"The professor! Why, that ain't likely, Ma. He's cut all to bits."

"I think a man would crawl out of his grave if Julie smiled at him. She always was like that." She suddenly laughed, and the laugh sounded like Julie's. "So was I, believe it or not."

Brodie turned and looked at his mother. "Really, Ma? I can't believe that." It was hard for him to picture her as a young woman courted by young men and acting like his aunt Julie. It bothered him to think she was anything like her sister when it came to men.

She turned to him and and saw his expression of unbelief at what she had said. Digging her elbow against him, she said, "Don't worry about it. Your children will look at you someday and say, 'Why that old codger, squiring around after girls and kissin' on 'em.'"

Brodie blushed and did not speak. His ma had the ability to embarrass him, and he did not say another word until they reached the spot where they were going to have the funeral.

Clay and Josiah had finished burying the men, for the grave was already covered as they approached. Brodie was glad for that, since neither he nor Clinton would have been up to it. Digging the large grave was hard enough. He already had bad memories of the horrible things he had seen yesterday, and he didn't want any more to think about.

The professor got down out of the wagon and came over to the grave, where Josiah and Clay were standing. He looked around and said, "I wish we had a bishop here, but

I suppose we'll muddle through. Maybe we could have a song."

The others gathered around and Jerusalem began singing a hymn. Those of them who knew it joined in. After the sound died down, the professor took his hat off. He looked very tall standing there, and he was as lean as a snake. His homely face puckered up, and he looked up directly at the sky and said in a conversational tone, "I say there, Lord, I didn't know these men at all, so to speak, but you know them. So, none of us can judge 'em, but you are always fair, so we leave them in your hands." And then the professor began speaking in some other kind of language.

Brodie didn't know what it was, and he could tell from looking around that no one else knew it either.

Finally the professor turned, and his face was sad. "Well, amen. We'll all be in a hole like this one day."

"Well, ain't that a cheerful thing to say!" Julie said out loud.

"Sorry, my dear. I didn't mean to offend you."

The professor had two wagons, both of which were the best money could buy, with canvas on the top. Brodie and Clinton had both peered inside and were in awe of one of them. It was made up just like a tiny room with a long bed that folded up against the side. It also had a desk, a bookcase, a wine rack, and all sorts of conveniences, some of which neither of them had ever seen before. The other wagon was loaded with plenty of food, clothes, and things that the boys could only wonder about. The professor's servant James drove one of them, and Clinton drove the fancy one with the bed in it. Clay and Josiah had tied the Indian ponies together so that they could all be handled in a line. As they left the clearing, Brodie looked back, remembering the horrible fight that took place here yesterday. He was driving the wagon his mother was in. Nothing much had been said about the fight, but he knew that Clay had told her that he had saved his life. She had not asked him about it, but he could sense she was only waiting for the right time.

Brodie looked straight ahead as the wagons moved out, then swallowed hard and said, "Ma, I . . . I don't ever want to have to see what I saw yesterday."

Jerusalem waited a moment before saying anything. Then laying her hand on his arm, she said, "It worried you that you killed that Indian?"

"Yes, ma'am."

"I'd be ashamed if you didn't, but it had to be done. It's a horrible thing to have to kill someone, but you saved Clay's life, and he won't ever forget it. I hope you learned somethin' from it."

Brodie could not answer. He had, indeed, learned something, but he could not explain exactly what it was. His mind couldn't seem to let go of it, and his thoughts drifted back to the vivid scenes from the day before. As they rode on in silence for a while, he knew he was grateful that he had saved Clay's life. He remembered the bad nightmare that kept him tossing and turning most of the night. He kept seeing the bullet strike the Indian and then seeing his face as he fell back dead. When the first rays of the sun had come up, he had gotten up to gather wood for the fire. He had tried to put it all out of his mind, but a somber restlessness continued to bother him. He had wanted to ask Clay, who had killed at least six Indians, or his great-grandfather, who had killed two, but he couldn't think of a way to put it. By the time they had dug the grave, packed up, and had the funeral, he didn't have the chance. At the sound of his mother's voice, his thoughts returned to the present. Somehow, he now understood a little of what it must be like when Grandpa's mind went off somewhere.

He turned and looked at his mother and said, "I guess I'll forget about it someday, Ma. I sure hope so, and I hope I don't ever have to do it again."

By the time they had traveled with the professor and Langley for two days, they had learned a great deal about Fergus Nightingale. He could speak a half-dozen languages, and he had studied at the famous Oxford University in England. Langley had told them this, although the professor hadn't mentioned it. He also told them that Nightingale's family was extremely wealthy and owned a great deal of land. Nightingale could have stayed in England and had the best of everything, but his immense curiosity to learn had led him to Africa, and now here to study the Comanches. Langley also informed them that when the professor's father died he would inherit a title and become Sir Fergus Nightingale III.

The professor was beginning to heal up well, for the cuts had only been superficial. None of them really knew what to make of him. He could look straight at you and make you feel that he was laughing, although his horse face would be sober as a judge. But something in his eyes twinkled from time to time, and his sense of humor took odd streaks. He talked more to Julie than to the rest of them, and the two of them drank freely from the bottles of champagne that he had brought along in his wagon. Around the campfire at night, he would tell them tales so tall that at times they were all amazed. One time he told them of living with a tribe in Africa called the Masai that killed lions with only a spear.

"I say, that was a bit much for me! A gun's one thing when you're up against a ferocious beast, but to see a black-maned lion running at you . . . and you with just a spear. I begged off on that one." After a while he told them about the Masai's favorite meal. "Their favorite meal was to take a jug and milk one of those big cows of theirs until the jug was half full. Then they would open a vein on its neck with a sharp knife and finish filling the jug with blood."

"What'd they do with it?" Clay asked.

"Why, they'd mix it up and drink it."

"Drink it!" Clay stared at him. "Sometimes I doubt that you're rememberin' things straight, Professor."

"Upon my word it's true. I tried it myself."

"What'd it taste like?" Brodie asked.

"Tastes like blood and milk mixed together. Wouldn't care for a steady diet of it."

As they continued on their journey, they discovered that the professor was *almost* as good a shot as Clay, who was an expert. He had four rifles in his wagon and some fancy dueling pistols that interested Clay. One day when the professor was showing them to Josiah, Clay had picked one of them out of its leather case, sighted it, and then looked at the tall Englishman. "Did you ever use one of these?"

"Oh, once or twice."

"What was the trouble over?"

"The blighter insulted me. He said my tie didn't match my trousers. Can't put up with that, you know."

"Did you kill him?" Julie asked, wondering if it was another of his tall tales.

"Kill him! Why, bless you, child, no! Just pinked him in the arm a mite. Can't kill a man because he's got poor taste."

"If you did that in this country, there wouldn't be nobody left," Josiah said and laughed.

Langley was talking one day about his employer as they approached Nachitoches. "Why, the professor's not afraid of anything. I've seen him stand right up to a charging elephant, I did. It bothers me. I think he's going to get himself in a fix someday that he can't handle."

"Well, he'd better be afraid of the Comanches," Clay said. "They're worse than a charging elephant."

As they pulled into Nachitoches the next day, Clay said, "Well, if this is the best they got in the way of towns, you can pardon me."

Indeed, Nachitoches was a sorry-looking place. The few scattered houses that made up the settlement were built with no appar-

ent plan. The tiny town had only a black-smith shop, a trading post, a small hotel, and two saloons. It didn't even have a church, which Jerusalem thought was strange.

When the caravan pulled up in front of the trading post and Clay jumped off of his bay, he heard a voice calling his name.

"Well, if that's not Clay Taliferro, I'll be dipped!"

Jerusalem was getting down off of the wagon and saw Clay turn and stare at a tall man wearing a fine-looking suit and smok-ing a long cheroot. She took the baby and stood beside Clay as the man walked down the steps of the trading post.

The man held his hands out from the guns at his side and said, "Don't shoot, Clay."

"Hello, Jim. Sure didn't expect to see you here." Clay put out his hand, and the other man looked relieved as he shook hands. "Let me introduce you to Miz Jerusalem Hardin. Jerusalem Ann, I'd like you to meet Jim Bowie. You've heard me speak of him."

Bowie had penetrating blue eyes, tawny hair and had a reckless air about him. He was a handsome man and bowed in a courtly fashion toward Jerusalem. "I'm happy to make your acquaintance, Mrs. Hardin."

"Miz Hardin's on her way to meet her husband in Texas. He's bought some land from a fellow named Austin."

"Oh yes, the Austin settlement. I don't believe I've met your husband," Bowie said.

"I doubt he's been there too long, sir," Jerusalem said. "Have you two met before?"

Bowie gave Clay a quizzical look, and for a moment the smile left his face. Jerusalem had the feeling that he could be a very dangerous man. She had heard he was a fighter and knew that the scar on Clay's chest had come from Bowie.

"I see you still got that knife I gave you, Clay."

"You didn't give it to me, Jim. I took it away from you. I guess old age has addled your memory a bit."

For a moment, a stormy look swept across Jim Bowie's face, and then he grinned and laughed aloud. "That you did. The only man who ever did it. The others didn't fare as well as you did. You still got that reminder on your belly."

"And you still got the one on your neck, I see."

"I got the one on my arm under here too. I thought I'd lose that arm for a while."

"What did you gentlemen disagree about?" Jerusalem asked.

For a moment both men were silent. "I disremember," Bowie said. "What was we fightin' about, Clay?"

"I think it was over a dog, but I ain't right sure."

"Well, in any case, it's all over now." Bowie's eyes took in the wagons and said, "It looks like you are gonna have a good start, Mrs. Hardin."

"We don't know much about the lay of the land, Jim. What about you?" Clay asked.

"Oh, I live in Mexico. I guess you'd call me a Texican. Married a beautiful Spanish woman. I've got two fine children."

"Glad to see you've finally settled down."

"Well, thanks, Clay." Bowie looked at Jerusalem and said, "I expect your women-folks are worn out. How far did you come?"

"All the way from Arkansas Territory."

"Some came a lot farther. Me and Clay came from Tennessee, and others came from Kentucky. But look. Why don't you make camp and let me buy you folks a meal."

"That would be very kind of you, Mr. Bowie," Jerusalem said.

"You can pull your wagons up almost anywhere," Bowie said. "Plenty of fodder to be had. That's a hotel over there. The food's not as good as I'd like, but it's the best there is here in Nachitoches. As soon as you set up camp and get cleaned up, I'll meet you there."

An hour later, they all came back to what Bowie had called a hotel. It was just a large building with a cook shack on the back. They sat down at a couple of tables and watched as Jim Bowie spoke in broken Spanish to the two Mexican girls who worked there. A few minutes later, when one of them brought out a large platter of crawdads, Clinton stared at it with horror and then shook his head stubbornly.

"I ain't eatin' none of them bugs," he said, scrunching up his face.

Jim Bowie laughed and said, "You won't have to eat many of them out on the plains, son. Just along the coast."

"What are things like where we're goin',

Jim?" Clay asked. "We'd be much obliged if you would lay it out for us."

"You know much about the politics of Mexico?" Jim asked as he put an ample portion of crawdads on his plate.

"Not much. I don't reckon any of us do."

Bowie took a sip of the fiery white wine that burned the throat of those who tried it and shook his head. "Well, here it is in a nutshell. Spain tried everything to settle this part of the world. I guess they own everything clear on up to Santa Fe, but they couldn't handle the Comanches. Every family that settled would get killed and burnt out. So Stephen Austin's father, Moses, had the idea of Americans settling there. So he got a big grant of land and aimed to parcel it out to whoever wanted to stake a homestead there. He died before it happened, so his son Stephen is trying to make his father's dream come true. And he's been doin' that now for quite a few years. Funny thing about Austin, though. He had to promise the Mexican government that the settlers would be responsible, law-abiding citizens."

"Well, that lets you out, Clay." Julie smiled. "You may as well hop on your horse and head back to the mountains."

"He can let Jake out too," Clay said, offended by the remark. "I'm as upstanding as he is."

"Well, not everybody that comes in fits up to Austin's high standards." Bowie smiled. "But there's some political winds a-stirrin' that I don't like. When Austin came here and got the land, Mexico was under Spain's rule. But they got their independence a few years ago, and since then it's just been one big fight after another. It seems like things change every other day, and they change the rules on us. Just last year some big muck-a-muck came down from Mexico City and took a look around Texas and decided there were too many northerly Americanos, so they said no more could come in."

"But my husband's already bought the land!" Jerusalem exclaimed. "Will they let us go in?"

"Oh, they don't pay too much attention. Somehow Austin's figured a way to take in just about anybody who wants to. You won't have any trouble gettin' in. The trouble is gonna come in two ways. One of them is the Comanches. You bump up against them much, Clay?"

"No, not so much. Our trouble was more

with the Cheyenne up in the mountains and the Sioux."

"Well, the Comanches are the worse. They're the littlest of all the Plains tribes and the meanest. Don't ever let 'em catch you alive."

At that point, Professor Nightingale spoke up. "I'm most interested, sir, in studying the habits of the Comanche. I've come a long way to learn all I can about them."

"Well, sir, you may have wasted your time, then. Ain't nothing particulary interesting to learn about 'em. Their *habits* are to catch people, torture them to death, steal everything they've got, and then burn up what's left."

Not knowing what to say, the professor sputtered, "W-what's the other thing you're worried about besides the Comanches?"

"Well, things are in a flux right now. I'm keepin' my eye on a man called General Antonio López de Santa Anna. He's an important general, but he's got big ambitions, folks. From what I hear and see, he's gonna be trouble one day." The conversation went on for a long time as they ate, for Bowie loved to talk about all he knew concerning what was happening in Mexico. He told them that he would never be going back to the States. He had decided to settle for good here with his Mexican wife and family.

"Well, Jim, we all thank you for the meal," Clay said as he stood up. "That was right kind of you."

"Don't mention it, Clay. Just make sure you keep your eyes out for trouble."

As they were leaving the restaurant, Clay turned back and asked, "How do we get to this Austin colony?"

"It's real simple. You take the El Camino Real and head south. Anybody can tell you where that is when you're on the road. It's about two hundred miles, I'd guess, from here." He snapped his finger and said, "Clay, I just thought of something. You and Gordon Lebonne, wasn't you partners for a while in the mountains?"

"We sure were. Best partner I ever had except for Jake, of course," he added quickly. "You know Gordon?"

"Well, he's been here in Mexico for a while, but he's had a pretty bad streak of luck."

"What's wrong with him, Jim?"

"He went into business with a slick oper-ator and lost everything he had about two years ago. Since then he's been tryin' to scrape through by herdin' up these wild longhorns and takin' 'em to market. But he got hurt pretty bad last month, I heard."

"What happened?"

"One of them longhorns charged him and knocked him off the horse, then rammed one of his long horns into Gordon's middle. It tore him up pretty bad." Bowie shook his head. "I heard he's not gonna make it. He's got a family too."

Jerusalem was watching Clay's face as Bowie spoke. She saw something change in his features and knew he was concerned for his friend.

"Where is he?" Clay asked.

"He's stayin' in a little village about seventy miles over the border. Wouldn't be hard to find. I don't know him that well, but he spoke of you, and I just remembered it."

"We grew up together, Gordie and I did," Clay said. "We ran off together and went to the mountains. Gordie saved my bacon a couple of times when the Cheyenne got pesky. Reckon I'll drop by and see if I can lend him a hand."

"You'd better hurry, from what I heard,"

Bowie said. "He might be gone already. When you plannin' on leavin'?"

"As quick as possible."

Bowie rose up and said, "I'll be leavin' early in the mornin'. What about you folks?"

"I think we'll be on our way too. I'm anxious to see about Gordie."

Jerusalem had kept her eye on Clay when they returned to the camp. She saw him go check the stock, and then he went and stood and stared up at the stars. She walked over to where he stood and said, "What are you thinking about, Clay?"

"Oh, nothing much. Mostly about Gordie. Looks like the plans he had for himself ain't gonna work out."

"Come on and sit down. I want to talk to you."

Clay gave her an odd look, wondering what she had on her mind, and shrugged. They went over and sat down on two boxes they used for seats around the fire. It was very late, and everyone else had gone to bed.

Jerusalem turned and said, "Clay, you

know something about Jake you're not tellin' me." She waited for him to reply. Instead, he changed the subject.

"You know, we're headin' to a dangerous place. Comanches can come out of nowhere, and they always hit those who can't fight back. Besides, from what Jim says, these Mexicans are going to clamp down on settlers here sooner or later."

"I have to go, Clay, but you don't. You can go back to the mountains or wherever you like."

Clay turned to face Jerusalem. The moonlight made her eyes bright, and he said, "You know what? You don't like to admit that you need people. But you need me if you ever hope to make it."

"Yes, I do," Jerusalem said without argument.

"Well, I promised Jake I'd help, so after I get you and your family settled, then I'll move on."

The silence ran on for a brief moment, then Jerusalem asked, "Why are you so nervous around me, Clay?"

"Why, I ain't!"

"Yes, you are." She laughed deep in her throat, a soft sound, and reached over and put her hand on his forearm and squeezed it. Then she got up and turned away, but something came to her. She wheeled and stood facing him. "You know less about women than any man I ever saw, Clay Taliferro." She hesitated, then said, "That song you been singing—about the rose from New Orleans. Tell me about it."

"There's nothing to tell. It's just a song."

"Was there a woman there who left you, like in the song?"

Clay straightened up and puffed his cheeks out as if he'd been insulted. "You don't reckon I'd lie about a thing like that, I hope!"

"Well, I thought it might be just a song you picked up."

"Picked up? I'll have you know I wrote that song my own self—right after I got my heart busted." He nodded and said sadly, "But you're only a woman, Jerusalem. You couldn't be expected to understand how a man's broken heart can hurt."

"What was her name?"

"What?"

"What was her name . . . the girl who broke your heart in New Orleans?"

"Why . . . it was . . . Juanita."

"You have to think hard to remember it?"

"Why, it just hurts me to say it, Jerusalem. Now, don't give me pain by bringing her up."

"Well, I guess I'll turn in for the night," Jerusalem said, then turned and headed back toward camp. Just before she reached the wagon, she heard him singing it again:

Deep in the heart!
O deep in the heart!
Naught can be lost
That's deep in the heart!

All flowers may fade
Their fragrance depart—
But my New Orleans maid
Will ever be deep in my heart.

CHAPTER
ELEVEN

Julie had been bored with the trip, for every day was the same monotonous routine: travel all day, set up camp, help prepare a meal, then pack up and leave in the morning. But the professor had livened it up for her with his never-ending tales of adventure. Professor Nightingale, whom she called Fergus almost from the beginning, was a fascinating talker. He spoke so rapidly that at first she had trouble keeping up with him, but it was worth the trouble. For two days she had sat beside him in his wagon listening to him rattle on, which helped keep her from getting bored. She was delighted to discover that the seat, both bottom and back, was well padded and covered with a rich tan leather. It was much more comfortable than riding in the other wagons that tossed her about all the time. Fergus also kept a bottle of French wine in a case at his feet, which he gladly shared with her. He sampled it liberally but never seemed to show any sign of it, and Julie found that the sparkling wine made the long hot days more bearable.

The professor's wagon was last in the line, and Julie glanced at him, admiring his fine clothes. He told her how Langley meticulously shaved him every morning. He even had a huge brass tub, which he bathed in every night. Julie glanced back at it and said, "I'd like to take a bath in that tub of yours tonight, if you don't mind, Fergus."

"Why, of course, my dear lady. Be my guest. After riding in this heat all day and being covered head to toe with this infernal layer of dust, a warm bath is an absolute necessity."

"Why, thank you, Fergus. You're a true gentleman." Julie laughed and took notice of his apparel. He was wearing a pair of white trousers, a pale blue shirt, and a string necktie. On his head he wore a top hat, which he insisted was the mark of a true gentleman.

He turned and gave her a smile and a wink. "I don't know much about you, Miss Satterfield."

"You can call me Julie, but there's not much to know." Not wanting to talk about herself, she said, "Are you married, Fergus?"

"No, bless you! No time for that. Not with my traveling so much."

"Any romantic ties to anyone back in England?"

He shook his head and said, "No, not at present. But tell me about you."

"Well, I'm what you might consider a *wild* woman."

"Really! Plan on being one permanently?" Fergus acted as if she had said she had blue eyes or brown hair.

"I never think about it. Tell me about Africa."

"Oh, that's ancient history. What I'm interested in now is the Comanches."

"Well, tell me about them," she said as she sipped some more wine.

Fergus began speaking in a didactic fashion as if he were addressing a class. "Well, the first people to Texas weren't Indians. Almost certainlya land bridge arose out of the northern sea connecting Asia and Alaska, and the first men to see America migrated down this land bridge. But that race probably died out, and a new group came in, probably Mongoloid. Scholars call them the Amerinds, or the American Indians as they were later called. They called themselves merely the People or sometimes the Real Humans. They spread all over North America and down to Mexico. Some of 'em scattered here in Texas. Somewhere along the line, some of them learned to cultivate maize, or Indian corn, but two things happened, my dear, that changed this country."

"What were they? What two things?" Julie asked, amazed at all the professor knew.

"The Apaches appeared on the scene. They were a fierce tribe who feared nothing that walked or breathed, but they were on foot. Their range was limited, but that all changed with the Conquistadores."

"What's that?" Julie asked.

"Spanish conquerors, my dear Julie. Spain sent them to conquer this new world,

and in the south, Central America particularly, they did just that. But they did more
than that. They brought horses with them all
the way from Europe, and some of those
horses fell into the hands of the Apaches
and other tribes. The Apaches mastered the
horses better thanthe Conquistadores and
became a fierce tribe."

"Are they the worst kind of Indians,
Fergus?"

"They were, but at some point not too
long ago a group of mounted Indians came
down into this country. They call themselves
the Human Beings, but other Indians called
them *Komantcia,* or Comanches. They became the greatest horse thieves of all. They
are known for spending most of their lives
on horseback."

"Have you ever seen one?"

"Not yet, but I trust I shall soon. They're
not too attractive, from what I hear. They are
the shortest and smallest of all the Texas
tribes, but they drove the Apaches from the
plains. The Western Apaches moved into
the north. Some of them moved east and
became farmers. But in all this land you see,
the Comanches defeated the Spaniards on
every hand. Their fierce reputation as war-

riors is enough to keep the Spaniards and Apaches out."

Julie shivered suddenly. "I heard enough about them to be scared to death."

"They are a bit frightening, but as John Calvin said in one form or another, whatever happens is going to happen. Or as the French put it, que sera sera."

Julie reached down and plucked another wine bottle out of its case. She popped the cork, tilted it up, and then popped it back in and said,"I hate to be overeducated, Fergus. You can give me another lesson tomorrow."

Jumping to the ground, Julie waited until Clay, who was riding his big bay behind the last wagon, came up beside her. He stopped, and she held her arms up. "Give me a ride, Clay. I'm tired of that wagon seat." She waited until Clay kicked his foot out of the stirrup, then swung up behind him. She wrapped her arms around him and pressed herself against his back. She felt him tense and said, "Don't worry. I'm not going to bite you. Besides, you enjoy havin' a woman hug you, don't you?"

Clay had never known exactly how to answer Julie. He felt much more at ease with

Jerusalem, but Julie was so outspoken that she often embarrassed him. She was pressing against him so tightly that he said, "You don't have to hold on so tight. You ain't likely to fall off."

"But I want to." Julie had discovered it was easy to tease Clay. She liked him a great deal and had spent considerable time trying to analyze him. Now she said the thing she knew would disturb him most. "I bet if it was my sister back here hugging you, you wouldn't fuss."

Clay stiffened even more and said, "You ought to be ashamed talkin' like that!"

"You think I don't know you're sweet on Jerusalem? I've seen you watchin' her when you thought nobody was lookin'."

"I never done such a thing!" Clay insisted

"You are a poor liar, Clay Taliffero."

"You got a wicked mind, Julie Satterfield! If you're not gonna be nice, you can get off and walk."

Julie relaxed her hold and sat behind him, swaying with the movement of the horse. Finally, she said, "I know what's the matter with you, Clay. You're worried about what will happen when we find Jake." When he made no answer, she added, "He won't live with Jerusalem. He never has . . . really. I told her before she married him she was making a big mistake."

"Do you have to talk *all* the time?"

"It's funny how well I know you. It's almost like we were married."

"Well, that ain't likely to ever happen."

"No, it's not. But I'm gonna tell you something. You're a tough hairpin, Clay. Brodie told me how you ticked off those six Indians with six shots, and he suspected you slit the throats of those that didn't die right off." She waited for him to deny it, but he said nothing. "But you've got a soft spot that's gonna get you hurt one of these days. Maybe killed." She reached up, ran her hand along the back of his head, moving upward, and then shoved his hat down over his eyes. She laughed, slipped off the horse, and ran to catch up with the professor's wagon. She moved quickly, leaping up into the seat with an easy movement and said, "Tell me some more useless stuff, Fergus. . . ."

By September the tenth, Clay figured they were at least halfway toward the Austin settlement, where they hoped to find Jake. But late that afternoon, he nodded toward a small settlement of eight or ten houses and said to Brodie, who was riding alongside him, "If I remember right, that's likely where Bowie said I could find Gordon Lebonne. You find a likely campin' spot. I'm goin' in and see what I can dig up."

As he rode into the settlement, Clay saw that the inhabitants, all of them Mexicans, were watching him suspiciously. He walked his horse slowly until he came to three men, who kept their dark eyes fixed on him. "I'm lookin' for a man named Lebonne."

The three men seemed to relax, and one of them said something in Spanish. Clay did not understand it, but the man turned and pointed to a house, and the word "Lebonne" came out again.

"Gracias," Clay said, which was one of the few Spanish words he knew. When he approached the house, he saw a young boy and a girl approximately the same age watching him. He pulled his horse up and said, "I'm looking for Gordon Lebonne."

Neither of the youngsters answered him but stood staring at him sullenly. They were both handsome young people, somewhere

around fourteen or fifteen. The girl had already begun to blossom into young womanhood. She had jet black hair but disturbing eyes—large, almond-shaped, and almost a violet hue. He had never seen such eyes in a Mexican before. The boy was taller and somewhat older, perhaps fifteen. He also had black hair but blue eyes. Clay waited for them to speak, and finally the boy nodded.

"Who are you, señor?"

"My name is Clay Taliferro. I'm a friend of Gordon Lebonne."

As he spoke, a woman came out of the house, and Clay stepped off of his horse and removed his hat. She was pure Spanish. She wore a simple dress, and her eyes stared at him with the same suspicion he had noticed in the youngsters.

"I am Lucita Lebonne, señor."

"I am pleased to know you, ma'am." He waited for some sort of invitation, but none came. "My party's on the way through. I thought I'd stop in and see how Gordon was doing. I hear he had an accident."

"He had an accident," she said evenly.

Clay stared at the woman. "Not serious, I hope?"

"Serious enough. He's dying."

The harshness of the woman's words struck Clay. He swallowed hard and then looked down at the ground, unable to meet her eyes. "I'm sorry to hear that, ma'am."

"He's asleep now, but he wakes up from time to time, if you want to see him."

"If it wouldn't be too much trouble."

Clay followed the woman inside the house, which was bare except for a table, three rickety chairs, and a door that led off to what was apparently a small bedroom. He followed the woman inside, and a beam of light from the small window illuminated the figure on the bed. Clay had never been particularly good around sick people, and the sight of his old friend lying there struck him hard. He stood still for a moment, noting that the strong form that he remembered was wasted away. Gordon's face had always been full, but now it was shrunk, and his eyes, which were closed, were sunken in deep cavities.

"When did he get hurt, señora?"

"Two months ago now. We had no doctor, but we did the best we could. You may sit if you wish."

Clay moved awkwardly over and sat

down on the stool beside the bed. The fetid odor stifled him, and he wanted to leave, but he knew he couldn't. He studied Gordon Lebonne's face and saw the pallor of death on it. He had been around death long enough to recognize it. "I'm plumb sorry about this. Gordon was a good friend to me."

The woman did not answer right away, then said, "I will bring you something to drink, señor."

After she left the room, Clay passed his hand over his clammy forehead. *I hope this never happens to me. Would've been better to get taken out at once by an arrow or a bullet than be helpless like this.*

Gordon's wife came back soon with a cup filled with water. Clay took it and said, "Thank you, señora."

The woman nodded, and the sunlight fell across her face. It was a strong face, beautifully structured with fine bones. There was none of the Indian in her. She was a *criolla,* pure Spanish. She stood there silent for a time, and finally she said, "You knew my husband a long time ago?"

"We grew up together, ma'am, in Tennessee."

"What did you say your name was?"

"Clay Taliferro."

"My husband has spoken of you often. You were partners in the mountains."

"That's right. We both ran away from home a long time ago." His eyes went back to the dying man's face, and with difficulty, he said, "Gordie, here, saved my life probably twice."

"He spoke of how you saved his too."

"I guess we were takin' turns. I never met a better man than Gordon Lebonne."

The two said nothing else, and after ten minutes of intense silence, Lebonne stirred slightly. A groan passed his lips, and the woman came over and spoke to him in Spanish. "You have a visitor, marido."

Gordon opened his eyes and blinked. He could not seem to focus, and Clay leaned forward. "It's Clay, Gordon. Clay Taliferro."

Lebonne licked his lips, and it took a moment to sink in, then he said in a weak, hoarse voice, "Clay, is it really you?"

"It's me, partner." Clay reached out and took his hand. He was shocked with the frailty of it. It was like holding a sack full of bones. "Sorry to find you in such poor shape," he mumbled.

Gordon stared at Clay. He obviously had a high fever, but recognition filled his eyes. "What are you doing here? Never thought I'd lay eyes on you again."

"On my way west, Gordie. Takin' Jake's family to the Austin colony."

"I'm glad to see you before I cash in, Clay. We had us some good times."

"That we did, partner," Clay said, squeezing his friend's hand.

Clay looked up and met the woman's eyes. She had an inscrutable expression and did not speak.

Clay continued to hold the sick man's hand, and then his eyes fluttered and closed.

"He will not wake up for a time, señor."

Clay got up, releasing Lebonne's hand. He walked out of the room, and the woman followed him. The boy and the girl were in the nextroom, and the woman said, "This is Mateo, and this is Serena."

"I'm glad to know you," Clay said. He got little response, and he could feel the antagonism of the two.

"You must forgive them," Señora Lebonne said. "It is not you personally, señor. But they have found it hard being half-Mexican and half-American."

"How is that, señora?"

"The Mexicans hate them because of their white blood, and the white people hate them because of the Spanish blood." The words were without emotion, but a fire burned in the woman's fine eyes. "I will fix you something to eat."

Clay started to protest, but she turned and went to a small table. He sat down in one of the chairs and looked at the two youngsters. "You don't have to be afraid of me," he said. "I think your pa's one of the finest men I ever knew." When they did not respond, Clay turned around and put his elbows on the table and thought about his dying friend. He did not speak until the woman put some tortillas in front of him and a cup of wine. She had not fixed anything for anyone else, and suddenly Clay realized that it probably was because there was no food. He knew it would offend her to refuse it, so he ate it and said, "That's mighty fine grub, ma'am." The youngsters went outside and Clay said, "Do you have relatives here, señora?"

"No. We have no one."

"Gordon has people back in Tennessee. At least he did have. Maybe you could go there."

"They would not want half-breeds."

Clay noted the bitterness on the woman's face. He stood up and said, "I'll be camped close by. I'd like to come back and check on Gordon from time to time."

Lucita Lebonne said quietly, "He may die at any time, Señor Clay."

"What will you do then?"

"I do not know. The good God, He knows."

Clay started to offer help but knew it was not the time. "Maybe I'll just wait, if I won't be in the way."

"No, you would not be in the way."

Clay stayed the rest of the afternoon, and just at sundown Gordon woke up again. He was more lucid this time, and Clay discovered that they had no resources at all.

"I lost everything in a bad business deal. This house we live in . . . it's not ours." Gordon's eyes turned bitter, and he twisted in the bed, his wasted frame writhing in pain. "I've made a real mess out of things, Clay."

Clay Taliferro leaned forward and said, "Look, Gordie, if you're worried about your family, I'll help them." Lebonne lay still and did not look at Clay, but when he did, Clay saw tears in his eyes.

"That's worried me more than anything. I put 'em through a rough time. Lord, but I hate to leave them helpless!"

"They won't be helpless. I promise you."

"It's askin' too much for a man to take on," Gordon said, his voice weak.

"Me and you are friends, ain't we? I ain't forgot the time you stopped that Blackfoot from puttin' a tomahawk right in my head. I wouldn't be here talkin' if you hadn't jumped on him and stopped his clock."

"You did the same for me."

"Maybe so, Gordon." Clay leaned over and took Lebonne's thin hand. "There's no preacher, but I hope you're right with the Lord. It sounds funny, me sayin' that."

"I am all right, Clay. I made my peace with God five years ago. Not your way, I guess. I joined the Catholic Church. That's the way it is down here."

"Now, you set your mind at ease about your wife and kids. I promise to help them."

Lebonne lay quietly for a long time, and then he whispered, "That's like you, Clay. It purely is!"

Clay had tried to convince Jerusalem and her family to go on, saying he would catch up with them, but Jerusalem had said, "No, we'll wait right here. And I'm going back with you. If they're short of food, we've got plenty."

"My yes, plenty!" Fergus spoke up. "Take what you need from my supply wagon."

Jerusalem rode back with Clay to Gordon's home, and when the two women met, Clay saw a stiffness in Lucita Lebonne. He could tell she had pride, but somehow Jerusalem had been able to bring the food in as if the woman were doing them a favor to accept it. Jerusalem stayed there, remaining quiet, even though the two youngsters stared at her with animosity. Somehow, her quiet and tender help softened them.

Lebonne woke up twice more that day, and the last time he had been with his wife and children. Clay and Jerusalem waited in the outer room. When Lucita came back out, Jerusalem went to her at once. "I'm sorry, my dear," she whispered.

"He is at peace, now. He is with God," Lucita said. She saw true compassion in Jerusalem's eyes and bowed her head. "Thank you, señora," she whispered.

Clay walked outside and away from the house for a few minutes, mourning the loss of his friend. As he looked back at the house, he said, "Gordon, I aim to keep that promise I made you. I'm gonna help your family."

He and Brodie dug the grave, but there was no priest. There was no church either, so the funeral was at the graveside. A few of the villagers, mostly women, gathered, and one of them spoke some brief words in Spanish.

After the service Lucita and her children turned away, and Jerusalem went back to the camp. When Clay returned a while later, she pulled him aside and said, "What are you going to do, Clay?"

"I'll have to stay around here, Jerusalem. I promised Gordon I'd do what I could for his wife."

"No, that won't do."

"I have to do it! I promised," he said determinedly.

"I talked to Lucita quite a bit, and she's miserable and unhappy here. There's no place for them. I've decided that we're going to take them with us."

Clay was continually being shocked by Jerusalem, and now he suddenly stood up straight and stared at her. "Take 'em where?"

"Wherever we're going. There's plenty of land there."

"She'd never do it," Clay said, shaking his head.

"I'll take care of that."

"Mamá, that woman's coming." Serena had been sitting outside on the bench. Mateo stood against the wall, his face fixed in a scowl. Both of them were crushed by their father's death. Now Serena stood up as her mother came outside.

"I'm sorry to come at such a time, but I must talk with you, Lucita," Jerusalem said.

"Come inside."

"No, I want your children to hear what I have to say."

Both Mateo and Serena stared at Jerusalem, but she looked directly at Lucita and said, "I want you and your family to come with us."

Lucita was taken aback. She could not speak for a moment. Grief had marked her face, and lines of worry showed the pressure she had been under for the last few months. "Go with you, señora? I . . . I don't understand."

"Yes. We've talked enough, and it is clear from what you say that there is nothing here for you. I must tell you, I don't know what we will find.I haven't seen my husband in a long time, but I know he has land, and I have money to buy more. We will make a house for us, and we will make another house for you."

Mateo suddenly spoke up. "Why would you do this for us? We are strangers."

Jerusalem turned to face the boy. He was a handsome lad with clear features, but bitterness filled his eyes. "Because Señor Clay promised your father that he would help you. He is practically a member of our family, and families must stick together." She

went over then and put her hand on Serena's face. The girl was lovely, but her eyes
were filled with grief. "I can't promise you
anything except we will be family." She
turned then to Lucita and said, "Please
come with us."

"We would be a burden."

"You would be more of a burden if you do
not come."

"How could that be?"

"Because if you do not come, Señor Clay
will stay here and do what he can. He's a
strong man, and he intends to keep his
promise."

Lucita stared at the woman in disbelief.
Her lips trembled for a moment, and then
she pressed them together. She looked
down at the ground and whispered, "Do you
want us to come?"

"Yes, very much," Jerusalem said, taking
her hands in hers.

Lucita looked up at Jerusalem for a moment, and then she went to her children.
She did not touch them, but a silent understanding passed between them. "We will go
with this family. They are more generous
than any I have seen among the Ameri-

cans." She turned then and said, "We will go, and we will try not to be a burden."

"Let me know when you are ready."

"We will be ready in the morning. We have little to take."

"We'll bring the wagons by then, and we will leave as early as possible."

Early the next morning when the wagons stopped in front of the house, it took only a few moments for the Lebonnes to load their few possessions. Clay had been standing beside Julie when Lucita came and stood before him. She fixed her eyes on Clay and said, "You are a kind man, señor. We will try not to be a burden on you." She turned and walked away quickly, and Julie moved closer, pressing her shoulder against Clay. He looked down at her, and she was grinning at him wickedly.

"Are you going to comfort the widow Lebonne, Clay?"

Clay's face burned. He hated it when that happened, and Julie had a way of causing it. "You'd try the patience of a saint, Julie Satterfield!"

"Well, you're no saint, Mr. Clay Taliferro, so watch yourself." Her eyes were laughing and she pulled his face around to hers. "Now you'll have three of us women to fight off."

Clay had never been able to get the best of Julie and knew that he never would. He grinned, however, and said, "Well, I heard a preacher say once that Solomon had seven hundred wives and three hundred porky-pines. I've always reckoned the porkypines gave him less trouble than all them women. Reckon if King Solomon could put up with seven hundred pesky women, I can put up with three!"

CHAPTER
TWELVE

A couple of weeks had passed since Gordon Lebonne's funeral. Clay and Jerusalem had done all they could to try to make Lucita and her children feel welcome. Even Professor Nightingale had tried to interest them in some of his stories about his travels, but they still kept to themselves most of the time.

"I don't like Serena, Clay," Moriah snapped one day. "She's so stuck up she won't even speak to me!"

Clay had been mending a bridle by adding a piece of new leather. Now he looked up from his work and said, "What if

you'd lost everything you had, Moriah? And what if you didn't have any place to go? Would you feel like laughin' and carryin' on with someone you hardly knew?"

Moriah was sitting on the ground across from Clay. She was, as usual, covered with dust, for she was not prone to much bathing except under pressure. "But she's so *mean!* I tried to be nice to her, and she won't have anything to do with me. And Mateo's no better. I tried to be friends with him, and so did Clinton and Brodie, but he won't even talk. He just mutters something in Spanish and walks away."

"Give 'em time, punkin. They'll come around. They're still grieving the loss of their father."

Jerusalem had been aware of the estrangement between the newcomers and her family. It did not surprise her, so she had given a lot of thought on how to make a friend of Lucita. She tried to put herself in the woman's place so she could understood her behavior. *If I had to take everything from strangers and didn't have anything to give in return, I'd be crushed myself,* she thought.

She had been thinking of this a lot the last few days, and when they stopped beside the road to camp for the night, she went to Lucita and said, "I need a little help, Lucita. Would you mind taking care of Mary Aidan while I cook the evening meal?"

Lucita seemed surprised, but a small smile turned the corners of her mouth. "Yes, I will keep her."

Jerusalem surrendered Mary Aidan, who looked up at the face of the other woman, then began to coo.

"She likes you already," Jerusalem said, smiling.

"Most babies like me. I lost three of them."

"I lost two myself."

"I am sorry for your loss. Nobody knows what that's like, do they, except another woman?"

"That's right." Jerusalem watched as Lucita cuddled Mary Aidan and said, "I want to ask a favor of you, Lucita."

Lucita looked up at her. "What can I do? I have nothing to offer."

"Well, that's not so, and I want you to teach me how to cook."

"But you are already a fine cook. Everyone says so."

"But I need to learn how to cook Mexican food. I don't know anything about that. Would you teach me?"

"Sí, of course. It is not hard."

"Maybe you can help me cook up something tonight."

"I brought some of my special seasonings and many kinds of peppers that you do not have. We use many kinds to flavor our food."

"Good. We'll work together, then. I will teach you how to cook Anglo, but there's something else I want to ask."

"What is that?" Lucita asked

"We all need to learn some Spanish. We need you and your children to help us. It's such a beautiful language," she said wistfully, "and I feel like an idiot not being able to speak with your people. If we're going to live here among your people, then we have to learn Spanish."

"Yes, it was hard for me to learn English, but I will help you all I can, and my children will also."

"I am glad you decided to come with us. When we finally reach our land, we will need to know what to plant or when. It is so different here than it was in my home. You will be a great help, you and your children."

Jerusalem saw that Lucita was happy to have something to do. She put her hand on the woman's arm and said, "We will make a good life for our children in this new place, and you will be a great help to us, Lucita."

"Gracias, usted es muy simpática," Lucita said.

"Well, I guess my first Spanish lesson might as well start right now. What does that mean?" Jerusalem asked.

"It means, 'You are very kind,'" Lucita said.

"Come along, Mateo." Clay pulled up his horse in front of the young boy, who was plodding along beside the wagon.

"What for, señor?"

"Time for you to starting pulling your share of the load. I saw you had a rifle. Was that your pa's?"

"Yes, señor."

"Go get it and bring it along."

Mateo went to the wagon and pulled out his father's rifle. He had a few balls and a little powder, which he grabbed also. He walked back to Clay, who kicked his foot out of the stirrup, and said, "Climb on behind me here."

Mateo swung up beside Clay, and Clay stirred the bay into a fast trot. "Hang on there, Mateo. I don't want to lose you."

Mateo steadied himself by holding on to Clay's side with one hand. With the other he clung to his rifle.

When they were about a mile from the camp, Clay stopped the horse and said, "Get down now." Mateo came to the ground in one leap, and Clay dismounted. He tied the horse to a sapling, pulled the Hawkin free, and said, "Can you shoot?"

"Of course I can shoot," Mateo said stiffly. "My father taught me."

"Well, you had a good teacher, then. Almost as good as me."

"I think my pa was better."

Clay grinned and shook his head. "I admire a man who stands up for himself. You stay here while I go put out a target or two."

Clay pulled some empty cans out of the

sack he had brought and walked out a ways and set them up on the top of some large rocks. When he came back, he said, "Well, let's see what you can do."

"I have only a little powder."

"I got plenty of that. Take your shot." He watched carefully as Mateo loaded the rifle and nodded. "I see you know how to load up fast. That will come in handy someday."

"Which can shall I hit, Señor Clay?"

"The one on the right. You'd better take a rest."

"I do not need to, señor." Mateo pulled the rifle up, and with an imperceptible pause, he pulled the trigger. The shot rang out, and the can went flying away.

"That was a good shot! Your pa would be proud of you."

Mateo beamed with pride. "He wanted me to be able to shoot well."

"Well, let's move back a bit and see what you've got."

The two shot all of Mateo's powder up, but Clay had plenty. Mateo was shocked at the shots Clay made with his gun. Whatever he aimed at, he hit. "I could never shoot like that, señor. I've never seen anyone who could shoot like that."

"You've got the knack for it too, Mateo. You just need some practice. Here." Clay handed him a full bag of powder and another bag of shot. "Now, I want you to practice every day." He stood in front of the young man and said, "We're gonna run into trouble one of these days. I've got to have a man who'll fight for his family."

"I will fight, señor. You will see."

Clay nodded. "I'm right pleased. You know, you remind me of your pa. Him and me went through some tough times together, and he never let me down."

Mateo flushed at the praise of his father. "I will never let you down, Señor Clay!"

"Well, that's fine. Now, you can do me one big favor."

"Anything, Señor Clay."

"I'm a little bit worried about Brodie." He saw the surprise wash across Mateo's face. "You see, he ain't like you and me. Both of us are tough, but Brodie's a little bit shy. He needs a tough young fellow like you for a friend."

Mateo pulled himself up to his full height. "Sí, señor! I will help him all I can."

★   ★   ★

Lucita watched the friendship blossom between Brodie and Mateo and was pleased.
She had learned from Mateo how Clay had
taken such an interest in him and was glad,
for her son needed a man to look up to.

She was disappointed, however, in her
daughter, who had always been prouder
than Mateo. She watched the attempts of
the Hardin youngsters to make friends with
Serena and was saddened when she saw
Serena continue to reject them day after
day with a stolid silence. From the day her
father died, she had retreated into a silent
world of grief and anger.

Lucita thought about it considerably,
wondering how to help her daughter. One
afternoon when they had paused to make
camp, she watched Brodie as he disappeared into the nearby woods with an ax.
Soon she heard the ax ringing out, and an
idea came to her.

"Serena, Brodie's chopping firewood. Go
help him bring it back."

"I don't want to."

"What do you mean you don't want to?
You've got to work."

"I'll work, but I don't want to be around
any of them."

"Why not? What's wrong with you?"

"They treat us like beggars."

"Don't be foolish! They have been kind to us. Now, you do as I tell you."

Serena glared at her mother but saw something in her eyes that she had learned to recognize. Whenever her mother looked at her like that, Serena knew she had better obey—and soon. She tightened her lips, whirled, and walked off stiffly toward the woods. She followed the sound of the ax, and when she came to where Brodie was, she did not speak but began to gather up the pieces of dead wood that he had already chopped off from a tree.

Brodie stopped working and turned to face her. "Going to help carry the wood?" he said. She did not answer, and he saw she was struggling to put more in her arms.

"Let me help you with that," he said.

Serena turned and started away with the load she had, but she stepped into a hole and was wrenched around. Brodie reached out, saying, "Look out!" and caught her as she fell.

The wood fell to the ground, and Serena pulled away from his grip.

She slapped Brodie in the face with a

ringing blow and cried out, "Keep your filthy hands off me!"

"Well, I was just—"

"I know what you were trying to do," Serena said, staring at him. "Stay away from me!" She bent over and picked up the wood and started back to camp.

When she got back she went to her mother and said, "That Brodie, he tried to touch me."

"What happened?" Lucita listened until she was finished, then said, "You stepped in a hole, and he tried to help you. That's what happened."

"I hate him! I hate them all!" Serena spit out.

Lucita stared at her daughter, and her hand moved quickly. She slapped Serena across the face, and her voice was low and filled with frustration. "You're a worse fool than I thought! You know what that makes me? The mother of the fool. Now, get out of my sight!"

Serena could not believe what had happened. Her mother had never put a hand on her since she had been a little girl. She put her hand up to her face and stared at her mother. Then she whirled and ran away.

For the rest of the day, Serena avoided her mother and everyone else. She saw her mother teaching Jerusalem how to make tortillas, and the two women were laughing. She also noticed that Mateo and Brodie were playing some sort of card game with the professor and Clay, and they were having a wonderful time. When her mother called her to come and join the others to eat, she turned and climbed into the wagon to settle down for the night. When her mother came to lie down beside her later, she finally whispered, "I'm sorry, Mamá."

Lucita rolled over and embraced her. "It's all right. And I'm sorry for slapping you. You've just got to be more understanding of people—especially these people. They want to be kind to us. And we must be grateful for all they have done. It is what your papá would want. Now you think about that and pray about it."

"Sí, mamá. Te quiero mucho," Serena said.

"I love you too," Lucita said then pulled a blanket over her.

Serena had trouble going to sleep, but before she did, she made a decision in her heart and looked forward to the morning.

★ ★ ★

"You're not very good at that."

Brodie looked up, surprised to find that Serena had approached and was looking down at him critically as he was milking the goat. After what had happened yesterday, he was sure she would ignore him for the rest of the trip. They were approximately the same age, but where he was still lean and gawky and awkward, she had begun to blossom into an attractive young woman. She confused him, and he said, "I never claimed to be a great milker."

"Let me do it."

Brodie was shocked when she came over and touched his shoulder. He got up, and she sat down on the stool and began to milk the goat with ease, squirting continuous streams of warm milk into the pail. At one point, she turned and smiled at him. He stood off to one side and watched her with admiration. "You sure do it good."

"I've had lots of practice."

When the pail was full, she got up with it in her hand and turned to him. He looked into her eyes and wondered at the color and the shape of them.

"My mother says I'm a fool."

"Why in the world would she say that?"

"I told her what happened, and how I slapped you. Well, she called me a fool and slapped my face."

"Why, she shouldn't have done that."

"She hasn't struck me since I was a little girl. But she says I was wrong. I'm sorry," she said abruptly.

"Why, it didn't hurt."

Serena handed him the pail, and he took it. She looked at him intently and said, "I've had boys trying to touch me for a long time now, and men too. I thought you were like them, but my mother says I was wrong."

"Touch you! Why, I never touched a girl in my whole life!" Brodie exclaimed.

Suddenly Serena laughed. Her eyes sparkled and she said, "Don't you like girls?"

"Well . . . I don't understand them. They make fun of me."

"Why would they do that?"

"Oh, I'm tall and skinny and gawky, and I don't know how to talk to them."

"You're talking to me."

Brodie smiled. "Well, I guess I am!"

"I'm sorry I hit you, Brodie."

"Why, that's all right," Brodie said as he nervously shifted from one foot to the other.

"What are you going to do now?"

"Nothing, I don't guess."

"Tell me about the place we're going to."

"Well, shoot, Serena, you know as much as I do."

"I don't understand about your father. Where is he?" Serena stood there listening while Brodie lamely tried to explain his father's absence all these years.

"So, we ain't seen much of him, you see . . ."

"No, I don't see. Why does he go off and leave your mother? She's so beautiful. And all of you kids. I don't understand it."

"Well, I don't rightly know." Then for the first time Brodie expressed the worry he'd had ever since his mother had announced they were leaving to find his father. "What'll we do if Pa won't promise to stay home? I'm afraid Ma will leave him."

"She should leave him if he won't stay with her."

"Oh no, a woman's not supposed to leave her husband!"

Serena smiled, and there was a wisdom

in her beyond her years. "Men should be faithful."

"I guess so."

Suddenly, Serena said something in Spanish, and Brodie said, "What does that mean?"

"I won't tell you now. Maybe if you're good, I'll tell you tomorrow."

Twenty feet away Serena's mother was watching them. She heard her daughter laugh and saw Brodie smile and felt a relief. "Maybe it will be all right," she whispered. "Maybe it will."

On September the fourteenth, Clay waved over toward a settlement with some scattered houses and said, "That should be part of the Austin colony." Jerusalem and Julie were sitting in the seat of the wagon with him, when Clay pulled the mules up and said to a young Mexican boy, "You know where Señor Hardin lives?"

The boy evidently could not speak much English, but he nodded and pointed to a dilapidated house a ways off the road. "Sí, Señor Hardin."

"He lives there?"

"Sí, Señor Hardin there," the boy said, nodding.

Jerusalem felt herself grow tense as she looked at the run-down house. "Oh no, Jake," she sighed.

Julie felt her sister's tension and saw the look of disappointment on her face. She turned to face her and said, "Are you sure you want to find Jake?"

"I've got to find him, Julie. I can't go on living like we have been."

Julie hesitated, then put her arm around Jerusalem. "I'm afraid you're going to be disappointed, but you've got to do it." She looked over and said, "Well, what are you waiting for, Clay?"

"Nothin'," Clay said. He had also felt Jerusalem's uncertainty, the first he had ever seen in her. He looked at the house and shook his head. "Well, here we come, Jake. It doesn't look like you've done too good." He slapped the mules and said, "Git up!" And they moved obediently forward.

PART THREE:

ROOTS
September 1831

CHAPTER
THIRTEEN

As Brodie pulled the team of mules to a halt, he felt his stomach tightening with fear. Ever since his mother had announced that they were leaving to find his pa, he had been thinking about what they would find when they finally got there. Now, bracing his foot against the floor, he stared out at the small ramshackle house. It was built primarily of logs, but an additional room had been added on with old warped boards. A small garden was off to the right of the house, and an Indian woman and two young people were pulling beans. As the rest of the caravan of wagons drew up, the three of them looked up and stared at the newcomers. A sense of doom seemed to settle on Brodie like an ominous cloud. He glanced quickly toward the lead wagon, where his mother sat with Julie, and saw her watching the woman carefully.

"I'm looking for Jake Hardin," Jerusalem said.

His mother's voice was not overly loud as she spoke, but Brodie knew her well enough to see that she was tense.

The woman came out of the bean patch before answering. She was pure Indian with dark brown eyes and black hair tied into twin braids down her back. She wore a deerskin dress with moccasins. "This is his home. Why are you seeking him?"

Jerusalem handed Mary Aidan to Julie and jumped down to the ground. She approached the woman until she was directly opposite her and said, "I'm his wife—one of them at least."

Her eyes went to the young girl and the boy who had come and stood a few feet behind their mother. They were obviously not full-blooded Indians, and Jerusalem said evenly, "I guess we've got something in common. I can see Jake in your children."

At that moment Jake came out of the house. He was wearing a pair of dirty brown trousers, and the top of his long underwear had holes and was dirty as well. He was barefoot, and his eyes were bleary. The sight of the four wagons drawn up in his front yard took away Jake's power of speech. He was a big man, six feet tall and over two hundred pounds, and his brown hair was uncut and hung down in his eyes. For a moment he stared at Jerusalem and blinked wildly. Finally, he started to speak and then coughed.

"What the devil are—"

"Good morning, Jake," Jerusalem said evenly. "You seem to be in good health."

Jake licked his lips and shook his head as if to clear it. "Jerusalem, what . . . what are you doing here?" He looked wildly at the wagons, and when he saw his other children, he started to get angry. "What are you doing dragging these children all the way across the country?"

Jerusalem did not move for a moment, and the awkward silence between them grew. Then she turned around and staunchly walked to the wagon and lifted up her arms. Taking Mary Aidan from Julie, she walked back and said, "I thought it was about time you met your daughter, Jake. This is Mary Aidan. You weren't there to name her, so I picked the name I liked." Jake stared at the baby, and his lips moved, but he could not form a single sentence. "Aren't you going to introduce us to your family—your other family that is?"

Jake swallowed and then mumbled, "Ah . . . this is Awinita, and this here is Rose . . . and this is Paco."

Jerusalem looked at the two youngsters and asked, "How old are you, Rose?"

"I'm thirteen," Rose said as she stood close to her mother.

Brodie saw his mother's face tighten, and he frowned as he did some arithmetic in his own mind.

"You've been living a lie a long time, Jake," Jerusalem said.

Jake suddenly shook his shoulders and straightened up. "We've got to talk private, Jerusalem. Not here!"

"No, we don't," Jerusalem said, her voice sharp and clear. "I want *all our* children to hear everything. No more secrets," she said loudly.

At that moment Clay started to turn his

bay around, obviously intending to leave. Jerusalem called out in a voice that caught him. "You stay put, Clay."

Clay pulled his horse up and stared at Jerusalem but made no other attempt to leave.

At that moment Professor Nightingale said, "I say, madam, this is most embarrassing."

Jerusalem turned to face the professor. "You're pretty easily shocked, Fergus. If Texas is anything like Arkansas Territory, everybody will know about Jake Hardin and his multiple wives soon enough." She turned to face Jake and studied him before saying, "Is this all of us, Jake, or do you have another wife stashed away somewhere?"

"Jerusalem, this ain't decent," he said, embarrassed as he saw everyone staring at him.

"This hasn't been a pleasure trip for me. I sold the house, packed up everything, endured a long trip with plenty of dangers just to come here and try to be a family again. And I've put up with your wandering ways for years, Jake Hardin. I've suspected that something like this was going on." Silence hung over the yard, and everyone seemed frozen in place.

Brodie took his eyes off his ma and pa and looked around at Clinton. For once Clinton was shocked into silence, and Moriah was staring at her father with her eyes wide open. Her mouth was open too. Lucita Lebonne was sitting in the last wagon, and both Serena and Mateo were watching the scene silently.

Well, Brodie thought, *it looks like Ma don't intend to have any privacy about this, but I wish she would.* Right then, he wished with all his heart they had never left Arkansas Territory. He could tell from the rigid set of his mother's back and the expression on her face that she was not backing down. But her next words shocked him so that he nearly dropped the reins.

"All right, Jake, choose your woman right now!"

Jake's eyes flew wide open, and he exclaimed, "A man can't decide a thing like that in a minute!"

"Maybe a man can't," Jerusalem said evenly, "but a woman can. It's simple enough. You get rid of your Indian family and vow never to go roving again, and I'll take you back. That's my last offer, Jake. Make up your mind," she said, glaring at him till he looked away at Awinita and the children.

"Listen, Jerusalem," Jake said desperately. "I had to claim Awinita as my wife to get this land."

"That's business, Jake. I'm talking about her or me as your wife. Which is it gonna be?"

Brodie had not been around his father enough to know him well. Jake had come back only a few times as he grew up, and those visits were always short. He remembered good times spent with him, and somehow Brodie had assumed that one day, sooner or later, his pa would come home and they would be a family again—that there would be no more roving. He had always thought of his father as one of the biggest, strongest men he had ever known, but now as he watched his father's face, he saw a weakness there. He watched as his father half turned and his eyes locked with his Indian wife. After a moment, Jake turned back again, and the look on his face said it all! Brodie knew that all his hopes of being a family were over.

Jerusalem, who knew this man better than anyone else, could sense his decision even though not a word was spoken. She sighed, and her shoulders seemed to sag for a moment, but then she turned to the Indian woman. "Awinita, it looks like you win." Without another word Jerusalem turned, walked back to the wagon, and handed the baby up to Julie. She climbed up into the wagon seat, took the baby, and said, "I'm finished here, Julie. Let's go."

"Wait a minute, blast it!" Jake called out. "We have to talk," Jake said as he walked toward the wagon.

But Julie struck the mules with the lines, and the wagon pulled out. The others followed suit, but Jake ran out and grabbed the bridle of Clay's horse as the wagons left the yard. He stared up and said, "Why'd you bring her here?"

"I didn't, Jake," Clay said. "She brought me."

"A fine friend you turned out to be."

"Jake, I reckon you've forgotten a few things about your wife. It'd be easier to stop a steam engine than it would be to stop Jerusalem."

"You got to talk to her, Clay."

Clay pulled his horse away and halted only long enough to say, "Jake, she's your wife, not mine. I told you a long time ago what I thought about the way you treated your family. Now it's caught up with you, so swallow your medicine."

Brodie's mind was spinning with feelings of anger, hurt, and disappointment as he sat on the wagon seat. He felt numb all over from what had just happened. Fortunately, the mules needed no guiding. They simply followed along in line behind the wagon in front. He could not make sense of all that was racing through his mind. It was as if his thoughts had traveled to another time just like Grandpa Josiah when he had a "spell." The only thing he could picture in his mind was the hope of ever being a family again was like a door that had just closed forever. When Clinton and Moriah came running alongside the wagon, he snapped back from the disturbed state he was in.

Both of them pulled themselves into the wagon, and Clinton demanded, "What's Ma going to do, Brodie? She can't just up and give up like that!"

"Did you lose your hearin' along with your brains?" Moriah said. "She's through with him. That's what she said."

"Why, she can't do that," Clinton said, his voice rising. "The Bible says when people get married, they're always married."

"Oh, shut up, you fool!" Brodie said, anger spilling out of him. "Just keep your mouth shut!"

Clinton and Moriah had rarely seen Brodie so angry, and now Moriah said, "But, Brodie, what are we going to do?"

"Why do you ask me? I don't know nothin'. Now either keep hush up or get off this wagon and walk."

Moriah jumped down, and Clinton remained long enough only to say, "You got to do somethin', Brodie. Talk to Ma."

Brodie did not answer. Nor did he speak again for the next two hours. Later that afternoon, he heard Jerusalem call out, "Clay, we'll camp out over there by that stream." He pulled his wagon in, stopped it, and began to unhitch the team.

"Did your ma mean what she said?"

Brodie turned to find Serena standing a

few feet away. Her eyes were curious as she waited for his answer.

"She *always* means what she says," he said as he worked the harness free on the lead mule.

Serena came a few steps closer. "I'm sorry," she said. "I guess both of us have lost a father, then."

Brodie shot her a quick look. "It's different," he said roughly.

"Will you go back to your home in the United States?"

"I don't know, Serena. Don't ask me fool questions right now." He turned and began unhitching the rest of the mules, jerking at the harness so that one of the mules shied.

Serena watched him and was not offended. She could tell that Brodie was very upset, and when she went back to her mother, she said, "Do you think Señora Hardin will do what she said?"

"Yes, she will. I have not known her long, but you don't have to know Jerusalem Hardin very long to know she's a strong woman." Displeasure filled her eyes, and she said, "Her husband is a fool."

★ ★ ★

Josiah had helped set up camp, and while the women were preparing the evening meal, he went over to where Fergus Nightingale was seated on the ground reading a book. Josiah squatted down on his heels across from the Englishman.

"What are you readin' there, Fergus?"

"Oh, words . . . words . . . words. A book written by a fool."

"Why you readin' it, then?"

"So that maybe it'll stop me from bein' a fool in the same way."

Josiah shook his head. "Books give people funny notions. Then them things git people into trouble."

Fergus laughed. "I think you're right, Josiah." Fergus was smoking a cigar and reached into his inner pocket and pulled out one. He handed it to Josiah, who rolled it between his fingers, then accepted the light the Englishman gave him. He settled back and watched Josiah as he took a long puff and the blue haze of smoke rose. Finally Fergus said, "Your granddaughter is a remarkable woman. She possesses a very firm mind." When the old man did not answer, he added, "I felt a little sorry for her husband today."

"He's doin' what he wants to do," Josiah said in a spare tone. At that moment Julie came up, and Josiah rose and walked away, puffing on his cigar.

"What were you and Grandpa talking about?" Julie asked.

"About your family situation. A mite delicate situation, I should say," Fergus said.

Julie stared at the Englishman. "Jake's never been a good husband to Jerusalem. I think she's well rid of him." She changed the subject abruptly. "Can I use your bathtub tonight, Professor?"

"Why, of course, my dear, I'll have Langley heat up some water."

Julie walked away and hurried to catch up with her grandfather. "What do you think about Jake, Grandpa?"

"Seen it comin' a long time ago," he said.

"Well, I'll tell you one thing. That sister of mine won't share her man. I think she'll go back home."

Josiah shook his head and chewed his lower lip thoughtfully. He turned to face Julie and said slowly, "I stopped tryin' to second-guess that female when she was ten years old. There ain't no point to even try."

CHAPTER
FOURTEEN

Two days had passed since Jerusalem had turned her back on her husband and walked away without another word. Now it was Wednesday morning. Clay had gotten up long before the others and left carrying a shotgun. A few hours later he returned to camp with a sack full of quail. The sun was now a quarter of the way up to its zenith, and as he approached the camp, he looked up and saw Lucita coming to meet him.

"Good morning, Señor Clay."

Clay stopped and set down the bag of quail and shook his head. "No, it's Wednesday."

"What is wrong with Wednesday?"

"Wednesday's a bad day. I never had any good luck on a Wednesday. Usually, I try to go off and stay by myself where nobody can bother me."

Lucita laughed. She was an attractive woman when she did this, her large lustrous eyes glowing, and she ran her hand down her black hair and shook her head. "That is an odd superstition, Señor Clay."

"It ain't no superstition at all," Clay said firmly. "It's just the way it is. Bad things always happen on Wednesday."

Lucita shook her head. "What do you have in your bag?"

"Somethin' good to eat." He reached down, picked up the bag, and pulled out a limp bird. "Never saw so many quail. In one shot I brought down four of 'em."

"Let me have them. I will clean them for you."

"That'll be good. I'll probably cut my hand off tryin' to dress 'em, bein' it's Wednesday."

Clay followed Lucita away from the camp and then watched as she easily dressed the birds. "You sure do that better than I can," he admitted.

"I'd be shamed if a man could clean a bird better than I. Women are better at some things."

"I reckon you're right about that." Clay watched with admiration as she cleaned the birds quickly and efficiently. He studied her and finally asked, "Are the kids grievin' themselves much over Gordie's death?"

Lucita stopped working on the bird and was silent for a moment. Then softly, she said, "They're handling it better than I am."

Clay blinked with surprise, for ever since the day Gordon had died, Lucita had not shown a great deal of grief. But now she turned to him, a bird in her hand, and plucked at it slowly. She allowed the feathers to fall to the ground, and then she looked up and said, "I miss him a great deal. He was a good husband to me, Señor Clay. And a woman needs a man."

"I reckon that's true."

"I don't know what will happen to us. I don't worry for myself, but my children . . . they have no father, and now they have no place to call home."

Clay shifted his feet and gnawed at his lower lip for a moment, then said, "I made Gordie a promise that I'd look after you."

Lucita suddenly looked up, and their eyes met. "That was kind of you, but it's too much to ask of any man."

"Don't rightly think so, ma'am. It'll be all right. We'll find something for you."

Lucita smiled. His words seemed to reassure her. She continued cleaning the quail, and finally, when they were done, she put them back in the sack. "What will Jerusalem do?"

"I don't think she knows. She's been quiet since she met up with Jake. That woman makes me nervous. Kind of like being around a keg of dynamite. You don't ever know when it's gonna go off."

The sound of an approaching horse drew Clay's attention. He looked, and Lucita followed his gaze. "It's Señor Bowie."

Bowie was riding a large roan stallion. When he swung down to the ground, he held the lines and bowed slightly, taking off his hat. He said, "Lo siento por la muerte de su marido, señora."

"Gracias, Señor Bowie."

Bowie nodded to Clay, then his attention returned to Lucita. "The neighbors told me you had left. Is that so?"

"There was nothing for us there. Señora

Hardin invited us to come with them. She said we could join with their family, at least until we find something. And Señor Clay has offered to help me."

Bowie turned and gave Clay an odd look. "Is that right, Clay?"

Clay seemed embarrassed. "Sure, it's right. Gordie was a good friend of mine."

Bowie smiled slightly and something flickered in his eyes, but he said nothing.

"I been wondering if it wouldn't be possible for Lucita here to find some land of her own," Clay said. "She needs a place for herself and Mateo and Serena."

"Well, that's entirely possible. If you're thinking of trying to get some land, Stephen Austin is the man to see."

Lucita listened as the two men talked about the land grants that were available, and finally she said, "I will go start cooking these birds. You will stay to eat, Señor Bowie?"

"Don't have time, but thanks for the offer, señora."

As Lucita left, Bowie turned to face Clay. "I been tryin' to figure this out, Clay."

"Tryin' to figure what out?"

"Well, I don't know Jake Hardin that well, but I understood he's already got a wife."

Clay grimaced. "He's got more than one. He's got two of them."

"Well, that's against the law, ain't it?" Bowie said with surprise.

"You know how it was in the mountains. A man would take up with an Indian woman and call her his wife, but there wasn't anything legal about it."

"That's what Hardin did?"

"A long time ago. He's got two kids now, and it looks like a pretty bad situation for Jerusalem. It didn't go too well when Jerusalem and the kids saw Jake had kids almost the same age as them."

"You think she'll go back to the States?"

"I don't know what she'll do."

Bowie slapped the lines of the horse in his free hand and thought hard for a moment, then said abruptly, "Let's go see Stephen Austin. He can tell you whether or not Lucita has a chance at getting some land. There shouldn't be trouble since she's a Mexican national, and he might even be able to work something out about Mrs. Hardin."

"I don't see how that could be. I don't

reckon she's gonna live with Jake knowing what he's done."

"What does Hardin say about all this?"

"I can't answer for him. Let's go see Austin."

"Might be a good idea to take Mrs. Hardin with us," Bowie said.

"You might be right about that, Jim. I'll go ask her." Clay stood there for a moment thinking about all that had happened in the last few months. "You know, Bowie, life was sure a lot simpler for me before I got involved with Jake Hardin and his family."

"Why don't you just walk away from it all, Clay?"

Clay shook his head. "I'd better not do that. Not today. Today's Wednesday."

"Is Wednesday a bad day?" Bowie asked.

"The worst day in the world. Everything bad that ever happened to me was on a Wednesday. Even our knife fight, remember."

"You're right! Maybe we should go see Austin tomorrow."

"That sounds good. We'll do it."

★   ★   ★

Stephen Austin was not an impressive man, at least to Jerusalem. His house was even less so. It was a simple two-room shack, one room for sleeping and one room for everything else. Jerusalem had accompanied Bowie and Clay to talk to the man, and he had made them welcome, offering them what little refreshments he had. He was a small man with none of the roughness she had come to expect from the frontier types. His manners were fine, and finally Jim Bowie brought him around to the business at hand.

"Steve, Mrs. Hardin here is in a hard place. She came here to join her husband—"

Bowie broke off and seemingly did not know how to continue.

"My husband has taken an Indian wife. That's the problem," Jerusalem said bluntly.

Austin glanced at her and then dropped his eyes. "I'm sorry to hear that, Mrs. Hardin."

"He told me he had to claim her as his wife to buy the land, so I asked Mr. Bowie to bring me here to see if it would be possible for me to buy any more land."

Austin moved uncertainly, not knowing

what to say at first. He picked up a pen, held it for a moment balanced between his thumb and forefinger as he tried to think of an answer. "It's not a good time for settlement, ma'am. Last year the government shut all immigration down."

Clay saw that Jerusalem was plainly disappointed.

She shrugged slightly and said, "Well, I suppose I'll have to go back to the States, then."

"Come on, Steve, you can do something to help this lady, can't you?" Bowie said quickly. He grinned broadly and winked. "You and I have seen some title changes that weren't exactly what the government would have approved."

Austin suddenly grinned. He was a tired man, worn down with all his duties of trying to carry out his father's dream, but the smile made him look much younger. "Now, Jim, we don't need to be talking about those things. Bending the rules might have worked before, but that's not the way things are now."

"But ain't there somethin' you can do?" Clay said. "There's plenty of land around here. I've never seen so much land in all my life."

Austin seemed to be making up his mind, struggling with the problem, and finally he said slowly, "I'm truly sorry, Mrs. Hardin, but the stipulations of the grant are very specific. And with the political situation right now, the Mexican government would not approve the sale. The . . . ah . . . situation with your husband already owning land only complicates matters. If you had a brother, or if your father could put his name on it, we could arrange that. Do you have anybody like that, Mrs. Hardin?" Austin asked, trying to work out something.

"I . . . I have a brother called Zane, but he's not here. I have a grandfather, but he is not well." Jerusalem watched Austin as he nervously looked at Clay. Somehow she knew that it wasn't going to work.

Before Austin could say anything, Clay asked, "How big a piece is it?"

"It's bigger than usual. The man was going to use it to run cattle on, so I put two pieces together. All in all, it'll be nearly four thousand acres."

"Four thousand acres!" Clay said. "That's one big chunk of land."

"How much is it, Steve?" Bowie said.

"I could sell it to the right couple for five cents an acre. But they'd have to be married and Catholics to fulfill the requirements of the grant," he said, looking at Jerusalem.

Austin saw the disappointment on Jerusalem's face, and he tried to explain the political situation so she would understand why his hands were tied. "Right now, Mrs. Hardin, things are in such a mess that nobody really knows what's going on. Since Mexico won its freedom from Spain, the government has changed leadership half a dozen times.

"Sometimes it's the Centralists in power. They want a strong central government. Sometimes the other group believes in more authority in the States. Someday, I suppose, they'll settle it all, but right now we just have to hope that they leave us alone as much as possible. If there was any other way, Mrs. Hardin . . . but I don't see how it could work."

Jerusalem was struggling with the disappointment she felt. When Clay and Bowie had asked her to go with them, she had really thought that maybe things could work out. But she had faced hard times before and managed to carry on. She swallowed hard and looked at Austin and said, "I thank you for trying, Mr. Austin."

Feeling bad himself, Austin turned to Clay and quickly changed the subject. "What was that you asked me before, Clay, about some land for someone else?"

Clay was about to argue, but he felt Jerusalem's hand touch his arm, and he turned and saw a look he knew only too well. Instead of pressuring Austin to change his mind, he said, "Ah . . . there's a couple I know. The man's American, but he's lived in Mexico and become a citizen. He's a Catholic. Of course his wife is too."

Jerusalem suddenly turned to stare at Clay. She knew he was talking about his dead friend, Gordon Lebonne, but he said nothing about the man's death. She kept silent and listened as Clay continued to explain the situation. "I don't know if it's possible for anybody to live in your colony that didn't come in from the States. I know that's what you designed it for. But this couple has had hard times."

Bowie was staring at Clay also. "Are you talking about Gordon and his wife?"

"Yes. Would it be possible to get any land for them?" Clay said.

"Well, the colony was designed to bring in Americans. But he is an American, and since he's already here, and they're both Catholics and citizens, there's one piece right next to the one that I just mentioned. What are their names? Have them come in, and I'll work something out," Austin said.

"Couldn't we just settle the payment and do the book work and get it done right now?" Clay asked.

Austin shrugged. "I guess that's fine with me. The simpler the better." Austin stopped and said, "What about you, Clay?"

Clay stared at him. "What about me?"

"Are you married?"

"No, I'm not."

"Well, that's too bad. If you were, you could take up this four-thousand-acre plot, then sell it to Mrs. Hardin in the future."

"I don't reckon I'd qualify," Clay said.

Steve Austin prepared the necessary paperwork for the land for the Lebonnes. As soon as the business was done, the men all shook hands, and Bowie left to head for his own ranch.

Steve Austin turned to Jerusalem and said, "I'm sorry I couldn't help you, ma'am."

"I understand, Mr. Austin," Jerusalem said and nodded, disappointment clearly showing on her face.

Jerusalem and Clay said good-bye and left. She was silent as they climbed into the wagon and started back to where they had camped. Halfway back, she turned to Clay and said, "Clay, thank you for trying. I guess what Fergus has been saying all along is right. Que sera sera. What shall be shall be."

Clay could hear the sadness in her voice, even though she was trying to accept it. He didn't have an answer and kept riding in silence.

After about five minutes, Jerusalem broke the awkward silence and asked, "Why didn't you tell Mr. Austin that Gordon was dead?"

"Oh, just an idea I had," Clay said, shrugging his shoulders.

"You could get into trouble, Clay, for things like that."

He grinned at her rashly. "Well, it ain't Wednesday, so I reckon I won't get in much trouble."

When they were almost back, Clay pulled

up on the reins and stopped. When Jerusalem turned to ask him why he'd stopped, Clay said awkwardly, "Sorry about, Jake . . . the way he's treated you. I didn't think it was my place to tell you about him and Awinita."

"No, you wouldn't do that. You're not one to carry tales."

Clay said loudly and with a trace of anger, "I told him plenty of times that he was a blamed fool, but he wouldn't listen to me!"

"What did he say?" Jerusalem asked.

"He didn't like my buttin' into his business."

As soon as they arrived at the camp, Julie could tell that something was bothering her sister. She pulled Jerusalem off to one side. "What'd you find out?"

Julie listened as Jerusalem explained how the land grants did not provide land for single women. "I guess we'll have to go back."

"Don't you want to go back?" Julie asked.

"No, to tell the truth, Julie, I'm played out. I've got no man. I've got no home, and my kids don't have a father."

Julie was shocked, for her sister had

always been the strong one in the family. Now she saw the lines of weariness traced in Jerusalem's face, and her shoulders were slumping. She put her arm around Jerusalem and said, "I wish I could help. I've never done a thing for you or anyone else."

"It's all right, Julie. We'll make out somehow."

Jerusalem pulled away and headed toward her wagon. And at that instant, Julie felt a great regret for all that her life had been. As she watched her sister walk wearily away, she spoke aloud in a fierce whisper, "There's got to be a way to get a place for Jerusalem and the kids. There's just got to be!"

CHAPTER
FIFTEEN

Mateo Lebonne had a brooding look in his eyes as he watched his mother, who was engaged in a serious conversation with Clay Taliferro. "What are they talking about, Serena?"

"I don't know." Serena had been watching the pair also, and now she turned to face her brother. "Maybe we made a mistake coming with these Americanos. They are no relation to us."

"I have been thinking that myself, but what choice did we have? With Papá gone, there was nothing for us back there."

"But why would Señor Taliferro want to help us? We're nothing to him."

"He was a friend of our father."

"So he says. We do not know that," Serena said.

"I think he's telling the truth about that. I heard Papá mention him more than once when he talked about his days in the mountains."

"Maybe we can go to San Felipe and find work."

"There are no jobs there. No work," Mateo repeated. He slouched back against the wagon and studied his mother's face. "I cannot tell what she is thinking, but she trusts this man."

"Mateo, I do not trust gringos, but what else can we do? There is nobody else."

Lucita was not unaware that her children were watching them, although she did not turn to face them. She kept her eyes fixed on Clay. He had called her aside after breakfast and now seemed to be having trouble expressing himself. He was not an easy man for her to understand. He was nothing at all like her husband, who had been strong but gentle. Clay was a rugged man and masculine in a strong way that she had seen in few men. Usually he was smiling, but now he seemed almost embarrassed by her presence.

"What is it you wish to say to me, Señor Taliferro?"

"Just call me Clay. I'd feel a little bit more comfortable."

"Very well. Clay, what is it? You seem to be troubled about something."

Clay was, indeed, troubled. With Jerusalem not able to get some land, Clay didn't know what to do. And now he had taken on the responsibility of his dead friend's wife and children, and he hardly knew the woman at all. The Mexicans were a proud race, he knew that much, and he was not sure how she would take what he was going to tell her.

He avoided her eyes, watching as four crows rose and beat their heavy wings, casting four shadows on the earth. With an effort he faced her and thought again that she had the blackest hair he had ever seen in his life. It had almost a blue sheen to it. "Well, I don't know how to tell you this exactly, Lucita, but I've been meddling in your business. My mama always said I was a meddler even when I was six years old."

"And how have you meddled, Señor Clay?"

"Well, I been thinkin' about a place for you and the kids. When I talked to Señor Austin yesterday about the situation with Jerusalem and Jake, I talked to him about a place for you. It didn't go too well for Jerusalem, though."

"But I thought he only took Americanos."

"That's true, but your husband is an American. So I asked him if there was any chance of getting some kind of land grant. And he said there was."

For a moment Lucita did not speak. She searched Clay's face, then said, "But my husband is dead."

"Well, I didn't exactly tell him that. I just let it slip, sort of, and he didn't ask. So when he made out the papers, they're made out to Gordie and to you."

"Isn't that against the law?" Lucita asked.

"Why, I reckon it might be against the rules, but nothin' we can be put in jail for." Clay ran his fingers through his hair and said, "We're in kind of a tough spot here. If Gordie had been alive when we got here and signed the papers, it would have been all right. I don't see that his dyin' a week early makes any difference to anybody."

"I would not want you to get into trouble over this."

"Why, shucks, Lucita! I been in trouble most of my life." Clay grinned. "What we'll do is get you settled down out there, and after a while, we'll let the news get back to Señor Austin that your husband died. I'm pretty sure it won't make any difference."

"But the land. It has to be paid for. I have no money."

"Well, it wasn't much. I paid for it myself."

"I can't let you do that."

"It's just a loan," Clay said quickly. "You can pay it back sometime when you can." Changing the subject, he said, "We'll have to build a house on it, adobe, I reckon. Me and Mateo can do it, and we'll hire some help." He glanced over at the children and said, "If it's all right, then, we'd better tell Mateo and Serena."

"Yes, that would be well." As the two walked toward her children, Lucita was aware that this man was not the usual sort of American. She knew that her husband had been kind and generous, and she saw the same qualities in Clay Taliferro. She spoke, saying, "Mateo—Serena, ven aquí. Tenemos algo que decirles."

Jerusalem looked up at Julie and saw that she was unusually serious. "What is it, Julie, a problem?"

"No, I wanted to talk to you about what's going to happen."

Jerusalem shrugged. "What's going to happen is that we're going to have to leave and go back to the States. I've thought about maybe buying the old home place back, although I hate the idea of it. Now that I cut the ties, I really don't want to go."

"Listen, Jerusalem. I've got an idea, and you've got to let me do it."

"What sort of idea?"

"It's simple. Clay said that there was a large tract of land that a man never paid for, but the papers were all made out. All he'd have to do is change the names, and it would be legally his."

"What does that have to do with us?" Jerusalem asked.

Julie took a deep breath. "Here's what I want to do. We need a lot of land, and if a man has a wife, he can get twice as big a grant. So, if Clay and I got married, we could get it. But it would be your land, don't you see?"

Jerusalem suddenly laughed. "That's crazy even coming from you, Julie."

"There's nothin' crazy about it. Look, suppose we get married here in Mexico. That doesn't mean anything in the States. Just a piece of paper. I'll be going back to the States, and I guess Clay will, too, as soon as he gets all of you settled. So there'd be a piece of paper somewhere in Mexico saying we're married. It doesn't mean a thing."

"No, I won't let you do it. It wouldn't be fair to Clay, and it wouldn't be right."

"I've never done one single thing to help you, Jerusalem, nor the kids. All I've ever done is give you lots of grief. Please let me do this," Julie insisted.

Jerusalem stared at her sister. Indeed, it was true enough that Julie had never caused her family anything but grief. But something about her proposal went against the grain. She shook her head firmly and said, "No, it wouldn't do, Julie. It just wouldn't do."

★ ★ ★

"Julie told me about this crazy idea about you and her getting married, Clay."

"Well, I admit it set me back on my heels when she mentioned it, but the way she put it, it seems like a pretty good idea, if you ask me."

"A good idea! Why, it's terrible. You don't marry someone just to get land."

Clay laughed. "You don't know much about the world if you think that. People marry for all kinds of reasons, not all of them having to do with romance."

Jerusalem turned to face Clay, her eyes direct and seeming to penetrate him. "I can't let you do this, Clay."

Clay hesitated, then said, "Maybe you'd better think of the kids. It'd be some security for them. Of course, someday you may go back to Jake."

"No, I don't think that'll ever happen," she said resolutely.

"Well, think about it, Jerusalem. I can't see no other way out."

Jerusalem nodded, but as Clay turned and walked away, she thought about all that it would mean. But the whole idea sounded wrong to her. She was confused and depressed after traveling so far to discover her husband had been unfaithful all these years. When Lucita came and asked her to come eat some dinner, Jerusalem said she wasn't hungry and went to the wagon to be alone.

Later on when Brodie came in, he said, "Julie told me about what she wants to do. That'll be good, won't it, Ma? We'll get the land, and we'll have our own place."

"I don't like it, Brodie."

Brodie blinked with surprise. "What do you mean?"

"It's not right. Marriage ought to be more than a business deal."

"But Julie said it was just kind of a game."

"Son, I hope you don't listen to your aunt in matters like this. It may be just a game to Julie, but marriage is a serious commitment."

Brodie obviously was disappointed. "What'll we do then, Ma?"

"I don't know. All I can think of is going back to Arkansas." She watched as Brodie's face became downcast and knew that since learning the truth about his father, these last days had been extremely difficult on him. He left without another word, and Jerusalem clasped her hands together and looked out across the flatness of the land and felt a helplessness such as she had never felt in her entire life.

CHAPTER
SIXTEEN

Jake arrived at the campsite early in the afternoon. Jerusalem had seen him coming, and when he got off of his horse, she waited until he came and stood before her. "Hello, Jake," she said. "Will you have some coffee?"

"No, I don't reckon. Where is everybody?" he asked, looking around.

"Clay took them all down to the river fishing."

"Who's that Mexican woman and the two kids that are traveling with you?"

"Her name is Lucita Lebonne. Her husband, Gordie, died a few days ago. He was a friend of Clay's, and Clay promised to look out for them."

"Seems Clay's lookin' out for lots of people these days."

"Yes, he is," Jerusalem said, noting the sarcasm. She matched Jake's gaze until he finally dropped his eyes. "What's on your mind, Jake?"

"Well, I been thinkin' about the situation, tryin' to find a way out of it." He waited for Jerusalem to speak, but when she did not, he blurted out, "Look, it ain't like I don't care about you and the kids. You know I do."

"No, I don't know that, Jake. Your being gone all this time speaks a whole lot louder than your words, I'm afraid," Jerusalem said evenly.

"Don't be foolish! Of course I do," he insisted.

"Jake, just say what's on your mind and be done with it."

"All right, here it is. I think I ought to find a place for Awinita and her kids to live, and I'll come back and stay with you."

"What makes you think I want you back under those terms?" Jerusalem said. "Let me ask you one question, Jake. Did you ever really love me?"

Jake Hardin could not face his wife's penetrating glance. Instead, he quickly shifted
his glance and looked to the mountains far
off to the north. "Well, there's different kinds
of ways to love a woman."

"I'm sure you found that handy."

"I can't give up Awinita and the kids.
They're my responsibility just as much as
our kids."

At that instant Jerusalem knew that talking
was hopeless. She felt angry and wanted to
tell him what all his years of negligence had
done to her and their children, but she knew
it would do no good. She knew Jake lacked
commitment, the very quality her heart had
longed for all those years. She realized she
had known about his unfaithfulness for a
long time, but she was a determined woman
and had set her whole personality to try to
make her marriage work. Looking back on it
now, she had experienced serious doubts
about Jake's long absences, which she
never permitted herself to voice. Now she
knew she should have faced up to it years
ago, but it was too late.

"I won't live like that, Jake. It's a lie, and
you know it," Jerusalem said with a finality.
She watched as Jake summoned up an ar-

gument and then seemed to wither under her direct gaze.

"Then I reckon it'll have to be your way," he murmured.

"I suppose I'll be going back to the States, Jake," she said. "So this is good-bye forever."

"Jerusalem, I won't get to see my kids grow up."

"You can watch your other family grow up," Jerusalem said. She turned her back on him and walked away.

Jake Hardin had no choice but to mount his horse and ride off. He had little enough hope when he came to talk with Jerusalem, and now he knew that a large part of his life had vanished.

Clay had come out to give some grain to his horse, which he had hobbled some distance from the wagons. The sun was high in the sky, but dark thunderheads were rolling in, and it looked as though rain was coming. He looked up and saw Julie walking toward him. He knew her well enough to recognize

she had something on her mind. "What is it, Julie?"

"I'm worried about Jerusalem," Julie said as she came up and stood before him. "Got an idea how we can help her."

"She won't listen to it if it's like your last one."

"She won't have anything to say about it, Clay. Look, I've been thinking. I've never done anything good in my whole life."

"Well, me either . . . I guess."

"Yes, you have. You pitched in to save our family, but me . . . I haven't done a lot to be proud about. Now, listen, Clay. Jerusalem's dead set against our getting married, and maybe she's right. She keeps saying that God meant marriage to last forever. You know how she is about things like that."

"I guess you're right. That kind of backs her into a corner with no way out, if you ask me. I mean, with Jake takin' up with another woman."

"Wouldn't bother me. I'd shoot him, at least in the leg." Julie's eyes glinted, and she shook her head. "I knew what kind of a scoundrel he was a long time ago, but Jerusalem just wouldn't listen to me. She said she wouldn't give up on him. But here's

what we can do. We don't have to actually marry, Clay. All we have to do is just *say* we are."

Clay stared at her. "What are you talking about?"

"You don't think these people go back and check county records or demand to see marriage licenses, do you? All you have to do is tell Austin that we're married. Then he'll sell us the land, and sooner or later we can transfer the title to Jerusalem."

Clay was caught with the idea. "You know, there's something in that. To tell the truth, I didn't like the idea of goin' through with a marriage."

"No, you're not the marryin' kind," Julie grinned, "and neither am I. But here's what we'll do. We'll go find Stephen Austin and buy the land, and then—"

"We have to become Catholics first. Steve Austin said it was one of the requirements of the grant," Clay said.

"I heard that the priest was down the road a ways havin' mass. He can baptize us and whatever else he has to do."

"I expect he has to give us a paper."

"Well, come on, then. Saddle up that horse and saddle up one for me." Julie suddenly grabbed him and threw her arms around his neck. Her eyes were dancing, and she laughed aloud. "I'm anxious to be Mrs. Julie Taliferro."

Father Michael Muldoon was a short, rotund man with black hair and merry blue eyes. He had been eating when Julie and Clay came in, and a pile of bones from a chicken littered his plate. He got up, and as soon as Clay explained the situation, that they needed to fulfill the law, Muldoon shrugged and said, "That is easy, my son."

Clay felt uncomfortable. "I'm not real sure that I'm fit to be a member of anybody's flock, Father."

"Who is fit?" Muldoon said. His eyes went from one to the other, and he smiled freely. "I am a renegade, of sorts. I was thrown out of Ireland for bad behavior."

"Is that right, Father?" Julie's eyebrows arched, and she leaned forward. "What sort of bad behavior?"

"Oh, nothing to do with the usual sins of money or women. I had a theological difference with my bishop. He ran me out of the country for it. This was the only place that would take me."

"I'm sure you do a lot of good," Julie said. "Is this going to be very complicated?"

"Not complicated at all. I baptize you and give you a certificate, and you sign a paper saying that you are members of the church."

"Well, let's get on with it," Julie said. "I like to try everything once, and I've never tried being baptized." *Especially if it helps me get some land,* she thought and winked at Clay.

Jerusalem was worried about Julie and Clay. They had been gone for two days now, and she was growing weary of making explanations for them to the others, especially the children. She and Moriah had just finished cooking the meal and were working on supper before the open fire when she heard Moriah say, "Look, there come Clay and Aunt Julie."

Jerusalem stood up from the fire and turned. Clay and Julie rode right up next to the wagon, both dismounted, and Clay took the reins from Julie. He had an odd look on his face, and Jerusalem thought again how easy he was to read.

Julie was smiling as she greeted them all. "Where have you been, Aunt Julie?" Brodie asked. "We've been worried sick about you."

Julie looked at Jerusalem but then turned to Clinton and winked at him. "Well, you ought to be happy, Clinton, strong as you are in your religion. Me and Clay just got baptized."

A silence fell over the group, except for Clinton, who said, "You got put under the water?"

"No, we got sprinkled."

Clinton's face wrinkled up. "Well, that ain't no good. You got to be put under. If you wasn't put down under, you ain't baptized at all."

Julie only laughed at Clinton. She turned from him and was watching Jerusalem. "Show her the paper, Clay."

Clay looked as if he would have rather gotten back on his horse and ridden out. He started to speak, but Julie said sharply, "Just show her the paper!"

Jerusalem waited as Clay pulled a folded paper out of his pocket and handed it awk-

wardly to her without speaking. She unfolded it and stared at it, then looked up.
"You two got married after all?"

"No, we didn't get married," Julie said
quickly. She looked around at the kids and
at Josiah, who had come in close. "We just
said we were married. And we got baptized.
That was all we needed to get the land
from Mr. Austin. Nobody will know the
difference."

"It's really Julie's idea, and I thought it was
a good one," Clay mumbled. "We'll let a little
time pass, and then we'll sign the place over
to you."

Jerusalem turned to Julie and could not
speak for a moment. Julie came over and
did something she had not done in years.
She put her arms around Jerusalem and
held her tightly. She pressed her cheek
against Jerusalem's and whispered, "It'll
give you a home, sis, you and the kids. It's
the only good thing I could do for you.
Please accept this and don't turn your back
on me, Jerusalem."

Jerusalem looked at Clay, who stood
there silently chewing on his lower lip. She
looked over at her children and at her
grandfather, and when she did speak, she

said, "I don't feel right about this, but I don't know what else to do. All right, we all understand that it must never get out that Clay and Julie aren't married."

"We get to stay!" Brodie said quickly, and his eyes lit up. "We've got us a place?"

"You got you a place," Julie said. "No more sleeping under a wagon."

Julie stepped back, and Jerusalem saw that her sister's eyes were damp with tears. "Well, it's not right, but if it works out that we get a home out of it, I suppose I'll have to put up with it."

Clay breathed a sigh of relief, for the whole way back he was worried about how Jerusalem would react. He walked over and dropped his hand on Brodie's shoulder. "It'll be your ma's land one day soon, and then down the pike, it'll be yours someday." Clay looked at Jerusalem and saw that she was upset, so he tried to smooth things over. "It's a bigger grant than usual, and it's right next to the land that I got for Lucita and her kids. It'll be big enough to make a cattle ranch, or big enough to grow plenty of cotton, if that's what we decide to do."

"And there's already a house on it," Julie

said with excitement. "You can move right in. It'll be your house."

Despite the guilt she felt about what Clay and Julie had done, Jerusalem Hardin felt a sudden lightness of heart. She had felt like a wanderer ever since she had left Arkansas Territory. And she was tired from the long trip, always wondering if they would get attacked by Indians. Now she had a place to call home and a chance to start over. She saw how happy Brodie and Julie were as they gave each other a hug. Even Moriah and Clinton looked relieved that their traveling might finally be over. Taking a deep breath, she said, "All right, let's go see this place."

As they pulled up to the house that sat only a few hundred feet from the Guadalupe River, Clay said, "Nobody's lived in the house for quite a time, but before I leave here, we'll get it all fixed up."

As she got down from the wagon, Jerusalem gave Mary Aidan to Moriah, then walked toward the house. Clay and Julie followed, and the others trailed behind. The

house was two-story, made of frame, an unusual thing out on the Texas plains. Most
houses were either adobe or bare logs that
had been cut down and trimmed. This one
had never been painted, and the wood had
weathered to a silvery tint. A porch ran
across the front. Jerusalem stepped up and
saw that the door was open. As she
stepped inside, she was startled, for something moved, and she almost cried out as
a big red rooster sailed by her, clucking
furiously.

As they stepped in, a dozen or more hens
started to cluck loudly. Brodie laughed and
said, "They just lost a house, didn't they,
Ma?"

"I guess they did, son."

They all went through the house excitedly.
The first floor had a large room, which could
be used for dining and living. Beside that
was a smaller room, where the wreck of a
stove still remained. Another door led to a
hall that separated two bedrooms. And at
the end of the hall, a rickety stair went up to
the second floor, where there were two bedrooms.

Jerusalem came down the stairs slowly
and found Julie watching her anxiously.

"It'll be a fine house. Just needs a little cleaning up, Julie."

"You think so, Jerusalem? Can you be happy here?"

"Of course I can."

Clay came in right then, and Julie walked over to him. "We did fine, Clay." She hugged him and suddenly kissed his cheek, then turned and winked at Jerusalem. "Now, where's the bridal suite for Mr. and Mrs. Clayton Taliferro?" She laughed at the expression on Clay's face and then ran out laughing.

"She's a handful, ain't she? I reckon this takes the rag off the bush," Clay said, looking awkward as his face turned red.

"Clay, be careful about Julie," Jerusalem said.

Clay grinned at her. "I'm always careful around grizzly bears and good-lookin' women."

"A wise notion. What about Lucita and her family? She's going to need a house too."

"We'll have to hire some laborers to build her an adobe house for now. Can't be too far away from this one."

"Why not?" Jerusalem asked.

"Because of Indians."

"But we haven't seen any Indians in weeks."

"You generally don't when they don't want to be seen," Clay said, then looked out at the land that stretched to the horizon. He smiled to himself. For once in his life, he felt good about helping somebody out, especially Jerusalem. He turned back to Jerusalem and said, "I know you didn't agree with all we done to get this place, but—"

"It's all right, Clay. You and Julie have done fine for us."

A week went by, and everyone pitched in and did an enormous amountof work on the house. Jerusalem was exhausted, and she sat down on the porch to rest. The moon was up, and the children were all in bed. Even Julie and Josiah were exhausted and had turned in for the night. Jerusalem had stayed up to finish cleaning the dishes and also waiting for Clay, who was working on Lucita's house.

As she sat there, she heard Clay singing

the song that had become habitual with him:

I found a rose in New Orleans,
Sweetest flower I'd ever seen.
Coal black hair and sparkling eyes
And rosy lips for telling lies.

Deep in the heart!
O deep in the heart!
Naught can be lost
That's deep in the heart!

Jerusalem smiled, for Clay was singing the sad ballad with all the gusto in the world as he unsaddled his horse and put him in the corral. When he stepped up on the porch, she said, "Go wash up, Clay, and then come inside and eat. I saved you a plate of food."

"Where is everybody?" he asked as he moved toward the washstand and began to wash his face.

"They've all gone to bed. Everybody's worn out. They've all been working from dawn to dusk to whip this place into shape. I suspect you are too. You've worked the hardest, and . . . well, thanks for all you've done for us."

" 'Twas nothing, Jerusalem Ann," he said as he dried his face and hands, then came over and sat down. They had managed to buy a few pieces of furniture, and now Jerusalem went into the kitchen and brought out a plate that had been left on the stove to warm.

"Steak and potatoes," she said, "and fresh biscuits and milk."

"I reckon I could eat anything about now." After taking a bite, he looked at Jerusalem and said, "Why, Jerusalem, this all looks good."

Jerusalem smiled and sat down and watched him as he ate hungrily. "How's the house coming?"

"We still got a ways to go, but it's coming along. Should be done before cold weather."

"We got here too late to plant a garden, but Awinita has a big one. She gave me some vegetables that we can put up for the winter. Next year we'll put in a big garden if you'll break up the ground."

"Sure," Clay said as he continued to eat.

"I've got a reward for you for all your hard

work." Jerusalem got up and went into the kitchen again. She came out with a plate in her hand and set it down on the table in front of him. "Fresh apple pie. Awinita had a few apples."

Clay's eyes shone as he lit into the pie and washed it down with the hot coffee she poured for him. Finally, he was finished, and she refilled his coffee cup and said, "Let's go out on the porch."

Clay rose and followed her out on the porch, and they stood there looking out over the land. The moon was enormous, and a peaceful quietness had settled on the land.

"The professor and Langley left today looking for Comanches," Jerusalem said, breaking the silence they were enjoying.

Clay shook his head. "I sure hope he don't find none."

They were silent again for a while as Clay sipped his coffee, then he put the cup down on the rail. Jerusalem said, "Julie's doing well. She's working harder than I've ever seen her."

"I had an ornery horse once," Clay said.

Jerusalem stared at him. Clay Taliferro had a way of making odd remarks that seemed to have nothing to do with the conversation. "Did you?" she said.

"Yep. Reminded me of Julie in a way."

"How was that, Clay?"

"Well, she'd be good for six months, just waiting for the chance when I wasn't looking to kick me or bite a plug out of me."

Jerusalem was amused at the comparison and laughed. "That's Julie, all right. She's got a good heart, but I'm worried about her. Her life is all wrong."

"So is mine, I guess."

Jerusalem did not answer. From somewhere far off a coyote yodeled toward the moon, one of the many night sounds she had grown accustomed to. The sound rose in the air and then faded away. She looked up at the moon, then turned to Clay and said, "You bit off more than you bargained for, didn't you, Clay?"

Surprised, Clay turned to face her. "What do you mean?"

"Well, look at what you've gone and done. You've got me and my four kids. You've got a make-believe wife, and you've got Lucita and her two youngsters to look after. That's quite a bit for a bachelor."

Clay grinned wryly. "Well, I wasn't cut out

to be a hermit. And it don't look like I'm gonna be one, does it? But I'll get everybody settled down before I leave for the mountains."

Jerusalem suddenly reached out and placed her hand lightly on his chest. Clay grew very still at her touch. As the silence ran on, he thought about what he knew about this woman. As he looked into her eyes, he suspected a woman's silence could mean many things. She was looking at him in a most peculiar fashion that made him nervous. He wasn't sure what it meant in Jerusalem Hardin, but it pulled at him. It caught at his own solitary thinking, and he felt a certain excitement, as if he were on the edge of a discovery.

He had been caught by the force of this woman's personality as he'd watched her day after day these last months. She was attractive, but it wasn't just her beauty that drew him. She had a strength of character that he admired. He was absolutely certain that if the need arose, she could lift a shotgun and shoot someone if it meant protecting her friends and family. She also had a temper that could either charm a man or chill him all the way down to his boots. The strength she possessed to face the difficulties of life square in the face in no way took away from the femininity he saw in her bathed in the moonlight in the pretty tan dress she was wearing.

The silence ran on, and Clay's heart began to race. Then he saw a look in her eyes that said more than words ever could.

The moment broke when she whispered, "Clay, I wish—" She broke off suddenly and removed her hand.

As she turned to walk away, he caught a glimpse of tears in her eyes.

Clay Taliferro stood astonished as she opened the door and quickly stepped inside. The door closed, and he heard her footsteps as she walked down the hall to the room she shared with Mary Aidan. "Well, plague take it! Now, I've went and upset her. What'd I do this time?"

He heard a thumping sound and turned around. He saw the big dog stretched out flat, leaning against the house. "Well, Anthony Wayne, you stay away from females. There's no way to figure them out."

Anthony Wayne thumped his tail on the floor, and Clay entered the house and went to bed.

Nothing changed on the landscape, except the heavy breathing of Anthony Wayne.

When the moon had risen high in the sky, something stirred on the horizon. Three mounted figures appeared—Comanche warriors sitting on their small rugged horses. They sat silently, watching the house for a long time, and then one of them pointed his lance toward the house. He spoke briefly and then turned his horse away.

Overhead the moon was round and luminescent. It was what some called the Comanche Moon, for it was the sort of moon that Comanches wait for to ride on their deadly raids.

The three disappeared, and inside the house some slept and dreamed, while others stayed awake and could not find the blessings of sleep as they thought of what was past and of what was to come.

PART FOUR:

THE TEXICANS
1833—1835

CHAPTER
SEVENTEEN

Zane Satterfield felt the cramps coming on in his legs again. Desperately, he pushed his feet as hard as he could against the end of The Box, although he knew it was useless. When a man was lying on a cot at night in a cell and a cramp came, all he had to do was roll off the cot and stand on the leg tip-toe until the cramp went away. But inside The Box, there was no room to stand up. As the cramp doubled the muscles of his right leg, Zane kneaded it with his hands, trying to make it go away.

A cold sweat covered Zane's emaciated body as he worked feverishly to get rid of the cramp. It was September now, Zane thought, but he couldn't be sure. He knew it was 1833, but that meant little to him at the moment. The weather was bearable, unlike those scorching days in August when the Louisiana heat could turn The Box into a furnace that dried every bit of moisture out of a man's body so that his tongue swelled up and pushed out of his lips. But even now, the agony of being forced into a stooped-over sitting position for three days with one pint of water twice a day and living in his own filth kept Zane in a continual state of insanity.

The Box did that to men. It caused most to become inhuman, a mere lump of twisting, knotting, suffering flesh with the passage of time coming to a halt. Zane could tell night from day by the sun that shone through the cracks, and now he saw the same pitch-black darkness outside that was inside The Box.

The cramp eased, and Zane tried to think of something pleasant. After three days of being locked up in The Box, a man was lucky to think at all. He willed his mind back to the hills of Arkansas, thinking of the verdant lushness of the mountains beside the home where he had grown up as a boy and left as a young man. He forced himself to picture in his mind the clear water of the river that flowed beside the cabin. By sheer force of will Zane managed to shove away the horrors of his surroundings, at least for a time.

The noise of voices, muted by the heavy, wooden sides of The Box, came to him faintly. And even muffled as it was, he immediately recognized the voice of Alf Renzie.

Renzie had a mushy voice, but at the same time penetrating, and Zane knew he would never forget it for as long as he lived.

"All right, open the door," Renzie ordered. "Pull that scudder out of there. He's had enough vacation."

The lock rattled in the hasp outside and the door swung open. Even though it was almost dark, the last fading rays of the sun struck Zane Satterfield, and he closed his eyes.

"Come on out of there, boy! You had enough of an easy life. Pull him out of there. He's actin' like he's hurt."

Rough hands seized Zane and dragged him out of The Box. He tried to straighten his legs, but all his strength was gone, and his limbs were sore and stiff. His eyes were shut tight against the fading sunlight, and he felt the butt end of Alf Renzie's bullwhip strike him against the shoulders. More than one man had died under the cruelty of that whip, but Zane could not obey. A burly guard swore at him and punched him.

"All right, Short. You and Williams drag him out of here. You get a good night's rest, Satterfield. I got a feelin' I'll be seein' you early tomorrow. Got a special little job that ought to suit you just fine."

Zane opened his eyes to mere slits and saw the beefy, red face of Renzie. He was a big man, well over six feet, padded with plenty of muscle and fat. He had the brutal face of a butcher and the reputation of being the toughest guard who had ever worked at Melton Penal Camp, which was quite a distinction, considering the stiff competition.

Zane felt hands under his arms lifting him up. His legs were like rubber, and he heard Bennie Short whisper, "Come on, Zane, you can do it. Here, put your arm over my shoulder."

By the time the two inmates had helped

Zane back to the cell block, he had recovered part of the use of his legs. The heavy thumping of the guard's feet behind him silenced the voices in the cells.

"Here we go. Just lie down on your bunk there, Zane," Bennie said.

Zane lay down and stretched his legs full-length, feeling tremendous relief in his cramped muscles. He heard Bennie begging the guard to bring him some water and food, and he heard the guard laugh harshly.

"All right, I figure he'll have a tough day tomorrow with Alf. I'll see if I can round up somethin'."

By now Zane's eyes had become accustomed to the darkness of the cell. Only one lantern in the middle of the hall gave off any light for the inmates. He could hear the breathing of the convicts and the muttered voices, a familiar sound that he had listened to now for almost three years. He did not try to move, but finally he heard the guard come back and shove a tin plate under the bars.

"Here, Zane, sit up and eat somethin'."

Zane sat up on the bench and took the plate that Bennie put in his lap. His tongue was so swollen he could barely eat it, and he had to soak it with the tepid water in the tin cup until finally he was able to eat the vile-smelling stew, the first food he had had in three days.

"That there stint in The Box was a rough one, Zane." Bennie Short was a small, young man of twenty-two, with hair white as the cotton he had spent most of his life working with. He had buck teeth and pale hazel eyes, and his skin was so fair the hot Louisiana sunlight constantly blistered it. His body was scarred from all the beatings he had taken in prison. But he was the closest thing to a friend that Zane had managed to make during his sentence. Bennie was in for a year, and he lacked only one month of fulfilling it, whereas Zane was looking at fifteen years and understood well that he would never live it out.

"You ought not to sass Renzie, Zane," Bennie said. "You just make it hard on yourself."

Zane sat there drinking the water, feeling the moisture slake his immense thirst. He could barely see the outline of the young man sitting on the cot next to his and did not have the strength to answer.

Bennie filled up Zane's cup three times,

then said, "That's all of it, Zane. I could try to get some more."

"No, don't get 'em stirred up," Zane whispered. "The way they are, they just might lock you in The Box." His voice was rusty, and he cleared his throat. "You've got to behave yourself and get out of this place next month."

"Shore will be good. I'm gonna get as far away from this here place as I can," Bennie said.

"Better go to sleep. They'll come and get us early in the morning."

"I do dread that. I don't know what Renzie's got on his mind, but it ain't never no fun. Good night, Zane. I'm glad you're out."

"Good night, Bennie."

Zane lay on the bed, his body tense, waiting for what he knew would come next. It never failed, and when it came he found himself flinching. The sound was always the same. The crack of a whip split the silence as it cut into a man's flesh, followed by horrendous screams, followed by Alf Renzie's laughing. It was the same every night. Inmates worked all day, and if they committed a fault, no one said anything. But at night, after they had put in a full day's work and were shoved in their cell, Renzie would come by later and take them out and say, "You didn't pick enough cotton today, boy. I'm gonna have to teach you a lesson." The brutal whipping seemed to go on interminably. Men screamed until they had no voice left. More than one man had died under the whip of Alf Renzie. Zane had tasted that whip half a dozen times during his sentence. And because of it, his hatred for Alf Renzie bordered on insanity. Zane's back would carry the scars from Renzie's brutality for the rest of his life. Zane spent hours thinking of ways he could kill him slowly and painfully.

Finally, Renzie gave a last laugh, and then silence fell over the prison. Zane Satterfield dropped off into unconsciousness, dreading the morning and Alf Renzie's whip.

When morning came, Zane and Bennie ate the meager breakfast provided, and then waited for Alf Renzie to appear. About a half hour later, Renzie swaggered out of the guard's quarters, his dreaded black whip coiled at his side. From time to time, he caressed it as a man might touch a woman, but today he evidently was in a better mood than usual.

"Come on, boys. We got some clearing to do in the bayou," Renzie said.

Renzie mounted his fine roan stallion, and the two convicts, carrying axes over their shoulders, hobbled along after him. The bayou was accessible by trails that led through the high ground, but it took more than an hour until Renzie pulled his horse up and said, "There, cut that tree down."

The tree was a massive cypress, surrounded by knobby knees. The undergrowth had to be cleared out before Zane and Bennie could even get to the base of the trunk. They fell to work, and from time to time Zane glanced over toward Renzie, who was sitting down, drinking out of a bottle. As the sun rose slowly, the first rays of dawn threw a light across the horizon that outlined the mud flats. The moss in the cypress and oak trees seemed to shimmer like gold in the morning light. As the sun slowly climbed to its zenith in the blue sky, it burned like a torch so that even September's coolness fled away.

By noon both men's arms felt like lead,

but they continued to flail at the massive trunk. It was like chopping at rubber, for the dull axes seemed to rebound off the trunk.

Renzie was working himself up into a rage, and finally he got up and lumbered toward them, limbering his whip. He cursed loudly as he approached. His eyes glowed with a brutal pleasure as he swung the whip back and brought it down across Zane's bare back. The lash burned like fire, and Zane flinched but held back from crying out.

Renzie turned on Bennie with the whip, lashing Bennie like a crazy man. Bennie went down on the ground, pleading and begging, but to no avail. Zane had seen this before, and he felt sick as he watched the red stripes appear on Bennie's pale body and then begin to bleed.

Suddenly, without any provocation, Renzie reversed the butt of the whip and swung it with all his force, striking Bennie in the temple.

The crunching sound turned Zane's stomach sick, and he knew Bennie was dead. Suddenly, all the hate he had buried inside started to rise in him like a bursting dam that could not be stopped. The insanity that had been growing in him for months turned on Alf Renzie. The sight of his friend's pale body criss-crossed with stripes, the eyes open but staring at the open sky, pushed Zane over the edge. With a growl deep in his throat, he flung himself at Renzie, throwing his arms around him and dragging him down. He flailed at the thick body, and Renzie, caught off-guard, shouted and began struggling to get loose. Ordinarily, that would have been easy enough, for he was brutally strong, but he was wrestling with a man driven by rage who had waited for this moment far too long.

Zane pummeled Renzie's thick face. His blows closed an eye and loosened a tooth, but he also felt his strength ebbing. He knew he wouldn't last long against his opponent.

Renzie had been shocked at first, but now his cries of rage scored the air. He reached for the pistol in the holster and pulled it out. Zane locked both hands around the wrist. The pistol exploded, and Zane felt the fiery blow as if someone had struck him in the left side with an iron rod. He felt the burly guard turning the pistol to shoot him in the middle, and with one final burst of strength, Zane twisted the guard's hand around. The gun fired again, and Renzie uttered a surprised sound, and suddenly his body went limp.

Zane's face was not a foot away from Renzie's as he kept his hold on the man's arm. He saw Renzie's eyes staring at him in disbelief, and when he looked down, Zane saw a crimson flower of blood spreading over the man's stomach. He wrenched the gun out of the hand that held it loosely. Alf Renzie was sitting down, and his eyes went down to his stomach. He pressed on it as if trying to hold the crimson flood in, then looked up and whispered, "You done kilt me, boy."

Zane nodded, and a smile turned the corners of his lips. "Good! The best day's work I ever did. Go on and die. For all the men you've killed with that whip, you deserve to die." Zane stood there watching as the blood poured out of the big man.

Renzie slowly slid to the ground, as if he were preparing for a night's sleep. He muttered, "The sun's in my eyes." He put his arm over his face. Suddenly his body loosened, and his arm dropped toward the ground.

For a moment Zane stared at the body, and then turning, he went over to where Bennie Short lay exactly as he had fallen. Reaching out, Zane touched the boy's neck and felt the stillness of it. A bitterness welled up inside, and he glanced over at Renzie's body. "I wish I could have killed you a dozen times. You cheated me!" He laid his hand back on Bennie's hair for a moment and then said, "I hate to leave you with that scum, but I got to git."

He hesitated, then found Bennie's shirt, tore it into strips, and made a crude bandage. He picked up Renzie's cartridge belt and holster, belted it on, and then took the money Renzie had in his pocket and a fine, gold watch that Renzie was particularly proud of.

Zane moved over to the horse, mounted, and for one moment looked down with great sorrow at the body of his friend, Bennie Short. He shook his head and whispered, "I wish you were going with me, Bennie," then turned and kicked the horse into a dead run.

★ ★ ★

Rhys Morgan was sitting loosely on the seat of the wagon whistling a tune when suddenly the sound of a horse's cry came to him.

"Whoa, boys!" Pulling back on the reins, Rhys listened. For a timehe heard only the singing of birds in the top of a tall tree, whose heavy growth shielded the road from the sun.

And then it came again. "Well, that's something," Morgan said, as he had gotten into the habit of talking to himself. He jumped out of the wagon, secured the lines, and moved off into the undergrowth. He was no woodsman, but he could faintly smell wood smoke. As he continued making his way through the undergrowth, he heard the thrashing sound of a horse grunting.

Cautiously, he moved ahead, wishing that he were armed in some way. Then he caught a sudden motion up ahead and stood still for a moment. Moving forward slowly, he pushed his way through the brush until he saw a horse tied to a sapling.

"Whoa there, boy," he said as the horse whinnied as he approached. It was a fine animal, saddled, and Morgan searched the ground quickly. He saw nothing, and then when he glanced over to one side at the base of a large hickory, he saw the form of a man. He waited for a moment, for he did not like to wake a man up out of a sound sleep. It was too likely to get a man hurt. "Hello," he called softly and then more loudly. "Hello, are you awake?"

Rhys Morgan heard a faint moan. He walked over to the tree and saw that the man's shirt was off, and a bandage soaked with blood covered his chest and side. At the sight of a gun in the man's hand, he stopped dead still. "Having a bit of trouble, you are. Let me help you, but don't shoot."

The eyes of the man opened slowly, and Rhys saw that he was feverish from the look in his eyes. "You look to be in bad shape."

After a few seconds, the man whispered, "Yes, afraid so."

Rhys knelt down beside the man and said, "You're in poor condition here. What happened?"

"Had an accident."

The voice was faint, and Rhys shook his head. "Man, it's a doctor you need."

"I need to get to Texas."

"To Texas, is it? Well, I'm going that way myself, but you're in no condition to travel.

I'll get you in my wagon and take you to a doctor."

What's your name?"

"My name's Rhys Morgan."

"Reese?"

" It's really R-h-y-s, but people in this country can't spell it. And your name is?"

The man hesitated, but then he shrugged and said, "Zane Satterfield. I'm tryin' to get to my folks in Texas."

"Well, you can't ride a horse, but I've got a wagon. If I can get you into it, I'll do my best for you, Satterfield."

"Get me there, Morgan. If I pass out, put me on your shoulder like a sack of meal and bring that horse. He's a fine one."

Morgan helped him up and started back toward his wagon, with the horse trailing behind. They hadn't gone ten paces before Zane Satterfield passed out, and Morgan had to load him over his shoulder like a sack of meal. He was a smaller man than Rhys, shorter at least, but Zane's emaciated body was no trouble for him, for the Welshman was strong and able. When he got Satterfield into the wagon and had tied the horse on securely, Rhys looked down at the man and said, "Well, Lord, I think I need a little miracle here. And it comes to me, Lord, that it's not just his body that needs savin' but his soul. You know it better than I, Lord. You do your part, and I'll do mine."

He climbed up into the wagon, sat down, and slapped the lines on the team of mules. "Come you, mules. We've got to get this man to Texas. . . ."

CHAPTER
EIGHTEEN

Brodie watched with envy as Mateo gave some sort of invisible signal to his horse, leaned in the saddle, and as easy as breathing dropped the loop over the front legs of the moving longhorn. He stopped the mustang and the loop tightened, throwing the steer to the ground with a mighty *thump!*

Brodie ran forward and grabbed the head of the steer, avoiding the horns and yelling, "Come on, Clinton, slap that brand on him!" He held on until Clinton ran forward from the blaze that made a fiery dot on the open prairie, touched the end of the branding iron to the bellowing steer, and backed off.

"Let him go!" Clinton yelled as soon as he finished.

Brodie released his hold on the steer and, dodging a sweep of the mighty horns, plucked the lariat off the steer's legs and backed away. The steer jumped to his feet, gave him a malevolent look, then trotted off, bellowing his outrage.

Mateo sat on his horse grinning as he recoiled the rope. "That's about it for today, compadres."

"About time! That's not fair, Mateo," Brodie said. "You've got the easy part. You ought to have to get down in the dust and wrestle these critters."

Mateo, at seventeen, was slim but at the same time muscular. He shoved his hat back off his head, and his dark eyes gleamed as he laughed at Brodie. "When you learn how to drop a steer with your rope, I'll change places with you. Come on. Let's get to the house. I'm starving."

Brodie did not argue, but he and Mateo had to listen to Clinton's complaining again. Mateo and Brodie both ignored him as they gathered the branding irons, let them cool, and then wrapped them in a piece of rawhide. Clinton was twelve now and broad as his father, Jake. He had mastered the art of bellyaching until he was an expert at it.

Brodie and Clinton swung into their saddles, kicked their mustangs, and headed toward Mateo's adobe home. As they rode across the open prairie, Mateo glanced at Brodie and thought, *He's growing like a weed. Up, anyway. If he ever fills out, he'll be quite a man.* He had a fondness for Brodie. For the past two years they had seen each other every day. Brodie had helped to build the house that Mateo, his sister, and his mother lived in. Clay had seen to it that the two boys lent a hand whenever it was necessary. When they approached the adobe house built near the elbow of the Guadalupe and shaded by cottonwoods, the three dismounted, tied their horses, and entered.

Mateo's mother looked up from the stove, where she was making fresh maize tortillas, smiled, and said, "I believe I have three hungry men here."

"Hungry!" Clinton said loudly. "I'm so hungry I almost ate up my saddle! Whatever you got, señora, I don't care what it is. I hope there's plenty of it."

"You boys go and wash up. It's almost ready."

The three trooped out to the back, washed in the stream, and came back with faces glowing. When they returned, Brodie's eyes went at once to Serena, who was putting the food on the table. "Hello, Serena," he said. He was glad that his voice did not break, for at the age of sixteen, he was not too far into manhood to have forgotten how embarrassing that was.

"How many cattle did you brand today, Brodie?" Serena asked as she set down a plate of fresh hot tortillas.

She was now out of adolescence and becoming a pretty young woman. Her hair was black as coal, and her skin was so smooth. It was her eyes, however, that dominated her features—well-shaped, large, and a dark violet color that Brodie had never seen in anyone else.

"I don't know," he said. "I wasn't counting."

"About a hundred, I think," Clinton said loudly, plunking himself down in a chair. He picked up one of the tortillas, put it on his plate, and then reached out and began to dump the beans into it.

"Help yourself, Clinton," Lucita Lebonne said wryly. She loved these boys almost as much as her own. For the past two years, she had grown close to the entire Hardin family. "Everyone sit down and eat."

Mateo filled his plate with rice and beans, and listened as Clinton dominated the conversation. He smiled as he saw how Brodie never took his eyes off of Serena. *He's going to stick those beans in his ears,* he thought. *I never saw anyone so lovestruck in all my life.*

Lucita and Serena were both aware of Brodie's infatuation, and when the meal was over, Mateo teased Brodie gently about it. "I think you enjoy looking at my sister more than you enjoy the food," he said, winking at Serena.

Brodie flushed and dropped his head in embarrassment. Lucita came over and put her hand on his head, smoothing the cowlick back from his forehead. "You leave him alone, Mateo."

It was too late, however, for Brodie quickly stood up and said, "Thanks for the food." Without another word he left, motioning for Clinton to follow him.

"You shouldn't have teased him," Lucita said to Mateo.

"Well, I'm sorry, but he needs to learn that my sister will never marry an Anglo."

"I married one," his mother said.

"Things are different now," Mateo said shortly. "My sister will marry a rich Spaniard, and she needs to stay away from that lawyer, William Travis. Everyone knows he's got a wife in the States, and they know he's a woman chaser."

Serena suddenly flared up. "All he did was speak to me, Mateo!"

"You stay away from Anglos, you hear me?"

Lucita suddenly reached out and grabbed Mateo by the hair and pulled his head upward. "You have a home here because of an Anglo. If Clay had not helped us, where would we be?"

Mateo did not move but sat in his seat looking at his mother. For the last two years, he had watched her carefully and knew that she felt a special fondness for Clay.

"Mother, don't you ever think of marrying Clay Taliferro," he said.

Lucita stared at him, shocked that he had

said such a thing. "Don't be foolish! Now, get out of here."

When he left, she turned to Serena and said, "He's wrong about me and Clay, but he's right about William Travis. That man is no good for young women, or older ones either, for that matter. Ten cuidado con ese."

"I will be careful, Mamá. I care nothing for him," Serena said.

"And try to be kinder to Brodie."

"It would not be kind to show affection." Serena shrugged, then got up and began to clean the table. "I can't help it if he's in love with me. He'll just have to get over it."

Moriah cupped the baby rabbit in her hands and made cooing noises over it. She was fourteen now, but still as foolish over animals as ever. She stroked the smooth fur and said, "Look at him, Clay. He knows me."

"That's a good idea you got, honey, keepin' a rabbit. I always said we ought to start keepin' edible pets."

Moriah stared at Clay, her eyes open wide. "What do you mean, *edible* pets?"

Clay kept a straight face and leaned back in his chair against the side of the house. "I mean, get pets when they're little and cute, and then when they get big enough you can eat 'em. They serve two purposes, don't you see?"

"You're not going to eat this rabbit! I'm gonna keep him forever."

Clay laughed. "Why, Moriah, I think you'd make a pet out of a rattlesnake!"

Moriah gave him a baleful look and continued to pet the rabbit and shoot questions at Clay as fast as she could. It never ceased to amaze Clay how she could think of more questions than he could think of answers.

Moriah stopped petting the rabbit and looked up at Clay. "You think Mama will ever divorce Pa and get married again?"

As accustomed as Clay was to Moriah's abrupt shifts of thought, this one caught him completely off-guard. "Whatever made you think of such a thing?"

"Well, she ain't got no husband anymore, and you ain't got no wife. But she could divorce him, and then she could marry anybody. Why, she could even marry *you,* Clay."

Clay suddenly rose to his feet. "No, she won't never get no divorce."

At that instant Julie and Jerusalem came out of the house. They were preceded by Mary Aidan, who, at the age of thirty months, had learned the art of walking, then running and getting into everything. She ran to Clay and threw herself at him. If he had not caught her, she would have fallen flat on her face. "Watch out there, honey, you're gonna fall!"

Mary Aidan laughed. She was a happy baby, with her mother's red hair and green eyes, but with her Aunt Julie's exuberance and foolishness.

Julie watched the pair, then said impishly, "Husband, I'm going to town." She delighted in calling Clay "husband." When strangers were around, she would wrap her arms around him, pat his cheek, and kiss him. She loved to see how embarrassed he would get. When Clay did not answer but merely nodded, she said, "I may get drunk."

Jerusalem glanced quickly at Clay and saw that he was as angry at Julie's behavior as she was. "That's no way to talk, Julie, and it's no way to act either."

"Clay ought to beat me as a good husband would do," she said, smiling.

Jerusalem's face reddened. "I've had about enough of your foolishness, Julie. It's one thing to shame yourself, but it's another thing to shame Clay."

Julie stared straight at Clay and said, "He knows how to stop me."

Moriah had been taking all this in, and now she piped up. "You'd better stay away from William Travis. He's been flirtin' with Serena. Mateo says he'll shoot him if he ever touches her."

Clay suddenly straightened up and stared at Julie. "He'll have to get in line."

Clay and Julie remained staring at each other, their gazes locked. Finally, Julie said in a steely voice, "I'll see Travis or anybody else that I want!"

Jerusalem stared at the two, grieved. *I knew this would never work. I never should have let them carry on this pretense of being married.* But at that instant Moriah spoke up.

"Looky, a wagon's comin'. I don't know that man in it. Who is it, Clay?"

"I don't reckon I know him either." Clay had the best eyes on the ranch, and he stared at the approaching wagon. "He don't look dangerous, though."

When the wagon pulled up, the man driving it lifted his hat. Jerusalem said, "How do you do?"

"Hello, ma'am. My name is Rhys Morgan."

"Well, Mr. Morgan, won't you get down? You must be thirsty."

"I'm looking for the Hardin home."

"Well, you found it," Julie said. She moved away from Clay and studied the man. He was of middle height and appeared to be a strong man. He had a deep chest and a flat stomach, and he had dark hair and dark blue eyes. "What's your business, Mr. Morgan?" she asked.

"I'm a preacher."

Julie suddenly laughed. "Well, go no farther, Reverend! If you're looking for sinners to convert, here's a whole passel of sinners right at your fingertips."

"Pay her no mind, Reverend Morgan," Jerusalem said quickly. "I'm Mrs. Hardin. What can we do for you?"

Morgan jumped out of the wagon and came around, taking his hat off. "I have your brother here, Mrs. Hardin. He's been hurt real bad."

For an instant Jerusalem stood absolutely stunned. "You mean Zane?" she whispered.

"That's the name he gave me."

Jerusalem ran to the wagon, and Julie was right beside her. They peered down at the pale face of the man lying flat on his back, and Julie let out a cry. "It *is* Zane!"

Jerusalem said quickly, "What's wrong with him, Reverend?"

"He's been shot, and I think the wound is going bad on him with infection. I tried to find a doctor, but there wasn't one. Devil fly off! This is some country—no doctors!"

"Why do you talk so funny?" Moriah piped up, coming to look up into Morgan's face.

"Because I come from a different place."

"What place?"

"A place called Wales."

"Stop pestering the preacher, Moriah. Clay, you and Reverend Morgan bring Zane into the house. Julie, go get the bed ready."

Clay and Morgan were as careful as they could be, but Zane groaned several times as they carried him into the house. When they laid him down on the bed, Morgan stood back and shook his head. "I tried to get him to go to a town, but he wouldn't. I don't know why."

"I'll go to San Felipe and get Doctor Heilmeyer," Clay said instantly.

As soon as he left the room, Jerusalem said, "You look worn out, Mr. Morgan. You'd better stay with us. Julie, why don't you make him some food and fix him a bed in Clay's room. I'll take care of Zane."

Julie nodded. "This way, Reverend." She took him into the dining room and pointed to a seat. "You sit right there. I'll heat something up for you."

"Oh, that's not necessary. I didn't catch your name."

"Julie Taliferro." She hesitated over the last name. "That was my husband who went to get the doctor."

Ten minutes later Morgan was eating in a famished fashion. Julie sat across from him, and when he had finished, she began to question him. "What are you doing in a place like this?"

"Well, Mrs. Taliferro, I was born in Wales. I worked in the coal mines, and then got tired of that and came to America. I was leading quite a sinful life, but one day God used a man to show me the error of my ways. I got converted that night. After that He called me to preach the same freedom He had given me."

"Weren't there enough sinners in the rest of the country?"

"That's speakin' straight out. I felt the call of God to come to Texas."

"You won't be allowed to preach here. Everybody in these parts has to be Catholic."

"God will provide a way," Morgan said plainly.

Julie stared at the man and said, "You're a good-looking man for a preacher. You got a wife?"

"No, Mrs. Taliferro."

Julie smiled at him. "Let me tell you all of our family's secrets. My sister's name is Jerusalem. Her husband is living on the next place with an Indian woman and his kids. I'm supposed to be married to Clay Taliferro, but I'm really not. We just say that so we could get the title to the land. And you won't be here long before you find out that my sister is more than half in love with the man who's supposed to be my husband."

Rhys Morgan stared at her for a moment, and then a light of humor touched his dark blue eyes. "There is confused! I would say there's plenty of work for a minister in this part of the world."

"Like I say," Julie said and gave him a wicked smile, "there's no shortage of sinners in Texas."

For three days Zane was in a coma from the high fever. When he finally opened his eyes, he found his sister Jerusalem watching him. He reached out his hand and was shocked to find out how weak he was. "Well, sister, I made it."

"Reverend Morgan came hauling you in here three days ago. We all thought you were going to die. Reverend Morgan says God healed you. I think he may be right. How'd you get shot?"

"It's a sad story, Jerusalem. I'd rather not get into it right now," Zane said, his voice weak.

Jerusalem put her hand on his forehead. "Your fever has gone down."

"I haven't heard from you since Ma died. I was surprised when I got your letter saying you were moving to Texas. Is everybody well?"

"Do you remember seeing Julie?"

"No."

"She's been helpin' to tend to you. She's a wild girl, just as she always was. Josiah's still alive."

"I thought he'd be gone long ago."

"He's not himself, Zane. He's harmless enough, but he just . . . he just seems to go to a different world with his thoughts from time to time and sits smiling at people, not saying a thing."

"Sorry to hear that. He was always a favorite with me."

"Jerusalem paused. I've got another baby now—Mary Aidan."

"And Jake? I guess he's about as usual?"

"No, he's not. He's got an Indian wife now. He lives close by, but we don't have anything to do with each other."

Zane saw the sorrow that marked the lines on Jerusalem's face. "I reckon things have gone downhill with all of us, sister."

CHAPTER
NINETEEN

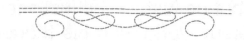

A thought came to Jerusalem as she pinned one of Brodie's shirts on the clothesline. She looked up into the steel gray sky. Removing the clothespin from her mouth, she spoke aloud her thought: "Well, here you are, 1834. I sure hope you're better than last year." She waited as if the sky could speak back, then shook her head. "I'm talking to myself now. That's the last stage, I reckon."

She hung up the rest of the wet clothes and turned to go to the house, but looking up she saw a wagon coming down the road. It had rained slightly the night before, so no dust arose as it did in the hot, dry summers.

She recognized Rhys Morgan and waited until he pulled up in front of the house. He jumped out, walked over to her, and removed his hat.

"Hello, Jerusalem," he said. "I think we have got some bad weather headed this way."

As always, Jerusalem was glad to see Rhys Morgan. It had been two months since he had brought Zane back, and in that time he had covered more ground preaching than any other man in Texas. He stood before her now, his black hair falling down over his forehead in a curly lock, and smiled at her. He was a cheerful young man of twenty-one, well-built and neatly dressed. *He's fine-looking, but he doesn't know it.* Jerusalem had thought this before, and now she said, "Come along. I heard a rumor that preachers like fried chicken. Anything to it?"

Rhys patted his stomach. "I've got a fried chicken graveyard down here, ma'am, but plenty of room for one more."

Jerusalem carried the basket to the porch, and as they walked around the house, Rhys spoke of his travels. He was not allowed to hold meetings, for Protestants were forbidden by law to do such in

Mexico, or in Texas for that matter. Still, he had made a habit of simply stopping by houses, and Protestants who had agreed to become Catholic gathered with neighbors and held services.

Reaching the backyard, Jerusalem stepped inside the fence. She'd had to fence the chickens in because of the coyotes, foxes, and other varmints. Now she stood in the middle and clucked to the chickens, tossing them some grain she kept in a can on top of a post. They came running and surrounded her in a flurry of feathers, clucking and pecking at the grain. For a moment she was undecided, then she waded through the bunch to find a mottled hen and reached down and picked her up.

Rhys opened the gate for her as she stepped outside, and he grinned, saying, "Why did you wade through all the rest to get to that one? It almost makes a man believe in predestination."

"I only kill the stupid ones," she said, laughing.

Jerusalem wrung the chicken's neck with one quick twist and stood there watching as it flopped around wildly for a few seconds. Jerusalem had a way of making odd statements and changing the subject, and she turned to Morgan and said, "The boys were breaking the garden, and they found some bones in it. Somebody was buried there."

"You know, I thought about that myself. With all the miles I've covered these last few weeks, I saw dried bones from buffalo and wild animals, and also people too." A strange look came into his eyes. "You know, maybe right now, Jerusalem, we're standing on the bones of a man and woman who fell in love and died together and were buried right under our feet."

Jerusalem turned to face Morgan. "You're too romantic to be a preacher."

"Oh, I don't think so. I think preachers should be romantic."

"Some of them are a mite *too* romantic, if the rumors you hear are true."

"You mean me?"

"Oh, of course not, Rhys. Just in general."

"Well, preachers should be romantic in a sense, believing in things that you can't see. That's romanticism. That's being romantic."

"You are one strange preacher, Rhys Morgan." Jerusalem suddenly laughed. "Go and talk to Josiah while I dress this chicken."

All the while Jerusalem was frying the chicken, she paid close attention to Rhys, who had sat beside her grandfather. It was one of Josiah's clear-minded days, and he talked quietly, answering Rhys's questions. She was glad when Morgan brought up the subject of faith in God.

"Have you ever met the Lord, Josiah?" Morgan asked in a nonoffensive way.

Josiah nodded quickly and said, "I did at a revival meeting back in Arkansas. I got plumb downright converted. Right to the core."

A real gladness filled Jerusalem's heart as she heard her grandfather describe how he had come to faith. As she continued to prepare the meal, she noticed that Mary Aidan had climbed right up on Morgan's lap. She called out, "Mary Aidan, don't pester the preacher."

Mary Aidan paid no attention at all to her mother. She sat bolt upright, staring into Morgan's face.

"Does she always stare at everyone like this?" Rhys asked. He reached out and touched the child's smooth face and shook his head. "You certainly never met a stranger, Mary Aidan."

"I don't know why she does that," Josiah murmured. "She looks at people as if she was trying to look right down inside of 'em. I think she's tryin' to figure people out."

"She does too," Jerusalem said as she brought a platter of fried chicken over to the table. "She knows people better than most grownups."

"Well, I wish I did," Rhys said. "Be nice for a preacher to have that gift. That way I'd know just what to tell them so they'd open their hearts and let God fill 'em with His love."

The three of them sat down, and Mary Aidan insisted on sitting on Morgan's lap. When Jerusalem tried to remove her, she clung to him and said "No!" in a very determined tone.

"Let her stay there. I'll give her a bite of chicken once in a while to keep her good." As Rhys began to eat, he said, "Tell me all about the family. How are they doing?"

"I don't have good news about Julie," Jerusalem said and shook her head, sadness marring her features. "She's been going into town, San Antonio and San Felipe. She's even got a room in San Antonio, where she stays. I hate to think about what she's doing, but I guess I pretty well know." She looked up and said, "Rhys, why don't you talk to her?"

"I have," Rhys admitted, "but she just laughed at me."

Jerusalem studied him for a moment. "Or flirted with you, I'd guess."

Rhys colored slightly. "Well, I guess you know your sister pretty well. A little of that, I guess."

When Rhys finished his meal, he got up, put Mary Aidan down, and said, "I think I'll go over and visit the Lebonnes."

Jerusalem nodded. "That's good. Those youngsters are growing up so fast." She walked with him to the door, and when he stepped out and put on his hat, she said, "Don't visit with Lucita unless the kids are there."

Rhys blinked. "Why's that?"

"People talk, Rhys. Haven't you discovered that?"

"I guess you're right. I'll be careful. Thanks for the meal."

"Come back tonight and preach at us a little bit. We can all use it."

"I'll do that."

As soon as Brodie walked in, Jerusalem saw that something was troubling him. She could always read his mind as if he had a piece of plate glass over his forehead. She knew it bothered Brodie a great deal, for he could keep nothing from her. When he sat down at the table, she gave him a chicken leg and said, "That's all you get before supper. Now, what's bothering you?"

Taking a huge bite out of the chicken leg, Brodie chewed it and then said reluctantly, "It's Uncle Zane."

"What's he gone and done now?"

"Mateo said he got into a fight with a man over cards and beat him up pretty bad. They put him in jail. He's out now."

"He hasn't changed. He was getting into

trouble like that when he was not much older than you."

"He sure is tough. Mateo said the man he whipped was the roughest man in San Felipe."

Instantly Jerusalem said, "Don't model yourself on Zane, Brodie."

Startled, Brodie looked up and blinked. "Why, I . . . I—"

"I know young boys admire tough men, but I don't want you to turn out like your Uncle Zane."

Brodie was about to answer when they heard the sound of horse's hooves. Moving over to the door, Jerusalem said, "It's Clay, and Jim Bowie's with him." Turning back to Brodie, she said, "Don't model yourself after Jim Bowie either, or that William Travis."

"Why not?"

Jerusalem did not answer but went to open the door. When the men came in, she greeted them. "Hello, Clay." Turning to Bowie, she nodded, "Hello, Mr. Bowie."

Mary Aidan ran straight for Clay and threw herself at him, crying out, "Papa!"

Clay caught her, and his face turned red. "Brodie, you taught this child to call me that!"

"I did no such thing!" Brodie said indignantly. "She just thought it up all by herself."

Jim Bowie was smiling, but Jerusalem could tell he was not happy. She knew he was pretending so nobody would know the grief that still ate at him. Jerusalem had been concerned ever since Jim had lost his entire family the previous year—wife, daughter, and son—in a cholera epidemic. She knew the devastating loss had nearly killed him, and she also knew that he drank too much to try to forget. "Come inside. I've got what's left of a chicken fried up. The good parts are mostly gone, but you can finish off what's left."

"Sounds good, Mrs. Hardin," Bowie said.

Every time Jim Bowie came around, Brodie would stop everything he was doing, as he did now, just to listen to him. The tales of Jim Bowie's wild deeds were known by everybody in Texas. And Brodie was hoping to hear another one.

The two men sat down, and Mary Aidan stared up into Clay's face with the same rapt attention that she had given to Morgan. Clay stared back at her and shook his head. "I don't know what this child is thinking. I'm afraid for her to grow up. She's gonna be one mighty discerning woman."

"Not hard to discern you, Clay," Jerusalem said. "You're the easiest man to read I ever saw."

"I am not!" Clay protested. "I've had women call me plumb mysterious."

Jerusalem sniffed. "Women! A lot you know about women. Never mind him, Mr. Bowie. Tell us what's going on. We never get news way out here."

Bowie had started in on the chicken, but he paused long enough to shake his head, and his face turned gloomy. "I don't have any good news. Steve Austin has been arrested by the Mexican government."

"Arrested!" Jerusalem stopped and turned from the stove, where she was taking out a fresh biscuit. "Arrested for what?"

"You remember that assembly they had at San Felipe last year? Well, they sent Steve Austin there to take our grievances. They paid no more attention to him than if he was an armadillo! So he cooled his heels, and finally he wrote a pretty hot letter back home. When he started back, somebody turned that letter over to the authorities. So now they're holdin' him in jail."

"They can't do that legally, can they?" Clay asked.

"They don't worry too much about legality down in Mexico. But I'll tell you one thing that they did at that assembly. They wrote a constitution. And you know why they done that? Because most of the people I know think one day Texas is gonna be taken in as a state. That's the way you do it. You give it a constitution."

"I hear Sam Houston's big on that," Clay remarked.

"Well, he was President Andy Jackson's righthand man. Fought for him in the Indian wars. Jackson thinks there's nobody like Houston. Everybody's startin' to rally around Sam."

"What kind of a man is he?" Jerusalem asked. "I've never seen him."

"Well, he's a big man. Two or three inches taller than me, and seems even bigger than that," Bowie said.

"He got in some kind of scandal, didn't he?" Jerusalem asked. "I remember reading something about it."

"When he was governor of Tennessee, he married a pretty young girl. Nobody knows why, but she left him after a few weeks.

Stories started going around, and Sam resigned from being governor. Went to live with the Cherokee Indians for three years. They called him The Big Drunk, or something like that."

"But he's practicin' law here in Texas now, isn't he?"

"Yes, he is, and everybody's got their eye on him. If trouble comes, he's the one we want on our side."

The talk ran around the table, mostly between Clay and Jim Bowie, and finally Jim said slowly, "That fellow Santa Anna is not gonna be satisfied until he runs every Anglo out of Texas."

"Why, I thought that scamp was on our side!" Clay said with astonishment.

"He was, but he changes his politics more often than a man changes his socks. Sam says we'll have to fight Santa Anna if we're gonna stay here, and I think he's right."

A silence fell over the room, and Jim looked around at the gloomy faces. "I hate to be the bearer of bad tidings, but sooner or later we'll have to fight if we want to stay in this country."

★ ★ ★

Evening had come now, and the wind had died down, but the night air was chilly. Jerusalem put on her heavy coat and left the house. She walked fifty yards away and stood staring up at the sky. It was clear, and the stars winked as if signaling a secret. She was startled when she heard Clay's voice behind her.

"Are you all right, Jerusalem?"

Jerusalem did not turn around. She was a strong woman and had borne her share of troubles, but all day long she had been struggling with a dark depression that she could not explain.

Suddenly, she bowed her head and put her fist against her mouth to choke back the sobs. But as hard as she tried not to cry in front of Clay, she couldn't stop the emotion that welled up inside her. Her shoulders began to shake and soon she was weeping loudly.

Clay stood there astonished. For months he had seen her face troubles with a strength most women did not have. Jerusalem was not a crying woman. But now he felt helpless and afraid for her. He stepped up and put his arm around her but said nothing. She turned to him, and her body sagged so that she almost fell. Her face was pressed against his shoulder, and he felt the tremors in her body. As much as he wanted to say something to comfort her, he could not think of one single thing to say. So he stood there holding her, not understanding what had broken her like this.

Finally, Jerusalem straightened up, reached into the pocket of her coat, pulled out a bandanna and wiped her face. After a moment she turned to him, and he saw the light of the silver moon reflected in her eyes.

"Most men would have left a weepy woman to herself. Thanks for staying, Clay."

"What's wrong? Something I don't know about?"

"It's everything. I'm worried about Zane. It seems every time he goes to town, he gets drunk and into a fight. And Julie . . . I . . . I don't even know what to say. Both of them are so lost. Brodie's unhappy. He thinks he's in love with Serena, but she doesn't seem to care for him. I don't have a husband, Clay, and the country's falling apart all around us with everyone wanting to control this land." She shook her head sadly. "I wish things would go wrong one at a time, but they never do."

Clay had learned to admire this woman's strength. Now that he saw that it wasn't limitless, he stood in front of her, wishing he could help.

"You know what troubles me, Clay, and it's so foolish."

"Tell me. Maybe I can help."

"No, you really can't. I miss the boys that I buried back in Arkansas Territory. I've told myself a thousand times that they're not really *there*. I know in my heart that they're with God. But when we lived there, every time I would get sad, I would go out and sit in that cemetery. I don't know why it was, but somehow it helped me. Every time you sing that song about the woman in New Orleans, I think of them. But I've got my boys deep in my heart, like the song says. Nobody can take that away from me!"

Clay did not speak, and Jerusalem shook her head and dashed the tears from her eyes. "I'm a foolish woman, Clay Taliferro. I don't know why you put up with me. Nobody else would."

She turned and walked away so abruptly that Clay was startled. He followed her, but she went into the house. When she didn't come back out, he stayed out on the porch. He sat down in the chair, tilted it back, and watched the moon and stars that dotted the sky. The stars, bright as they were, seemed cold like ice, and it troubled him that Jerusalem Hardin could hurt so much.

CHAPTER
TWENTY

At some point liquor stopped making Julie Satterfield feel good and brought up a mean streak in her that disgusted her. As she sat slumped in a chair in Pete Border's saloon, she knew she had passed that mark some time ago. All around her flowed the sound of raucous men who had come to Pete Border's place to get drunk. The room reeked from the smell of stale tobacco smoke, wine, raw whiskey, and unwashed bodies. Most of the men who sat at the tables scattered around the room were dressed in animal skins or sweat-faded Eastern clothes. Few of them were shaved, and their faces were raw from windburn and the alcohol they poured down their throats day after day. Almost all of them wore pistols and knives. A hand touched her knee, and reaching down, Julie grabbed the little finger and bent it back with all her force.

"Ow! Blast, Julie, you almost broke my finger!" The man sitting beside Julie was Jack Catchall, better dressed than most, for he was able to afford it. He was one of the many land speculators who had flooded into Texas to make money. Now he sat there glaring at Julie, holding on to his finger. "What'd you go and do that for?"

"If I want you to put your hands on me, Jack, I'll let you know."

Catchall stared at her, anger bringing a flush to his face. He had a thick moustache and thin, brown hair, which he combed over the top of his head to try to cover a bald spot. He had a habit of brushing it continually, and now he tried to smile. "You shouldn't try to break a feller's finger just for being friendly, Julie." He brushed his moustache again and leaned closer. "After all, there aren't that many pretty women like you out here."

Julie turned and watched Catchall brush

his moustache. It was thick and droopy and covered his lower lip completely. "Is that a moustache, or are you trying to eat a muskrat, Jack?" Julie laughed as Catchall blinked and his face flushed. "You ought to cut that thing off, or I'll do it for you if you like. Let me borrow your knife, Charlie."

Charlie Hillhouse, seated across from Julie, pulled out a huge bowie knife and said, "Here. You want me to hold him for ye?"

"Put that pig sticker away, Charlie," Catchall snapped.

Hillhouse laughed and put the knife back in the sheaf at his side. Then picking up a bottle, he filled the three glasses with whiskey.

"I t-think I've had enough," Julie slurred.

"There ain't never enough whiskey," Charlie said. He was a huge, brawny man, with a broad face and a thick neck. He wore buckskins, and a livid scar marked the left side of his face, running from his eyebrow to under his collar. He tossed the liquor off as if it were water and then filled the glass up again.

"Who's that, Charlie?" Catchall said. "Never seen him before."

"Don't know. He looks like a lawyer, don't he now?"

Julie turned in the direction of the door and saw Rhys Morgan coming through the door. She sat up straighter, and her lips drew together in a tight line. She was drunk enough that she did not want to talk to him, but she said, "That's Rhys Morgan. He's a preacher."

Hillhouse grinned. "A preacher! How come you know him, Julie? I don't reckon you spend a lot of time in church."

"What's he doin' in here?" Catchall said.

"He's looking for me." Julie took the bottle, poured her glass full, and held it up as Rhys crossed the floor. Everyone in the saloon had turned to watch him, but when he reached the table where Julie was, his face was pleasant and he made no mention of Julie being drunk.

"Hello, Julie," he said.

"What do you want, Rhys?"

"I would like to have a talk with you."

"She's busy," Catchall said. "Are you blind or somethin'?"

Julie drank the whiskey off and slammed the glass down on the table. "I don't want to talk to you," she said, knowing it would do no good. She had learned that Rhys Morgan was always kind, but when he got a notion in his head, he had a stubborn streak.

"It won't take but a few minutes, Julie, if you'd just come outside."

"You go outside. I'm staying here."

Charlie Hillhouse laughed, but there was no humor in it. "Mister, I can't stand preachers. Get out of here before I bust you up."

"I wish you wouldn't do that. All I want is a talk with this lady."

"You got a hearing problem, Preacher?" Hillhouse said, his face turning red with anger. "Get out of here!"

"I just came from talking to your sister, Julie," Rhys said. "I thought you might like to know how everyone's doing."

"If I want to know, I'll go to the house and find out for myself. Now leave. This is no place for you."

"Oh, I've been in lots of saloons like this with plenty of whiskey. And I always woke up the next day with a splitting head. But the Lord showed me that life was more than getting drunk all the time. He delivered me from all that." He looked around and surveyed the room with interest. "All you fellas need to give your hearts to the Lord."

Charlie Hillhouse stood up so abruptly his chair fell over. He came around the table swiftly for a big man and cursed as he, without warning, threw a roundhouse right that would have knocked Morgan flat out if it had landed.

Julie cried out, "Leave him alone, Charlie!" But it was too late. Whenever he got drunk, he would get angered by the least little thing. She had seen Hillhouse demolish two men already in fights in the last week. And after he had pummeled them to the ground with his huge fists, he'd had no compunction about kicking them repeatedly.

Amazingly, the second blow did not connect either. Rhys simply moved his head a couple of inches. The punch went over him, and the force of Hillhouse's rush drove him forward. Rhys stepped aside and let the big man lumber by.

"Bust him up, Charlie!" Jack Catchall said. "We didn't send for no preacher to spoil our fun."

Julie started to get up, but Jack grabbed her arm. "Let him alone, Julie. I ain't seen a preacher whipped in quite a spell. This is gonna be good."

Julie struggled to break free, but at the same time she kept her eyes on the two men. Hillhouse was incensed that he had missed again. And now he came back more carefully, eyeing Rhys with a calculated look filled with more anger.

"I'm gonna mess you up real good, Preacher," he said. His eyes looked red under the yellow lantern, and he made a fearsome sight, for he had huge muscles that bulged against the leather shirt he wore. He swung again, but this time he took more care. But once again he could not land the blow on Rhys. "Why don't you stand still? What are you, some kind of a dancing master?"

"I'd rather not have any trouble," Morgan said. But at the same time, he lifted his hands with fists closed. "I'll just step outside if my presence bothers you."

"You ain't steppin' nowhere!" Hillhouse roared and rushed again.

Julie did not see exactly what happened. Morgan's hands moved too fast. They seemed to be pumping, and she heard a *splat!—splat!—splat!* as three blows caught the big man in the face. The first one stopped Charlie dead in his tracks, and the second and third drove him backward so that he fell full-length on his back. Everyone in the whole saloon gasped at the sight of Hillhouse sprawled out on the floor. They'd never seen him take a blow before in all the fights they'd watched. He stared up dazed. His right eyebrow was split open, and blood was running down his face and over his shirt. He seemed confused and shook his head, wiping the blood from his face.

"Quit foolin' around with him, Charlie!" Catchall called out.

Hillhouse slowly got to his feet. He stood staring at Morgan. "What'd you hit me with?"

"Nothing but my fists," Morgan said. "Come on, Charlie, let's quit this foolishness before somebody gets hurts."

"Grab him, boys; he's too slick!" Hillhouse shouted.

Julie watched helplessly as several men rushed forward and grabbed Morgan, holding him as Charlie stepped in front of him, sneering with rage.

Hillhouse laughed and said, "Here, see how this fist suits you." He struck Morgan square in the face with a powerful blow that drove the preacher's face around. Then Hillhouse began to pummel him repeatedly with his huge, meaty fists.

"Let him alone, Charlie, you'll kill him!" Julie called out.

"I aim to!" Charlie said as he punched Morgan in the face again.

Julie reached over suddenly with her left hand and pulled the revolver out of Jack Catchall's belt. She aimed it carefully at Charlie and pulled the trigger. The explosion rocked the saloon.

Hillhouse yelled and stepped back, reached up and grabbed his ear, which was bleeding. "You shot me!"

"The next one will be right in your stupid head, Charlie! Now, everybody back off!" she yelled.

As the men who were holding Morgan upright released him, he slumped to the floor, his face bleeding.

Julie stepped around, and her eyes were flashing. "All right, Charlie, you and Harry there pick him up."

"Pick him up! What for?"

"Take him to my room." When Hillhouse

hesitated, Julie pulled the hammer back and aimed right in his face.

"Wait a minute! Be careful with that thing," Hillhouse said.

"Come on, Harry, pick him up—now!" Julie ordered.

Julie followed the two men as they carried Morgan's limp body outside. Turning, she said, "I'll keep the gun in case I have to shoot Charlie." She turned then and left, and the saloon at once burst into loud talk.

Pete Borders, who had watched the whole thing, came over and sat down beside Catchall. He was a small man with a dark face and black hair. "I think she'd have shot him, Jack."

"I think so, too." Catchall shook his head. "She sure is a hard woman to figure."

Julie leaned over and mopped Rhys Morgan's face with a damp cloth. "Well, congratulations, you're not dead." Rhys blinked his eyes and tried to sit up, but Julie put her hand on his chest. "You lie down there. You're in no shape to be getting up after the beating you just took from Charlie."

Rhys licked his lips, then said, "Where am I? How'd I get here?"

"Well, you sure didn't walk here. I made Charlie and one of his thugs carry you." Julie put her hand on his head and turned Morgan's head sideways. "I don't guess you'll need any stitches, but you're lucky you still have all your teeth. I've seen Charlie knock a feller's teeth right out with one blow."

"Let me sit up," Morgan said.

"No, you need to stay there for a little bit and rest."

Rhys lay still for a time. He looked around and commented, "This is a nice room. Is it yours?"

"Yes."

The room was nicer than usual for Texas. He had been in a lot of homes on his travels that didn't have much of anything, just the bare essentials. Julie's room contained a settee, a rocking chair, a dressing table with a mirror over it, and a bed with a colorful quilt that was pushed back to make room for the reverend. "I messed your bed up,"

Rhys muttered. Reaching up, he touched his face and winced. "I can't open my eye."

"It's all swollen shut. I been puttin' cold wet packs on it, but I imagine it'll stay closed for a day or two until the swelling goes down."

Morgan shook his head and suddenly sat up. "I thought I heard somebody shooting."

"That was me. If I hadn't put a bullet in that ornery Charlie Hillhouse, he might have killed you. He's done it before, you know."

"You shot him?"

"Just a piece of his ear. He's so mean nothin' would kill him but a slug between his eyes. How do you feel?"

Morgan smiled lopsidedly. "Wonderful. Thanks for saving my life."

"You're a fool, Rhys Morgan! Why didn't you leave when you had the chance?"

"I needed to talk to you."

Julie moved over, sat down on the bed, and stared at him. "Talk about what?"

"About your family. They're worried about you—and so am I."

"I'm none of your concern," she said as she got up to get more cold, wet cloths.

"Why, sure you are, Julie," Morgan said.

"So, now I guess you've come to preach at me."

"That's my business, but I don't guess you'd listen, would you?"

"No."

"I just want to tell you that Jesus is the best friend you'll ever have. You can go to all the saloons you want, but you're not going to find anything that can match what He can give you."

"I don't want to hear it, Rhys." She came back over toward the bed and reached out and put her hands behind his neck, locking her fingers. A wicked smile came to her lips. "You know, even beat up like you are, you're a handsome fella. If you weren't a preacher, maybe you and I could get to know each other better."

Rhys shook his head and pulled her hands loose. "That's mighty tempting, but I guess I'll be moving along now," he said, then quickly stood up. He moved over toward the door and stopped. "Where's my hat?"

"Back in the saloon, but I wouldn't go back for it, if I was you."

"I guess I won't." Rhys hesitated. "I want to be your friend, Julie."

Julie stared at Rhys Morgan, and then

something passed over her face. "I've had men want to be my *friend* before."

Rhys shrugged. "I'll be seeing your family tomorrow. Anything I can tell them?"

"Tell them I said not to send you to see me anymore, and if you know what's good for you, you'll stay out of saloons. I'm not always going to be there to save your hide."

Rhys grinned and said, "I'll be coming back. Good evening to you, Miss Julie."

As soon as Rhys closed the door, Julie sat down on her bed and started to tremble. It was not liquor, she knew that, but rather what Rhys Morgan had said that disturbed her. She did not want to think about it. She went to the window and watched Rhys as he mounted his wagon and drove away.

"The crazy fool could have been killed," she said aloud, then turned away abruptly from the window.

Jerusalem had been thinking about Julie, for Rhys had told her he'd gone and visited her. When Jerusalem saw his battered face, he had laughed and said he had run into a "little" trouble, but it was nothing to worry about. The thought bothered her, but before she could ask him anything else, she heard a knock at the door. The next thing she knew, the door flew open and Jake stepped inside and came over to where she stood.

"I gotta talk to you, Jerusalem."

"All right, Jake. You want to sit down?"

"No, this won't take long."

Jerusalem studied this man who had been her husband for so many years. In many ways he was like a stranger to her now. He had been gone from her life more than he had been with her. Now she saw something was troubling him, and she couldn't imagine what it was. "Somebody sick, Jake?"

"No, it ain't that, but I come to ask a favor."

"What kind of a favor?"

"I've got to go to Santa Fe."

"Why would you be going there?"

"I've always thought I might like to get into the freightin' business. I heard of a fellow there who wants to sell out. The thing is, I want to ask you to keep an eye on Awinita."

Jerusalem had heard that Awinita was pregnant, and she was honestly concerned for the woman. "You're going off and leave her at a time like this?" Jerusalem said bluntly.

Jake's eyes shifted, for he could not meet her gaze. "I've got to go. Will you look out for her?"

As much as she wanted to tell him he hadn't changed, she knew it would fall on deaf ears. "Yes, I'll see to it."

"Thanks. I knowed you'd do it." Jake started to go. He put his hat on his head and then turned to face her. "Why don't you get a divorce, Jerusalem? I won't fight it."

"I can't do that, Jake."

"I don't reckon we'll ever be together again. You might as well have another man."

"Good-bye, Jake. I'll look after Awinita and the kids."

Jake stared at her and then, without another word, turned and left the house. Jerusalem went to the window and watched him go. As he rode away, she thought, *He'll always be riding away from whatever woman he's with.*

★ ★ ★

Brodie was saddling up alongside his great-grandfather and listening to him talk. He was always happy when Josiah had one of his good days, and this morning the old man's eyes were bright and clear. He was reminiscing about his earlier days for a long time after breakfast while Brodie did his chores. The old man was fascinating to listen to, for he had known some of the heroes of the Revolution. It made Brodie sad whenever his great-grandfather lost the light in his eyes and his mind seemed to wander to another distant time in the past. But today was not one of those days, and Brodie was hanging on to every word as Josiah told another story about George Washington.

Brodie slipped the bridle onto his horse. As he was fastening it, he turned and said, "Grandpa, can I ask you something?"

"Why, shore, boy. Anything you'd like."

"You think you'll go to heaven?"

Josiah laughed heartily. "Why, boy, I'm plumb sartain of it."

"That's good. Maybe I'll get saved someday."

"You'd better, boy! 'Cause the Bible says the other option ain't too appealing."

"What do you think heaven will be like?"

Brodie started leading the horse over to where Clay was mounting up.

Clay turned to listen as Josiah said, "Heaven? Well, I've studied on that a heap, son. I think it's gonna be green fields and high mountains with pretty white snow on top of 'em. And there'll be clear streams ten feet deep that look like they're a foot deep, just like the Yellowstone."

Brodie saw that Clay was listening, and he said, "The Bible says it'll be golden streets. You think that's so?"

"I don't care nothin' about them golden streets. Never was a town man. What I really think, boy, is that if Jesus is there, He'll make it all right. If you got Him, you don't need anything else." Josiah reached out and slapped Brodie on the shoulder with his hand, still strong after eighty-five years of living. "Don't miss heaven, boy." He glanced over and winked, "You, too, Clay."

Brodie stepped easily into the saddle and said, "Good-bye, Grandpa. Tonight maybe you can tell me some more about that heaven of yours."

"I'll do 'er, boy. I'll do 'er."

Brodie spurred his horse, and as he galloped off beside Clay, he said, "You reckon that stuff about heaven is for real?"

"I ain't no expert on heaven, Brodie, but your great-grandpa's a pretty smart man."

Brodie said no more, lost in thought as the two rode over the ridge. He looked back once and saw his great-grandfather waving at him. Brodie waved back and then turned, and the horses plunged down the ridge, and the house was lost to view.

Clinton watched the cork carefully, and when it went under with a noisy plunk, he yanked up and tried to pull the fish out. "It's a whale!" he yelled. "It's a whale, Anthony Wayne!"

The big dog began barking in staccato fashion, and when finally Clinton dragged the fish to shore, the dog came over and sniffed it cautiously. The fish flopped, and Anthony barked and jumped back.

"Reckon that's all the fish we'll need to feed us. Boy, he is a beauty, ain't he, Anthony Wayne?"

Clinton put the fish on the stringer and the pole over his shoulder. "Let's go home," he said. "I hate to clean these things, but they'll sure taste good tonight."

Clinton felt satisfied with himself, for he had managed to get out of doing chores long enough to come fishing. His mother had agreed, saying, "I got a taste for a bit of fish myself. If you don't catch any, though, don't come draggin' back here."

Clinton had seen the twinkle in her eye and quickly ran off to the river before she thought of any more chores for him.

"She'll be mighty glad to see these, Anthony Wayne," Clinton said as he headed back toward the house.

The big dog suddenly stopped dead still and lifted his head, sniffing the air. "What is it? What you got, boy?"

Anthony Wayne bared his teeth, and a snarl came from deep in his throat. He threw himself forward at a dead run, and Clinton said, "Hey, wait a minute!" He galloped after the racing dog, running clumsily with the pole in one hand and the fish in the other. He had never seen Anthony Wayne take off like that. "Somethin's got him mad," Clinton gasped. He came to the rise of the hill, and when he topped the crest, he halted as if he had run into a wall.

Down below, a group of Indians was approaching the house. They were wearing war paint, and at that instant the door to the house opened and Josiah stepped outside, carrying a rifle. In one smooth motion, he leveled it and shot one of the Indians off his horse.

Clinton's legs seemed to turn to jelly. He had heard stories about the fearful Comanches, and he knew somehow, without being told, that these were the ones he had been afraid of. He cried out, "Grandpa!" as the Indians rushed toward him. One of them had fallen when Josiah had swung his rifle like a club, but two of them jumped him, bearing him backward. Clinton saw the tomahawk rise and fall, and suddenly he vomited. When he straightened up, the Indians were pouring into the house. One of them stopped to shoot Anthony Wayne, and he fell dead at Josiah's feet.

"Ma!" Clinton cried out and started toward them. But he knew that would be useless. There was nothing he could do. Dropping the fish and the pole, he turned and ran along the line of the hill, staying out of the Indians' sight. He was crying and did not know it as he raced along toward the pastures where he knew Clay and Brodie would be.

Brodie looked up and blinked. "There comes Clinton on foot."

Clay turned and took one look. "Somethin's wrong, boy."

Clay spurred his horse into a fast run, and Brodie followed. He heard Clinton calling his name, and he piled off his horse. Clinton could hardly speak. His breath came in great gasps.

"Indians! They killed Grandpa!" he blurted out, tears running down his face.

Instantly, Clay jumped on his horse and galloped off toward the house, and Brodie yelled, "Wait on me!" He mounted and got Clinton on behind him. Clinton was holding him so tightly he could hardly breathe. "Are they all dead, Clinton?" Brodie cried, but Clinton did not answer. Brodie spurred his horse to a dead run. He could not catch up with Clay, but when they crested the ridge, the house was on fire. He pulled up, and even before he got down, he saw Josiah lying on the porch face up. He had been tomahawked and scalped. The rest of his family was gone.

"Let's get this fire out quick!" Clay called out.

The boys piled off, but Clinton simply sat down and could not move. The fire had been started in the living area, but Clay and Brodie put it out quickly.

Clay stepped outside and said, "They've taken the horses and the rifles. Brodie, I want you to go get Mateo and his family. They'll take care of your grandpa."

"What are you going to do?" Brodie asked, his mind numb.

Clay did not answer. He ran inside the house and came out, buckling on his cartridge belt with his six-shooter in it and holding his Hawkin rifle. "They missed this one," he said with grim satisfaction.

"I'm going with you," Brodie cried.

"No, you're not. You do what I tell you, you hear."

"We got to get a bunch together, Clay, and go after them."

"By the time we do that, those Comanches will be a hundred miles away from here. You go tell Mateo, and then you go to town. They'll get a good tracker. Try to get

Will Spivey. He can cut sign better than most."

"But I want to go with you. You can't go by yourself."

Clay shook his head and said, "Brodie, I'll catch up with 'em. Somehow I'll get your ma and your sisters back. One more thing."

"What is it? I'll do it."

"Find that preacher and get him to prayin'."

Without another word Clay ran to his horse, and without a backward look, drove him out of the yard at a fast gallop.

Brodie stood there helplessly and watched Clay ride away until he was out of sight, and then he walked over to where his great-grandfather lay. He knelt down and put his hand on the old man's chest. Tears filled his eyes, and he bit his lip to cut off the sobs.

"Well, Grandpa, I guess now you're in that green grass, sure enough."

CHAPTER
TWENTY-ONE

The scene exploded before Jerusalem's eyes like a shell going off. She was sitting at the table peeling potatoes and answering questions Moriah was firing at her, when suddenly the door burst open. She looked up to see Josiah, who had been on the porch, race in, his face stretched with tension.

"Injuns! It's Injuns!" he shouted. "Get your gun, Jerusalem!" Josiah snatched the rifle off the pegs where it hung over the front door and rushed out again.

Jerusalem leaped to her feet and ran across the room to get the other rifle hanging over the fireplace. "Girls, go out the back way!" she cried. Even as she spoke, she heard a rifle shot from outside and then the wild screams of the Indians. The rifle was not kept loaded, and she raced across the room to where the powder and shot were kept. She had picked up a powder horn and was pouring it into the muzzle when suddenly a short, broad Indian came through the door. His face was marked with red and yellow paint, and he moved quickly across the room and snatched the rifle from her hand. He had dark eyes that seemed to glitter, and even as he spoke, more Indians came pouring through the door.

"No need gun," he said.

Jerusalem released her grip on the rifle and ran across the room and snatched up Mary Aidan. "Stay with me, Moriah," she said. With her free hand she pulled Moriah close to her, her arm around her shoulders. She faced the Indian who was watching her, trying not to show the fear she felt.

"That old man was brave. Was he your father?" the Indian asked.

The fact that he spoke some English shocked Jerusalem. She felt her heart beating rapidly, for she had heard the horrific stories of what happened to white female captives. "He was my grandfather," she said. "Take what you want and go."

One of the Indians cried something and dashed for Moriah. She had been helping her mother with the potato peeling, and when he yanked her away, she slashed at him with a knife. It sliced his upper arm, and he yelped and reached for the tomahawk in his belt. He raised it, but even as Jerusalem cried out, the short Indian who had grabbed the rifle barked out a command. Evidently he was the chief of the war party. He gave another command and came forward and held his hand out. "Knife," he said to Moriah.

"Give it to him, Moriah," Jerusalem said quickly. She watched the Indian take the knife, test its edge, and then look at her.

"I am Red Wolf."

A chill went through Jerusalem then, for she had heard of this Indian. From what other settlers had said to Clay, Red Wolf was more vicious than most Comanches. He was watching her steadfastly and waiting, she knew, for her to break down.

"Where are your men?"

"I won't tell you anything," Jerusalem said.

Suddenly Red Wolf laughed. He had a broad mouth, and like most Comanches, he was short and broad. Of all the Plains Indians, they were the most feared. "You make good wife after you learn to hold tongue." Still holding the butcher knife, Red Wolf turned and walked around as the members of his band went through the house. They tore the curtains down, opened drawers, overturned the furniture, all the time laughing and shouting. As they ransacked the house, they acted like naughty children, but they were killers glorying in the thrill of the hunt. From what Clay had told her, Comanches did nothing but hunt either animals or men. The women and the young ones did all the work.

Mary Aidan was clinging to Jerusalem now. "What are they, Mama?" she whispered.

"They're Indians."

"Will they kill us, Mama?" Moriah said, her voice strained.

"I don't know. We'll pray that they won't."

The Indians appeared to be in a hurry, and finally Red Wolf gave a short command

and most of the band rushed out of the house. Red Wolf turned to Jerusalem. He came close to her, so close she caught his rank smell. He waited for her to flinch and cry out, but she had determined that she would not show fear. He reached out, took a strand of her hair, and rubbed it thoughtfully.

His eyes met hers, and he said, "We go now."

"Leave us here," Jerusalem said, but she knew that was hopeless.

Red Wolf jerked her hair and started dragging her toward the door. "Come," he said.

Though he was short of stature, he was a powerful man and pulled Jerusalem out the door. As soon as they were outside, he gave another command and one of the Indians yelped and ran inside. The others had gathered up the seven horses that the family had and looped them together with a long piece of rope.

Motioning toward the horses, Red Wolf said, "Get on."

There was no point arguing, and Jerusalem said quietly, "We have to go with them, Moriah. Get on one of the horses."

Jerusalem went to her favorite horse, a blazed-face sorrel, and put Mary Aidan on. Without help she jumped astride and turned to see Red Wolf watching her. He said nothing but called, and a brave came out from the house. Through the open door, Jerusalem could see that he had set the room on fire. Her heart ached, for this house had become a home for her.

Red Wolf ran to his pony, swung on with an easy motion, and yelled out, his rifle held high in the air. The Indians circled the house screaming and whooping, then rode out of the yard.

Holding Mary Aidan with one hand and the mane of the horse with the other, Jerusalem suddenly prayed aloud, "Jesus, only You can help us now, and I ask You to watch over my girls."

Jerusalem slipped off the horse and lifted Mary Aidan down. She was trembling with weariness, for the band had ridden hard all day. They had stopped only once to drink beside a stream. Now darkness was beginning to fall. One of the braves yanked

Moriah off and was saying something to her. She broke free and ran and held on to Jerusalem tightly.

Red Wolf was barking commands, and the Indians began to gather firewood. Others walked a short distance away with their rifles in their hands and stood as guards.

From time to time, one of the Indians would come by and speak, grinning at the captives. Sometimes they would reach out and touch their hair. Moriah would slap at their hands and say, "Let me alone!" which amused them.

Finally, when the fire was blazing, they produced some sort of meat and began to roast it on sticks.

Moriah stayed very close to Jerusalem. Once she whispered, "Mama, will we have to be squaws?"

"Whatever happens," Jerusalem said quietly, "God will be with us. We'll be home again one day."

"They'll come after us, won't they, Mama? Clay will come with men to rescue us?"

The pleading look Jerusalem saw in her daughter's face almost broke her heart. She took her face in her hands and said, "Yes, Moriah. It may take a long time, but they will come."

Red Wolf brought some chunks of meat over and handed them to Jerusalem. "You cook," he said. She took one of the sharpened sticks that one of the Indians had whittled and shoved it through the meat. As she cooked it, he stood there watching her curiously. Jerusalem was intensely aware of his gaze.

"I had white squaw once. She was not strong. Not like a Comanche woman."

"What happened to her?" Jerusalem asked as she put more meat on another stick.

"She died." Red Wolf moved closer. Jerusalem's red hair seemed to fascinate him. "You look like a strong woman. Most white women cry and scream when we take them, but you're not afraid."

"I'm afraid for my girls," she said, looking him straight in the eyes.

Red Wolf said nothing and wandered off. The Indians had stolen some whiskey—not enough to make them crazy, but enough to loosen them up. They began telling stories, and Jerusalem was amazed at how they acted like a pack of young boys. She had always thought of Indians as being solemn, but these Comanches were not. It was hard to believe that they were vicious killers who often slowly tortured their victims to death.

Red Wolf came back to where Jerusalem had sat down with Moriah right beside her and Mary Aidan in her lap. "You have hair like the sunrise," he remarked. "Maybe I will take you as my third wife."

Jerusalem did not even look at him. With a swift movement, he reached across and pulled her head around. She looked deep into his eyes and forced herself to remain perfectly still.

"You're not afraid. Are you a Jesus woman?"

Up until that moment in her life Jerusalem Hardin had been a believer in Jesus Christ, but it had been a nominal belief. She did not have the strong faith of many she had known. But as she sat there in the midst of a band of savage Comanches, she realized a moment of decision had been set before her. She knew that what she answered would direct her the rest of her life. She looked directly at Red Wolf and said clearly, "Yes, I am a Jesus woman."

Red Wolf considered her words and then shook his head. "Your Jesus God cannot save you."

"Yes, He can," Jerusalem said, surprised at the sudden peace she felt inside.

Red Wolf sneered at her. "I've seen many white eyes of your people die under the knife. Some of them cried out for Jesus to save them, but He never came for any of them. He is weak."

Jerusalem had always been silent about her faith, but now it was as if she had stepped through a door, and an assurance flooded her heart. "Red Wolf, we must all die. Even you. If Jesus decides to kill you and let me live, that is what will happen. If He decides that it is my time to die, then that will happen. But whatever happens to me or to you, Jesus is the Creator of all things, and He is the one that you and I must stand before someday and explain how we lived our lives."

They were interrupted then, for one of the Indians who had drunk more of the whiskey than the others lurched across the ground and made a grab at Moriah. Moriah did not cry out, but she fought him silently as he reached out and ripped her dress.

Jerusalem threw herself forward and struck the brave with her fist. It did not hurt him, but it angered him. He struck her in the face with his fist, and she fell backward.

As the warrior turned again to grab Moriah, Red Wolf spoke sharply. The warrior argued with him, and as Jerusalem got back to her feet, she was aware that their fate lay in the hands of the short, muscular savage. Obviously, the brave was claiming Moriah as his share of the spoils, but Red Wolf finally fell silent, and the hard look in his eyes brought the other Indian to his senses. He turned away, and Red Wolf watched him go.

"That is Mantua. He wants the girl for his squaw."

"I know what he wants."

"I told him the girl is for my son."

Red Wolf watched to see what effect his words would have on the two and was pleased when neither of them began to beg. "He was wounded and could not come on this raid. I promised him I would bring him a white woman for his squaw." A look of pride came into the chief's face. "He will be chief one day. You will have a good man, girl." He turned to Jerusalem and said, "Maybe I will take you as my own squaw." He reached out and touched Mary Aidan's hair. "This one I will adopt."

Red Wolf was waiting for Jerusalem to answer, and when she did not, he said, "Don't you know what would have happened to you if you had been captured by any other Comanche war party? You and your oldest daughter would have been shared by all the warriors, and your little one would have been knocked on the head."

"I know that, and I thank you, Red Wolf," Jerusalem said calmly.

Red Wolf was puzzled by this white woman. She behaved like none he had ever seen, and he had taken many white captives. He stared at her for a while and then said, "Your Jesus cannot save you, but you will have a good life as a Comanche squaw." He turned and went back to the fire and took a piece of meat that one of the warriors offered him.

"Mama, do you really believe that Jesus will save us?" Moriah asked.

With a newborn strength she had never experienced before, Jerusalem looked her daughter in the eye. "Jesus is able to do

anything, and I'm asking Him to save all three of us."

On the afternoon of the second day, the Comanche raiding party encountered a small herd of buffalo grazing on the plains. At Red Wolf's word, his warriors began chasing the herd. Red Wolf sat on his horse and watched the hunt. He had not spoken to any of the captives since yesterday, but it was obvious to Jerusalem that only his iron authority had kept them from being abused. Turning to Red Wolf, she said, "Thank you for being kind to me and my daughters."

Red Wolf looked at her, but he did not smile. His face was expressionless for a moment, and then Jerusalem saw some dark humor glitter in his dark eyes.

"You will be kind to me. A man needs squaws to take care of him."

Jerusalem did not respond, and she knew that only the power of God had kept the three of them safe. She watched as the men slaughtered a number of buffalo and began to dress the meat. Red Wolf rode out toward them, leaving Jerusalem, Moriah, and Mary

Aidan alone. The distance was nearly a quarter of a mile, and Moriah said, "Mama, let's run away."

"It would be no use. They would catch us," Jerusalem replied. She watched with disgust as the warriors gutted the buffalo, pulled the warm entrails out, and ate them raw.

Finally, Red Wolf came back and said, "You two find wood and build fire. You learn about how Comanche women live."

Red Wolf led the women to a growth of small, stunted trees, and Jerusalem and Moriah began gathering sticks. They worked quickly, and when Red Wolf made a fire with matches, she was surprised. She knew they must have taken the matches on one of their raids, but she said nothing.

The warriors were bringing in huge chunks of buffalo meat, and Red Wolf said, "You cook. I like the tongue best."

"Very well," Jerusalem said.

As Jerusalem began to roast the meat over the fire, Moriah stayed by her side. As the Indians laughed and talked while she prepared a meal, she thought of home and wondered what was happening. She knew Clay would form a rescue party, but it would take time. Red Wolf had traveled like the wind, driving the horses hard for two days. By the time a rescue party was gathered and set out on the trail, they would be days behind in their pursuit. She knew that Moriah was frightened, and more than once she reached over and touched her and said quietly, "It'll be all right. The Lord is going to deliver us."

This newfound faith of hers was an amazing thing. Always before, when she had sought something from God, it had been a struggle. When her boys had been sick, she had prayed as hard as she knew how. And when they died, something died within her. Now, however, the calmness that surrounded Jerusalem was a miracle. She remembered something Rhys Morgan had said. It came back to her mind. *The peace of God passeth all understanding. No matter how many troubles there are outside, we are inside with Jesus.* She thought about this statement as she continued to turn the meat on the sticks. She marveled at what had happened. Though she should be terribly afraid of what could happen to them, God had replaced her fear with an amazing confidence that He was with her and her daughters.

The Indians loved to gamble, and that night they were gambling in some fashion that she could not understand. Jerusalem watched them, thinking again how childlike they acted at times. Moriah was sitting beside her, and Mary Aidan was lying on the blanket that Red Wolf had given them to share. Red Wolf had eaten a lot of buffalo tongue and was now sitting across from them by the fire, smoking a long pipe. Her thoughts were interrupted when he spoke suddenly.

"You have no sons?"

"I had four sons. Two are dead," she said.

"I also have two sons," he said, taking a long drag on his pipe.

Jerusalem turned then to face him. "Red Wolf, I will buy our freedom. If you will let us go, I will give you two hundred horses. Very good ones."

"You do not have that many horses. We took all you had."

"But I have land, and I will sell it and use all the money to buy fine horses."

Red Wolf studied her intently. "My people do not lie, but white people do. I can't trust your word. Besides," he added, "I can steal horses anytime." Then he laughed. His lips and broad mouth spread wide as he did so. "We let the Mexicans and your people live on our land just to raise horses for us. When you get them raised, we come and steal them."

The moon was enormous overhead, and it shed its silver beams down over the camp. They had moved under the trees, but two of the Comanches walked off a ways and stood as guards for a few hours until they were replaced by others. From far off a wolf howled, a lonesome, melancholy sound.

"That is my brother Wolf," he said as he continued to smoke his pipe and stare into the fire. The silence ran on for a long time, and then Red Wolf said, "We captured a white woman once who was a bad squaw. Most white women, after a time, forget their white blood, and they become one of us— Comanche. This one never did, no matter how hard her husband beat her when she tried to escape. He was Bear Killer. After a while he got tired of her running away and traded her to a Pawnee." He pointed at Jerusalem with the pipe and shook his head. "The Pawnee are not so kind to white women as the Comanche." He waited for her to speak, and when she simply looked at him, he shook his head. "Better if you forget. No one will come for you." As soon as Red Wolf had spoken these words, a voice to his right broke the silence.

At the sound of it Jerusalem stiffened and wheeled to face the man who had appeared.

"You are wrong, Red Wolf."

Red Wolf had iron control, and he simply turned his head and stared at Clay Taliferro, who had managed to sneak past the guards and walk into the camp undetected. He simply watched the intruder, and finally Clay spoke again.

"I have come for my women."

Jerusalem cried out, "Clay!" and at her cry Mary Aidan stirred. When she looked up and saw Clay, she ran to him and threw her arms around him.

Red Wolf watched the child embrace him and still did not speak. The other Indians were sleeping, for it was late. "You walk softly like a spirit man."

"Your warriors do not have sharp ears."

"They have become careless. I will have to speak with them."

"One of them you won't have to speak with," Clay said. "His ears were better than the rest, and he tried to stop me."

"That would be White Elk. He never was much of a warrior, but his squaw will grieve." Red Wolf seemed interested and showed no trace of fear. "You are alone?"

"Yes."

Red Wolf called out sharply, and at once the band of sleeping Comanches was alert and on their feet. He spoke again, and the warriors came rushing toward him. When they saw Clay standing there, they fell silent. They had their weapons in their hands, some with rifles and others with tomahawks raised high. They made a complete circle around the small group. Red Wolf got to his feet. He still had the pipe in his hand, and he moved to stand directly in front of Clay.

Clay bent over and said, "Mary Aidan, go to your ma."

"You come into my camp alone. That is foolish."

Clay had no rifle, but he had the six-gun,

which was in the holster on his right side. "I come to buy back my people, Red Wolf."

Red Wolf interpreted his words, and the Indians laughed. "My men think that you are very foolish."

"I've been foolish enough in my day. Probably you have, too, as a young man. But now Red Wolf is older and wiser. He will know a good trade when he hears one."

Red Wolf spoke Clay's words in Comanche, and his warriors muttered among themselves. "They want to know what will you give for your women."

"Your life, Red Wolf."

Red Wolf looked around at the warriors, and when he had interpreted Clay's words, the warriors started shaking their weapons and moved in closer. "My life is not easy to take. What is your name?"

"You can just call me the White Ghost."

"A fine name for one who moves like a silent ghost in the night. My warriors would not let you kill me."

"They cannot stop me," Clay said as he looked directly at Red Wolf. He knew if he did not show courage, they would fall on him in an instant with their weapons.

When Red Wolf translated this, all the

braves made sharp cries. One of the warriors raised his tomahawk and cried out, obviously asking permission to kill the man called White Ghost, who had dared challenge their chief.

Others were fingering their knives, barely containing their desire to torture this challenger. One brave drew the hammer back on his rifle, making a sharp clicking sound.

"I think, Ghost, you will be the one to die slowly under our knives. I see that you are a brave man, but under torture many brave men cry out like children."

"Hold up your pipe, Red Wolf, and I will show you why you will not kill me but trade with me."

Red Wolf laughed and then spoke to his braves. He held up his pipe and said, "Now, show me."

Jerusalem could barely breathe, for she knew at the least little provocation, the circle of Comanches would fall on them and kill them all. She saw Clay hold up his right hand and wave it. "You see this hand?"

"I see it."

"Watch it closely, Red Wolf."

Red Wolf fixed his eyes on Clay's hand, which he held in front of him to his side.

Then suddenly, with a move so fast that Jerusalem could barely see it, Clay drew his revolver. It leaped into his hand, and she heard the clicking sound as he pulled the hammer back. But the action was so smooth that the explosion seemed to come from nowhere. The bowl at the end of Red Wolf's pipe disappeared as if by magic.

Clay moved the gun until it was pointed right at Red Wolf's heart. "You see, you're an easy man to kill." He lifted the muzzle of the revolver and said mildly, "Your life is what I trade. I give you your life. You give me my people."

Red Wolf stared at the pipe. "I've never seen such a fast hand, but you cannot kill us all."

"No, I can't. They can kill me, but if I touch this trigger, you will be dead."

The Indians surrounding them were murmuring, but the gun in Clay's hand remained steadily pointed at Red Wolf. "You are a brave man, Red Wolf. All the Comanches and white men out here know that. You have nothing to prove."

Red Wolf remained silent, as well as his braves. They seemed to sense that if any one of them made a move, their chief would die. Jerusalem held tightly to Mary Aidan. The night birds had fallen quiet, and the only sound was the faint crackling of the fire. Jerusalem kept her eyes fixed on Red Wolf's face. She saw not the slightest trace of fear, and she knew that Comanches feared nothing, not even death. *He won't take the bargain*, she thought.

But then Red Wolf smiled and nodded. "There are many things I would miss on this earth. I would miss hunting the buffalo on the open plains. I would miss the raiding parties. My squaws would mourn for me, and I would not see my son grow up and become a strong Comanche chief."

"You can do all of these things," Clay said. "Lots of things I'd like to do, too, so I hope you take my bargain."

Red Wolf tossed the pipe aside. "I will take your bargain," he said abruptly.

Relief rushed through Jerusalem, and she squeezed Mary Aidan so hard that the child cried out.

"Do I have the word of Red Wolf that we will all go free with horses?"

"Yes."

The gun disappeared in Clay's holster, and the Indians rushed forward. Two of them seized him, but Red Wolf cried out something and they let him go. He came to stand before Clay and had to look up at him. He smiled broadly and said, "We will both see the sun come up."

"Maybe. No man knows about that," Clay said.

"Your woman. She offered two hundred horses if I let her go."

"You should have taken her bargain, but that's not what we agreed on. Your life is worth more than two hundred horses."

Red Wolf turned to Jerusalem. "This man is your husband?"

"No."

"Where is your husband? Why did he not come to rescue you?"

"I don't know, Red Wolf."

Red Wolf shrugged. "This one called White Ghost is better than the coward who did not come for you. You better get rid of the other one." He called out something to his braves, then said, "They will bring your horses." He turned and faced Jerusalem, taking a step closer and peering into her face. "Your Jesus, He is a strong warrior. Now go."

When the Indians brought their horses up,

they all mounted quickly. Clay had swung Mary Aidan up to ride with him. Clay held up his hand and nodded. "A good bargain for both of us, Red Wolf." Then he turned and rode out with Jerusalem and Moriah riding at his side.

Red Wolf watched them head off into the darkness, then he turned around and faced his warriors.

"You let a white man walk past you. You are nothing but a woman," he said to one warrior.

"But he is a ghost, Red Wolf," one of the warriors protested. He had been one of those on guard. "You can't fight with a ghost."

Red Wolf did not answer. He turned to face the darkness and watched as the White Ghost disappeared into the night.

Clay made them ride hard for half an hour, putting as much distance between them and the raiding party as he could. Then he slowed the horses to a walk. Jerusalem came up to his side, and Moriah trailed a horse length behind her mother.

"I knew you'd come, but I didn't think it would be so soon."

"They trouble you or Moriah?" Clay

asked, his face taut with concern. He was well aware of what Comanches often did to the women and children they captured.

"No, thank God."

"That's a miracle."

"It is. A *real* miracle." Suddenly, Jerusalem reached over and took Clay's hand. She held it, squeezing it hard. "Thank you, Clay," she whispered, her voice filled with emotion.

Clay Taliferro was very much aware of the warmth and strength of Jerusalem's hand. He looked at her and saw she was watching him intently. "Well, shoot, I didn't want to have to go to all the trouble of breaking in a new ma for Brodie and Clinton and Mary Aidan."

Jerusalem squeezed his hand as hard as she could. "I'll be glad to get home," she said and did not release his hand. She held on to him as if he were an anchor, and from behind, Moriah watched them and wondered at it.

CHAPTER
TWENTY-TWO

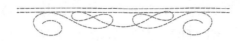

"Well, there comes your rescue party," Clay said and pointed.

Jerusalem looked up surprised and only saw a cloud of dust far off in the distance. "How do you know, Clay?"

"Because nobody else would be comin' that fast. They made better time than I figured."

Jerusalem looked back at Moriah and saw that the girl was shading her eyes and squinting, watching the group gallop toward them.

"There they come, Mama," she shouted, "but we're saved already."

Jerusalem was holding Mary Aidan in front of her, astraddle the horse. "I don't think I'll ever forget this, Clay. You know, for a long time my religion didn't mean that much to me. But something happened to me in Red Wolf's camp the other night. I found out Jesus is real." She turned and asked abruptly, "What about you, Clay? You never talk about religion."

"Don't have enough to talk about," he muttered as he watched the riders approach.

Jerusalem studied Clay's face. He was not facing her, and she knew he was embarrassed by her question. "I'm sorry to talk this plainly."

"Well, you never was put off by plain talk before." Clay suddenly turned and smiled briefly. "Reckon I'll be gettin' a lot of preachin' out of you from now on."

"I think you might," she said, smiling.

"I guess preachin' never hurt anybody. Come along. Let's meet 'em halfway."

As they got closer to the rescue party, Clay, who had the best eyes of any person Jerusalem had ever seen, said, "There's Brodie right up in front along with Zane. I figured they'd be with 'em."

"Who else is there?"

"Well, there's Mateo—" and then he gasped. "Well, I'll be dipped! Jim Bowie's there! I reckon he's been the tracker." Clay pulled up, and the others followed suit. The band of men, about twenty in all, were whooping as they rode toward them. "Reckon we're about to get welcomed," Clay said.

The party surrounded them, yelling and waving their hats in the air. They all dismounted, and Brodie came running forward. "Ma, are you all right?"

"Yes, I am. We all are."

"I was so scared, Ma! And Grandpa didn't make—"

"I know, son," Jerusalem said, trying to hold back the tears. "But I do know where he's at right now. He's with Jesus."

Jerusalem saw her son's face twitching, and she knew that the worst thing she could do would be to put her arms around him and hold him as she longed to do. She reached up and patted his cheek. "There now. We're all safe. God protected us, Brodie."

Jim Bowie walked up and struck Clay on the arm hard enough to set him back. "Well, you son of a gun! How in the world did you get 'em back, Clay?"

"Oh, I surrounded them, Jim. They gave up pretty quick when they seen it was me. They call me the White Ghost now. My new Indian name."

"White Ghost." Zane grinned. "Why do they call you that?"

"Because he came through all their guards at night and took us away from them," Jerusalem said. Then she proceeded to tell them how Clay had faced Red Wolf and drew a pistol on him as fast as lightning. When she finished, she enjoyed seeing the awe in the eyes of the men from the rescue party.

Jim Bowie laughed and said, "Wait'll Sam Houston hears about this stunt! He'll sign you up for his army, Clay. Maybe make you a general. If you can bluff a Comanche war party, you won't have no trouble whippin' that little old Mexican army of Santa Anna's."

"Well, I reckon bein' a general wouldn't be too bad. You fellows could all be privates and wait on me hand and foot."

Everyone laughed, and Zane came over and put his arms around Jerusalem. "Well, sister, I'm mighty proud to see you. I've been worried something fierce."

Jerusalem felt the strength in her brother's arms. "I knew you'd come, Zane."

"Too late, I reckon. You didn't need anything but that one-man army. White Ghost—he'll never get over that."

"I'm tired, Mama," Moriah said. "I want to go home."

"I don't reckon there's any home to go to. The house was on fire when we left," Jerusalem said.

"Ma, it went out almost by itself. Some of the front room was burned," Brodie said, "but the house is fine." Seeing his mother and sisters safe filled him with emotion. He moved away from the men then, for tears had come to his eyes. He kept his face turned away, and Mateo moved to stand beside him.

"It is not unmanly to weep," he said, "not over a mother restored from the dead, or for losing your great-grandfather."

Brodie felt Mateo's arm go around his shoulders, and he leaned against his friend. "I can't hardly believe it, Mateo. It's a miracle they weren't killed too."

"Yes. You will never forget this. A man

only needs to see one miracle to know that the good God is in heaven."

Rhys Morgan was speaking with Jerusalem inside the house. The smell of burned wood still lingered, but little damage had been done to the rest of the house. Wood was charred around one window, but that could be easily repaired.

"We didn't know what to do about Josiah, Jerusalem," Rhys said. He was wearing a black suit despite the hot weather, and his smooth face was even as he spoke. "We didn't know how long it would be before we got you back, so we went ahead and buried him. We thought we'd wait and have the funeral when you were rescued."

"That was the right thing to do, Rhys. Thank you," Jerusalem said. "I appreciate all you've done for us."

"Do you have any particular scripture you'd like for me to read at the service?"

"Grandpa always liked the twenty-third Psalm. He used to recite it to me when I was a little girl. I think it would be nice if you read that."

"That's always good. Anything else?" Rhys asked.

"No, let's have the funeral. It's time now."

Rhys Morgan followed Jerusalem out of the house. The two walked fifty yards to the grave where her grandfather was buried. Brodie had picked the spot in the shade of a large pecan tree that he had often sat under with his great-grandfather and listened to his tales. The crowd was not large. Jake was there with his Indian family, Lucita had come with Serena and Mateo on each side of her. About twenty of the neighbors had gathered, and Jim Bowie had remained to pay his respects before returning to his home.

Rhys waited until Jerusalem took her place beside Zane. Zane was holding Mary Aidan, and Brodie and Clinton stood on one side of her. Moriah was holding Zane's free hand. Rhys looked around and said, "A beautiful day. This is the day that the Lord has made. We will rejoice and be glad in it." He looked over the crowd and said, "We rejoice over the life of our departed brother Josiah Mitchell. I had many a long talk with Josiah. He had a hard life. Most of you know that he fought under George Washington, serving with General Anthony Wayne. His life was filled with activity, but the last time I spoke with Josiah, he told me that the one regret of his life was that he waited so long to take Jesus Christ as his Savior. . . ."

The crowd was silent, and Brodie listened carefully and fought back the tears. *I'm gettin' to be a regular crybaby,* he thought. *I can't let anybody see that.* He glanced around and saw Clay standing beside Julie. He knew they weren't man and wife, but he saw that Julie had tears in her eyes and was shocked. *I didn't know she loved Grandpa that much.*

Rhys Morgan read several scriptures, including the twenty-third Psalm, and then he said, "In the eleventh chapter of John, there's a story that I never cease to marvel over. A man named Lazarus had died. He and his sisters were dear friends of Jesus. . . ." He read the entire chapter aloud, speaking plainly in his clear, tenor voice. "The thing that always moves me in this story is when Martha came to Jesus and said, 'If you had been here, our brother would not have died.' And then Jesus said, 'Thy brother shall rise again.'

"Martha believed in the resurrection. She said, 'I know that he shall rise again in the resurrection at the last day.'

"And then in the twenty-fifth verse, Jesus said to her, 'I am the resurrection, and the life: he that believeth in me, though he were dead, yet shall he live.'"

Rhys closed his Bible and spoke for a while about the Lord Jesus Christ, stressing His own resurrection from the dead. Finally he said, "I was speaking with a member of the family, one standing here. Talking about all the people buried in this land and all over the world. The world is one huge graveyard, but for those who believe in Jesus, those bodies will rise one day, and Josiah will be one of them. He will be with the Lord forever."

Rhys then bowed his head and said a brief prayer. As soon as he said, "Amen," he went over and took Jerusalem's hand and whispered a few words of comfort. Others came, and Jerusalem knew a strange sense of joy. She turned to Julie, who had come to embrace her. "He's with the Lord, Julie. I'm so happy for him."

Julie could not answer. She bit her lips and turned away without another word.

Jerusalem felt her sorrow and a grief. "God help her," she said. "She needs Jesus."

After all the visitors had gone, Jerusalem stood with the family, looking down. Brodie said, "What's the matter, Mama?"

"I wish—" She broke off and then shook her head. "I wish my boys were here." She turned quickly and walked away.

Clay, who was standing beside Brodie, muttered, "She sure misses that little cemetery she had back in Arkansas."

"I wish they was buried here with Grandpa," Brodie said. "It would be a real comfort to Mama."

Clay turned away but stopped long enough to put his hand on Clinton's shoulder. "You had a good great-grandpa there, boy. I hope you'll be as good a man."

"I hope so, too, Clay."

"Clay, Mama's not talking hardly at all," Brodie said. The two were out planting in the new garden, and Brodie's face was troubled. "You reckon she was so scared by gettin' kidnapped by the Indians, and she can't get over it?"

"Scared? Not your mama." Clay took his handkerchief out, wiped his face, and leaned on his shovel. "She is in a funny mood, but don't push her, boy. You can't understand women. No way to do that."

"You think she'll be all right?"

"Just give her time, boy, and be good to her."

"Clay, I cried over Anthony Wayne. You think it's wrong to cry over a dog?"

"Not me! I've cried over dogs and horses myself!"

Jerusalem was more aware than anyone of the dark mood that had gripped her. She could not understand it, but she knew that two things were happening. One thing was her newfound faith. She found herself reading the Scriptures more and more often. Verses spoke to her as they never had. To be able to read God's Word and understand it better pleased her. She found herself sharing things from the Bible with her children and knew that she had somehow passed into a new stage of her life with God.

On the other hand, she was experiencing a strange moodiness, which was not at all like her. She knew it had something to do with being kidnapped, and she knew that Clay Taliferro was part of it.

Clay had not spoken about any of it. He kept himself busy with all the work that had to be done on the new homestead. But when he was not around, Jerusalem often became nervous for no reason at all. The more she thought about it, she realized it had to do with how much she depended on Clay. Ever since they had left Arkansas, and even before, she had been drawn to his strength, although she had not wanted to admit it even to herself.

The night he had appeared like magic at Red Wolf's camp and saved her and the children, she realized how much she needed a man out here to protect her. The Indians were still there, and another raiding party could appear again tomorrow. War was looming on the horizon with the Mexicans. Jake had never been a help to her with the family, and she had borne the burden of raising them alone. The constant threat of danger surrounded them every day, and now she felt it more than ever.

Without realizing it, she found reasons to keep Clay close to home. She felt apprehensive when he rode over to help Mateo with work, as he often did. She found herself looking for his return with a strange nervousness. She chided herself for worrying, for she had never been one to worry much in her life!

Others sensed it too. Brodie had already mentioned it to Clay, and more than once Moriah would say, "Why are you so worried, Ma?"

Jerusalem had always been the anchor of the family, and now she found herself needing someone, and with each passing day, this longing grew stronger and stronger.

Brodie had practiced his speech for days, and finally he was alone with Serena. He had ridden over to help Mateo, and the two of them had worked on a new smokehouse. But Mateo had gone inside, and Serena had come to bring him a dipper of water.

"Thanks, Serena." He drank it, and then as he handed the dipper back, he blurted out, "You know they're having a celebration in San Antonio."

"Yes, I heard about it. What are they celebrating?"

"Oh, it's something about Stephen Austin's colony. Anyhow, would you go with me?" Serena turned, and for a moment Brodie's heart sank like a plummet. He thought, *She's gonna say no.*

But instead she said, "I wouldn't mind, but I can't leave Mama alone. She gets lonesome, you know."

"Well, that's all right," Brodie said. "Clay wanted me to ask your mother if she'd go with him." The lie fell easily from Brodie's lips, so easily he could not believe it. He almost opened his mouth to contradict himself, but Serena beat him to it.

"Why, that's wonderful, Brodie! I know she'd love to go. I'll go tell her."

"Well," Brodie said quickly, "I've got to get on back home."

"I'll be ready to go on Tuesday morning," Serena said, smiling.

Brodie got on his horse and rode away from the Lebonnes' farm feeling miserable. "Why did I have to lie like that? What am I gonna do now?" he said in a plaintive tone. "I've got to find Clay."

He rode at a fast gait all the way back and found Clay napping in the shade beside the house. Scrambling off the horse, Brodie went up and said, "Clay, wake up."

"Why, hello, boy. What mischief you been up to?"

Brodie swallowed hard and squatted down beside Clay. "I done a bad thing, Clay. I told a lie."

"Why, I told one once myself. I think it was back in 1822, if I remember correctly."

"I'm not foolin', Clay."

"What'd you lie about?" Clay was sleepy-eyed as usual, and he listened as Brodie stammered for a time and finally came out with it.

Clay reached out and pulled Brodie's hat down over his eyes. He laughed and shook his head. "Well, if that's the worst thing you ever done, I reckon you'll make it through the pearly gates."

"But Serena won't go unless her mama goes."

"Why, you done settled that, didn't you? I'll put on my best clothes, and we'll take those ladies. It'll be good for both of us to get away from all this work and celebrate a little."

"Will you really, Clay?"

"Shore, boy. Be glad to go."

Brodie rose and went into the house. He burst out, saying, "Mama, Serena's going to go to the celebration with me in San Antonio. First time she's ever let me take her anywhere."

Jerusalem saw the happiness on Brodie's face. She came over and reached out and ruffled his hair. "Why, that's wonderful. You'll have a good time."

"Well, she wouldn't go unless her mama could go, so Clay's takin' Lucita."

Brodie did not notice that something changed in his mother's face. She simply said, "Oh, is that right?"

"That's right. And, Mama, you ought to go too. It'll be a fine thing."

"I'm not going, Brodie," she said evenly.

Brodie stared at her. "Why not?"

"I'm just not. That's all."

Brodie stared at his mother and then turned and walked out of the house. *Women sure are funny. You think she'd be glad to go and enjoy the entertainment.*

Maybe I can convince her of it. He put the idea out of his mind, however, for he could barely contain one idea, much less two. And all he could think of now was that he was taking Serena to a celebration.

CHAPTER
TWENTY-THREE

Stripped to the waist, Rhys Morgan brought the razor carefully down the side of his cheek. He had come to the back porch of the Hardin house, where he'd spent the night. He was in the midst of his shave when Moriah came out to watch him. She began to pepper him with questions, which he answered as best he could. Now as he wiped the lather off on a bit of cloth, she asked, "Well, where did Cain get his wife, Preacher?"

Well, devil fly off! Rhys found Moriah fascinating. At fourteen she was between adolescence and womanhood, but she was the

most direct person Rhys had ever met—with the exception of her mother. He looked into Moriah's deep brown eyes and smiled. "Why would you ask a strange thing like that?"

"Because there was only Adam and Eve. If Cain got a wife, she must have been his own sister. Ain't that right?"

"Don't say *ain't*. And I'd appreciate it if you'd let me finish shaving without asking any more questions."

"But you said in your sermon we ought to study the Bible and learn to ask questions. Well, why won't you answer me?"

"Because I don't have a good answer, Moriah. Of course Adam and Eve started the race, but they may have had children and grandchildren and great-grandchildren. It may be that by the time Cain got married, he had plenty of second or third cousins to choose from."

Moriah stared at him and then smiled. "I knew you'd say that." She narrowed her eyes and said, "How come you have muscles that are so strong? Most of the preachers I've seen have been either fat or skinny as string beans."

"I'm what I am from working in the coal

mines. It either kills a fellow or muscles him up."

"You look real strong. When I get married, I'm not gonna let my husband get fat."

Rhys Morgan laughed. "I'll bet you don't," he said. "That young fellow will have a fine time being married to you. Now, go and help with the chores!"

Moriah did not obey. She sat quietly, watching intently as Rhys finished shaving. He finally washed his face, put on his shirt, and tucked it into his pants. "Now, let me get my tie and coat, and we'll be ready for the celebration."

Moriah's face suddenly grew long. "We're not going."

"Not going!" Rhys said, staring at her. "Of course you're going. Everybody's going."

"Mama says she won't go. Please go in and make her let us go."

"Why, I can't make your mother do any-thing," Rhys protested, "but I will ask her." He came forward and, reaching out, pulled Moriah's earlobe. "I'll turn my charm on her. We Welshmen can do that, you know. Why, I can charm the birds out of the trees. Come along and watch."

Going inside the house, Rhys found Jerusalem changing the sheets on one of the beds at the end of the hall. "Now, Sister Hardin, I think it's time you had a vacation. Go get yourself ready, and I'll drive you to that celebration myself."

"I'm not going, Rhys," she said as she straightened out the sheet.

Rhys quickly surveyed Jerusalem's countenance. He saw that her lips were set and did not understand why she wouldn't want to go to the celebration. She led a dull life in many ways here on the ranch, and now he said lightly, "I think it would be good if you went. I'd like some company myself, and the children need a break. They'll be disappointed if they don't get to go."

"Rhys, I got too much work to do around here to be trotting off to some celebration. Besides, it's foolish," Jerusalem said as she finished making the bed.

"Suit yourself, Jerusalem, but I think you're going to miss a real fun time. And the kids were really looking forward to going," Rhys said as he followed her to the kitchen.

As she worked in the kitchen, Rhys continued to try to convince her to go.

Jerusalem started to mull over what Morgan had said about the children. *They do work hard, always helping Clay out with all the work,* she thought as she swept the kitchen. Twenty minutes later, she threw up her hands and said, "All right, I'll go! You'll drive me crazy, if I don't. I declare, Rhys Morgan, you're worse than one of the children!"

"So you'll go, then?" Rhys smiled. "Good."

"You did it, Preacher!" Moriah said. She had followed the pair around and listened in. "You really did it. I didn't think you could."

"What did he do?" Jerusalem demanded, turning to stare at Moriah.

"He said he could charm the birds out of the trees and that he could certainly make one woman go to a celebration."

"Now wait a minute," Rhys protested. "I didn't exactly say all that."

Jerusalem's eyes flashed, but when she saw the guilt in Morgan's face she laughed. "All right. I believe you Irishmen can charm a woman."

"I'm not Irish, bless you. I'm a Welshman, but I'm glad you're going."

"Can I wear my new dress, Mama?"

"Yes."

"I'll go get ready."

★ ★ ★

As Clay helped Lucita into the front seat of the wagon, she asked, "Where's Jerusalem?"

Clay jumped up in the wagon and took the lines and looked back at Serena and Brodie, who had seated themselves in the back. "Well, she wouldn't come."

"Wouldn't come?" Lucita said. "Why not?"

"I don't know. I can't figure it out."

"I can't either," Brodie said. "We told her there'd be plenty of room in the wagon for her, but she just got stubborn. Ma does that sometimes. I think she needs some kind of a tonic or somethin'."

"I always consider myself an expert about women, but Jerusalem puzzles me sometimes," Clay said.

Serena laughed aloud and reached forward and touched her mother. "Better be careful, Mama. You're sitting beside an expert in women." She sat back and glanced over at Brodie. "Why, you look nice, Brodie."

Brodie was wearing a new shirt he had saved up and bought for the occasion. He had even shaved, which he scarcely needed to, but it made him feel more grown up. He flushed with pleasure and said, "You look real fine, Serena. Is that a new dress?"

"Mama and I made it." The dress was made out of a shiny green material and fit Serena well. Her black hair was glossy and shone in the sun, and she smiled and whispered, "I'm glad you asked me to go, Brodie. It'll be fun. We can dance and everything."

"Dance! I can't dance."

"It's easy. We'll probably do a fandango. I'll show you how."

As they approached San Antonio, Clay remarked, "Never saw so many people in town. Might have trouble findin' a place to park this rig."

They drove past the San Antonio River, formed by a number of springs several miles above the town, as it wound its way through the flatland surrounding the settlement. Usually, at this time of the day, lots of people flocked along the river to wash clothes and bathe and fish.

San Antonio itself was laid off in streets crossing each other at right angles. In the center of the town, about midway, was an oblong space where the church and public buildings dominated the scene. Clay pulled the wagon up at a plaza and got out, handing Lucita down. He looked at her and smiled. "Why, you look pretty as a pair of red shoes with green strings, Lucita."

Flushing, Lucita dropped her eyes. "Thank you, Clay," she said. "I haven't been anywhere to dress up for in a long time."

"Well, looks like everybody's dressed up and ready for the frolic to begin." Clay turned and said, "Well, I'll be. Look who's coming. It's Rhys and Jerusalem—and Moriah too. Let's go say hello." They walked over to where Rhys was helping Jerusalem and the baby out of the wagon, and Clay said, "Glad you changed your mind, Jerusalem."

Jerusalem gave Clay an odd look. "It's Rhys's fault. He can charm the birds out of the trees and make a woman do anything."

"Oh, come now, Jerusalem!" Rhys protested. "I was only joking."

Moriah walked up to Clay and pulled on

his arm. "You've got to dance with me, Clay."

"Sure I will, Moriah! Why, the day I turn down an offer to dance from a good-lookin' woman will be the day they put me six feet under the posies!"

Indeed, the event turned out to be quite a celebration. The settlers who had come and staked out homesteads worked hard from dawn to dusk every day. But when it came to having a *fiesta,* as Lucita called it, they knew how to let down and have a grand time. Clay and Lucita, accompanied by Serena and Brodie, enjoyed all the food and participated in some of the games being held. There were horse races and shooting matches, and the highlight was a speech by Sam Houston. He was a tall man with penetrating eyes and had a way of carrying a crowd with him.

As Clay listened, he leaned over and whispered to Lucita, "That fellow's dangerous."

"What do you mean dangerous, Señor Clay?"

"I mean he could talk a man into doin' things that could get him into trouble. I've seen a few of those fellas before. Jim Bowie's one of them. Have to be careful, or

I'll find myself volunteering for some foolish thing."

Later in the afternoon Clay excused himself, saying, "Brodie, you look out for these ladies. I'm gonna take me a little break."

"I know what you're going to do," Serena said. "You're going to a saloon."

"That's a bad habit you got there, Serena," Clay said sternly. "Mindin' a man's business. I'll be back before you know it."

Clay had seen Jim Bowie go into a saloon, accompanied by Houston, and he wanted to know more about this big man who had already made his mark in the world. Clay knew about Houston's political career in Tennessee, where he had been governor, and wondered why the man had come to Texas. He had heard he had filed for divorce from his young wife, which puzzled everyone.

Entering the saloon, Clay saw a small group of men sitting at a table off to the side. Jim Bowie was one of them.

Bowie looked up, and seeing Clay, he said, "Clay, come over and have yourself a seat. I want you to meet some folks."

Clay walked over and was introduced to William Travis. He knew Travis was a lawyer and land speculator. Travis was a tall, pleasant-looking man, handsome, with reddish hair and a direct gaze.

"This here's Deaf Smith. Best scout in all of Texas," Jim Bowie said.

"Pleased to meet you," Smith said. He spoke in a strange off-key voice and cupped his ear as Clay spoke. "Can't hear thunder. Have to excuse me."

"He can't hear much, but he's a-thunderin' good scout," Bowie said. "And this is Mr. Samuel Houston. Sam, here's one of your fellow Tennesseans. The Comanches call him the White Ghost."

"Are you indeed, sir!" Houston said as he got up and extended his hand.

When Clay took it, he found his hand almost crushed by the man's strong grasp. "Glad to meet you, Mr. Houston."

"And you, too, sir. Sit down and join the conversation." He winked at Bowie, saying, "We've got to have young fellows like you if Texas is ever going to make it."

"Well . . ." Bowie grinned. He touched the scar on his neck. "He nearly eliminated me from that process. And I left my mark on him too."

"A knife fight?" Houston said.

"I think we used everything—knives, fists, feet, thumbs."

"What was you fightin' over?" Deaf Smith inquired curiously.

"I forget," Bowie said. "Do you remember, Clay?"

"Done faded from my memory completely."

"Clay here's the best shot I ever saw, pistol or rifle," Bowie said. "Better sign him up if you ever lead an army, Sam."

Houston suddenly grew sober. "That may come sooner than you think, gentlemen."

"Have you heard from Steve Austin?" Bowie asked.

"He's still in that jail in Mexico City. That's enough to fight a war over right there. They had no right to grab a citizen and stick him in jail with no charges filed. That's the way it is with those loyal to Santa Anna," Houston said.

"What's happenin' in the government?"

"Santa Anna took over in April, and he's made himself a dictator. I said all along he was the man we had to watch. He's slicker than goose grease, men. He's changed sides so many times nobody knew where he stood, but we know now."

"You think it'll actually come to a fight, Mr. Houston?" Clay asked.

"Bound to, but the problem is, we don't have an army," Houston said, shaking his head.

"Oh, come on, Sam," William Travis said. "A few years ago we didn't have ten thousand citizens here. Now we got over thirty thousand. Most of those men have rifles, and they know how to use 'em."

"That's right," Bowie nodded. "We got enough men to make a good-sized army."

"But there's no order to them," Houston said. "If a fight comes, it'll be against the army Santa Anna's raising, and he'll have trained, disciplined troops."

"They can be kilt," Deaf Smith said, "same as anybody else."

"Deaf, you ought to know better than that. Sooner or later the trainin' tells. They already have an edge over us. That's why I'd like to see Texas have more than just a militia. We need to have men who've had some training and can follow orders from a leader."

"If we did anything like that," Bowie said, idly fingering the drink before him, "Santa

Anna would come charging in. Just the idea of an American army could touch off a war."

"You're right, Jim, but that's exactly what we've got to have," Houston insisted.

Clay sat listening for a time, very much impressed with Houston and his ideas. After seeing what a small war party of Comanches could do, he didn't even want to think of a trained army of thousands to fight against.

Houston had a unique ability to state his views in such a way that men were drawn to him and wanted to do what he asked. Travis, he noted, had some of the same strength of personality as Houston. Travis was already known as an impulsive firebrand and had almost touched off a war once when he challenged Mexican authority. That had passed, but he had become a marked man among the leaders of Texas.

Finally, Clay rose and left the group. Jim Bowie followed him out, saying, "Clay, we'll need fellows like you when the trouble comes around here. Can I count on you?"

"I don't know whether I'll even be here."

"Why, Clay, I thought you'd come for good, takin' up land and all with a family."

Clay could make no answer without revealing the true situation between him and Julie. "If I'm here, Jim, you know I'll stand with you."

"That's good enough for me." Bowie clapped Clay on the shoulder and winked. "Watch out for yourself. The señoritas are out tonight."

Clay almost said something in the same vein, but he saw the sadness that hung on Bowie like a garment. *He's still grieving over his wife and family,* Clay thought. "I'll see you later, Jim. Don't be a stranger."

The largest building in town had been cleared of all furniture except for a few tables along the edge where refreshments were being served. The crowd was composed of equal numbers of Mexicans and Texans. Most of the men wore broad-brimmed hats, a reddish or white color, with the band ornamented with silver or gold beads. They wore calico shirts, wide trousers with fancy-colored sashes, and jackets thrown about the shoulders. The women wore their brightest dresses, adding a dash of color to the affair. As Brodie stood beside Serena, he felt awkward and out of place. Serena was dancing, and although she had tried to get him on the floor, he had stubbornly refused, saying, "I'd make a fool out of myself and step all over you."

Brodie stood at the side of the dance floor, watching Serena as she danced with a tall man. Soon he found himself getting angry. He did not know the tall man, but he knew she had danced with him three times ina row.

Finally, he could stand it no longer and made his way across the dance floor. When he got to the couple, he said, "I'm ready to dance now, Serena."

Serena looked at him startled, and the man turned and stared at him with displeasure. "Son, that's no way to act. Go back and wait your turn."

"I've waited, and now I'm telling you that I'm dancing with Miss Serena."

"Brodie," Serena said, her face showing displeasure, "I'll dance with you later."

Brodie was a gentle young man as a rule, but he had looked forward to being with Serena for weeks, and now it was all going wrong. He had never started a fight in his life, but the sight of the well-dressed, middle-aged man who had such assurance that he himself lacked made him angry.

"I'm dancing with Serena, and you can go scratch for it," Brodie said rashly.

"On your way, son," the man said impatiently, then turned to Serena and took her hand to start the next dance.

Brodie, goaded beyond his measure, reached out, took the man's arm, and whirled him around. "Take your hands off her and don't turn away from me when I'm talking to you."

"What's the trouble here, Brodie?"

Brodie turned to see Clay standing beside him. "This fellow, he's—" Brodie was so angry and embarrassed that he could not speak.

Clay looked at the man and said, "Well, Mr. Travis, we meet again."

"Hello, Clay. We're having us a little disagreement here."

"Mr. Travis was just dancing with me, and Brodie objected," Serena said. "Brodie, you need to go outside and cool off."

Brodie felt his face flush red at Serena's rebuke. "All right," he said. "I will." He turned and shoved his way through the dancers.

"I'm sorry about that," Travis said. "I expect the young man's a little jealous. I can't blame him with such a fine young lady."

"Maybe you wouldn't mind if I finished this dance," Clay said in an offhanded manner.

William Travis did not like to be challenged. He stared at Clay for one moment and seemed inclined to argue. But then he laughed. "Why, of course. Be my guest."

"Thanks." Clay took Serena's hand and said, "I'm not much of a dancer."

Serena was upset. "We weren't doing anything wrong."

"Well, Brodie's mighty fond of you, Serena, and he's awkward. When I was his age, I didn't know my right hand from my left where girls were concerned. Just be patient with him. He's a good young man."

"All right, Clay. I'll try."

Jerusalem had watched the scene from the side of the dance floor and went to intercept Brodie as he was leaving. She understood what had happened but didn't speak of it.

"Would you dance with an old lady, Brodie?"

"Ma, I can't dance."

"Yes, you can. I'll teach you."

Brodie dropped his head. "I made a fool out of myself, Ma. Serena wasn't doing anything wrong, and I just butted in."

"Well, it'll turn out all right. Come along. I'll give you a dancing lesson."

Clay pulled the team up to Lucita's house and sat in the wagon seat for a moment. Mateo had taken Serena home an hour before they themselves had left. As they sat there on the wagon seat, Clay said, "Mighty fine dance. Good to be foolish once in a while."

"I guess it wasn't too foolish, Clay," Lucita said.

"I reckon not." Clay sat holding the lines as the two spoke of the day's activities and the dance. Neither of them mentioned the problem that had come up between Brodie and Serena, but they were both aware of it.

"I've been meanin' to talk to you," Clay said. "I'd like to take a bunch of cattle, some of ours and some of yours, to Shreveport to sell. We could use some hard money right about now."

"You'd take Mateo?" Lucita asked.

"Yes, maybe Brodie, too, although I'd rather leave him at the house with his ma."

"I will go with you, Clay," Lucita offered.

Clay turned with surprise. "Why, Lucita, you can't do that."

"Yes, I can. You'll need somebody to cook for you on the way. Besides, I'd like to make the trip. It would be something different."

"Well, I'd sure rather eat your cookin' as mine. But what will you do with Serena?"

"She might like to go over and stay with your people. Maybe she could stay at your house for a while."

"Well, Brodie wouldn't be agitatin' to go with us if Serena was there." He grinned.

Lucita was silent for a time, and then she said, "Clay, do you think you will ever marry?"

"Me, marry?" Clay shoved his hat back on his head and gave her a wry grin. "I've kind of got sort of a wife in Julie."

"She is no wife to you," Lucita said, and her meaning was not lost on Clay.

Clay blinked with surprise. "Well . . . er . . . Lucita—"

"I know you get lonely for a real wife."

Clay did not know what to say. He thought of Lucita as Gordon's wife, even though the man was dead. He avoided the issue, saying, "I don't reckon I'll ever marry. It'd take a heroic sort of woman to live with me."

"No, I do not think so." Lucita then moved, and Clay hurried to help her down from the wagon. As he took her hand, she held it for a moment and smiled up at him. "Thank you for taking me."

"Well, we'll do it again sometime."

"Maybe there will be a celebration in Shreveport when we get there with the cattle."

"If there ain't, we'll make one. Good night, Lucita."

Lucita watched as Clay got back in the wagon and drove away. She did not move for a long time, but finally she smiled secretly, turned, and went into the house.

CHAPTER
TWENTY-FOUR

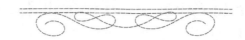

Brodie stepped forward and took Julie's hand, helping her down from the buggy she had driven up to the front door. He was beaming as he said, "Why, Aunt Julie, you look pretty!"

"Why, thank you, Brodie. And you look downright handsome. My, you're growing up so fast." Julie stood in front of Brodie, reached up, and put her hand on his shoulder. "Why, you're taller than your pa now, I'd bet."

"A little bit. I'll put your mare up for you."

"I'll probably stay all night if your ma will have me."

Brodie's face changed, and he said, "Well, Ma's a little bit touchy right now."

"What about?"

"I don't know. She just ain't herself lately." His face brightened, and he said, "Serena's comin' to stay for a while with us while her ma's gone."

"Oh, where's Lucita going?" Julie asked.

"Clay and Mateo are taking a bunch of longhorns to Shreveport to sell. Lucita's going along to do the cookin'. I thought it'd make Ma happy, but she didn't seem to like the idea too much."

Julie chewed her lower lip thoughtfully and then said, "Well, you won't have any competition here with Serena."

"You're talkin' about how I made a fool of myself in town at the dance. Well, I plumb did it. I just don't know how to act around girls, Aunt Julie."

Julie reached up and put her hand on Brodie's cheek. "A young fellow has a certain amount of foolishness, and it's got to get out. I'll tell you what. Later on after supper, you can take me down to the river for a walk, and I'll tell you how to make women happy. Julie laughed at Brodie's expression and shook her head. "Go put up that horse now." She turned and walked into the house, calling out, "Where are you, Jerusalem?"

"Here in the kitchen," Jerusalem called back.

Julie found her sister churning butter and pulled up a chair where she could sit facing her. "I came for a visit. Going to stay all night, maybe longer."

"That'll be nice, Julie. Always good to have you."

Julie knew that Jerusalem did not approve of her way of life, so she did not mention any of her activities in town. Instead, she wanted to know what all was going on out at the ranch. She listened as Jerusalem spoke and noticed her sister had a soberness about her that was unusual. "I hear that Serena's coming to stay while her ma goes with Clay to sell the cattle at Shreveport."

"That's what they plan," Jerusalem said as she continued to churn the butter.

Julie stared at Jerusalem carefully. "What's the matter with you? You mad at me?"

"No, of course not."

"Well, what is wrong with you, then?"

Jerusalem continued to move the plunger up and down and did not speak for a moment. When she looked up, her lips were drawn into a tight line. "We don't need to sell any cattle. We're getting by. And besides that, there's a lot of work for Clay to do around here. He doesn't need to be going all the way to Shreveport."

"Maybe Clay thinks Lucita needs the money. I hear she's going along to do the cooking."

Jerusalem applied more force than was necessary to the plunger, and her face grew more tense. "She doesn't need to be going. It doesn't look right."

For a moment Julie didn't speak, and when she did, her voice was sharp. "Sister, I've had about a hundred lectures from you, and I deserved every one of them! So you can take one from me now. Stop that churnin' and listen." She waited until Jerusalem looked up and met her eyes, then she said, clearly enunciating every word, "You need to turn Clay loose."

Jerusalem stared at Julie. "What are you talking about?"

"You've become way too dependent on him, Jerusalem. It's not like you. It's natural

enough, since he got us all out to this place when nobody else could, and then he saved you and your daughters from Red Wolf. But I've noticed that ever since you came back, you've been afraid to let Clay out of your sight."

"That's not so!" Jerusalem insisted.

"It is so."

"No, it's not! And I'll tell you right now, Julie Satterfield. I don't need any advice from a woman who lives like you do!" Jerusalem said, glaring at Julie.

Julie got up and said, "I reckon I'd best go back to town. It's a little bit uncomfortable around here."

"You don't have to do that."

"Sister, you're the strongest woman I've ever known, but all women get a blind spot sometimes where men are concerned. I think you need to wake up and face the truth." She turned around and walked out the door without looking back.

Jerusalem opened her mouth once to call, but then she closed it abruptly. "It's not so," she said. "Julie doesn't know what she's talking about!"

★ ★ ★

For the next two days while Clay and Mateo were getting ready to make the drive to Shreveport, Jerusalem found herself struggling in a way she had never known. Something had happened to her that night in Red Wolf's camp. It had looked as though she and her daughters could end up as Comanche squaws. Yet when she openly confessed her faith in Jesus to Red Wolf, her spiritual life had been transformed right in the face of danger. And her life had been different since then. She now experienced a deep joy that she didn't have before. But for some reason, she felt absolutely miserable when she thought about Clay leaving. She went over Julie's words time and time again but could not bring herself to accept them.

On the morning when Clay was leaving with Mateo and Lucita, she got up early and started to make breakfast. She couldn't explain why, but she felt an uneasiness that bordered on fear. The more she tried to ignore it, the more it grew. She began thinking how hard life would be if something happened to Clay. She thought about how they all could have died a slow death at Red Wolf's hands. Out here on the plains of Texas, the Indians were a constant danger.

But then another thought came to her mind. *Lucita has always had something in her eyes for Clay. She's grateful to him, but it's more than that. She doesn't need to go. Clay doesn't know anything about women. He's weak like all men are.*

Finally, this thought became intolerable. She called Moriah and said, "I'm going over to Lucita's. You take care of Mary Aidan while I'm gone."

Jerusalem went outside, hitched up the buggy, and left at once. All the way to Lucita's house, she went over what she was going to say. "It's not right for him, but he ought to see it. But men are blind. She's an attractive woman, and she likes him more than he knows. And Clay's not handsome, but women are drawn to him. I can't let him put himself in this kind of danger."

As she neared Lucita's adobe house, she could see the dust raised by the cattle that had been gathered to drive to market. When she pulled up, Clay left the small herd and came riding over. He looked excited as he came alongside her and the buggy.

"Come to see us off? We've made a good

selection. They should bring us a good price."

"No, Clay, I didn't come for that." The speech was in her mind, and she knew that if she didn't make it immediately, she would not be able to. "Clay, I've tried to talk to you about this. I think it's the wrong time to take any cattle to market. There are some things that need doing around the place, so I've decided that you're not to go."

Clay stared at Jerusalem with astonishment. "But I've explained all that, Jerusalem. We do need cash, and what's more, Lucita needs it a lot more. Look," he said, "we can get a good price for these cattle, and we won't be gone more than a couple of weeks. I can bring back some of the things we've been needing from Shreveport."

Jerusalem shook her head and said brusquely, "No, Clay, you can't go."

Something changed in Clay Taliferro at that moment. He was an easygoing man with a ready grin, but he had no smile on his face, and his lips drew into a tight line. For that instant, he had the same hard look on his face as when he had challenged Red Wolf. His eyes were fixed on her, and he said, "I'm going, Jerusalem. Make up your mind to that. Besides, there's something I need to take care of."

A mixture of anger and fear took hold of Jerusalem, and she said, "Clay, it's not fit for a single man and a single woman to make a trip like this together." The words seemed to hang in the air, and Jerusalem knew at that instant that she had said too much.

Clay gave her an odd look and said, "I'm going to take these cattle to market, Jerusalem, and I have an errand of my own to do."

And then Jerusalem blurted out without thinking, "If you do go, Clay, don't bother to come back!" She was appalled at her outburst, and she felt the blood leave her face. She had never spoken to Clay like this before.

For a moment Clay did not move, and then he shrugged his shoulders. "You don't know everything that's in a man," he said, then turned and rode away.

Jerusalem sat there, knowing that she had made a complete fool of herself! For a fleeting moment, she was ready to chase after him in the buggy and try to make it right. But the look on his face had been like the closing of a door. She spoke to the horse and turned around, heading back home. Her shoulders were slumped, and she had to blink the tears away. *Why did I say such a thing as that? What a fool I am!* As she rode back to the house, she realized she would never be able to face Clay again in the same easy way they had always had toward each other.

For the next week Jerusalem made it a point to keep her feelings to herself. Every night she lay awake, remembering the last scene with Clay and thinking of how she had said things that should never be said by a woman to a man. She had tossed and turned and gone over and over the scene in her mind. The more she thought of it, the more ashamed she grew of her words and her actions. For most of the time, she managed to keep her feelings from showing, but once Mary Aidan asked, "Why don't you laugh, Mama?" And she knew that even the child had sensed the difference in her. Clinton had not. He was not a discerning young man, and Brodie was too occupied with shining up to Serena to even notice.

On Thursday night she awoke at three o'clock, and after tossing in bed for an hour, she got up and dressed and went into the kitchen. Lighting the lamp, she began to read in her Bible. She was reading the sixty-ninth Psalm, which began, "Save me, O God; for the waters are come in unto my soul. I sink in deep mire, where there is no standing; I am come into deep waters, where the floods overflow me. I am weary of my crying: my throat is dried: mine eyes fail while I wait for my God." She felt the cry of the psalmist deeply, and then she read verse five, which seemed to leap out at her: "O, God, thou knowest my foolishness; and my sins are not hid from thee."

The words burned into Jerusalem's heart, and she bowed her head and began to pray. For a long time, all she could say was, "Oh, God, forgive me. I've been a foolish woman." Finally a peace came to her heart, and she got up and washed her face. She went out on the porch and sat down. The night was cool and refreshing, just like the refreshing she found in her soul. She knew God had heard her prayer and forgiven her.

She sat there until the dawn began to break in the east, and she was able, for the first time, to think clearly about Clay.

"I can't marry Clay because I have a husband. I know Clay's lonesome at times. If he loves Lucita and she loves him, then it would be good if they married." Even as she spoke these words, she realized how painful it was to see the truth. She reminded herself to have a talk with Julie. Her sister was right. She also realized how a large part of her life had been influenced by Clay Taliferro. She sat there watching the sun come up and then suddenly stood up, for someone was riding along the road. She stood there peering until she recognized that it was Jake. She waited until he stepped off of his horse and came up on the front porch before speaking.

"Hello, Jake. Surprised to see you here. When did you get back?"

Jake was wearing his buckskins, and there was a nervousness about him as he came and stood before her, taking off his hat. "I've been back for two days."

"Was your trip successful?"

"I guess you might say that," Jake said as he turned the hat around by the edges. "I

came to tell you something, Jerusalem. I've been thinkin' a lot while I was off in the mountains. It's a good place for a man to think and see things clear. When you're on the top of a ridge, looking out across a valley, your thoughts have a way of speaking to you. I thought about you and the kids, and I thought about what a sorry, trifling, no-account husband and father I've been."

Jerusalem was shocked at Jake's words. She had been married to this man for years, and suddenly she realized that she had never really known him. "Jake, I . . . I don't know what to say. You ought not to be too hard on yourself."

"Yes, I should. That's been the problem all these years. I ain't been hard enough on myself. But we can't go on like this. I know it, and you know it. So while I was out in the mountains, I made a decision." He reached into his pocket and pulled out an envelope. "I want you to have this. It's for you and the kids."

"What is it, Jake?" Jerusalem asked as she took the envelope.

"It's a deed to the land that I bought. I want you and the kids to have it."

"Why, I won't take it, Jake. You paid for

that land fair and square, and your family needs it. You've got to look out for them. You've got a new baby now."

"I'll take care of Awinita and the kids, but this is for you. It ain't enough to make up for all the hard years when I wasn't much of a husband to you—or a pa to the kids when they needed me . . ."

Jerusalem shook her head. "I can't take it, Jake."

"You got to take it. That's all there is to it. I'm leavin' here with Awinita and the kids. She's miserable and wants to go back to her own people. So that's what we're going to do."

Jerusalem could not think clearly. She held the envelope in her hand and looked into Jake's face. She tried to recall the first time she felt love for this man. They had shared the same house, the same bed, and although it was true he had never been a good husband or a good father, still they had shared life for many years. She realized as she stood there that whatever that youthful feeling had been, it was completely gone, or what was left was only a faint memory.

"I'm gonna say good-bye to the kids,

and we're leaving first thing tomorrow. You take the house and everything that we leave in it."

"This isn't right, Jake. I need to pay you something."

"No, you don't." Jake reached out suddenly and put his hand on Jerusalem's shoulder and squeezed it. "You got to take it, Jerusalem. It'll make me feel halfway like a man. I can't leave Awinita now. She'd be helpless, but you're a strong woman. If you want a divorce, you can sure have it. You deserve a good husband, but it ain't me."

"I hate that it's come to this, Jake."

"So do I. Well, get the kids up, and this is good-bye. Try not to think too hard of me, Jerusalem."

"I'd never do that, Jake." She put her hand over his, and in that instant, she knew she was saying good-bye to a lot of years. "I'll get the kids. They'll want to say good-bye to their pa."

CHAPTER
TWENTY-FIVE

Jerusalem had seen Lucita drive up and went out on the front porch. She waited until Lucita was close and then said, "It's good to see you back. When did you get in?"

Lucita was wearing fresh clothes, but she looked tired. "Just yesterday."

"Come in and tell me about the trip." Jerusalem held the door open and then led Lucita to the kitchen. "I've got some lemons, and I made lemonade. It won't be cold, but it's good."

"That would be nice," Lucita said as she sat down at the kitchen table.

Jerusalem busied herself with pouring the

lemonade into glasses and then sat down at the table across from Lucita. The two women talked for a moment, and then Lucita reached into her pocket and handed over an envelope. "There is your share of the money for the cattle. Clay got a good price for them."

"Why didn't he bring it himself?"

Lucita gave Jerusalem an odd look and then shook her head slightly. "He didn't come back with me. He said he had something to do, and he told me to give you the money."

Jerusalem made no attempt to open the envelope. She stuck it in her pocket as if it were of no importance and then sat up straight and cleared her throat. "Lucita," she said evenly, "I have an apology that I owe you."

"An apology? For what?"

"I behaved very badly before Clay left on the trip. I told him not to go and . . . I said it wasn't right for you to go. That was very wrong of me, and I apologize."

"I know you didn't want me to go, Jerusalem." She smiled, and sipped the lemonade while the two women sat silently. Finally, Lucita said quietly, "We are much alike, you and I. We have lost our husbands. Mine is dead, and yours is the same as dead. It's the way of a woman to wanta man to hold on to, but you needn't worry. Clay never thinks of me as a woman he might love."

Jerusalem stared at Lucita but said nothing.

"I have seen how you look at him, Jerusalem, as a woman looks at a man."

"No, Lucita, that is not how it is."

When Lucita did not answer, Jerusalem knew that her words were hollow. She had thought the apology might make her feel better, but it did not. "Did Clay . . . say when he'd come back?"

Lucita sipped again from the lemonade and then set the glass on the table. "I must go," she said. She stood up and went to the door, but before she opened the door, she turned and answered Jerusalem's question. "No, he didn't say anything about coming back."

A week had passed since Mateo had returned with his mother from Shreveport.

Clay had given him part of the money for helping with the drive, and he had invited Serena to go to town, saying that he would buy her something pretty.

The two of them got dressed, and while Mateo went to hitch up the horses, Serena went to tell her mother they'd be back in a couple of hours. When they entered town, Mateo said, "I'm going to look at a gun that I may want to buy. Where will you be?"

"I'm going to look at cloth. Maybe you will buy me some to make a new dress."

"Try to find red. You look good in red."

"I will see."

Serena entered the general store, and for the next forty minutes, she looked at every bolt of cloth the clerk had to show her. She finally decided on a brilliant red satin and said, "I will go find my brother. He will buy this for me."

She left the store and turned to go down to the gunsmiths, when she heard someone call her name. She turned to find William Travis walking up behind her. He was smiling and took off his hat as he came to stand before her.

"Well, señorita, it's good to see you again. You here with your family?"

"Just my brother. He is looking at a gun, but he may be a long time."

"That's my good fortune," Travis said.

Serena continued to speak with Travis. He was a fine-looking man, but she knew that he was married and had a wife somewhere in the United States. She had learned that the day of the celebration and Sam Houston's speech, when everyone was talking at the dance. She also understood that he was a womanizer, as rumor had it. But he was well-spoken and seemed to appreciate her company.

When Serena finally mentioned that her brother was back from Shreveport and was going to buy her a dress, Travis put his hand out and touched her shoulder. "Why, this is a pretty enough dress right here. Couldn't be any prettier."

At that instant Serena heard her brother's voice coming from behind her.

"Take your hand off my sister!"

Serena turned and saw that Mateo's face was etched with anger. "Mateo, it is nothing," she said, but he was not listening.

He stepped in front of Travis and said, "You've insulted my sister for the last time,

Señor Travis. If you ever speak to her again, I will come for you with a gun."

Travis blinked with astonishment. "Why, I was just carrying on a pleasant conversation with your sister."

"I won't trade words with you. You are a womanizer and a married man. Stay away from my sister, or I will kill you."

Travis flushed with anger, and for one terrible moment, Serena thought that he might pull the gun that hung in the holster at his side.

Instead, he bowed slightly and said, "I'm sorry that you feel that way, young man. I meant no harm." He bowed to Serena and said, "Good day, señorita."

Mateo watched Travis move away, and Serena pulled at his arm. "Come, Mateo. It was nothing."

"Nothing! He treats my sister like a common woman!"

"Let's go look at the material," Serena said quickly. She knew Mateo had a terrible temper when stirred, and others had been watching.

Two of the observers were tall, raw-boned Texans wearing buckskins. They were burned by the sun and unshaven, and they had a rather fierce look about them.

One of them said, "Come on, we're not gonna let that greaser get away with that."

Mateo whirled just in time to face the two. One of them snarled, "You dirty greaser! You can't talk to a white man that way." Without warning, he threw a blow that caught Mateo high on the head.

Serena screamed and turned to go to him, but the other man laughed and grabbed her. He held her clear off the ground and said, "Teach him a lesson, Bill."

The man named Bill leaned over and kicked Mateo in the side, and Mateo cried out and rolled over. He tried to get to his feet, but the rangy hunter knocked him down again.

"That's enough from you."

The hunter turned quickly and saw who was coming. "What's that you say, Bowie?"

Jim Bowie had walked out onto the street, and now he drew the famed knife from his side and said, "You get out of here, and take your friend with you. If I catch you in town again, I'll cut your gizzards out."

Serena gasped, for the two were larger

than Bowie and looked very dangerous. But the one who had done the kicking said hurriedly, "Why sure, Jim. We were just tryin' to teach this fella a lesson about respect."

"You heard what I said," Bowie said coldly. "Now git!" He did not even turn to see the two scurry away but came over to where Serena was kneeling beside Mateo. "Here, young fellow. That was a mite rough." He helped Mateo to his feet, and Mateo had a dazed look. Blood was running from his nose, and Serena took her handkerchief and began to wipe his face.

"I'll see those two don't bother you anymore," Bowie said.

"I don't need your help," Mateo said, grabbing his sister's arm. "Come on, Serena."

"Thank you, señor, for your help. My brother is not himself."

"Better take him home," Bowie said.

Serena got into the wagon, and Mateo struck the horses with the lines. "Git up!" He did not speak all the way home but sat burning with anger, despite Serena's pleas that he should forget it.

★ ★ ★

Brodie came sailing through the front door, his eyes wide, and said breathlessly, "Ma, Mateo has run off."

"Run off?" Jerusalem turned from what she was doing and said, "What do you mean run off?"

"He had a run in with that fellow Travis in town. Two white men beat him up, and he's run off to join Santa Anna's army."

"That can't be," Jerusalem said. She shook her head. "He would never do a fool thing like that."

"That's what Serena said. She's all broke up about it, and so is her mama."

Jerusalem took off her apron and said, "I'd better go and talk to Lucita."

"I'll go with you, Ma."

"All right." She turned and said, "Moriah, you get supper started. We may be a little bit late coming back."

"Sir, a young man is outside. He says he wants to volunteer."

General Santa Anna looked up from the map he was studying. The tent was large, and the map was spread out on a table. Two other officers had looked up when the aide had come in.

"A volunteer? You mean for a private soldier?"

"Yes, sir."

Santa Anna frowned with displeasure. "Why should I be interestedin enlisting a private soldier?"

Lieutenant Gomez said quickly, "I think you might be interested in this one, My General. He has just come from San Antonio. He lived there a long time, and he knows the area well. He says he has important information and that he wants to serve."

"That might be helpful," one of the officers said. "If he knows the lay of the land, he can be a valuable scout."

"He could also be a spy," the other officer said. He was a tall, thin man, with dark eyes and a thin mustache.

"I will talk to the man," Santa Anna said.

"He's really very young, sir, but he speaks well," Lieutenant Gomez said.

Santa Anna stepped outside the tent and saw the trim, young man standing there. "I am General Santa Anna, and your name is?"

"Mateo Lebonne, General."

"Lebonne? That is not a Spanish name, I think."

"No, my father's an Anglo, but my mother's pure Spanish."

"And you have come to join with us?"

"Yes, sir, if you will have me."

Santa Anna was a tall, thin man with a fine bearing. His uniform was impeccably clean, as always. As a military man, he had proven himself to be an able soldier. He had also proven himself to be more than an able politician, for now he ruled all of Mexico with an iron hand. Part of being a good soldier, he had learned, was always being alert to opportunities, and this young man interested him.

"Tell me about yourself, Mateo."

Mateo began to speak of his family and how his father had died. He also told of the unrest the Texans were starting to feel about the Mexican government. At this information, Santa Anna had looked at one of his lieutenants, who nodded.

Finally, Santa Anna shrugged, saying, "Well, if you know the area well, we could, indeed, use you."

"There's one more thing, My General,"

Mateo said. He looked at the other two officers who had come to stand beside Santa
Anna. "How far do your muskets shoot?"

"What would you say, Colonel?" Santa
Anna said, turning to the tall, thin officer.
"Perhaps eighty or ninety yards?"

"Less. Sixty or even fifty."

"Have you ever seen anyone shoot a rifle
like this?" Mateo asked.

Santa Anna looked at the long rifle that
the young man held out. He was interested
in weapons of all kinds and shook his head.
"No, what is it?"

"It's a Hawkin rifle. If you would permit
me, sir, I would like to give you a little
demonstration of how accurate it is."

"By all means. Choose a target."

They walked a short distance to the east
of Santa Anna's tent. Mateo then turned to
the general and said, "How far away would
you say that pile of trash is?"

The shorter of the two officers said, "Perhaps two hundred yards."

"Do you see that bottle over to the right?"
Mateo said.

"Yes, I can see it. You don't propose to hit
that!" Santa Anna exclaimed.

Mateo lifted the rifle, held it very still,

aimed, and pulled the trigger. The bottle exploded, and Mateo turned to face the general with a smile. "That is the kind of rifle fire you will be facing, General."

Santa Anna's face was grim. "Are there many of those rifles in the hands of the Texans?"

"Almost all of them have one like it, sir."

Santa Anna turned to face the two officers. "What do you think?"

The tall colonel rubbed his chin thoughtfully. "We would not want them to pick us off at long range. We must somehow get very close."

"I think you are right, Colonel." Santa Anna turned to Mateo and smiled. "You are a bright young fellow. Suppose I make you a sergeant and a scout?"

Mateo's face shone. "That is why I have come, sir."

"But you are half Anglo. Could you fight against your own people?"

"My own people are Spanish, General. I want every Anglo driven out of Texas."

General Santa Anna laughed aloud and then slapped his hands together. "That is exactly what I intend to accomplish." He turned and said, "Lieutenant Gomez, find this young man a uniform and explain his duties to him. . . ."

Twilight had fallen, and some bats flew out of the trees that sheltered the house. They fluttered across the landscape, but Jerusalem, after one glance, did not notice them. She had been to see Lucita and was depressed, for Lucita was crushed over the loss of her son. Mateo had left despite her protests and tears, and there was little that Jerusalem could say to comfort her friend. This was the second visit she had made, and now, as she rode back down the road toward her house, she suddenly saw a wagon traveling in that direction. She had ridden her mare instead of taking a wagon. As she approached, a shock ran through her when she recognized the man sitting in the wagon. She kicked the horse into a gallop and pulled up beside the wagon. "Clay, is it you?"

"Whoa, boys, stop there!" Clay said and pulled the team to a halt. He turned and nodded. "Hello, Jerusalem. What are you doing out here?"

"I've been over to see Lucita."

For a moment she could not think of what to say, but she knew she had to talk to Clay privately. She had done a lot of thinking since he had left, and she wanted to try to clear the air. "Let me ride back with you." She got off the horse, tied her to the rear of the wagon, and then climbed up to the seat beside Clay.

When she sat down Clay spoke to the horses. As they moved forward, he turned and studied her. "A little bit late for you to be out."

"I'm worried about Lucita."

"What? Is she sick? She got back all right, didn't she?"

"Yes, she did, but it's Mateo."

"What's happened?"

"Mateo almost got into a fight with Travis in town, and now he's run off to join Santa Anna's army. It's hit Lucita hard."

Clay shook his head and said, "I wish that boy hadn't done that. It's going to make it hard on them all."

When Clay didn't say any more, Jerusalem began to talk about all the things that had taken place on the ranch. "The cow had a new calf, a fine one."

"That's good. I could drink about a gallon of buttermilk right now. It's been a long and thirsty trip."

For the next ten minutes, they rode in silence. Jerusalem had seldom felt more awkward. Finally she said, "I missed you, Clay. I was wrong to say what I did."

"Well, you just lost your grandfather and was drug off by Indians. You was upset."

Jerusalem was grateful for his words. He did not seem angry, and she said, "When Lucita came back and told me you left her, it frightened me."

"It scared you? Why's that?"

"I didn't think you'd ever come back, Clay."

"Well, I had me a chore to do."

By this time they were in sight of the house, and Clay did not say anything until the horses pulled up in front. Darkness had fallen completely, and a pale sliver of a moon hung in the night sky. When he drew the horses to a halt, he turned and faced Jerusalem. "I didn't like seeing you grieve, Jerusalem, about your boys back in Arkansas."

Jerusalem was surprised. "I didn't know it showed so bad."

"I could tell it. It really hurt you, so—" Clay turned sideways and gestured toward the back of the wagon. "I went back to Arkansas. I brought 'em back so they could rest with Josiah."

Jerusalem could not move. She stared at Clay in disbelief, then turned and looked at the bulk in the wagon bed covered by canvas. She did not speak for a long time, and finally it was Clay who spoke.

"I didn't bring your ma because—well, it seemed right that she was right there beside your pa." He waited for her to reply, but when she sat looking straight forward and not moving, he said, "Maybe I done a wrong thing, but I meant well."

Jerusalem turned around and looked at him, and even in the darkness, Clay could see the tears in her eyes.

Her voice was a whisper as she said, "Nobody could have done anything to please me more, Clay."

The two of them sat there, and the bats fluttered overhead, and from far off came the lonesome sound of a wolf.

Clay could say nothing. Jerusalem had turned away, brushing the tears from her eyes. When she turned to face him again, he saw the old smile that he liked so well. He gave a gusty sigh of relief. "I got to thinkin' about it on the way back. I thought maybe I was doin' the wrong thing. I almost turned back a couple of times, Jerusalem. It's awful hard to know how to please a woman."

Jerusalem reached out and took his right hand. She held it between both of hers and for a moment regarded him in a way that he had never seen before.

"You know how to please one woman, Clay, and that's more than most men learn in a lifetime." She looked back at the shape of the coffins covered by canvas and was silent for a time. Finally she said, "You know that song you sing sometimes, about the rose from New Orleans?"

"Just an old song I picked up."

"I find myself singing the chorus:

Deep in the heart!
O deep in the heart!
Naught can be lost
That's deep in the heart.

"I guess that foolish song has some truth in it after all."

"Yes. My boys are deep in my heart. And, Clay, I didn't think I'd learn to love this place, but Texas is deep in my heart too. Do you think it's foolish to let a place come to mean so much?"

"No, I don't think it's foolish. Matter of fact, Texas has kind of come to mean a lot to me too. It took a while. I didn't like it much at first. It's a place where there are more rivers and less water, and where you can see farther and see less than most any place I know. But it's a good land—and going to be a free land someday."

Jerusalem squeezed his hand and said, "Sing me a little of that song, Clay." She leaned back as Clay began to sing.

"I found a rose in New Orleans. . . ."

Overhead, a big horned owl drifted silent as a candle in a tomb. He banked into a sharp turn, his eyes on the two in the wagon, and then straightened up and flew over the silent land.

PART FIVE:

THE ALAMO

1835-1836

PART FIVE:

THE ALAMO
1835-1836

CHAPTER
TWENTY-SIX

The morning sun broke in the east, shedding crimson rays that reflected off the river. The silence of the morning was broken by the three individuals in the flat-bottomed boat who had crossed the river. Clinton jumped out of the bow and pulled the boat up onto the shoreline.

Clay stood up, balancing himself easily, and smiled at the two boys. "Well," he drawled, "we done got enough fish here to feed everybody, I reckon."

Brodie stood up and picked up one of the burlap sacks, opened it, and looked down inside. "This is the best we ever did on this here trot line." Reaching down, he carefully pulled up a huge catfish and laughed as it thrashed around, trying to free itself. "You just wait until we get you in a fryin' pan. You'll stop thumpin' then."

"Hurry up, I'm tired!" Clinton complained. "I had to do all the rowing to get us back to shore . . ."

"I swear, Clinton," Clay said as he leaped ashore, "you'd complain if they hung you with a new rope." He picked up a second sack of fish and stood looking for a moment at the river. "You know what?" he observed. "This wouldn't be a bad time for us to get a bath."

"I ain't takin' no bath," Clinton said. He picked up one of the sacks and said, "I ain't gettin' in that dirty ole river."

"Why, Clinton," Clay grinned. "I figured a good Baptist like you would be the first in, seeing how you Baptists love water so much."

Clinton glared at Clay, then turned and without another word trudged away. Clay laughed aloud. "That boy hates bathin' about as bad as any young'un I ever saw. Well, you and me can have a nice swim."

"Oh, I don't want to," Brodie said as he

stepped out of the boat. "I got to ride over and help Lucita build a fence. Now that Mateo's left she needs the help."

"Yeah, I know how much you love to build fences, Brodie. The last time we built one I could just hardly stay out of your way you were so anxious to get at it." He laughed at Brodie's expression and said, "I think the fence building has more to do with the fact you're sweet on Serena. Come on. Let's have a swim. You'll smell a little bit better when you get there. As a matter of fact, if you'd wash off a bit, she'd be a mite happier to see you."

Brodie's feelings were hurt, for he was a sensitive young man. He muttered something to himself, then grabbed one of the sacks and said, "You go on and take all the baths you want to. I'm going back to the house."

Brodie turned and left, and Clay stared after him. As the two young men disappeared, he shook his head. "I keep forgettin' how downright sensitive Brodie is. Can't take any joshin' at all about Serena, but I reckon I was about the same way when I was his age."

June had brought blistering heat to the

Texas plains, and Clay's smelly clothes clung to him, damp with sweat. He looked at the river and then hurriedly kicked off his boots, stripped, and ran out and threw himself into the river. He let out a yelp as he hit the water and then began to swim with strong strokes. The river was not overly deep at this point, but there were potholes in it where the big catfish lay. The coolness of the water was refreshing, and Clay, who had always been a strong swimmer, reveled in his swim. He dove down beneath the surface, holding his breath, until his lungs began to ache and spots danced before his eyes, then propelled himself back up to the surface. Rolling over on his back, he spit out a mouthful of water and contentedly bobbed along, caught by the gentle current. Overhead the shredded white clouds decorated the sky, and a red-tailed hawk wheeled and turned sharply, then dropped like a plummet, headed for a prey that Clay could not see.

Clay finally turned and headed for the bank, once more plunging down and swimming underwater. He came up sputtering where the water was waist deep. As he pushed his hair back out of his eyes, he was shocked when he heard Jerusalem's voice.

"Having a little swim, are you, Clay?"

Instantly, Clay ducked back into the water and spit out a mouthful as he saw Jerusalem. She had come to dump a load of bedclothes on the big flat rock that extended out where she sometimes came to wash clothes. She was wearing a light blue dress and a flat-brimmed straw hat, and her eyes were filled with laughter as she looked at him.

"You get away from here, Jerusalem Ann, right now!"

"I've got to get these bedclothes washed," she said, a smile on her face.

Clay knew that Jerusalem Hardin had a mischievous streak in her, and he saw it now in the glint of her green eyes. Her lips twitched slightly,and he knew she was laughing at him.

"Woman, get away from here. I've got things to do."

"So have I." Jerusalem bent over, picked up one of the pillowcases, and shook it out. Then she stooped down and swooshed it around in the water.

Clay never knew how to handle Jerusalem when she was in one of her playful moods like this. He stood up and said, "All right, then. I'm comin' out." He took a tentative step forward and saw her turn her head to one side and stare at him. "That scar Jim Bowie gave you wasn't sewed up too good, was it? I could have done it better."

Clay considered rushing out, but something about the humor in Jerusalem's face stopped him. "It ain't respectable for you to act like this, Jerusalem. Now get away!"

"After bein' married and raisin' a crop of boys, I don't think I'll be too shocked." She suddenly laughed and said, "All right, I'll give you five minutes to get dressed."

She turned around and faced the bank, and Clay took her at her word. He scrambled ashore, pulled his pants on, and immediately complained. "You'd drive a fellow to drink, Jerusalem Hardin! Plain take it, you do get on my nerves sometimes!"

Jerusalem laughed and said, "Your hair is gettin' too long. You need a haircut. I reckon I'll shear you today."

Clay pulled his boots on and came over and looked at her. "You are a bodacious

woman! I'll find a way to put you in your place for this little trick. You see if I don't!"

As Brodie pulled up into the Lebonne homestead, he found Serena and Lucita working in the garden. Slipping out of the saddle, he pulled the sack off of the saddle horn, where he had knotted it. When they turned to meet him, he held it high, saying, "Look what I got." He put the sack down, reached down, and carefully grabbed a large catfish by ramming his thumb down its jaw. He had been stabbed enough by the spines on the fish to be careful. When he held it up, he shook his head. "Ain't this a gollynoster of a fish?"

"Oh, that is a fine one, Brodie!" Lucita said. "I've been hungry for fish for a week now."

"I'll go clean it for you," Brodie said.

As Brodie hoped, Serena left the garden and came along with him. He went to the back of the house, where he had driven a nail in about five feet off the ground. Slitting the lower jaw of the catfish, he forced the tough surface of the tissue over it and then pulled out his sheath knife. He then slit the smooth skin of the catfish all the way around the head and stripped the skin off.

Serena watched and shivered slightly, saying, "I think a catfish is about the ugliest fish in the world."

"Well, they taste good when they're all fried with some cornbread and onions to go with it." He pulled the fish down, cut the head off, and then proceeded to cut it up into fillets. The whole time Brodie worked, he was telling Serena about how they had caught the fish. Finally, when he was through, he carried the fillets to the back porch. She put them in a dish, carried them inside, and then came back a few minutes later. Brodie was washing his hands, and she brought a towel for him.

He wiped his hands on the towel and turned to face her. "You're looking mighty pretty this morning."

Serena laughed at him. "So are you, Brodie."

As Brodie stood there, he wished he had followed Clay's advice in taking a bath. He smelled strongly of catfish, and although Serena had a bead of perspiration on her forehead, she looked fresh. Feeling a little bold, Brodie said, "Serena, don't you reckon I ought to get some kind of reward for bringing you that nice fish?"

"What kind of a reward are you thinking about?" Serena asked, teasing him.

"Well, maybe a little kiss," he ventured.

Serena stared at him in surprise. "Why, Brodie, you're getting to be quite a ladies' man."

Brodie had dreamed about kissing Serena, but he had never had the nerve even to hold her hand. Now he moved forward and said, "Aw, Serena, surely a big catfish like that is worth a little kiss."

Serena suddenly moved forward and kissed him right on the cheek. "There," she said. "There's your reward."

Brodie was caught off-guard, and before he could speak, he heard a voice behind him.

"So this is how you take care of my sister."

Brodie wheeled around quickly and saw Mateo, who had silently come into the yard. There was no sign of a mount, and Brodie saw that Mateo was smiling.

Serena ran forward at once and embraced Mateo, calling his name and lifting her voice. "Mamá, Mateo is home!"

Mateo kissed her on the cheek, squeezed her, and then turned to Brodie. "So you have a suitor here, Serena." He saw the stricken look on Brodie's face and laughed. He was covered with dust from the travel on the trail and was wearing what seemed to be a uniform of some sort. He came over and slapped Brodie on the shoulder. "Don't worry, Brodie. I've kissed a few pretty girls myself."

"Mateo!" Lucita came flying around the house, and Mateo stepped forward to greet her. She clung to him fiercely, kissed him, and then stepped back and tilted her head. "Why didn't you tell us you were coming?" she said, scolding him. "How long can you stay?"

"I couldn't tell you because I didn't know, but I'm starved to death."

"You're thin. Serena, come. We must feed this boy."

"Come on in, Brodie. Maybe they'll have enough for you too."

Brodie followed the three inside and sat down at the table with Mateo. Serena brought them cool water to drink, and then the two women hurriedly began to fix a meal.

Brodie was dying to ask what Mateo had been doing, but he didn't have a chance, for Mateo kept plying his mother and sister with questions as they prepared the meal.

Soon they set plates on table with beans, tortillas, and fried catfish. Lucita watched as her Mateo ate hungrily. Finally Lucita asked, "You're back to stay, my son?"

"No, Mamá, I am a soldier now under General Santa Anna."

At Mateo's words, a cold chill ran down Brodie's spine. He had heard of Santa Anna and knew enough to know that he was the archenemy of the Texans. He said nothing, but he saw that Lucita was dismayed. She protested, but Mateo was firm.

"I am one of his scouts now." He turned then and said, "Brodie, this will be bad news for you."

"What will be, Mateo?" Brodie asked, yet he had a good notion that any news about Santa Anna was not going to be good. Brodie had heard enough of Sam Houston's concerns about Santa Anna from Clay.

"The general has organized a huge army, at least over five thousand soldiers, and he will be coming north soon. And when he does, there will be a war against the Texans." Mateo leaned forward and said, "Brodie, you must get your family out of here. It's going to be bad. The general says that all the Texans have got to go."

"Why, he can't shove all of us out!" Brodie protested.

"This is Mexico, and he is now the president," Mateo said. He shook his head. "You are my friend, you and your family, but it would be best if you would leave."

"Ma would never do that!"

"I was afraid you'd say that, but please try to talk to them. A few hundred Texan men with no training will not to be able stop Santa Anna's five thousand trained soldiers."

Brodie felt a touch of anger. He had been friends with Mateo for a long time. He knew he had to leave, so he got up and said, "Will I see you again before you leave, Mateo?"

"No, I will be going back right away." Mateo stood up and came over and put his arm around Brodie's shoulder. Grief filled his dark eyes, and he shook his head sadly. "You have no chance against the general and his fine army. Leave while you can before you get killed. I would grieve over that, my friend, but it is what is going to happen."

As Julie walked down the street, she saw Rhys Morgan talking to Ruby, one of many of the young prostitutes who hung around the saloons in San Felipe. The sight caught her by surprise at first, but then she realized he would talk to anybody about God. Right then Rhys turned and spotted her.

When Ruby saw Julie, she said with irritation, "Why don't you preach at Julie? You're her friend, not mine."

As she turned and walked away, Julie stopped and went over to stand beside Rhys. "Is this your day to save bad women, Preacher?"

"I feel sorry for Ruby. She's so young and doesn't have much going for her." He looked down suddenly and saw the bandage on Julie's hand. "What's the matter with your hand? Are you hurting?"

"I burned myself cooking this morning. Hot grease popped all over." She held it up and shook her head. "Burns hurt worse than any other kind of hurt."

"I've got just what you need to fix that up, Julie. You wait right here."

Julie did not have time to answer, for Rhys turned and ran down the street. He had taken a room upstairs over the hardware store. Julie did not wait but continued to walk. The streets were filled with people, men mostly, and plenty of loud arguments were going on. It was almost like a meeting had been called.

Rhys caught up to her. He was holding a small clay pot in his hand with some kind of plant. "Here, take that bandage off." He bent over and broke off one of the thick leaves of the plant. When Julie removed the bandage, his mouth grew tight. "That is a bad burn, but this will make it feel better." He took her hand with his left one and with the right began squeezing the juice from the plant over the burned area. He moved carefully and gently. When he was done, he looked up, saying, "Is that better?"

"That *does* feel better. What is that plant?" Julie asked, looking at the strange-looking plant.

"I don't know. We don't have it in Wales that I know of, but I got it from a Mexican woman south of town here. She told me it was great for burns."

"Why, thank you, Rhys. The burn doesn't sting as bad now."

"Here. You take the plant with you. I'll get some more."

"I think I'll just leave that bandage off for a while," Julie said. "The air feels good on it." She waved her hand in the air, enjoying the freedom from the bandage and looked around. "Look, there's Brodie."

"Hi, Rhys. Hello, Aunt Julie," Brodie said as he walked up to them.

"I was just leaving, Brodie," Rhys said. "I'll see you later, Julie."

Brodie stood there, then noticed that William Travis was leaning against one of the posts that held the awning up over the store. Travis turned and came over and pulled his hat off. "Lots of folks in town today."

"What's everybody doing here?" Julie asked. "Is there some kind of a meeting going on?"

Travis liked to explain things. "Well, it's like this. Texas has got two political parties now, a peace party and a war party . . ."

"A war party? War against who?" Julie asked with a puzzled frown.

"Everybody knows there's going to be trouble with the Mexicans sooner or later."

Brodie thought immediately of Mateo's words, and he said to Travis, "I heard that Santa Anna has got an army of five thousand soldiers."

"Where'd you hear that, son?" Travis asked, concern showing on his face.

"Oh, I just picked it up."

"It could be true. I heard somethin' like that. So have all these fellas. The trouble is," he said thoughtfully, "there's no leader."

Even as Travis spoke a shout came from down the street. All three of them walked out into the center of the street to look, and Travis said, "It looks like they've caught somebody. I don't know him, though."

Brodie watched as a number of men milled around the rider they had stopped and pulled off of his horse. Travis suddenly recognized one of the men in the crowd and said, "That's J. B. Miller!"

"Who's he?"

"Oh, he's the Political Chief of the Department of the Brazos."

Miller came rushing down the street, and

looking up, he called out, "Travis, look at this!"

"What is it, J. B.?"

"That fella we pulled off the horse was one of General Cos's couriers. One of the fellows knew him, and look what he had in his saddlebag. It's several messages straight from General Santa Anna himself. We've got to do somethin' about this!"

"Let me have a look at that." Travis took the papers and read through them. "It looks like they're sendin' support down to Anahuac. We can't have that."

"Look at the other two. Look at this one," Miller said. He held up another paper and waved it in the air. "It says civil government in Texas has been suspended. You know what that means. General Santa Anna's taken over."

"What's the other one?"

"This is the worst," Miller said grimly. "He says Santa Anna's coming to lead troops all the way across Texas. This means war, Travis."

"Well, the first thing we'll have to do," Travis said quickly, "is to send help down to Anahuac."

"Just what I thought. Can you go, Travis?"

"Of course."

"Good. I'm authorizin' you to raise all the men you can. Go down there and intercept anybody heading north. We've got to put a stop to this."

"I'll do it," Travis said.

As he rushed off, accompanied by Miller, Julie said, "Travis has been looking for something like this. He's just itchin' to see a war start. He sees himself as a general, I think."

"This is getting bad, Aunt Julie," Brodie said. "Don't tell anybody, but I saw Mateo. He told me the same thing. General Santa Anna has got an army of five thousand trained men and is heading north. Mateo says we ought to tell Ma to get out of Texas."

"She'll never do that!" Julie said.

"I don't think so, but I've got to tell her." Brodie turned and made for his horse. As he got on it and rode off, Julie turned and saw that Travis was gathering a group of men, who all seemed to be excited about keeping General Santa Anna out of Texas. "Men," she whispered vehemently, "they like nothin' better than a fight."

★   ★   ★

Sam Houston studied the man across from him and said, "What happened with Travis and that bunch he took to Anahuac?"

Jim Bowie had ridden in as soon as he had some news of Travis's expedition. That had been two weeks before, and he shook his head in disgust. "Why, nothing really happened. Travis took two dozen men down. They found a little brass cannon somewhere. I guess the sight of it scared the Mexicans. The commander surrendered about fifty soldiers, and Travis let them go."

"I guess Travis wants to be a military hero of some kind," Houston said.

"Well, he ain't no hero this time," Bowie said coolly. "When he got back to San Felipe, he found out that the peace party was mad as hops."

"I heard General Cos wanted to shoot Travis when he got back."

"That's what he said he'd do." Bowie laughed. "Texas may denounce Travis for a fool, but it would be another thing to turn him over to a Mexican firing squad."

The two men were talking in Sam Houston's office in Nacogdoches where Bowie had come to meet with Houston. Bowie was a fiery man who loved action, and ordinarily so was Houston, but in this case Houston seemed reluctant.

"What's the matter, Sam? Don't you want to see Texas fight for their rights?"

"It's not the right time for it, Jim."

"I don't think it ever will be," Bowie said. "There's nothin' that'll tie Texans together. They're all just too blasted independent."

"Well, I've got some good news for you. It may make a difference," Houston said. "Stephen Austin's been released."

"He has? Well, that *is* good news! They had no right to arrest him anyhow."

Indeed, Austin had been held for more than eighteen months. No Mexican court or judge would accept the responsibility for freeing him or shooting him, and finally he had been released under general amnesty. He was neither pardoned nor cleared, but now he was free.

"Where is he now, Sam?"

"They put him on a boat and shipped him off to New Orleans. I got a letter from him somewhere." Houston dug around in a pile of papers in a drawer and pulled one forth. "He's changed his tune a lot, Jim. He's always bent over backward to get along with the Mexicans, but a year and a half in one of their jails has convinced him that Texas has got to be an American state. Look, he says here, 'We need to get a great immigration from Kentucky and Tennessee, *each man with his rifle.*'"

Bowie was excited. "Does this mean he's gonna help us break free from Mexico?"

"We've got to do it, but the timing's got to be right." Houston shook his head. "Santa Anna's started calling himself the 'Napoleon of the West.'"

"Texans can beat anything Santa Anna can throw at them," Bowie said.

"He's got a big force, Jim. We know that much. We have no organized army."

"There's enough of us if we pull together."

Sam Houston ran his hand through his hair. "The trouble is Texans are so *independent* that they don't want to take orders from anybody. And, Jim, we've got to have a trained army, or we don't stand a chance."

Bowie looked steadily at Houston. "We'll get one, Sam. We'll have an independent Texas sure as you sit there!"

CHAPTER
TWENTY-SEVEN

The fall of 1835 brought a smoky blue-gray haze over the Texas plains. The sun was warm, but the smell of winter was in the air. Those sensitive to weather changes recognized the coming crispness of winter. The cornstalks stood bare now, and hunters ranged the plains and the hills for winter meat to store in their larders. News came to Texas, as it did to all places, passing from mouth to mouth and making ripples of disturbance. Sometimes it would fade away, and sometimes it would gain momentum. A man murdered his wife and three children on a farm close to San Antonio, and the tale grew into a horror tale recounted from place to place during the long evenings. There were infidelities, and marriages broke up, but other families began with a young man and a young woman who faced the problems of this new country with faith and hope.

The first bloodshed of what would be the beginning of the Texas revolution for independence came in October. A Mexican colonel by the name of Ugartechea got wind of a small brass cannon—a six pounder—that was stored in Gonzales and used for defense against the Indians. The Mexican policy under General Santa Anna was to seize any military arms in Texas hands. Ugartechea sent a Captain Castañeda with two hundred men to seize the weapon. The captain demanded that the cannon be handed over, but John Moore, a leader in the neighborhood, was elected colonel and collected a small force. The cannon was mounted on a wagon, and two yards of white cloth was painted with the bold words "COME AND TAKE IT."

On October the second, Moore's militia met the Mexican force. After a short parlay with Captain Castañeda, Moore returned to his own lines and ordered the Texans to open fire. A brief skirmish took place, and as the Mexican forces abandoned the field and rode back toward San Antonio, there was no question about who fired the first shots in the Texas revolution.

This incident aroused the entire countryside. Hundreds of men began pouring in as volunteers for a fight. Soon the word spread over all of Texas, and the threat of war was in the air.

Moriah was outside playing with her pet coon she had named Bandit. She had tried to teach him tricks but had failed miserably. The only trick Bandit would perform was eating whatever was put before him.

"Here, Bandit, sit up," Moriah commanded. To her dismay Bandit remained on all fours, looking up at her with his bright black eyes, but apparently resistant to any sort of commands.

"You are a dumb old coon! I've got a good mind to let you go hungry for a week." As soon as she said the words, Moriah looked up and saw Brodie driving the wagon out of the barn. Forgetting Bandit, she jumped up and ran across the yard. Moriah trotted alongside the wagon, saying, "Where are you going?"

"I'm going to town to get some things for Ma."

"I want to go with you."

"You have to ask Ma."

Moriah dashed into the house, and Jerusalem gave her permission. Moriah grabbed her bonnet, ran back outside, and scrambled into the wagon, sitting beside Brodie.

"Get up, you lazy mules!" Brodie said, snapping the reins. He was sprawled in the seat loosely, lean and lank, still growing at the age of seventeen. "I don't know what you want to go into town for."

"I want to see Aunt Julie. Maybe she'll take us out to eat at the cafe."

Brodie drove the mules at a fast pace, but not at a faster clip than Moriah shot questions at him. She was sixteen years old now, and Brodie glanced at her and noticed she was no longer a girl but a young lady. With a grin he remembered when she was only twelve she had been sick with fear that she would never have a figure. *She's sure got one now. It's just a matter of time before fellas start linin' up at the front porch tryin' to court her.*

By the time they were almost to town, Moriah had asked enough questions to fill a book. Most of them Brodie had simply shrugged off, but she began to get more personal.

"Brodie, did you ever kiss a girl?"

Brodie turned to his sister with disgust. "Moriah, blamed if you ain't nosier than that fool coon of yours!"

"But did you?"

"What do you want to know for?"

"Well, a girl needs to find out about things like kissing. Did you ever kiss Serena?"

"No."

"But you like her, don't you?"

"Of course I like her. We all do."

"No, I mean you like her like a fella likes a girl, don't you now?"

Brodie fended off her questions, and Moriah said, "Brodie, can I ask you a question?"

Brodie suddenly broke out with a short burst of laughter. "Can you ask me a question? You've asked me about two thousand since we left the house."

"But I mean a special question. Somethin' I been worried about."

Brodie turned to face Moriah and saw that she was serious. "Sure, sis, what is it?"

"Do you think Ma will ever divorce Pa and get married again?"

"No, she never will," Brodie said curtly. He himself had thought of this many times, but he knew his mother's strong feelings about marriage. "Ma will never divorce Pa. It's against what the Bible teaches."

"I guess so. Do you think Pa will ever come back and live with us again?"

"No, I don't think he will."

The two of them fell silent then, neither speaking until they entered town. Brodie said, "I've got to go by the blacksmith shop and get these horses shod. You want to stay with me?"

"Well, you tell the blacksmith what to do, and then we'll go find Aunt Julie," Moriah said.

"All right. We'll do that," Brodie said as he headed to talk to Cal Solder, the blacksmith. When he reached the smithy, Solder was stoking up his fire. He was a big, burly man with bright blue eyes and enormous forearms.

"Hi, Mr. Solder. I was wondering if you had some time to shoe my horses?" Brodie asked.

"Why sure, Brodie. You're in luck, boy. I'm not that busy right now. I can have 'em both shoed in a couple of hours, I guess."

"Thanks, Mr. Solder. We'll be back and get 'em a little later, then. Come on, Moriah."

"You're lookin' mighty pretty, Miss Moriah." Cal winked at her. "You got a fella comin' to see you now?"

"Lots of 'em. They have to get in line, though," she said, smiling.

Brodie shook his head as the two walked out of hearing distance. "You are a story," he said.

"Well, I don't have any fellas now, but it won't be long."

The two went to find Julie, who invited them to eat, but she had other business to finish first. They agreed to meet her at the cafe at noon. To kill some time, they began walking up and down the street. There was not much to see in San Felipe, it was true, but after fifteen minutes Moriah said, "Look, there's Jim Bowie, and ain't that Sam Houston with him?"

"Ma says for you to stop sayin' 'ain't.'"

"Well, you say it."

Brodie ignored her. "Come on. Let's go see if we can get anything out of 'em about this war." The pair approached the men, and Bowie turned and grinned as the two of them stopped in front of him.

"Hello, Brodie. Hello, Miss Moriah. You're lookin' mighty pretty."

"Who me?" Brodie said.

"Not you, you clown," Bowie laughed. "I meant your sister."

"I don't believe I have met these two young people." Sam Houston had obviously had a few drinks in the saloon that he and Bowie had just left. His nose was red, and his speech was somewhat slurred.

"Why, this here is Brodie Hardin, and his sister Miss Moriah Hardin."

"I am pleased to know you," Houston said. Despite his obvious condition, he was a courteous man. He was not a handsome man, and his face looked as if it were carved out of stone. But when he smiled, he looked right at you with a humanness and a warmth that made people feel comfortable around him.

"We'd like to know what's happening, sir,"

Brodie said. "Are we gonna fight Santa Anna or not?"

"Well, as a matter of fact, fellas, it's lookin' that way," Bowie nodded. "General Cos is in San Antonio now. He's got fourteen hundred troops there."

"That's true enough. That's a large force," Houston said. "But some of our men heard that the Mexicans have taken Goliad."

"That's right," Bowie nodded. "The cry now is 'on to San Antonio!'"

Sam Houston shook his head. "That'll be another sort of fight, Jim."

"We can do it. Our men are the best shots in the world," Bowie said confidently.

"They may well be, but they're not that well-organized. We need to join our forces together and train them," Houston said.

"Well, I'll have to admit our fellas don't take orders too good," Jim Bowie said reluctantly. He turned and said, "What about your pa? Is he gonna be in this fight, Brodie?"

Brodie shifted his feet and mumbled, "Pa's gone back to the mountains. He ain't here no more."

"So, what about Clay? He's still here, isn't he?" Houston asked.

"Yes, sir, he's still here."

"Well, you can count on him, Sam. Clay's a fierce fighter." Bowie touched the scar on his neck and laughed. "I got the scar right here to prove it. And if he can face up to that Comanche Red Wolf, then he sure has the courage to fight Santa Anna."

"Mr. Houston, I want to join up," Brodie spoke up.

Houston smiled broadly. "That's a good spirit there, son. We can sure use brave young fellas like you. Can you use a rifle?"

"Yes, sir, I can."

"Brodie, you can't join the army without talkin' to Ma," Moriah said.

"That's right," Bowie said quickly. "You talk it over with your mother, but there'll be a place for you."

"It's good to have met you, young folks. I like your spirit." Houston smiled. Then the two men turned away and headed back toward the saloon.

"Ma will never let you join the army," Moriah said. "And I don't want you to either. You might get shot."

"I won't get shot, but I might do some shooting. Come on, Moriah. Let's walk some more and work up an appetite for that meal Aunt Julie promised."

"I'm hungry enough to eat a horse right now," Moriah said.

"You always are. You sure ain't got no dainty appetite for a young lady."

"Don't say 'ain't,' Brodie. Ma don't like it."

Brodie drove his horse at a fast pace toward Serena's house. He and Moriah had gotten back with the supplies late in the afternoon, but he rode over to see Serena and tell her about his conversation with Sam Houston and Jim Bowie. As he pulled his horse up, he noticed a strange horse there, a fine one that he didn't know. Puzzled, he tied his own horse, went up to the door, and knocked. It opened at once, and Serena, wearing a new yellow dress he had not seen before, stood there for a moment.

"Oh, it's you, Brodie."

"Hello, Serena." He waited for an invitation and then said, "Can I come in?"

Serena hesitated, then said, "Brodie, it would be better if you would come back some other time."

"What's the matter with now?"

"Well, I've got company," Serena whispered.

Brodie turned his head toward the horse, and then it all became clear to him. "Some fella's calling on you?"

"Is that unbelievable that a young man would want to call on me?"

"Well no, but . . . Serena, I need to talk to you."

"Brodie, it would really be better if you would come back tomorrow, if you don't mind."

Brodie flushed in a mixture of anger and embarrassment and said huffily, "All right, if that's what you want." Then he turned and headed for his horse.

Serena called out after him. "Brodie, don't be mad."

But Brodie did not answer. He jumped on his horse and kicked the animal into a dead run. He had looked forward to sharing his day with Serena, and now jealousy boiled up within him. "If she wants somebody hangin' around her all the time, then she can have him!"

★   ★   ★

Clay stretched out lazily in the chair, putting his feet toward the blaze. The fire crackled and snapped, sending fiery yellow and orange sparks up the chimney. He had just eaten a tremendous supper and had dozed off for a time, but now he awoke and straightened himself up. "I'm going to sleep in my boots here," he muttered.

Jerusalem, as usual, had been busy with chores. Now she sat across from Clay mending one of Clinton's shirts. "What did you do in town?" she asked.

"Oh, just the usual stuff."

Jerusalem smiled. "I believe you've got a girl there."

"I've got lots of 'em," Clay said.

"Have you got any particular one?"

"Oh no, I couldn't afford to do that."

"Why not?"

Clay turned to her and grinned. This was the kind of moment he liked. Most nights he and Jerusalem sat here in the quietness of the room after the children had gone to bed, talking about all sorts of things. He had told her many stories of his trapping days and of his youth in Tennessee, and he had listened as she had spoken quietly of her own life.

"Well, why can't you settle on one woman?"

"Why, because," Clay said, "if I settled on one, look what would happen. Why, there'd be jealous women shooting themselves all over Texas because of me."

Jerusalem laughed at the sort of humor that lay beneath the surface of Clay Taliferro. "You sure don't lack self-confidence. I don't believe you, though. I think you're scared of women."

"What's to be scared of?"

"If you'd read the Book of Proverbs, you'd find out," Jerusalem said. "A strange woman is a deep ditch. He that falls in will regret it. That's what the Scripture says."

"Well, I ain't got no strange women, Jerusalem, so I ain't likely to fall in."

Jerusalem looked at Clay's long hair and said, "It's time you had your hair cut. You look like a shaggy buffalo."

"I don't want to fool with that."

"I don't care what you want. I'm the one who has to look at you every day." She got up and moved with certainty, as she did most things, and came back with a straight chair, which she put before the fire. She reached into her pocket and pulled out a pair of shears and said, "Now set!"

Reluctantly, Clay got to his feet and sat down. Jerusalem produced a well-worn towel and tied it around his neck tightly. "Now, you sit real still. I don't want to cut your ear off."

"Woman, be careful with them shears!"

Jerusalem was an expert barber. She had had plenty of practice. She began trimming Clay's hair with swift, sure motions, holding it up with a comb and snipping it to a shorter length. She worked quietly for a while, intent on her task. When she had to move around in front of him, she was unaware that Clay's eyes were fixed on her.

She was so intent that she was a little startled when he said, "I seen a bird die today."

Jerusalem held the scissors away and stared at him, waiting for him to finish. It was the kind of remark that Clay Taliferro often made. Coming from nowhere, he would mention a subject that no one had spoken of. It was as if he had a sack full of thoughts somewhere and occasionally would bring one out at odd moments and toss it out without any preamble.

"What's odd about that? I've seen lots of birds die. Did you shoot him?"

"No, I didn't shoot him." Clay shifted on the chair and brushed his hand across his face. Then he turned his head to one side and said, "I was out over by the woods to the east when this bird came flying across. He was all by himself, and he was flying just as fine as you could imagine in a straight line, headin' north."

Jerusalem waited, but he seemed to have finished. "Well, is that all the story? How did he die?"

"It was the most peculiar thing I ever saw. He was sailing along, then all of sudden he just dropped out of the sky. He started tumbling over and over until he hit the ground. It was so peculiar I got curious. I got off my horse and went over and picked him up. I don't even know what kind of bird it was. He was kind of gray with some reddish stripes on his back."

"And he was dead?"

"Dead as Moses, and there wasn't a mark on him, Jerusalem."

"I never saw anything like that."

"Neither did I." Clay's face was caught by the flickering reflections of the fire. His skin took on a copper tan in the firelight, and his deep-set blue eyes seemed almost hidden in the shadows formed by the sockets. He reached up and touched his chin, passing over the deep cleft that gave him a manly rugged look, then he said, "I got me to thinkin'. I seen lots of death, and none of it was very pleasant. But most of the time you could see it comin' on. I mean, we were surrounded one time by a bunch of Cheyenne. There must have been fifty of them, and there wasn't but nine of us. When it was over, there were five of us left, and I expected any minute to get an arrow in my liver or a tomahawk in my skull. But this was different."

"Were you scared those times when you were fighting Indians?"

"I been scared green lots of times, and somehow this bird, such a little tiny feathery thing, scared me."

Jerusalem lowered her hands now and stared at Clay. "Why did it scare you?"

"I don't know. It just occurred to me that that bird, when he left his nest or wherever he came from, didn't have no idea he'd never make it to his next stop. He was just flyin' along one second, and the next second he was dead. No warnin' whatsoever.

That can happen to a fella. It kind of frightens me to think about it."

"Clay, did you ever feel the presence of God?"

Clay's eyes met hers, and he seemed to be thinking hard. "I did once, at least. It was in the middle of winter, and I was pushing hard through some deep snowdrifts. I didn't have any business bein' out in that weather, but I was. I came to a friend's cabin. His name was Cable Johnson. I hollered, but I didn't get no answer. So I went in and found Cable in the bed. He was in pretty bad shape."

"What was wrong with him? Had he been shot?"

"No, he was an older fella than most of us, and somethin' had happened to his insides. He didn't know what. His heart, I guess."

Clay grew pensive and troubled by his thoughts. "He died that night, Jerusalem, and he died hard."

"What do you mean hard?"

"Cable was a fella who was never afraid of anything, but he was mighty scared that night. He kept cryin' out 'don't let 'em get me—don't let 'em get me, Clay.'"

"What did he mean?"

"I don't know. I couldn't see anything, but Cable was scared to death. He died just before dawn, and he died screamin' as he went out." Clay shifted on his chair and shook his head. "I ain't never forgot that."

"I'd like to go the way my own ma went," Jerusalem said. "She went so easy. It was just like she was getting ready to go on a pleasant journey, and she said good-bye and then left."

"That's the way I'd like to go, but most folks don't go that easy."

"I'd like to see you find the Lord, Clay."

"I guess I'm too tough a sinner for that, Jerusalem."

Ignoring this statement, Jerusalem began to speak. She brushed a few of the hairs that had fallen on Clay's forehead away and then rested her hand on his shoulder. "I was converted when I was fifteen years old, Clay. It was so easy. I was at a camp meeting, and the preacher preached about Jesus dying on the cross, and somehow I knew that it meant something to me. So I went down front, and they prayed over me, and I prayed too. And something happened that day."

"That's good, Jerusalem. I'm glad for you."

"But when my boys died," Jerusalem continued, "I got mad at God. I didn't speak to Him for a long time. Not until I was in Red Wolf's camp." She saw Clay lift his eyes, and something came to his face. "That changed me. I called on the Lord to save my girls, and He saved all three of us. You know about that, Clay, because you were His instrument. But since that day, something's been different inside. It's almost like getting saved again. I've been so conscious of the presence of the Lord ever since."

Whatever Clay was going to say, he did not finish, for the door suddenly opened and Brodie came in. Both of them turned to look at him, and Jerusalem said, "Where have you been, Brodie?"

"Nowhere." He stood there, looking sullen. "I'm going to join the army," he burst out. "I talked to Sam Houston and Jim Bowie. They say a fight's comin'. And I'm gonna be in it." He saw his mother start to speak and then said, "Don't try to talk me out of it, Ma. I'm going." He dashed out of the room, and they heard the door to his room slam.

"Something's happened to him," Clay said. "Never saw him that riled before."

"He's been to Serena's."

"Well, what would upset him about that?"

"He's all mixed up. He's seventeen years old, almost a man. He is a man in body, but he's still a little boy on the inside. He's not like my other boys, Clay. Brodie has always had a tender and sensitive side to him, and now he's in love with a woman, and he's all mixed up about it. I wonder if something happened when he was over there. . ."

"Well," Clay said slowly, "I guess a woman can do that to a man."

Jerusalem brushed the hair from his face and removed the towel. She tossed it on the chair and then began to comb his hair. She was thinking about Brodie, worrying about him, when suddenly she realized Clay was staring at her. She looked at him and saw a certain look in his eyes that any woman could recognize. Clay tried to conceal his feelings for her, but Jerusalem knew they were there.

For a moment they stood looking into each other's eyes. Jerusalem felt a weakness in her own heart. She still held the strongest beliefs about her marriage vows, even though Jake had abandoned her. But she was still a woman and had had little attention or romance from the man she had married. Clay was looking at her steadily, and the wall that Jerusalem had put between them suddenly seemed very fragile. She knew with one word from Clay, it would crumble, and the thought both tempted her and frightened her. Quickly, she stepped back and said almost breathlessly, "What . . . what did you do with the bird, Clay?"

Clay shook himself slightly, as if the words had shocked him. He'd been caught up in the strong feelings he had for this woman. She had an irresistible drawing because of her beauty and strength of character. He swallowed hard and passed his hand over his face. "I . . . I buried it."

"You buried it?"

"Yep. I felt plumb foolish, but I somehow had to do it." Then, as if he could not trust himself, he mumbled, "Good night, Jerusalem. I'm going to bed."

Jerusalem watched him go and then began to clean up the hair scattered on the floor. For one moment she held a tawny lock in her hand, and a thought came to her, but she pushed it out of her mind. "Time to go to bed, girl," she said quietly and put the moment behind her.

CHAPTER
TWENTY-EIGHT

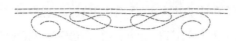

The sound of a horse approaching awoke Jerusalem out of a sound sleep. She had been dreaming of her life back when she was younger, but now that all faded as she heard the horse pull up in front and expel his breath with a slobbering sound. She swiftly threw the cover back, grabbed her robe, and slipped her feet into the shoes beside her bed. She stopped long enough to pick up the pistol Clay had given her, which he had insisted on teaching her how to use. She kept it loaded, and now she pulled the hammer back as she moved quickly into the large room and stood before the door. For a moment she stood there very still, and then she heard a movement outside on the porch. She lifted the pistol in both hands and spoke. "Who's there?"

"It's me—Jake."

A sense of relief flooded through Jerusalem. She lowered the pistol, slipped the bar that held the door, and opened it. All she could see wasthe outline of Jake's bulk, but she said quickly, "Come in. Let me light the lamp." Stepping back, she turned, and laying the pistol on the table, she found a match and lit the lamp. The corona of yellow light illuminated the room. Turning, she took one look at Jake's face and knew that something was terribly wrong. He looked worn, tired, and he had lost weight. "Sit down, Jake," she said quietly. "I'll heat you up something to eat."

"Not hungry."

"You can eat something, and there's coffee."

The business of stirring up the fire occupied Jerusalem, but she was thinking rapidly, wondering why Jake had suddenly appeared from nowhere. She stole glances at him as she prepared some food. He didn't speak. He just sat at the table with his hands out before him clasped together. He seemed to be in a daze, and he had a laxness in his body that warned her that he had changed.

When the food was ready, she brought a plate of potatoes and a large chunk of beef, along with a cup of scalding coffee, and set them on the table. "Here, eat this," she said and then sat down beside him.

Jake stared at the food for a while, then he shrugged and began to eat. He must have been terribly hungry because he ate all the food and drank two cups of coffee.

"That was good, Jerusalem," he said when he finished.

"What's the matter, Jake?"

Jake's eyes were deep pools of grief. Jerusalem had never seen him like this before. They had had hard times, but he had always been one to face it head on. Now she saw that he was drained of the vitality that had been such a part of his tough makeup. He tried once to speak but could not seem to find the words, and then he said simply, "It's Awinita and the kids."

"Are they sick, Jake?"

"They're all dead." The words seemed to be ripped out of Jake Hardin. He clasped his hands together and squeezed them powerfully, yet they were shaking. "Small-pox. We just started gettin' settled down in the mountains, and it got 'em. There was nothin' I could do, Jerusalem."

Seeing the misery in Jake's face, a wave of compassion rose up in Jerusalem. She had not loved Jake as a wife for a long time, though she had been faithful and obedient as far as she could. Now, however, noting the agony of grief that he kept back by sheer force of will, she rose up and walked over to him. Leaning over, she put her arms around him and drew his head down to her. She held him tightly, saying nothing, but feeling the trembling in his body. As she held him he struggled for control, and she simply stroked his hair, saying nothing, but thinking. *Lord, you showed me mercy that night I thought we could all die in Red Wolf's camp. How can I withhold it now from Jake when he's hurting so bad?* Though it seemed strange that she could be trying to comfort him for the loss of another woman and the children she bore, Jerusalem knew she had settled this in her heart long before. When Jake moved, she stepped away and went back and sat down, looking at him across the table. "Have you come back to stay with us, Jake?"

She knew the answer before he gave it, but for her sake it had to be spoken.

Jake shook his head, and it was as if he were having difficulty hearing her. Finally, he said hoarsely, "I heard about this war that's coming up with Santa Anna. I was worried about you and the kids being caught in it."

"We'll be all right, Jake."

"I thought you might want me to get you out of it. I've come to ask if you want me to take you back to the States. Maybe back to Arkansas Territory."

"No, we're staying here, Jake. Texas is our home now. We won't be driven off our land. We worked too hard to lose it all now."

"I knowed you'd say that, but I had to come anyway and offer." Jake straightened up, picked up the empty cup, and stared at it as if collecting his thoughts. "I got nothin' to do now. I thought the best I could do for you and the kids was to join up with this bunch that's going to fight the Mexican army."

"You can come back, Jake, and I'll take you back as a husband." Jerusalem knew what she was saying was hard for her, and

the memories of all the years when he wasn't there for her or the children came back right then. When she had married him she had had high hopes, and for a very brief time she had been happy. But that had been ephemeral, and the memory of his long absences and his infidelity tried to flood her thoughts. Still, she had made the offer freely, and as she did, that same peace flooded over her just as it had that night in Red Wolf's camp.

Jake shook his head and said, "I messed up your life enough, Jerusalem, and the kids too." He hesitated for a moment, then said, "When the war is over, I'm going back to the mountains. You don't need me." He waited for Jerusalem to speak, and when she did not, he said, "I'd like to stay here tonight and say my good-byes to the kids tomorrow before I leave."

"You're welcome, Jake."

Without another word Jake got up and went outside. He came back soon with his bedroll, threw it out on the floor before the fire that had almost died down. "I'll be all right here." He turned to her and then something came to him. He walked over and took her hand and looked into her eyes for a long time.

"Jerusalem, I know what I did to you and the kids. And . . . well . . . I'm sorry about everything. You've been a good wife, and you deserve better than me." He turned then, lay down on the bedroll, and pulled the blanket over him.

Jerusalem turned and went back to the bedroom. It was cold in the room. She undressed, got into bed, and pulled the covers around her. Her mind raced as she tried to understand what had just happened. She thought of the long years that she had been married to Jake, and one thing came with a grim finality. "That's all over," she said. "He'll never come back to his family now."

When Brodie walked into the room, followed by Clinton and Moriah, a shock ran through him at the sight of his father sitting at the table with Clay. He stopped so abruptly just inside the door that Clinton ran into him and then gave him a shove.

"What are you stoppin' fer? Get out of the

way!" But Clinton, too, halted, and Moriah as well, when she entered the room.

"Pa, you're back!" Brodie said and watched as Jake got up and came over to him. Jake was staring at him in a strange way.

"Boy, you're growin' like a bean. How tall are you now?"

"I don't know, Pa."

"He's about six-three, I think, if I figured right," Jerusalem said.

"You're gonna fill out one day and be a considerable man," Jake said as he looked up at his son. He squeezed Brodie's shoulder and kneaded the lean muscle. "You growed up all at once, boy. You know you look a lot like my own pa. You never got to see him. He was tall and lean like you and a better man than I ever was. I think you're gonna be just like him."

Jake turned to Clinton and grinned. "Well, Clinton, nobody'll ever need a picture of me as long as you're around."

Clinton swelled up with pride. He had always been proud of the fact that he looked like Jake much more than Brodie, who took more after his mother in some ways.

Jake then turned to Moriah. He stared at

her for so long, and she met his gaze. "What are you starin' at me for, Pa?"

Jake shook his head, and a look of wonder filled his eyes. "You know, Moriah, you look exactly like your ma did the first time I ever saw her. She's the finest lookin' woman I ever seen, and you're just like her." He reached out and ran his hand over her dark red hair, something he had not done for a long time. "I hope you turn out to be as fine a woman as she is."

Moriah was startled by her father's gentleness. Jake had never been one to give caresses to his children. Moriah could not speak but watched him intently, something in her expression that Jerusalem caught.

"Everyone sit down to eat," Jerusalem said. The children all sat down, and Jake sat down beside Clay. Clinton plunged into his food, but Moriah and Brodie could not take their eyes off Jake.

"Where is Awinita, Pa?" Moriah asked.

Jake did not answer at once, and all three of the children looked up at him to see the reason for his silence. Jake had a fork in his hand, and now Brodie saw that he clenched it so tight that his fingers turned white.

"She's gone, daughter, and both the kids.

They died of smallpox." Jake struggled with his words and then said painfully, "Paco went first. I buried him, but then Awinita . . . she died three days later. And then two days after I buried her, Rose died."

Brodie could not speak, and he saw that the others were struck dumb also. "I'm real sorry, Pa," he said quietly. "I was real fond of Awinita and the kids."

"I appreciate that, son," Jake said. He put the fork down and then looked down the table, studying the three. "I got me a chore to do. I'm goin' to join up with the army and stop this here Santa Anna."

At once Brodie straightened up. "I'm goin' with you, Pa."

Jake shook his head. "You're a man now, Brodie, and I'd take it as a favor if you'd stay with your ma and your brother and sisters. I'd be right pleased if you'd do that for me."

Brodie longed to go with him, but something in his father's eyes stopped him. His father had given him plenty of orders during his lifetime, but as far as Brodie could remember, he had never received this kind of request. Brodie thought, *Pa's changed. He ain't the same as he was.*

He struggled for a brief time with what his father had asked of him, but then he looked at him and said, "All right, Pa, if that's what you want."

"I appreciate that, son."

Jake rose to his feet. "I guess I'd better go." Instantly everybody got up, and Jake stood before them looking at them strangely. He came to Brodie and put out his hand. Brodie felt the large hand close around his, and then his father reached out and embraced him. Brodie could not remember his father ever doing a thing like that, and he held him tightly for a fleeting moment.

Jake turned and embraced Clinton and then turned to Moriah. "You're a beautiful girl. I'm right proud of you." He reached out, and she came to his arms and held on to him tightly. When she stepped back, Jerusalem saw tears in Moriah's eyes.

"I'm proud of all of you," Jake said. And then he turned to Jerusalem and stood before her silently. The silence seemed to run on for a long time, and finally Jake reached out and put his hand on her shoulder. "I wish . . ." he said and then broke off. "I wish

I'd been a better man for you, Jerusalem Ann."

At once Jake turned and left. Clay picked up the bedroll that Jake had apparently forgotten and hurried out after him. By the time he got outside, Jake was putting the saddle on his horse. Clay stepped up and threw the bedroll over and tied it down with thongs on the saddle. As he stepped back, Jake turned to face him, and Clay said simply, "I hate to see you go, Jake."

Jake Hardin stood for a moment looking into Clay's eyes. He was worn down, and fatigue had etched its lines on his face, but he smiled. "We had some good times together, didn't we, hoss?"

"Fine times, Jake."

Jake put out his hand, and Clay took it. "You done everything I asked you, Clay. Now let me ask you one more thing."

"You just name it."

"Watch out for Jerusalem and the kids."

"Sure I will. You can count on it."

Jake crushed Clay's hand with his powerful grip, and then he swung into the saddle. He looked at the family, for they had come outside and stood watching him. He leaned forward and said so quietly that only Clay could hear him, "Stay out of this war, Clay, as long as you can." He straightened up then and looked at his family one more time. Something passed between him and Jerusalem that could not be spoken. He tore his eyes away from her then, turned the horse around, and kicked his sides. His horse, a big, powerful bay, cantered down the road, and Jake Hardin did not look back one time.

CHAPTER
TWENTY-NINE

As Jake approached the town of Gonzales, he pulled up his bay and stared at a large body of mounted men, followed by men on foot, coming toward him. Jake watched them for a moment and shook his head. "I must have met the army right on." He waited until the leaders reached him, and he saw Jim Bowie in the front, riding a light gray stallion. Jake pulled his horse up beside Bowie and said, "What's going on, Jim?"

"Why, hello, Jake." Bowie grinned. He was wearing a gray wool coat, and the knife that bore his name was suspended in a leather thong at his side. "Did you come to join up?"

"I was lookin' for the army."

"Well, this is it, Jake," Bowie said and waved his hand back at the group. "We're going to whip up on the Mexicans."

"What do I have to do to join?" Jake asked.

"Consider yourself joined. You'll be with me. I need some good men for scouts."

Jake grinned and looked at the rag-tag group of volunteers. "This don't seem a whole lot like an army to me. More like a party of some kind."

"Well, we don't have the uniforms, and most of these fellas wouldn't know an about-face from a right face, but they've all got rifles, and they can all shoot. I guess that's about all we'll need."

One of the volunteers later described the march in colorful terms:

> Words are inadequate to convey an impression of the appearance of the first Texas army as it formed in marching order. It certainly bore little resemblance to the army of my childhood dreams. Buckskin breeches were the

nearest approach to uniform, and there was wide diversity even there, some being new and soft and yellow, while others, from long familiarity with rain and grease and dirt, had become hard and black and shiney. Boots being an unknown quantity, some wore shoes and some moccasins. Herea broad-brimmed sombrero overshadowed the military cap at its side; there the tall "beegum" rode familiarly beside a coonskin cap, with the tail hanging down behind, as all well-regulated tails should. Here a big American horse loomed above the nimble Spanish pony, there a half-broke mustang pranced beside a sober, methodical mule. In lieu of a canteen, each man carried a Spanish gourd. A fantastic military array to a casual observer, but the one great purpose animating every heart clothed us in a uniform more per-fect in our eyes than was ever donned by regulars on dress parade.

Before the army got halfway to San Anto-nio, the Gonzales cannon and its slogan, COME AND TAKE IT, lost a wheel and was abandoned. Jim Bowie said, "Jake, we could have used that cannon."

"We don't need it, Jim." Jake shrugged. "How many Mexicans you figure we got to kill at San Antonio?"

"Hard to say. Reports don't always agree. There's more of them than there is of us. We got three or four hundred here if nobody leaves. I reckon they've got about fourteen hundred."

Jake laughed. "Sounds like them odds are about right. We only have to kill about three or four Mexicans apiece."

The two men rode side by side, and Jake became more and more convinced that Jim Bowie was the man to command the expedition. Bowie was a fighting man, and Steve Austin was a businessman, a man of books and paper. He mentioned his thoughts once to Bowie, who simply replied, "We've got to have Austin. He's the man people look to—him and Sam Houston." Bowie would have said more, but suddenly a scout came thundering in on his horse and shouting.

"Jim, there's a bunch of Mexicans out ahead of us there!"

Jim Bowie proved his worth as a fighting man. He took ninety men from the main army and rode out to meet the Mexicans. Jake was one of them. Bowie let his instincts take over, and when they were in sight of the opposing army, he yelled, "Charge!"

Jake laughed and primed his rifle, then drove his heels into his horse's sides. The ninety men charged down on the startled Mexicans. Jake fired his rifle when he was no more than fifty feet from a Mexican. The man was wearing a fancy uniform and waving a sword, trying to get his men into action. Jake's bullet caught him right under the nose and drove him backward. Jake joined his voice with the other screaming Texans and rode right into the fray.

The Mexicans were driven back, and Bowie called his men to take cover under the bank. Jake fell down with the others, and Bowie ordered a steady skirmishing fire. The Mexicans returned the fire, but their muskets were no match for the Texans' long rifles.

"Look out! They're going to try to rush us!" Bowie yelled as the Mexicans attempted a feeble charge. Many of them fell as the long rifles picked them off.

The battle soon became a rout, and the Mexicans began to fall back to the Alamo.

"We got 'em on the run!" Bowie yelled. "Follow 'em, boys!"

The Mexicans retreated, throwing down their guns as they ran for their lives. Bowie's men followed them all the way to the walls of the Alamo, and Jake said, "Jim, we can't take San Antonio, can we, not without more men?"

"That's right, Jake," Bowie said. "You're a sergeant now, so start slowin' these men down."

Jake laughed. "Never thought I'd ever be a sergeant in no man's army." He began riding up and down the lines, stopping the men from advancing any farther.

"We can take it!" some of them yelled.

But even Jim Bowie, as reckless as he was, knew they could not take fourteen hundred trained soldiers with only ninety men.

"We'll wait for the rest of our men to come up, Jake, and then we'll find a way to get at 'em."

The rest of the army arrived shortly, but after a brief conference, the Texans began collecting their booty. They had lost four men, and Bowie believed the total Mexican casualties ran up to sixty.

"Them fellows was out after grass for fodder," Jake said after examining some of the pack animals the Mexicans had left behind in haste. He laughed and winked at Jim. "They'll be callin' this thing the Grass Fight."

As a matter of fact, "Grass Fight" is exactly what it was called. But for the Texans, it was another victory, which boosted their morale. They settled in around the walls of San Antonio, waiting for more reinforcements to come. They were a confident army now, ragtag as they might be, and knew that there would be a reckoning with Santa Anna sooner or later.

Julie had come out on the streets of San Felipe and was shocked at the crowds milling about. As she made her way through them, many of the men who had been drinking made rude remarks to her, which she ignored. When she started across the street, she saw Rhys Morgan and went over to him at once. "What's going on, Rhys?"

Morgan was wearing a faded brown coat

and a low-crowned hat. He shoved it back on his head and smiled at Julie. "Why, Julie, this is a Texas convention. Thought you'd know all about that."

"Men are always havin' meetings of some kind."

"This one's different, Julie. I think they might really do something this time."

"Tell me what's going on. I don't understand any of it."

"Well, there's two parties right now among Texans. One's the Peace Party, and the other is the War Party. The War Party is the biggest. It wants to declare independence from Mexico. But Sam Houston, he's against it."

"What are they going to do?" Julie asked.

"Houston's been named commander of all troops except for those at San Antonio." Rhys shook his head, and his lips twisted in a grimace. "Which is about all the army there is right now."

"I thought Austin was in charge of everything."

"I hear he's going back to the States to raise more money and men."

Julie walked down the street holding Rhys' arm. She was thinking hard, and fi-

nally she pulled Rhys around. "I'm afraid," she said. "I don't understand all this."

"Well, you're not the only one. There's going to be a war, Julie, and it will be a bad one. Look at those Texans out there. They think they can walk all over Santa Anna, but word's out that he's got an army of five thousand and more, and they're trained troops with artillery. It's not going to be easy. Without reinforcements, the Texans don't stand a chance against that kind of military strength."

The two stood there watching as the debates went on with citizens yelling at one another. Sometimes the animosity was so great it almost erupted into violence. Rhys saw that Julie was nervous. "Is there anything I can do for you, Julie?"

Julie made up her mind on that instant. She turned and faced him. She knew Rhys Morgan was unlike most of the others she had met. He possessed a strength and a goodness that puzzled her. Most men she had ever been around were only interested in taking advantage of her. Ever since she had known Rhys, she had waited for him to kiss her, but he never had. It was for this reason she said, "I do want something. Take me out to see Jerusalem and the kids, Rhys."

"Why, sure, Julie."

"And will you do this? Will you stay with us for a while? I'm . . . I'm afraid of the Indians."

"I guess you have good reason. They know our men are going to fight the Mexicans, and raiding parties will have easy pickings on isolated farms and ranches."

"Will you do it, Rhys? Stay with us for a while."

Rhys grinned. He pulled his hat off and ran his hand through his black hair. He had shaved that morning, and his skin glowed, and his teeth were white against his tan. "I may preach a little," he warned.

Julie squeezed his arm. "That's all right, I guess." She laughed suddenly. "You're too good-looking to be a preacher, Rhys. You should have been a gambler."

Julie straightened up in the wagon and said, "Look, there's Fergus Nightingale!"

"Who's that?" Rhys asked, looking at the two wagons they were rapidly approaching.

They were headed in the same direction, but Rhys had driven the team at a fast clip.

"He's some kind of a crazy Englishman come over to study the Indians. That's his man Langley driving the second wagon there. And look, there's a couple of Indians with them."

"They must be peaceful, I guess. I don't know what tribe they're from. I don't know that much about Indians."

"Neither do I."

When they drew alongside the first wagon, Julie saw Nightingale, who was driving. When he recognized her, he pulled up and took his hat off. It was an odd hat, a derby that was fashionable enough in London but looked oddly out of place on the open plains of Texas. Otherwise, he was dressed as always as a fashion plate.

"Why, Miss Julie, I do believe. What a pleasant surprise."

"Hello, Fergus. It's good to see you again."

"A delight to see you."

"This is my friend, Reverend Rhys Morgan."

"Pleased to make your acquaintance, Reverend," Fergus said.

"The pleasure is mine, sir," Rhys said.

"Where are you going, Fergus?" Julie asked.

"I've been to San Felipe to get some supplies. Now I'm going to look for some more Indians. I've had a delightful time with them. I've learned a lot from my research. Facinating people, they are."

Julie stared at him. "I never heard of anybody ever having a delightful time with Indians. Who are these you got with you. Are they Comanches?"

"Oh, dear no, my lady! They wouldn't be interested in being servants. These are Cherokees. That is Long Legs and this is Firewater."

"Long Legs and Firewater? Did you name them yourself?" Julie grinned.

"No, I did not! Their people did."

"Fergus, I have a favor to ask."

"Just name it, my dear Julie." He listened while Julie explained the rising tension and fighting that had been happening, then said, "Well, we'll be glad to stay for a time with your people."

"Jerusalem will feed you good, but then you always eat better than anybody else."

"Lead on, Miss Satterfield," Fergus said,

lifting his hat again. "I look forward to seeing your family again."

They were only six miles away from the ranch, and when they pulled in, Clay and Moriah came out with the other children. They greeted Fergus warmly, and when the Englishman got down and shook hands all around, Julie stepped down and said, "I brought you some reinforcements, husband."

Clay flushed at Julie's casual use of the word *husband.* He saw Rhys look at him with a startled expression and shook his head. "I wish you'd stop callin' me that," he complained. "I might take it seriously."

"No, you won't. But I brought you some reinforcements here."

Clay nodded in Fergus's direction. "That'll be good. Can them Indians shoot, Fergus?"

"Fairly well, I must say."

"Good. Then we'll have eight men to shoot and some women to reload. We'll be ready for Red Wolf or any other hostile that comes our way."

Julie went over to her sister and said simply, "Jerusalem, I'm worried about all the talk about fighting with Santa Anna and the constant threat of Indian attacks. I wanted to be with you."

Jerusalem put her arm around Julie and said, "I'm glad you're here. Now, everyone, I hope you've got a good appetite. We're going to fix a big supper."

"I have some tins of caviar inside my wagon if you think they'd go well," Fergus said.

"Caviar?" Clay said. "What's that?"

"Fish eggs, my good man, and they are considered a delicacy," Fergus said.

"Fish eggs!" Clay made a face. "Why would a man eat that when he could get good food? You eat the fish eggs. I'll take a big steak."

When the convention in San Felipe discovered they did not have a quorum, Sam Houston mounted his horse, a little yellow Spanish stallion, and rode at once to San Antonio. He explained the situation to the leaders there and took away all the men they could spare. He took back with him Austin, Jim Bowie, and William Travis, the actual strength of the army there.

As soon as they returned, they tackled the issue of whether Texas was fighting for independence and whether they should write a declaration clearly stating their intentions. In a powerful speech, Houston argued that it was not the proper time, so the convention declared support for the Mexican Constitution and established a Provisional State Government. Houston himself was appointed commander of the troops, and Austin was authorized to go to the United States to appeal for war funds and volunteers.

While all this was going on, however, conditions in the Texas camp began to fall apart. They had little organization and no strong leadership. The food was running out, and most of the men were ill clad for the cold December weather. Murmurings began, and some men began to drift back to the safety of their home and their families. Others were even saying that it was time to disband because nothing could be done.

At this moment a man named Ben Milam came to the front. Milam was a Welshman from Kentucky. He had been in Texas for a long time and had been allowed to vehemently voice his insistence for Texas independence. The idea of walking away and leaving their advantage was more than Milam could bear. He began to shout, "Who will go with old Ben Milam into San Antonio? Who will follow old Ben Milam?"

Something about Milam's challenge caught the attention of the Texans. They began to bellow in response, and on the morning of December 15, 1835, three hundred Texans, led by Milam in two columns, drove into San Antonio—Milam in charge of one, and a man named Johnson in charge of the other. They fought the Mexican troops all through the town. The Mexicans had cannons, but their aim was so poor that they knocked down more Mexican walls than they hurt Texans.

On the third day of fighting, Milam was shot dead, and Johnson took over as commander of all the troops. The loss of Milam had infuriated them, and the Texans fought like demons.

General Cos was not accustomed to this kind of fighting. Though the Texans were outnumbered, they fought with more courage and tenacity than Cos had ever seen. His nerve slipped, and many of his men deserted and fled. At the sight of his men retreating in fear, Cos lost courage and sent out a white flag and surrendered eleven hundred officers and men to the Texans.

The victory was brilliant, but a serious mistake occurred when an officer name Burleson accepted a pledge from General Cos that he and his men would never fight against Texans again. Burleson even provided Cos and his troops with enough weapons and powder to protect themselves against the Indians, and they disappeared, headed for the Rio Grande.

News of the victory quickly spread through the land and made Texans ecstatic. It was an overwhelming triumph, and all of Texas went wild with celebration. The Mexican army had been soundly whipped! All the Texans had to do was establish statehood within the Mexican Republic. The provisional government called for a new convention to meet at Washington-On-The-Brazos in March of 1836 to form a new government. With an important victory behind them, the Texas army began to drift back toward their homes.

One man in Texas, however, knew that the fight with General Santa Anna was far

from over. Sam Houston realized that Santa
Anna would see the humiliating defeat of
Cos as a spark that would ignite the Mexi-
can advance.

Houston issued a call for troops, saying,
"Our habitations must be defended. Our
countrymen in the field have presented an
example worthy of imitation. Let the brave
rally to the standard."

But Houston's fervent plea was ignored.
Content that they had shown their ability to
defend themselves, no one rallied to the
standards. Almost all of Texas was sure that
their relations with Mexico could be easily
handled—and they were wrong.

The battle for independence was just beginning, and the worst lay ahead.

CHAPTER
THIRTY

Henry Smith, the governor of the Provisional State in Texas, was an irascible man even when at his best. Now as Smith walked the floor muttering under his breath, his face flushed, he whirled suddenly as his door opened. At the sight of the man in the door, relief spread over his tense features. "Sam Houston! I'm glad to see you here!" he said as he went over to greet him. "Things are literally going to perdition. I could shoot that idiot Grant!"

"Doctor James Grant, you mean?" Houston said. He towered over Smith, as he did over most men, and studied the smaller man. "What's Grant done now?"

"Do you know about that scheme he cooked up down in San Antonio?"

"I heard he was going to attack Mexico, but that can't be true."

"Close enough!" Smith snapped as he cracked his knuckles, a nervous habit he had when something was bothering him. "He's got this hairbrained idea of attacking some town called Matamoros."

"Why would he want to do that, do you suppose?"

"Oh, you know Grant. He knows there are a lot of Mexican liberals down there who are opposed to Santa Anna. He thinks they'd welcome an expeditionary force."

"But that would be insane! It would take men we need to stay here and defend our own people—especially at San Antonio."

"Exactly what I think. And even worse, they've appointed a clown called James Walker Fannin to command the expedition down there."

"I don't know him," Houston said.

"Oh, he's a tall, gangling fellow from Georgia. Served well enough in the attack on San Antonio, but he's got an exaggerated sense of his own ability." Governor Smith whirled and almost ran over to his desk. Feverishly, he pawed through a stack of papers and came up with a single sheet, which he handed to Houston. "I sent Colonel James Clinton Neill to command at the Alamo, and look at what he writes."

Houston read the words aloud, squinting down at the paper:

Things could not be worse, Governor! Two hundred men have already left here for the rendezvous at Goliad. That only leaves me about a hundred men to defend both San Antonio *and* the Alamo. They took the pick of the supplies, most of the food and virtually all of the medicine. It will be appalling to you to learn our weakness. Many of my men are destitute and have but one blanket and one shirt. I must tell you that I do not feel that we can hold this position with the force that is left here.

"But this is terrible!" Houston exclaimed. "We've got to do something."

"You'll have to go down to Goliad. You've got to stop them, Sam."

"But I have no authority to do that. Not over Fannin."

"Find a way!" Smith said frantically. He popped his knuckles again and shook his head. "The only men I can trust are you, Colonel Neill, and William Travis. We've got to do something, Sam."

Houston handed the paper back and said vehemently, "The Alamo isn't the place to fight, Governor. Santa Anna will march along the El Camino Real all the way from the Rio Grande to the Sabine River. He could have as many as five thousand men or more, if our information is true. We simply can't defend a place like the Alamo."

"Are you saying we should abandon it?" Smith asked in surprise.

"Yes. We need to pull the walls down and take all the supplies, including the cannon and get out of there. We've got to get Santa Anna out into the open where our long-range rifles can cut them down. It's the only thing that'll work. We've got to feint, strike, fall back, and cut them to pieces with our Hawkins."

"But that's guerrilla warfare. We're up against troops in well-trained formations."

"Yes, exactly!" Houston nodded vigorously. "That's what we have right now, Henry, a guerrilla force! We don't have a trained army, and it would take a large one to hold out at the Alamo. If I know Santa Anna, he'll bring plenty of cannon along. They'll blow the walls down, and he'll leave a force there to starve out the men while he comes straight down El Camino Real."

Smith shook his head. "I hate to abandon the Alamo, but I can see that you're right. I'll write out an order for Neill to move the guns, blow up the walls, and get away."

"Write it out," Houston said grimly. "I'll have Jim Bowie take the order in. I know he could do more good there than he can anywhere else. Tell Neill to trust his judgment."

Governor Smith sat down, wrote out the order, and handed it to Houston. "I'll locate Travis. Perhaps he could help some there at the Alamo."

"What's he doing now?" Houston asked.

"I put him to recruiting men, but it hasn't been going well. He'll do more good at the Alamo helping Bowie and Neill with the men to destroy it. We'll fight this battle your way,

Sam." He handed the sheet over and said, "I been worried about those men in the Alamo. If they got trapped in there and ringed by Santa Anna's big army, there would be no hope. They'd be lost."

"We mustn't let that happen," Houston said. He took the sheet of paper and turning quickly left the room.

Two years of military dictatorship had given Santa Anna a great deal of confidence. He was the absolute ruler in Mexico now, controlling the government with an iron fist. Even as he dressed, he admired the brilliant uniform he had designed himself. He also had separate coaches to carry his linen bed sheets and gold ornaments, and courtiers arranged for pretty women wherever he went. Power corrupts, and Santa Anna had been thoroughly corrupted. Anyone who challenged him was struck down immediately. He had destroyed the state government of Zacatecas with a cruelty that shocked even his own men. He was, however, a charismatic man, and despite his

harsh treatment, his troops admired him and feared him.

As Santa Anna gave a final brush to his hair, he thought about the large army he had formed. He had spent seven and a half million dollars to build this force and train them into a disciplined and loyal group, unlike the ones the Texans had faced and defeated so easily. He had amassed six thousand of these troops, and now most of them were gathered at Saltillo, in the state of Coahuila, two hundred miles south of the Rio Grande. An advanced force of fifteen hundred men was already camped near Laredo at the Rio Grande.

"General, are you ready for the review?" came the voice of his aide from outside the door.

Santa Anna clapped a hat on and went outside at once. "Yes, are the men ready for inspection?"

"Yes, Your Excellency, they are indeed!"

"Get me that young scout. What's his name?"

"You mean Mateo Lebonne?"

"That's the one."

The aide turned and rushed away, and Santa Anna was greeted by his staff as he stepped outside into the bright sunlight. They all greeted him with smiles, and he said, "Well, gentlemen, I think our men are in excellent shape."

"They are indeed!" General Sesma smiled. "We are ready to annihilate these North Americanos."

Santa Anna walked along to the field where the troops had been gathered. Before he got there, he saw Mateo Lebonne and motioned him to come over so he could speak with him.

"Your Excellency." Mateo beamed. He was wearing a uniform with a shiny sword at his side. He saluted and said, "I'm at your service, Your Excellency."

Santa Anna had the ability to command intense loyalty despite the fact that he was an evil man in many ways. He smiled and said, "Mateo, I am glad to see you. Are you ready for our attack?"

"Yes, sir. Ready and anxious," Mateo said as he stood at attention. He felt honored that the general had singled him out to be a scout.

"I will depend on you a great deal to scout out the territory. You will need the best horses. I want you to find the enemy and report back to me personally. Do you understand?"

"Yes, sir. I can do that."

Santa Anna leaned forward and spoke so quietly that only Mateo could hear him. "You know, Mateo, some of my officers tell me that I am wrong to trust a man who is not one hundred percent Spanish, but I do not believe them. You have told me that you will be completely honorable in this matter, even though you are going against some of your own people."

Mateo stiffened. "Sir, I have sworn my loyalty to you. I feel no compassion for the Texans, for they have ruined our glorious country. After all, this is Mexico, and the North Americanos need to be driven back to their own land."

"Exactly what I wanted to hear! I feel the same way. I want you to go now. After this review, my army will be on the march. Find out where the strength of the Texans is and come and report it to me."

"I will not fail you, sir." Mateo saluted, whirled, and dashed away.

General Sesma had been watching their exchange, and now he came over and said, "Are you certain you can trust that boy?"

"Absolutely certain. I have his complete loyalty, and we need him. He knows that land like the back of his hand. He's lived there all his life. Furthermore, I have given him orders not to wear his uniform. He can go and mingle among the Texans. He will be the best of all possible spies."

Sesma shrugged. "As you will, Your Excellency."

"The plan is simple. We will march four hundred and forty miles along El Camino Real all the way to the Sabine River. We will have to pass by the Alamo. We understand by our reports that there is a force there."

"They would not be foolish enough to get themselves trapped inside those walls, facing an army such as this one," said General Sesma.

Santa Anna waved at the amassed troops. "They will flee and destroy the place. When we attack, everyone will flee. You will see, General!"

Julie was standing inside the kitchen looking out the window. "Look at that Fergus, will you? Sometimes I think he's crazy as a coot."

Jerusalem moved over and stood beside Julie. Fergus evidently was learning more of the customs of the Indians he was studying. The two Cherokee Indians were showing him how to do an Indian war dance. The three of them were going around in a circle, bending and stooping and making strange cries as they did so.

Jerusalem shook her head. "You'd think a man as highly educated as Fergus would have a little dignity, but he doesn't."

"He certainly doesn't. Isn't he ridiculous?" Julie said.

The two women stood there watching the antics of the tall Englishman. He had long legs and arms like a spider, and his long, homely horse face was lit up. Having him around brought a sense of security to Jerusalem, and Clay had mentioned that he had enough hunting rifles stashed in his wagons to hold off a tribe of Comanches. His three hired men were good shots also, but it was ludicrous to watch him as he spun around outside.

"Those Indians eat like there's a famine

comin'," Julie said. "I don't know how the food's going to hold out."

"They do eat a lot, but we've got plenty put away. Clay says they'll fight if the Comanches come. He's got them out all night long running around scouting. He says that no Indians could come within ten miles of the place without them finding out about it and giving us warning."

"That's good. I hope they don't come, though," Julie said as Jerusalem went back to her work. After a few minutes, Julie came over and sat down on a chair and looked at her. She studied her sister's face and said, "You're plain tuckered out, Jerusalem, and you're worried. Is it about Jake?"

"No, Jake can take care of himself. He always has. It's Brodie I'm worried about."

Julie gave her a surprised look. "But he didn't go with Jake. He wanted to. You could tell that."

"Yes, he did. You know how young men are. They've got romantic ideas. He sees war as a big adventure."

"Why are you worried about him, then?"

Jerusalem came over and sat across from Julie. She put her hands out and clasped them together and stared at them for a moment, then looked up. "He's so in love with Serena he forgets to eat."

"Oh, that. He'll get over that," Julie said carelessly.

"Most young men go through it, I suppose, but you know Brodie's always been different. He's not like most other young men."

Julie, of course, had been well aware of Brodie's sensitive feelings. He was mooning around and hardly had a word for anyone. Still, Julie was not too concerned about it. "He's young. Does a young fellow good to break his heart once in a while. Don't worry about him. He'll come around."

Jerusalem did not answer, and the two sat there listening to the whoops of the two Indians and the Englishman coming from outside. Finally Julie said, "Did you and Jake come to some kind of understanding?"

"What do you mean?" Jerusalem asked.

"Well, I mean Awinita's dead. I know everybody's wondering if you'll have him back as a husband."

"He'll never come back, Julie."

Julie looked up sharply. "But why not?"

Jerusalem did not answer right away. She thought for a moment, then said, "Sometimes, when someone bends over to pick up something and then straightens up, the whole world has changed. It took a lot longer than that, but somehow, whatever love Jake and I had when we first met just isn't there anymore. He hasn't wanted me for a long time. I see that now."

"What about you?" Julie asked. "What will you do for a man? You're a young woman."

Jerusalem looked Julie directly in the eyes. "I'll do without."

Julie immediately shook her head. "A woman can't do without a man."

Jerusalem said in short, clipped words, "As long as Jake Hardin is alive, he's my husband, Julie. Let's not talk about this anymore."

Clyde Biddle was a tall young man, limber and active. He piled off the mule he had ridden into the yard and said, "Hey, Brodie!"

"Hey, Clyde. What are you doing?"

Biddle's eyes were sparkling with excitement. "Me and Tim Beringer are going to join up with the army."

"Ah, your folks won't let you do that. You ain't but sixteen."

"I ain't tellin' 'em. Me and Tim have got it all figured out. We'll wait until everybody goes to sleep tonight, and then we're sneakin' off and join up with Jim Bowie and his army."

"Jim Bowie! Where's he?" Brodie asked.

"We heard he was at Goliad. That's where the whole army's gathered together now. They're gettin' ready to fight the Mexicans. Me and Tim are gonna get in on it. You want to come with us?"

"I promised Pa I'd stay here."

Clyde was disappointed. "Shoot! We counted on havin' you. Look, we won't be gone long. We go down, we fight those Mexicans, run 'em back to Mexico, and then we'll come right back. Why, shucks, we'll be back in two or three weeks! No more than a month at the most."

Brodie longed to go with his friends, but he had given his pa his word. He listened as Clyde kept urging him and said, "I just cain't do it, Clyde, much as I'd like to."

"Well, I wish you was goin'," Clyde said. "Me and you and Tim have had a lot of fun together, and this is gonna be a humdinger."

He got on his mule with an easy leap and said, "Hey, did you hear about Serena?"

Instantly, Brodie was alert. "What about Serena?"

"You didn't hear? Why, Tim told me about it. Serena told him she was gonna marry Albert Watkins."

"That old man! Why, he must be thirty-five, if he's a day, and he's got two kids anyway!"

"He's got a mighty big fancy place, though, and lots of money. Anyhow, I know you used to be sweet on Serena, but she's just like all other women, I reckon. She's out for the fellow with the big money. If you change your mind, me and Tim will be out at the river sometime around midnight by the two big oaks where the swing is."

Brodie watched Clyde ride off, but his mind was elsewhere. "Albert Watkins! That can't be right," he muttered. He stood there for one moment, then with a resolute motion, he ran toward his horse. He didn't wait to saddle it but leaped across him bareback and tore out of the yard at a gallop.

The minute he came riding into the yard, Serena could tell Brodie was upset. He piled off his horse and came straight toward her.

She was standing outside the house, where she had been mixing maíze flour for tortillas. "What's wrong, Brodie?"

"I heard somethin' about you, Serena. What's this about you and Albert Watkins?"

Serena had been expecting Brodie's coming. She loved to tease him and now said, "Oh, you heard about him asking me to marry him."

"He's an old man! Put that dough down and look at me when I talk to you!" Brodie walked over and pulled Serena to her feet. She was taken off-guard, for he had never been harsh with her before. He was so tall she had to tilt her head up.

"Why, Brodie, take your hands off me!"

"I'm telling you, you can't marry him, Serena! I want you to marry me!"

Serena's eyes flew open. She had known for a long time that Brodie was infatuated with her, but his declaration came as a complete surprise. "Why, Brodie, you're only seventeen years old! We're not old enough to get married."

"You thought you were old enough to marry Albert Watkins."

Serena was very fond of Brodie, but she was also a stubborn young woman who did not like to be told what to do, especially by a young boy no older than she herself. She had no idea in the world of marrying Albert Watkins, who, in her eyes, was a homely old man. Pulling her hands free, she said, "I'll marry anybody I please, Brodie."

Suddenly Brodie came forward. He wrapped his long arms around Serena and held her close and kissed her soundly. Serena had been kissed before, but it was Brodie's first real kiss. He was shocked at the softness of her form, and he lost control of the emotions that swept through him.

Serena put her hand on his chest, not displeased with the kiss, but still determined to control the situation. "You just calm down, Brodie Hardin."

"Serena, you know how I feel about you. You're not marrying him. You're going to marry me."

Anger flared in Serena. "I told you I'll marry anybody I please!"

Brodie stared at her, taking this for an admission that she intended to marry Watkins. He felt something die within him, and without another word, he turned and walked back to his horse. He did not speak nor look back as he leaped astride the horse and drove the animal out of the yard at a hard run.

"Brodie, wait! Come back!" Serena called.

"What's all that about, Serena?"

Serena turned to see her mother, who had come outside. "It's Brodie. He was mad because he heard that Albert Watkins wanted to marry me."

"Why is he riding off like that?"

"Oh, I teased him a little bit, Mamá. He should have known I would never marry that old Albert. I don't care for him."

"You shouldn't tease him, Serena. You know how sensitive he is."

Serena felt a touch of shame. "I did make him feel bad. He's so shy and sensitive. I don't know how to act without hurting his feelings." She looked in the direction of the horse as it disappeared in the distance. "I'll make it up to him tomorrow, Mamá. I promise."

The first thing Jerusalem saw when she went into the kitchen after getting up was the note. It was in the center of the table and weighed down with the porcelain sugar bowl, her prized possession. At once she went over to it and picked it up. There were only a few lines, which said, "Ma, I'm sorry to disappoint you. I'm sorry to have to break my word to Pa, but I've got to get away for a while. I wish I could stay, but I just can't. Please don't be mad at me, Ma. Brodie."

Jerusalem knew instantly that his running off had something to do with Serena. She had found out that Brodie had gone to see her, and when he had come back last night, he had refused to say more than a few words. She crumpled the note up in a ball and shook her head. "God," she prayed aloud, "take care of my boy. I've lost two, but I put this one in your hands. "Please, Lord, bring him back safe to me . . . !"

CHAPTER
THIRTY-ONE

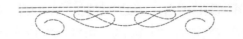

February had come to the land with a sharp, pinching cold that gripped the plains and hills that surrounded Jerusalem's land, wrapping the earth in a mantle of bitter cold. As she sat in her tiny cemetery, the world seemed to be a barren ball rushing through empty space. The trees that surrounded the house reached their stiff, bare branches into the cold sky, as if trying to grab at something they could not contrive. Jerusalem shivered and pulled her wool coat more closely about her. In the wintry atmosphere sound carried easily, and she heard a rifle shot far away. Seconds later the cry of a hunter who had made his kill floated to her on the crisp air as a tinkling sound. Jerusalem leaned forward, her eyes fixed on the small cluster of markers, studying those of her two sons and her grandfather. The pearl-colored air tinged the sky as Jerusalem sat there, and her plain features grew stern and dark as memories had their way with her. Her chest rose and fell softly to her breathing. As the wind whipped across the open plains, she quickened her breath, and a strictness gathered around her mouth.

She heard no sound, but a shadow, darker than the other shadows, fell across her. She turned quickly to see Clay, who had come to stand silently beside her. He did not speak but was watching her with a peculiar expression. His mouth was a long streak across the weathered bronze of his skin, and now it narrowed to a gentle, but strained, half smile. The last of the afternoon light struck against the solid ir-regularities of his features, and a scar on his temple showed white. In that one glance, Jerusalem got a renewed impression of Clay. She knew he was a man wholly confi-dent of some things, but greatly troubled by

others. At times like this, he could be quite homely, and as he moved closer and sat down on the small bench beside her, she admired the strength he had to offer. The silence ran on, and Jerusalem said nothing. But she knew he had come to give comfort. Somehow he had known of her grief, and it had troubled him.

Suddenly, Clay reached over and took her hand in both of his. He held it firmly and was looking down at it. His face was smooth, and his eyes had that sleepy, half droop look when he was thinking of something. It was such an unusual thing that Jerusalem was startled. Clay had never made any sort of move to touch her. She allowed her hand to remain in his, tightly grasped as a man would hold an object he treasured. A moment of shared silence passed, then Jerusalem said quietly, "You're a comfort, Clay Taliferro. Most men don't have sense enough to do things like this."

Clay shifted his head slightly so that he was looking right into her face. "I was taught to be nice to ladies."

"And who taught you that?"

"My mama did."

"You had a good teacher."

A coyote came trotting by with a bird in his mouth. He did not even glance at them but was intent on his errand. Jerusalem watched it go but was thinking about Clay coming to take her hand. She made no offer to remove it, and then she gently gave a pressure with her own. "I can't tell you how much comfort it's been to me to have my boys here. I know it's foolish," she said in the same intent tone, "but I'm a foolish woman."

"No, you ain't."

The whining wind almost carried Clay's words away. He was still looking down at her hand, then he lifted his eyes. "Are you worried about Jake?"

"No, not really. Jake is mighty handy. He could always take care of himself." The next words came without thought. "But he'll never be a husband to me, Clay. He made that clear."

At her words Clay released his grip, and she pulled her hand back. The moment had been brief, but Jerusalem knew it was a special moment she would guard in her memories. Somehow she knew that when she was an old woman, she would still remember this time sitting in the winter by the graves of her loved ones and Clay Taliferro holding her hand to give her comfort.

"What will you do?" Clay said.

"That's what Julie asked."

Out of nowhere a private and ridiculous thought came to mind. It amused her, and Clay could see the effect it had on her face. He watched her face, drawn by the full swell of her lips and the humor in her eyes.

She said, "I suppose I'll do without a man the same as you do without a woman."

"Not the same thing."

"I don't see why not." She turned then and said, "Why have you never married, Clay?" As he sat there silently, Jerusalem knew that he didn't intend to answer.

Clay let the moment go and avoided her question, saying, "I know what's the matter with you. You're worried about Brodie."

"Yes, I am. He's not tough like Jake. I couldn't bear it if I had to bury him here beside my other boys."

Clay thought hard about the danger Brodie was in, and what it would do to the boy's mother if something happened to him. "I been thinkin', Jerusalem Ann, about Brodie. I'm gonna go find him and look out for him a little bit."

"Clay, I can't ask you to do that."

Clay stood to his feet, and Jerusalem rose with him. "I'll be leavin' early first thing in the mornin'. I don't want you worried about him."

Jerusalem looked at Clay with a startled expression, her eyes widening at his offer. Color filled her cheeks, and she leaned toward him, wanting to reach out and touch him. Instead, she put her hands with a strange abruptness into her pockets. She whispered, "Bless you, Clay," and then turned and walked away.

Clay watched her go and then straightened up. He made a firm decision to do whatever it took to protect Brodie from the foolishness he and his friends were getting into. Action was a way of life that came natural to him, and the waiting had gotten on his nerves. He looked toward the west and nodded, "First light, I'll head out of here and we'll see what happens."

Clay said his good-byes in the evening, and long before dawn, he had left the house and headed for San Felipe. When he got there he stopped long enough at the store to buy a few supplies before continuing on to San Antonio. Stepping outside, he packed the supplies in his saddlebag. Before he could swing into the saddle, he turned and saw William Travis riding out. Travis saw him and stopped his horse.

"Hello, Taliferro."

Clay stepped into the saddle and pulled his horse over beside Travis's. "It looks like we're goin' the same way."

"I'm headed for San Antonio," Travis said. "Governor Smith has just appointed me commander of the forces there."

The words caught at Clay, and he turned to face Travis. "I'm goin' there myself. Maybe I can ride along with you."

"You're signing up?"

"Mostly I'm goin' to look for a young fellow who's run off to join the army. Don't know exactly where he is, but wherever he is, I'll be with him."

"We need every man we can get, Taliferro. I forgot your first name."

"Clay."

"Well, Clay, I'm going to try to gather some other men along the way, but the situation is pretty bad there, I understand. We'll have to ride fast."

Clay had a good horse and so did Travis. The two of them rode hard from San Felipe. Along the way, Travis was able to comman- deer a few more men to join his cause. By the time they arrived in San Antonio and pulled upin front of the Alamo, Clay had formed some definite impressions about Travis. From what he picked up, he had been under the impression that Jim Bowie was in charge at the Alamo, but Travis did not seem to feel that way. He talked freely about the commission he had received from Governor Smith and seemed confident that he was in complete command of the fort.

Travis left his small band without a word of thanks, and Clay dismounted and began to examine the Alamo itself. It was a large enclosure, running north and south, built of thick adobe walls. The central area was large enough to house hundreds of cattle and a great many men. He walked around studying the place, aware of how few men there seemed to be. At the southeast corner of the compound, he stopped to look at the mission church—or what was left of it. The church was a two-story building without a roof, built of stone. Next to the church were large enclosures that had apparently been added on later. The southern one was filled with horses, and the northern filled with lowing cattle.

Clay walked around slowly, noting that a number of cannons had been mounted at crucial spots. The best he could figure, the entire compound covered at least three or four acres. He shook his head and thought, *It would take seven or eight hundred men to man these walls against a heavy assault.*

As he kept surveying the place, he kept looking for either Jake or Brodie. As he walked across the open court of the Alamo, he suddenly saw Jake standing in front of one of the buildings that formed the western part of the wall. He was leaning back against the wall smoking a pipe, paying no attention at all to the other men as they came and went with their various duties. As Clay walked over, he saw Jake's eyes take him in, widening in surprise. Jake took his pipe out of his mouth and came forward at once to greet him.

"Clay, I sure didn't expect to see you," Jake said as he stretched out his hand.

"Howdy, Jake. Didn't expect to be here."

"You come to join up?"

"No, I came to find Brodie. Is he here?"

"Brodie?" Surprise washed across Jake's face. "No, he promised me he would stay at home."

"Well, I guess he intended to, but he got kind of a rough bump, and some friends kept asking him to join the army with them."

Jake listened as Clay tried to explain that because of a lover's spat Brodie had left. Jake spat on the ground and shook his head. "This ain't no place for him, Clay." He looked around and said, "It ain't no place for any of us. We're gonna be cooped up here like coons up a tree when Santa Anna's army comes. This place wasn't made to defend."

"Well, if he's not here," Clay said, "he's probably either at Gonzales or Goliad. Why don't you come with me, Jake? We'll run him down. He'll be more likely to listen to you."

"No, I'm stayin' here. You find Brodie and get him out of this place and back to the ranch where he belongs."

Clay did not argue, for he had expected no other answer from Jake. Somehow a darkness lay over Jake Hardin. Clay had known him for years, and though Jake had his mean spots, usually he was pleasant enough. Now his face seemed to have been frozen into a scowl, and Clay did not know what to say to him. "Whose idea was it to defend this place anyhow?"

"From what I hear, Houston sent Bowie down here with instructions for Neill to blow it up, and I wish they would. Jim Bowie's a fighter, not a soldier. Besides that he's sick."

"What's wrong with him?" Clay asked.

"Don't know, but he's gettin' weaker every day."

"Well, you got a new commander. From what Travis told me on the ride here, Governor Smith has put him in charge. It looks like Travis will be headin' things up here from now on."

"Doesn't matter much who's the commander here. If Santa Anna comes up from the Rio Grande with five thousand soldiers, we won't last long."

Clay made one more attempt to convince Jake to go with him. "Pile out of here, Jake, while you still got the chance. Houston will raise an army, and you and me can join that one. Take Brodie with us, maybe."

But the heaviness in Jake Hardin's face did not change. "No," he said. "I'm stayin' right here. You go to Gonzales. If Brodie ain't there, then for sure he's got to be at Goliad. Do your best to get him to go home, Clay. If he don't, try to keep him out of trouble."

Clay nodded. "I might as well leave now. I'll see you when the smoke clears."

Jake did not smile when he took Clay's hand. "Maybe, but I got a bad feelin' about this. If you can get my boy out of this hole, that's what I'd like."

Clay turned and walked away. Jake's heaviness had affected him, and as he mounted his horse and rode out of the compound, he thought, *Jake's gonna die in that place. All of them are.* The thought oppressed him, and he kicked his horse into a fast run and headed for Gonzales.

Jake, along with the other defenders of the Alamo, were disturbed by the arrival of Travis. Not many of them were aware that

Jim Bowie was coming down with some sort of intestinal trouble, but they had put their faith in Bowie and looked up to him as their leader. Now with the order that had come from Governor Smith, Travis and Bowie tried to work out the command of the fort, but it was a difficult time for all of them.

The only bright spot that came was the arrival of Davy Crockett, who was by far the most famous man in the Alamo. Crockett was a spellbinding backwoods orator and humorist who loved spinning tall tales. So popular had he become in Tennessee that he had been elected to Congress in 1827, 1829, and 1833. His career had ended bitterly when Andrew Jackson had been elected. Jackson and Crockett did not get along, and Crockett, after his defeat, told his constituents that he was done with politics and was going to Texas. But even though he lost the election, Davy Crockett's *Almanac,* which featured a number of illustrated fantasies by Davy, brought him huge attention. No matter wherever he went, his fame always proceeded him.

Jake had been standing by when Travis had offered Crockett a commission. Crockett had shaken his head and refused the command, saying, "No, sir. I intend to be just a high private among these my Tennessee boys." When Travis asked him to help defend the most dangerous and exposed part of the wall, Crockett accepted it as an honor.

Jim Bowie and Travis had both spoken of Houston's instructions to blow up the Alamo, but neither seriously considered carrying out the order. Bowie wrote Governor Smith early in February:

> The salvation of Texas depends in great measure on keeping the Alamo out of the hands of the enemy. It stands on the frontier, and if it was in the possession of Santa Anna, there is no stronghold from which to repel him in his march to the Sabine. Colonel Neill and myself have come to the solemn resolution that we will rather die in these ditches than give them up.

The rumors concerning the movements of Santa Anna abounded, but many of them were false. Some said that he was not coming at all, but Santa Anna and his vanguards were now camped on the Rio Grande only a hundred and fifty miles away. The dictator had firm plans for a swift and merciless retribution. He had given orders that all leaders of the Texas revolt would be executed, all rebellious settlers would be expelled, and all the land of Texans would be restored to Mexico.

Santa Anna's army was five thousand five hundred men and twenty-one cannons strong. As they began crossing the Rio Grande, they formed a long, dusty train that looked more like a freight outfit than an army on the march.

The nights were already brutally cold, and many of the oxen froze to death, leaving a trail of abandoned equipment and dead animals strung out behind them as they moved north.

Santa Anna was a man with a mission to drive the Texans out of Mexico at whatever cost. In one sense his move was totally unexpected. The Texans felt sure that Santa Anna would wait for the new crop of spring grass before attempting to cross the winter plains, in which case he could not possibly arrive before the middle of March. Santa Anna, however, was profligate in his use of men and animals, for his ambition to rid Mexico of all Texans drove him forward. General Santa Anna, the Napoleon of the West, as he styled himself, was enraged over the defeat and surrender of his brother-in-law General Cos at San Antonio and was determined to destroy everything in his path.

As Santa Anna approached, both Bowie and Travis sent out appeals for reinforcement troops. There were men in Texas who could have helped in the confrontations at Gonzales, Goliad, San Felipe, and even as far east as the Louisiana border, but the appeals went unheeded. And the Alamo stiffened for the assault by the Napoleon of the West.

CHAPTER
THIRTY-TWO

"Well, I'm glad to see you young men. Welcome to Goliad."

"We come to sign up with your army, Colonel Fannin," Brodie said eagerly. He had arrived, along with Tim Beringer and Clyde Biddle, late on a Thursday afternoon. The three were weary and hungry, but they all were eager to join themselves to Colonel Fannin's force.

Clyde Biddle broke in at once, saying, "When do you reckon we'll go to San Antonio?"

"San Antonio!" Fannin exclaimed, staring

at them. "What gave you the idea we're going to San Antonio?"

Biddle was intimidated by the colonel's harshness. "Why, we reckoned that that's where the Mexicans are gonna attack first."

"My force is organized to go to Matamoros."

Brodie stared at the colonel in dismay. "Matamoros, where's that?"

"It's a very important town on the border. We're going down there and take it, men. You're going to be part of a great victory," Fannin spoke eagerly.

He had attended the West Point Academy for a time. Though he had not finished his courses there, he had a burning desire to put into practice on the field what little he had learned of military strategy. He was, in fact, a martinet who stubbornly refused any new ideas that were not in line with the training he had absorbed from the Point. Now he said, "We're not going to wait. Once we hit Matamoros, the Mexicans will think twice before attacking. Now go and tell the cook I said to feed you men. I'll be expecting great things of you. Have you had any drill exercises?"

"No, sir," Brodie said, "but we can all shoot."

"That's all very well. We need good marksmen, but you've got to learn how to do close order drill. I'll give orders to Sergeant Rains to give you some training. Good to have you with us on this glorious expedition."

Colonel Fannin turned and walked away as stiff as a ramrod, and Brodie turned to his two friends. "I don't like this."

"I don't either," Tim Beringer said. He was a tall and lanky young man with piercing blue eyes. "I didn't come here to learn how to salute and all that kind of stuff. I came to see some real action."

"Give him a chance," Clyde suggested. "He's been to West Point. He knows what he's doing."

Brodie shook his head. "Well, I'll stick it out here for a while, but if nothin' happens, I'm going to join up with my pa at the Alamo. If I'm gonna be in this army, I want to do some good. Come on. Let's go get some grub. I'm famished."

Colonel Travis looked down at the letter he had just written. He had sent messages before for help, but now he realized how critical their situation was. For all practical purposes, he was commander of all the forces in San Antonio. Jim Bowie's sickness had gotten worse, and he could hardly raise himself from his cot. He had confided to Travis that he thought it was a bad case of scarlet fever, and so he had surrendered his command.

"I can't do anything to help you, Travis," he said. "You'll have to make out without me."

Travis got to his feet and read over the letter one more time. He was a man who loved drama, and he had spent much time writing the letter, hoping that his art with words would encourage others to come to his aid to defend the Alamo.

To the people of Texas and All Americans in the World—
Fellow Citizens and Compatriots:
I am besieged with a thousand or more of the Mexicans under Santa Anna. I have sustained a continual bombardment and cannonade for twenty-four hours and have not lost a man. The enemy has demanded surrender at discre-

tion, otherwise, the garrison is to be put to the sword, if the fort is taken. I have answered the demand with a cannon shot, and our flag still waves proudly from the wall.I shall never surrender or retreat. Then, I call on you in the name of Liberty, of patriotism, and everything dear to the American character, to come to our aid with all dispatch. The enemy is receiving reinforcements daily and will no doubt increase to three or four thousand in four or five days. If this call is neglected, I am determined to sustain myself as long as possible and die like a soldier who never forgets what is due his honor and that of his country.

VICTORY OR DEATH.

William Barret Travis
LT. COL. COMD'T.

Travis had made up his mind. Folding the letter and putting it into a leather case, he got to his feet and held it for a moment. "They've got to come," he whispered. "They've just got to."

★　★　★

Clay's horse was weary from the hard ride all the way to Gonzales. When he could find no sign of Brodie after a few hours, he had immediately continued on to Goliad. As he rode into town, he saw evidence of the army, for there were men everywhere with their rifles. When he reached the center of town, he dismounted and watched some of the men as they drilled, listening to the discontent among the men. He heard one tall recruit dressed in buckskin complain.

"What good is all this marchin' around? Let me draw my bead on them Mexes. That's all I come here to fight for."

For a time Clay simply wandered around, hoping to find Brodie, but there were at least four or five hundred men in town. Finally, he saw a tall officer and walked up to him. "Excuse me, sir. I'm lookin' for a young fella named Brodie Hardin."

"Brodie Hardin. Yes, he's here. I'm Colonel Fannin. Might I have your name, sir?"

"I'm Clay Taliferro."

"Did you come to join our forces, Taliferro?"

"Well, I came to look it over. I may be, but I need to find Brodie, my friend, first."

"You'll find him over there drilling with that group of men, he and his two friends. I hope you'll stay with us. We'll be seeing some action soon."

"I'll think on it, Colonel Fannin."

Still leading his horse, Clay moved over closer to where the men were drilling. He spotted a barn and led his horse over there. A heavyset soldier was leaning on the bars of the corral. "Got a tired horse here, soldier. You reckon I could get him a feed?"

"Shore, we'll take care of that. We've got plenty of fodder. Are you joinin' up?"

"Thinkin' on it."

Clay left his horse with the soldier and went back where the men were going through their drills. He leaned against the wall of one of the buildings. When the sergeant finally dismissed the men, Clay walked forward and said, "Hey, Brodie!"

Brodie, hearing his name, turned, and Clay saw his eyes brighten. The boy came running forward and grabbed Clay and hugged him.

"Clay, what are you doin' here? I'm glad to see ya. How's everybody at home?"

"Whoa there, boy!" Clay grinned. He had to look up now, for Brodie had shot up like a weed. "Everybody's fine at home. But they're just a little worried about you."

"You remember Tim and Clyde here."

"Hello, fellas. You watchin' out for this young scamp?"

"I don't need any lookin' out after, Clay," Brodie said.

"Shore not. I was just tormentin' you. What's goin' on here?"

"Well, Colonel Fannin keeps sayin' we're goin' into action," Brodie said. "But so far I haven't seen any sign of it. All we do every day is drill and drill. I didn't come here for that. Clay, I'm thinkin' of leavin' here and goin' on to find Pa."

"I just come from there—San Antonio. I talked to Jake, and he said for you to stay where you are."

"Was he disappointed I didn't stay at home?"

"Well, he wasn't too happy about it, but he figured you're a young buck and anxious to get into things. But I think you ought to do as he says."

"What about you, Clay?" Tim said quickly. "You signin' up?"

In that instant Clay made up his mind and said, "I thought I might stay here and see what Colonel Fannin's got on his mind. That sounds like a pretty ambitious job hittin' this town called Matamoros."

"Colonel Fannin thinks that if maybe we attack them and show some strength, Santa Anna would think twice before coming after us. Come on, I'll show you where you can sleep. Maybe you can get in our company," Brodie said eagerly. "I'd like that a lot."

"Me too," Clay said.

"But I don't need a keeper," Brodie warned.

"You don't? Well, I shore do."

For three days Clay waited along with the rest of the men for some sign of action out of Colonel Fannin, but Fannin seemed content to simply spend hours each day drilling the troops. Early afternoon on a Thursday, a man named Bonham came riding into Goliad with a message from Travis. Everyone knew he had brought a letter from San Antonio.

When Brodie saw a group of men gather around Bonham, he said with excitement,

"I'll bet we'll leave soon to go and support Colonel Travis and Colonel Bowie there. I sure hope so."

But late that afternoon Bonham was mounting his horse again, and Clay saw the downcast frown on his face. He walked forward and said, "Howdy. I'm Clay Taliferro."

"My name is Bonham."

"You brought word from the Alamo?"

Bonham seemed weary and discouraged. "Colonel Travis has sent several messages urging Colonel Fannin to come to the Alamo, but he won't do it."

"How are things there, Bonham?"

"No better. We've got fewer than two hundred men, with no help coming, it seems. Travis has sent out letters asking for reinforcements, but nothing is happening."

"You know a fellow named Jake Hardin?"

"Jake? Sure, I know him."

"When you get back, tell him his boy is here, and I'm doin' all I can to watch out for him."

Bonham nodded. "I'll do that." He looked at the men milling around and shook his head. "It's a tragedy, that's what it is. All these men doing nothing, and the Alamo needs them. If they don't get some reinforcements, they won't have a chance when Santa Anna arrives with his army," he said, then spurred off, a cloud of dust trailing him.

Clay looked after him and shook his head. "Somethin's not right about all this. I think Fannin's the wrong man for command."

Jake stepped outside and saw Davy Crockett watching a group of men who were leaving. He walked over to him and said, "What's going on, Davy?"

Crockett turned and said, "Hi, Jake. It looks to me like people are pullin' out of here."

"I don't blame 'em. If what I hear is so, there's a whole passel of Mexican soldiers on their way." The two men watched as the civilians piled their belongings onto wagons. Most of them were Mexicans, and they were obviously filled with fear. Finally, Crockett said, "Looks kind of like rats leavin' a sinkin' ship, don't it, Jake?"

"I reckon so."

Crockett suddenly turned and said, "Have you got a family anywhere, Jake?"

"Sure do." He started to speak and then

shook his head. "But I got to admit that I ain't been the husband I should have been."

Crockett cleared his throat. "Well, I ain't either. I got a family I haven't treated right. "So does Travis, for that matter."

"Well, there's a lot of us. Even Sam Houston didn't turn out to be much of a husband."

The two men stood there occupied by their own thoughts. Finally Crockett said, "Let's go down and see how Jim's gettin' along. He looks right poorly."

"I don't think he's gonna make it. If that's scarlet fever, he sure won't be any help to us when the fighting starts."

"Well, we'll fight 'em til we drop, but I don't aim to do that," Crockett said as they went to the room where Bowie was.

When they knocked on the door, they were met by a Mexican woman, who said, "Señor Bowie says for no one to come in. He doesn't want them to get the fever."

Crockett laughed. "I don't think that matters a bit, señora. Just stand aside."

"I don't reckon we need to be afraid of a little fever with eight thousand Mexicans on the way," Jake said, laughing along with Crockett.

The two men went inside, and Jake was shocked at the sight of Jim Bowie. Bowie lay on a cot with a cover over him. He obviously had a chill, for he was trembling all over. His face was flushed, and his eyes were cloudy.

When he saw who had come to visit him, Bowie said, "Well, hello, Davy. Hi, Jake."

"Well, Jim, doesn't look like you're doing too good. You've got to do better than that. We need you out there telling the men what to do," Crockett said as he went over and stood by the cot.

Jake joined him and saw that Jim Bowie's magnificent strength was gone. He hardly looked able to get off of the cot. Jake forced himself to smile. "Well, you got any orders for us, Colonel, until you get back on your post?"

"Fight 'em till you drop, boys," Bowie said feebly. He tried to smile, but it was a weary effort. "I wish I could be with you."

The two men did not stay long. They wished the colonel well, then left and went outside. "Bowie's not going to make it," Jake said abruptly, "but then I don't think any of us are." Right then they saw Bonham ride in from Goliad and said, "Look, there's

Bonham. He rode to get help from Colonel Fannin. Let's see if he did any good."

The two ran across the grounds, and as Bonham stepped off his horse, Davy said, "You find us any help, Bonham?"

Bonham's face was answer enough. He said in a spare tone, "No, it's just us, it looks like." He turned and said, "Jake, your boy is at Goliad, and a fellow named Clay said he'd look out for him."

"Well, that's good news," Jake said. "Thanks for the message."

Jake walked away and watched as the last of the civilians left the compound. He was glad to hear about Brodie and murmured, "I'm sure glad Clay's there to watch out for him."

Later that afternoon someone shouted, "The Mexicans are here!" Everyone ran to the walls to see Santa Anna's army. Far off in the distance, on the horizon, they could see a thin line of soldiers approaching.

Colonel Travis walked out and said, "All right, men, shut the gates."

Bonham was standing beside him, and he turned and said, "Do you think Colonel Fannin will change his mind and come?"

"I don't think so, Colonel Travis. It looks

like to me that he's either scared, or he just doesn't know what to do. He's no soldier. He never should have been given that post."

Travis gritted his teeth. "All right, it'll just be us then, but we'll stand 'em off."

The next day twenty-five men came in from Gonzales. They had had to fight their way through Mexicans to get inside the fort, and Colonel Travis stood watching them as they filed in. "I wish there were a thousand," he said. "Only twenty-five." He knew they were hopelessly outnumbered, but he could not let his disappointment show. He put a smile on his face and went forward to greet his new recruits.

Clinton came stomping in and marched right up to Julie, who was standing and staring out a window. "Aunt Julie," he said in a truculent tone, "you know what that crazy Englishman says?"

"What does he say?"

"Why, he says that the Indians are good as us."

Julie turned and could not help but smile

at Clinton. Her nephew was growing up, and he looked enough like Jake to startle her. When he was fully grown, he would be the exact replica of his father. "You don't think they are?"

"Why, no. They're just savages."

"I'm surprised at you, Clinton. A good Baptist like you! I thought you was supposed to love everybody. At least that's what Rhys keeps telling everyone. He tells them that God loves everyone, no matter what. Maybe you better have a chat with him and get your theology straightened out."

Clinton stared at her, not knowing what to say at her. Embarrassed at being corrected, he blurted out, "Well, it's hard to love them scalpin', red devils!"

"But you liked your pa's Indian wife and his Indian family."

"Well . . . that's different," Clinton said, trying to argue, but his aunt wouldn't say any more on the subject. Finally, he changed the subject, saying, "I been thinkin' about leavin' here."

"And going where?"

"Going to find Brodie and Pa. I'm old enough to fight."

"You're not going to do any such thing," Julie said quickly.

"Well, who's gonna stop me?"

Julie knew Clinton well and had a special affection for him. He was loud and argumentative, but she knew he had a tender heart. Going over to him, she put her arm around his shoulder and squeezed him. "Clinton, you've got to remember one thing."

"Well, what's that?'

"You're the only son that your ma has left here. The very last. It would break her heart if you would go."

Julie continued to speak softly, and Clinton began to shuffle his feet. His features softened, and when Julie mentioned his two dead brothers, he blinked hard and said gruffly, "Well, I reckon I'll stay around for a while."

Julie kissed him on the cheek, gave him a hard squeeze, and said, "That's my good nephew. Now, let's you and me go see if we can knock down some quail for supper."

By the time darkness had fallen, and things had grown quiet on the ranch, Julie was restless. She had not regretted her decision of coming to stay with Jerusalem and the family, but she had a sense of doom that seemed to hang over her. She spent some time each day listening to Fergus. The Englishman was cheerful and witty in a sly sort of way, and he never lacked for interesting stories to tell anyone who would sit down and listen. Julie sensed he had a fondness for her, and he made her feel confident.

Ever since Brodie had run off, Julie knew that her sister was worried about him and Clay. Jerusalem had been very quiet all day. Before going outside for some fresh air after supper, Julie had said, "Jerusalem, maybe we ought to leave this place while we still can."

"I thought about that," Jerusalem had said, "but I found out one thing after all these years. And that's never to run away from problems. As sure as you do, a worse one will meet you."

Julie had understood exactly what Jerusalem's words meant. The night air was cold, and she hugged her coat tightly around herself. She stood there looking across the land they had all worked so hard to make a home. She knew it could easily be taken away from them if Santa Anna's forces pushed farther. She had a sudden impulse to get into a buggy and ride away from here. But then she thought, *That's what I've done all my life—run away when things get hard and when I don't get my own way.* The thought depressed her even more, and she was about to turn and go inside, when she saw Rhys Morgan standing out beside the big oak tree in the front yard. For a moment he seemed to be doing nothing, just standing there looking off into the distance.

Julie had puzzled long over Rhys Morgan. She could not figure him out. In many ways, he was unlike any man she had ever met. He was a preacher, and yet there was nothing solemn or gloomy about him. On the contrary, he was one of the happiest men she had ever seen. There seemed to be an inner joy in him that only grew stronger when he faced hard circumstances.

The other thing that puzzled Julie about the Welshman was that he had never made any attempt to touch her as other men had tried. Ever since she was fourteen, almost every man she knew had tried to take advantage of her in one way or another. Now as she stood there, a startling thought came to her. *Maybe I'm losing my looks. Maybe he doesn't think I'm pretty.* The thought troubled her. She had always liked men and had enjoyed playing her game with them. Yet Rhys Morgan did not seem to know the rules of the game. He was always polite and cheerful with her, ready to help at any time. Even when she'd flirted with him, he had treated her with respect.

I could make him want me. The thought came to Julie as a challenge. She made a sudden decision and then walked up and said, "Hello, Rhys."

"Oh, hello, Julie. Come out to see the moon?"

"It is pretty, isn't it?"

Overhead the moon was a huge silver disc, and the stars were already winking in the skies. The air was cold, and Julie moved closer to Rhys. She deliberately pressed against him and whispered, "It is cold out here, isn't it?"

Any other man she knew would have taken this as an invitation, and when Rhys moved away from her just enough to avoid her touch, Julie grew slightly angry, and she did not know why. She put her arm through his and said, "Let's walk a bit."

"All right."

Julie pressed herself firmly against Rhys, and the two spoke of the beauty of the night. When they paused, Julie said, "Rhys, I get so lonely." He had turned to face her, and she was standing directly in front of him. She looked up into his face and whispered, "Don't you ever get lonely, Rhys?"

Rhys did not answer for a moment, and then he cleared his throat. "Sure, I guess every man does."

Julie put her hands on Rhys' shoulders and said, "You don't have to be lonely, Rhys. And I don't either." She pulled his head down and kissed him. After one moment of resistance, Rhys passionately returned her kiss.

Shocked, Julie put her hands on his chest and stepped back, suddenly angry with herself. She knew he was just as shocked, for she could see a self-disgust in his eyes.

"Julie, I . . . I didn't mean to—"

"I'm a rotten woman, Rhys!" she said bitterly.

"What? Why would you say that?"

"I wanted to see if I could make you want me."

Rhys shook his head and said, "I didn't take much temptation, did I? But I've always found you attractive, Julie."

The words came as a shock to Julie. "You never showed it."

"A man has to fight against things like that if he's trying to serve God." Rhys' face showed shame, and he started to turn away from her. "I thought I was stronger than this, but I guess not."

"You're a good man, Rhys," Julie said quickly. She caught him by the arm and turned him around and looked at him. "You're one of the few good men I've ever known."

"I wasn't very good just now."

His words were bitter, and Julie could tell Rhys was disappointed with himself.

"Any woman can stir a man up. I'm no good. That's the problem."

"I think there's something good in you, Julie."

Julie glanced up at Rhys, startled at his words. Her eyes widened, and color came to her cheeks. She leaned toward him with a sudden intent and whispered, "Me good?

Don't be foolish. I'm not a good woman, not after all I've done."

"I've always seen it in you beneath that behavior you put on. You've made a lot of bad choices," Rhys said quietly, regaining his composure. "But deep down in you there's a fine woman waiting to be set free. Julie, God can set you free. All you have to do is ask Him."

Julie's hand came up uncertainly and touched the lapel of his coat. She thought of all the mistakes she had made, and at that moment, she realized that the way she had been living had not left her happy. A strange feeling sliced through her, and she suddenly felt tears come to her eyes. She wanted to believe what Rhys Morgan was saying, but she couldn't. "I wish I was good like Jerusalem," she whispered. "But I'm not." Turning, she ran back toward the house.

Rhys knew he had seen a longing in Julie to be real and good and pure. He wondered if he would ever see it again, and he turned and looked up at the sparkling stars and murmured, "Lord, there's a good woman there, but she needs Your help."

CHAPTER
THIRTY-THREE

General Antonio López de Santa Anna cele-
brated his forty-second birthday on February 21, 1836. The following day he sent for
Mateo Lebonne to commend him on all the
valuable information he had gathered. The
young man came and saluted smartly, waiting for his orders.

"You have done well, Sergeant Mateo,"
Santa Anna said. "Your reports have been
accurate and most helpful."

"Thank you, Your Excellency!" Mateo had
ridden hard these last weeks, sending back
reports on the movements of the Texans.
Twice he had brought the reports back

personally to the general. He looked down at the tall tower of San Fernando Church just across from the Alamo and said, "There are no more than two hundred fighting men inside the Alamo. Colonel Fannin has five hundred men at Goliad, but he refuses to come here. They do have some cannon, however."

"I have a job for you, Sergeant." Santa Anna turned to the man behind him and said, "Lieutenant, let me have the flag."

A tall lieutenant stepped forward and handed a folded piece of cloth to Santa Anna, who unfolded it and smiled at Mateo. "I want you to hang this flag in the top tower of the church there. You understand its significance?"

Mateo looked at the flag, which was close to twelve feet long and wide. It was a bright red color with no symbol at all. "No, sir. What does it represent?" Mateo asked.

"It means no surrender. No prisoners. Anyone who fights against this flag will be killed."

Mateo was shocked but did not allow it to show in his face. He took the red flag and swallowed hard. "I will obey your orders at once, My General."

"I have sent out a proclamation. Every American colonist who takes arms against us will be shot. There will be no trials. Every Mexican who fights against us will be hanged without a trial. There will be no further immigration of any kind from the American States into Texas or any other part of Mexico. Any foreigner in Texas who is found in the possession of arms will be arrested, severely judged, and treated accordingly. Now, go."

After Mateo had left, Colonel Ortez said, "What is our battle plan, General?"

"We will not use our entire force against this rival. We will use siege warfare. We will strangle them, starve them, blast them with the cannon, and shoot them as they collapse."

The shelling of the Alamo began at daybreak the day after the red flag appeared in the church. The rounds were fired from nine pounders dug in on the river bank four hundred yards from the Alamo. The shells battered the walls along with the five-inch howitzer that hurled shots into the Alamo.

Despite the constant barrage, the walls were firm and solid, and the shells that fell inside were ineffective. During a lull in the bombardment, Travis sent a message to Gonzales, which eventually found its way to New Orleans, New York, Boston, and even to Europe:

> I shall have to fight the enemy on his own terms. The victory will cost the enemy so dear that it will be worse for him than defeat. I hope your honorable body will hasten reinforcements. Our supply of ammunition is limited.
> God and Texas. Victory or Death.
> Colonel William Travis

Jake had eaten a scanty breakfast and then had gone over to stand beside Davy Crockett. Crockett grinned at him and nodded toward the gunners. "I don't think them fellers over there are much punkins. Can't even hit this fort half the time with cannonballs."

"I hear tell you're a pretty good shot, Davy."

"Well, just fair. I killed forty-seven bears in one month. It took me forty-six bullets."

Jake grinned, knowing one of Crockett's tall tales was comin'. "How'd you do that?"

"Two of them bears was misbehavin'." Crockett grinned. "Most the time when I hunted coons, they throwed up their paws and just crawled down out of the tree when they saw me."

Jake was amused at his humor even at a perilous time like this. He looked over and said, "I can see the head of some of them gunners over there. Why don't we try a shot at 'em?"

"Good idea, Jake. You all primed and loaded?"

"Yep."

"Let's get two of 'em for the price of one. Here, rest your rifle real steady. I been watchin' them fellers. One of 'em keeps his head up most of the time, but the other one, an officer, I reckon, only pops his head up every now and then. You take the first one, and as soon as the officer's head pops up, I'll get him."

"All right, Davy." Jake rested his rifle on the stone wall and centered directly on the head of the soldier whose entire top of his body was in view. He held his finger steady on the trigger and waited. In less than sixty seconds, the officer popped up. Davy said, "Now!" and both men fired simultaneously. The two Mexicans fell backward, and Davy Crockett straightened up. He beat Jake on the shoulder and said, "That was some shootin'."

"It was right fair. I wish they'd all stand up, and we could knock 'em off as long as the ammunition held out."

"I hear Martin rode out this mornin' with a letter from Travis to try to get us some help," Davy said. "The way I heard, there's plenty of men at Gonzales and Goliad. Maybe five hundred in all. If they'd come, we could wipe these fellas out."

Jake looked around at the compound. "We need 'em," he said soberly. "It'd take a thousand men to defend these walls."

Rumors ran through the hundreds of men gathered at Goliad. One day someone would proclaim, "We're marching to Gonzales." The next day it was, "We're going to the Alamo to help Travis." On still another day it was, "We're gonna stay here and wait for the Mexicans to come to us."

Brodie listened to these rumors with a growing anger. On the twenty-sixth, he said to Clay as the two of them wandered through the camp, "I'm gettin' sick of this, Clay. I don't think Colonel Fannin knows what he's doing."

"You better not say that to anybody but me," Clay said quickly. "Fannin would consider that insubordination."

Brodie looked at Clay with a strange look and said, "Now that's some big fancy word Fergus would say."

Clay slapped him on the shoulder and said, "It may sound fancy to you, but it means you could get hanged for questioning his ability to lead."

"I still don't think he should have been made a colonel. What's the matter with that man anyhow?" Brodie demanded. "We sit here doin' nothin' while the war's goin' on. And the men at the Alamo need us."

Brodie was not the only one who had started to question Fannin's indecisiveness. Others throughout the ranks were wondering the same thing. Colonel Fannin's failure to graduate from West Point with a commission was already a strike against him. When he left the Point, he had become a slave trader for a while, then finally came to settle in Texas. Now he was looking for a promotion to general. Those closest to the situation believed that he refused to march to Travis's aid not because he was afraid, but because he would be forced to serve under Travis, whom he despised. Between the two of them, Travis was more of a fighting man than Fannin.

"Look, something's up," Clay said, pointing to a group of men who were gathered and listening as Colonel Fannin spoke to them from his chestnut stallion. "Come on, let's find out what it is."

When they crossed the parade grounds, they heard Fannin saying, "Men, we're marching to the Alamo tomorrow to help save our army. Get those supply wagons packed and be ready to leave at dawn."

A cheer went up instantly, and Brodie said, his eyes shining, "Now we're getting somewhere."

Shortly after dawn the next day, the soldiers marched out, followed by a line of wagons with what supplies they had. They had gone but a few miles when one of the supply wagons broke down. It took some time to repair it, which only delayed the column's progress. Not long after, they encountered a river that proved difficult to navigate. On the twenty-eighth, Colonel Fannin proved his ineffectiveness by announcing that he would take a vote on whether to continue or turn back.

"Take a vote!" Clay murmured in shock. "What kind of a leader is he that he would take a vote on a decision?"

Fannin addressed the group and gave such a pessimistic report about the difficulty of making a seventy-mile march without sufficient food that in the end the vote was to return to Goliad.

As the column returned back to Fort Defiance, as it had been called, Fannin gave orders to strengthen the walls so that they would be impregnable. His second order was to slaughter plenty of oxen and cure and dry the meat so that the men would never be short of rations.

All the time, Clay had been waiting for an opportunity to talk to Brodie about the situation. A few days after they had returned to Goliad, he said, "You know, it'd be a mighty good time to leave this place and go back to your ma and your family."

Brodie shook his head stubbornly. "I'm gonna stay here and see it out."

Tim and Clyde added their voices. "We ain't gettin' nowhere," Tim said. "Let's pull out."

Clyde nodded. "I'm about ready. It ain't like I thought it would be, Brodie."

Brodie had developed a stubborn streak. Surprised that his friends wanted to leave, he turned to them and said, "We ought to leave here and go to the Alamo."

"Fannin would shoot us if you tried to do that," Clay said, then tried to talk some reason to him about returning home.

In the end Brodie compromised and agreed to think it over if the others would stay a few more days.

Clay listened, then said, "All right, Brodie, but I'll hold you to that."

Miraculously no one inside had been killed during the daily bombardment that fell on the Alamo. Santa Anna's forces made one concerted attack but had been driven back.

The men of the Alamo peppered them with rifle fire from the walls and cannon loaded with grape. By the time they pulled back, a host of wounded and dead Mexicans lay in the fields outside. But Santa Anna's army was growing as more and more units arrived, and the odds narrowed with each passing day.

Inside, Travis kept the men working hard to reinforce the fort. Despite the gravity of the situation, Davy Crockett was, perhaps, the most cheerful man at the Alamo. He played his fiddle and even played a few duets with John McGregor, a Scotsman who played the bagpipes. He even challenged McGregor to a goodhearted contest. Davy set the terms. The winner would not be the one who played the best, but the one who played the loudest and the longest. And to his grand delight, Davy Crockett won the contest.

Jake watched every day as the new Mexican reinforcements arrived all the way from Saltillo, farther south, where Santa's Anna's main contingency had first formed. Jake felt encouraged, as had others, when the small group arrived from Gonzales. As the days dragged on, he speculated when larger troops would arrive, but by March 3 Jake realized that no more help would be coming. They were on their own against a disciplined army that numbered in the thousands.

Travis showed no fear, and on the third, he sent out a last letter pleading for supplies and more men. He still hoped for reinforcement, and many of the men scrawled notes to their friends and families, knowing that the outcome looked grim. Smith left at midnight while some of the men distracted the Mexicans by firing on them from the north wall.

The next morning the Mexican cannons were advanced to less than two hundred fifty yards away. They pounded away at the stone walls all day long and resumed on the morning of the fifth. The walls, tough as they were, were beginning to crumble, and Jake, who had been firing at the enemy, raised his head and peered across the distance. "Look there, Davy, they're makin' scalin' ladders."

"I reckon they'll be comin' at us pretty soon," Davy said. He drew a bead, fired carefully, and nodded. "Got him. There's one that won't be climbin' no ladder!"

Later that afternoon Travis marched out and called all the men, except for a few lookouts, to come to the center of the compound. His face was grim, and Jake noticed that Jim Bowie had been brought out on his cot. He went over to stand beside him and said, "How you feelin', Jim?"

"Not too pert, Jake."

Jake had no comfort to give him and stood with the rest of the men as they listened to Travis.

"Men, as you all see, Santa Anna's army is increasing every day. He's moving up his big guns. The big attack's coming. You know what that red flag means. No quarter. And Santa Anna will do exactly what he says." He paused and looked out over the dirty, weary men who faced him. "His army is forty times as large as ours, and he's got the cannon to cover it. I think the attack will come tomorrow, on Sunday, and I want to offer every man here one last chance to leave if that's what you want to do."

Travis took his sword and drew a long line in the sand. "Every-one who wants to stay here and take their chances fighting beside me, step over it."

"Jake, I can't make it," Jim Bowie whispered. "Carry me across that line."

"Sure, Jim. Here, you fellows, grab hold of Jim's cot." He and the others picked up the cot and walked across the line.

Travis was watching them, his face fixed in a stern expression, which broke for a moment into a smile. "I might have known you'd come, Colonel Bowie."

One hundred eighty-two men stepped across that line. Jake saw Louis Rose standing still, the only man left. He looked across the line silently for a moment, then he shook his head. "This place can't be defended, Colonel Travis. I'm leaving. I'll fight again somewhere."

"You'll never make it, Louis," Davy Crockett spoke up. "Better stay and die with us."

"When it gets dark I'll be gone," he said. "Any of you fellows want to give me a message, I'll take it."

Jake Hardin kept his eye on Rose, and as the shadows began to fall, he went over and said, "I don't think you'll make it, Louis."

"I'll make it, all right."

"Good luck to you, then."

"Why don't you come with me, Jake."

"Guess not."

Rose stared at him. "Are you mad at me for leavin'?"

"Every man has to hoe his own row, Louis. I'm stayin' here." He reached out his hand, and Louis Rose shook it, then turned and walked rapidly away.

Jake stood for a moment in the silence. He knew as soon as the first rays of dawn came up the air would be full of cannon roar and the crackling of musket fire and the screams of dying men. He was not afraid, but he felt a great sadness. After a time he turned and went to the room where Bowie lay on his cot. He pulled the chair up and asked, "How you doin', Jim?"

Jim Bowie was so weak he could hardly speak, but he managed to whisper, "Since I lost my wife and kids, Jake, nothin' has meant much to me. I don't much mind dyin'."

Jake Hardin sat in silence for a long time, thinking of his own life. Then he looked at his friend and said, "I lost my wife and kids, too, Jim, so I guess dying doesn't mean much to me either."

The two men sat bound together by strange ties. Both of them knew they had come to the end of everything.

CHAPTER
THIRTY-FOUR

Santa Anna sipped his coffee and carefully went over his plan as he looked down at the map spread on the table before him. He had decided that his infantry would be divided into four columns, with eight hundred men in each. The cavalry would hold back, ready to pick off the Texans if they tried to break out and flee. The air was chilly, and Santa Anna shivered. He glanced over to the east and saw a faint glow, and suddenly he heard one man cry out, "Viva Santa Anna!" Others began to echo the cry, and Santa Anna laughed aloud as he heard the sound of thousands of feet as his army rushed toward the Alamo. "Now we will see," he cried, his face exultant at the victory soon to be his.

Travis was sleeping when he heard his name being called. In one motion, he came up off the cot and grabbed his sword and his double-barrel shotgun. He ran to the north wall and saw the enemy approaching. It looked as though a massive wave of torches was rushing toward the Alamo as the rays of the sun glinted off thousands of raised bayonets.

"Hurrah, my boys, hurrah!" Travis yelled as he cheered his men to their posts. Some of the men had stacked a half-dozen loaded rifles by their side, and as the rifles crackled all along the walls, Mexicans fell like ripe grain. The men manning the cannon on the church waited until the column attacking from the east was dangerously close. Then Travis signaled for them to fire, and the cannon roared murderous shots on Santa Anna's army. The first ranks went down, and then the ranks behind them. Officers and privates fell and were trampled as the surge of soldiers pressed forward. The first assault never reached the walls, but mass musketry had knocked many Texans off the walls. Travis was crying out to his men, when suddenly a shot struck him in the head. He pitched over backward into the dusty yard and made no further movement.

Jake had taken his place with the small group where Davy Crockett was firing and reloading like a deadly machine. His Tennessee riflemen were laying down a constant fire, but the Mexicans kept pouring in. A cry went up then. "Travis is dead! Colonel Travis is dead!"

"I reckon it was his time to go," Davy said. He rammed a ball into his musket, replaced the percussion cap, and fired before adding, "I shore wish we was outside. I hate to be all hemmed in."

Just then they heard strange music coming from the Mexican army band. Jake looked over at Davy Crockett and said, "I don't know what the music is all about, but I sure don't like the sounds of it."

"It's the *Deguello*," Crockett said, a grim look on his face. "One of the Mexicans fighting on our side said it's the fire and death knell, signaling total annihilation.

Santa Anna has ordered his troops to give no quarter."

As the somber music continued, a deafening roar went up from Santa Anna's reserve that came rushing toward the Alamo. The Mexicans struggled up the wall, and at the same time attackers hurled themselves at the northwest corner and poured over faster than the Texans could work the guns.

Jake fell back along with Crockett and the other defenders until they stood alone. He glanced at Davy Crockett and saw the light of battle and no sign of fear at all.

Jake did not have time to reload. He grabbed his musket by the barrel and smashed a private dressed in white who came rushing toward him. Suddenly Jake felt a searing pain as a bayonet struck him in the stomach. He gasped and swung his musket again, smashing the man who had bayoneted him. He saw Crockett go down, bayoneted many times, and then he felt nothing as the great roaring in his ears faded to total silence.

The Mexicans now went mad shooting and bayoneting the helpless Texans, their cries of victory echoing throughout the Alamo.

Jim Bowie heard the sound and moved feebly, knowing what it meant. The door burst open then, and Bowie, who had been a fierce fighter all his life, lay helpless. He saw the Mexicans come pouring in, and a dark-faced man with fierce eyes raised his rifle with its bayonet, but Bowie could not move as it descended into his chest.

Susannah Dickerson, the young wife of an Alamo defender, held her daughter tightly. The screams of the Mexicans and the roar of battle had struck her almost dumb. She had no hope now, for she knew that the church where she had taken refuge would be broken into. She and a handful of women and children had fled there. Now the door burst open, and a party of soldiers ran in. Susannah held her child, shielding her with her body, expecting instant death. She was shocked when the soldier's strong hand grabbed her, and an officer said, "You come with me."

"Where are you taking me?" she cried.

"You will see."

The officer dragged Susannah outside of

the church with her daughter clutched tightly in her arms. As she looked around, she saw Mexican bodies sprawled all over the compound. As she left she saw Jim Bowie's body being carried outside. The Mexicans screamed and tossed him high on their bayonets. She turned her head away quickly, and as she was hurried along, she saw Davy Crockett's body stretched out among a host of his foes. For twenty minutes she was terrified, fearing that death would come at any moment. Then suddenly a group of officers came through the gates.

"General Santa Anna will speak with you now," the officer said. He grabbed her by the arm and pulled her over in front of Santa Anna, then saluted. "General, here is one of the captives, as you commanded."

Santa Anna stood there in his full military garb looking exultant. He knew that hundreds of his men had been killed at a terrible price in taking the Alamo, but the Napoleon of the West seemed happy. His order for "no quarter" had been carried out, and he proudly held his head high as he looked around the Alamo.

"Woman, what is your name?"

"Susannah Dickerson," she said, holding her daughter tightly.

"What are you doing here?"

"My . . . my husband, he was here."

"He is dead with every other man who was foolish to stay here and fight. I am releasing you. I want you to go to Gonzales and tell whoever leads your ragtag army that this is what will happen to them. You understand me?"

Unable to believe what she was hearing, Susannah whispered, "Yes."

"Take her out and give her a horse. Let her have our guide if anyone is left."

"There is also a slave, sir," the officer said.

"Let him go with her. Leave, woman," Santa Anna ordered.

Susannah Dickerson stumbled out of the compound like one in a nightmare. She did not look back but mounted the horse, scarcely aware of the slave who was behind her.

He came close and said, "Come, ma'am, I'll take you to Gonzales."

Inside the compound, Santa Anna walked around looking at the bodies strewn everywhere. He saw Mateo and said, "Today has been a great victory, Mateo."

"Sí, Your Excellency," Mateo said, but he was sickened by the slaughter. He saw that Santa Anna had no thought for the hundreds of men who had died to win his victory for him. Mateo had found Jake's body and was determined to give him an honorable burial. He could not help but think of the Hardins, who had been so kind to him and to his family. He hardened himself, and then he turned to take Jake's body outside but stopped when he heard Santa Anna's next words.

"I want every Texan burned," the general said loudly to all his officers who had gathered around him.

Colonel Francisco stared at Santa Anna. He was a short, husky man with a fierce fighting spirit, but this order stopped him dead in his tracks. "Burned, My General?"

"You heard what I said, Colonel. Send men out to find firewood. Make a fire and put the Texans on it. Bury our men, but I want all of these Texans burned."

Something changed inside Mateo at that moment. He was superstitious about burying people properly, but he knew now that there was no hope of burying Jake Hardin.

Turning, he walked away, appalled at

what he had just heard. As he slowly made his way toward the gate, he saw the body of William Travis. He stopped and stared down at the man, thinking of how strange it was. *Here is the man that drove me to leave my family and join Santa Anna, and now he is dead and I am alive.*

He did not dare leave the compound, for Santa Anna had ordered all his men to witness the burning of the Texans. He watched as a huge pile of firewood was dragged in by privates. The bodies were stacked on it and more wood on top. Then one of the men started the fire. The dry wood crackled, and soon a huge blaze lifted upward. The smell of burning flesh sickened Mateo. He stood there watching, and one of his officers, Lieutenant Rio, came to stand beside him. "Well, Mateo," he said, "this is the end. The Texans will run like rabbits when they hear what we have done here."

Mateo turned and gave the officer a cold look. "These men fought like demons, Lieutenant. Texans are not afraid to die, and when we meet them in battle again, we will meet an army of them. No, it's not the end."

Lieutenant Rio was taken aback. His jaw

dropped, and he said harshly, "I think you admire our enemy!"

Mateo did not answer for a moment, then he whispered, "I fear them, Lieutenant, and so should you—and so should General Santa Anna!"

CHAPTER
THIRTY-FIVE

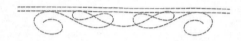

While Bowie, Crockett, and Travis were bat-
tling at the Alamo, Sam Houston was engaged in a different kind of struggle at
Washington-On-The-Brazos. The convention that met there was not the first of its
kind, but the men who had gathered for the
purpose of settling the fate of Texas knew
that Colonel William Barret Travis had given
all he had, and that the Alamo was lost. Sam
Houston was instrumental in defeating a
wild motion that the convention adjourn and
hasten, gun in hand, to the Alamo. Houston
denounced this seemingly patriotic move as
folly and treason and convinced the mem-

bers that the Alamo was in its present danger because Texans had not formed a government sooner.

Santa Anna's invasion and victory at the Alamo had made one thing clear in the minds of all. It had forever broken whatever ties bound the Texans to Mexico. The commission worked all night, and on March 2 they came out bleary-eyed but determined. The document they had produced was modeled after the words of Thomas Jefferson back when the Republic itself was being born. With a united vote, Texas declared itself an Independent Republic the morning of March 2, 1836.

For the first time the fate of Texas was set forth in clear terms. There would no longer be a Mexican state, but an independent nation. Sam Houston was appointed commander in chief with complete power to command all armed men in Texas, regular or volunteer. On the very next day, Houston set out on his mission, and Texas was never the same after this historic day.

Riding to Gonzales, Houston was shocked to find no more than thirty-seven men who had organized to help Travis. To his dismay he realized he had no army, at least not yet.

He wrote an urgent letter to Colonel Fannin at Goliad, saying simply, "Blow up the fortress and join me at once. I need your five hundred men."

At Goliad Colonel Fannin seemed to have lost his mind. He had certainly lost all military judgment, and most of the men under him realized it. Consequently, the morale of the men was low. He foolishly sent one-third of his force to Refugio, a nearby town, to help civilians to flee the Mexican forces headed their way. Fannin's men were immediately snapped up under General Urrea, who was one of Santa Anna's better officers. Those who were not taken captive scattered and fled through the woods and the swamps. At this point Urrea turned toward Goliad.

Brodie and Clay had been lounging against the wall of a building, when Clay suddenly looked up. "There comes somebody ridin' in mighty hard."

"It's probably another messenger from Colonel Travis," Brodie said hopefully.

The two men got up and moved closer,

and the scout came off his horse in one swift movement. He ran quickly to meet Colonel Fannin. "Colonel, the whole body you sent out has been taken by General Urrea."

Brodie saw Fannin's face go pale and his lips tremble. "All taken! How could that be?"

"That Mexican general ain't no dummy," the scout said, shaking his head. "And he's headin' here. I think we'd better get out of here quick, Colonel."

Fannin seemed to have lost his powers of thought. He simply stared at the scout, then nodded and turned around and walked away. As he disappeared inside the hut that he used for his headquarters, Clay said, "That man's lost it, Brodie."

"I think he has," Brodie nodded.

"Be a good time for us to cut out and leave here," Clay said.

"If we do," Brodie said stubbornly, "I'm goin' to the Alamo and fight with Pa."

Clay grinned and said, "You're one stubborn cuss, Brodie. I guess I have no choice but to stay and see what happens."

Late that afternoon, Fannin called all the men together and announced his plans in a loud voice. "Men, we're going to leave here, and we're going to take every one of the heavy guns with us."

"That's a mistake," Clay said quietly to Brodie. "If we want to move fast, we'll have to leave those guns. Why, there's not enough oxen to pull 'em."

Some of Fannin's own officers tried to tell him the same thing, but he stubbornly refused to heed their advice.

Indeed, when they got ready to march out, Colonel Fannin totally ignored his own orders. "We'll start our withdrawal today. It'll be a speedy retreat. We won't take our cannons with us."

"Well, I'm glad of that," Clay said. "We'd never have made it trying to haul them with General Urrea barreling after us."

But as soon as he had given the order, he told his troops to bury the cannons so the enemy could not use them.

At dawn the next day the column pulled out, but to everyone's shock Fannin had changed his mind again and decided to go back and take the cannons with him. It was a time-consuming process to dig them up, load them on wagons, and secure them with ropes. The whole time the men worked, they grumbled at Fannin's incompetence as a leader. His officers again tried to convince Fannin that they were losing precious time, but Fannin would not listen to any advice from his officers. Even as they were struggling along, pulling the unwieldy supply train, scouts came in with reports that General Urrea was on his way to Goliad.

"We'd better move out of here and fast," Clay said to Brodie. "Fannin will get the whole bunch of us caught."

Brodie did not answer. He seemed to be sunk in some sort of deep thought, and Clay made no more attempt to persuade him. The shambles of the army struggled across the plains, and at high noon the two rear scouts came in, and Brodie heard them give their report.

"General Urrea will be here with a large force before the sun goes down."

One of the scouts said, "I know this country. You can't let yourself get trapped in this open field, Colonel. Head for those trees along the river. You may be able to get away."

"I never divide my army," Fannin shouted. "I don't respond to panic. Now, we'll double-time."

But it was too late. The oxen were no

longer able to haul the useless cannon, and Fannin finally had to order a halt. Clay looked around and shook his head. It was one of the bleakest stretches of the route. "There's no protection at all out here in the open. Why are we stopping?" he complained. "No trees, no water. Not even a gully to use for a trench. Brodie, let's get out of here."

"All right," Brodie said. "I think you're right, but we'll have to get Tim and Clyde. They'll want to go with us."

Brodie went off to find his two friends, but by the time he found them, Fannin had commanded his officers to have the the men form a square in the middle of the field. Brodie, Tim, and Clyde were caught up by the officers and forced into position. Clay saw them and came to stand beside them, saying, "This is crazy! They'll surround us and cut us to pieces."

Fannin had three hundred and sixty men, whereas Urrea commanded well over a thousand trained soldiers. As Brodie watched, the Mexicans arrived and did exactly what Clay had said. They surrounded the entire force of Texans and began to fire. Nightfall came quickly, and many Texans were down. Those who knew how to work the cannons were wounded, so the cannons were useless.

Brodie came over to Clay and said, "You were right, Clay." His face was drawn and white, and he shook his head. "We should have left here when we still had the chance. Let's try it now."

"Too late," Clay said. "Anybody that steps outside of this square gets shot dead." Several Texans had tried it and had gotten nowhere. "We'll just have to wait and see how the cards fall."

Dawn came, and Clay peered out and shook his head. "Urrea's brought up his heavy cannons. He can cut us to pieces now."

He had no sooner spoken than the Mexican cannons exploded. Fragments of metal ripped through the camp, killing and maiming. The Mexican gunners had the exact range, and Fannin's officers went to him and said, "We'll have to surrender, Colonel."

"Never! We'll fight to the death!" he ordered.

One of the officers shook his head. "You've lost your mind. Men, raise a white flag."

Clay nodded. "That's a smart thing to do. We'll go to a Mexican prison, but there's always a chance to escape," he said as the flag went up.

At the sight of the white flag, General Urrea halted the attack, and the surrender went well. Colonel Fannin, still confused, asked that his troops receive all of the honors of war—that they would lay down their arms and there would be no executions and no reprisals.

General Urrea did not accept those terms in writing, but he did agree to an amiable surrender.

Less than an hour after the surrender, Clay was marching along, prodded by the rifle butts of the Mexicans, who were laughing at them and taunting them about their surrender. "Just hold your temper, boy," Clay said quietly to Brodie. "We'll get our turn."

"Clay, I ain't gonna stay in no Mexican prison."

"Me either," Tim said. And Clyde Biddle agreed.

"We'll stay together, and we'll bust out," Brodie said. He glared at Colonel Fannin, who was leading the group. "That's the stupidest man I ever saw. He ain't fit to command a herd of pigs!"

Since the Alamo had fallen, General Antonio López de Santa Anna had reveled in the glow of victory. He had lost an enormous number of men, but loss of life did not seem to matter to him in the least. He realized that his army had been bruised, so he contented himself with patching it together again and dallying with young, native girls as if he were on a holiday.

Mateo had been brooding over the heinous treatment of the defenders of the Alamo. He was proud of his uniform and convinced that he had done the right thing, but he could not forget the sight of the bodies being thrown like animals onto the fire. For many nights he had bad dreams about the fire itself.

"Mateo, the General wants to see you."

"Yes, sir." Mateo saluted the lieutenant and went at once to Santa Anna's tent.

Santa Anna shoved the young Mexican girl off of his lap and slapped her on the leg. She giggled at him and left the tent. Santa Anna laughed loudly and said, "Good news, Mateo. General Urrea has taken the entire force at Goliad."

Mateo's face lit up. "Wonderful, My General! Now the way is clear all the way to the Sabine River!"

"Exactly! And you will be asked to scout again, although there should be nothing to stop us along the way." He waved at an aide and said, "Send this order on to General Urrea. Tell him to shoot them all, every last one of them."

The aide stared at General Santa Anna but said instantly, "Yes, sir." He turned and left the tent at once.

Mateo was shocked. The callous order had robbed him of speech for a moment, and then he said, "My General, I think you should think more before letting that order get to General Urrea."

Santa Anna glanced up, surprise on his face. "Why should I? By decree of December the thirtieth, it clearly states that any foreigner taking up arms against the Government of Mexico will be shot."

Mateo felt helpless, for here was the Emperor of Mexcio, and he was only a humble sergeant. Still, he knew something dreadful was wrong with this order. "I think it would be a grave mistake, Your Excellency. Pardon me for speaking so plainly, but such an action would cause problems for you later on."

"No, I think not, Mateo. You do not show mercy to a beaten people. It only encourages them to wait and resist again. After all"—he stared at Mateo with displeasure on his face—"you did not complain when all that were in the Alamo were killed."

"But, My General, that was different. It was a battle. Those men had guns, and it was our duty to kill them, as they killed many of us. But when the North Americanos hear that we have executed all of those men who surrendered, they will become very angry."

"Let them! What can they do? With San Antonio and Goliad in our hands, we can sweep all the way to the river. All we have to do is pin down this Sam Houston. As I understand, he's now their commander. But he has no army. We've won, Mateo. Don't you see it?"

"Pardon me, My General. I would not argue with you, but something about this seems dangerous. To wipe out the Alamo was a battle, but if you shoot all of these men, these Texans will rise up. They will come in from the United States, and they will create an army. They may forget the Alamo, for it was a fair fight, but they will never forget a massacre like this."

Santa Anna was not a man to listen to anyone, much less a lowly sergeant. "I'll hear no more about this. I changed my mind about one thing. I want you to take the order to General Urrea."

"Me, sir?"

"Yes. It will be a test of your loyalty. After all, you're half Texan yourself. You must prove yourself, Mateo. Now, get ready, for I want you to leave at once. The order will be written out so there will be no mistake. I want every one of those prisoners shot."

For one brief instant Mateo considered walking away, but he had burned all his bridges behind him. He could not go back home again. Everyone knew that he had fought with Santa Anna. He found it hard to speak, but finally he whispered, "Yes, sir, it shall be done."

"Good, and you will see that I am right. These Texans will run like rabbits when they find out what sort of a man I am!"

Colonel José Nicolas de la Portilla's hands trembled so that he could barely read the order that the young sergeant had put into his hands. He looked up and said hoarsely, "But this order is to kill all the prisoners."

"That is what it says," Mateo said evenly. All the way on his ride from San Antonio to Goliad, his hope had been that General Urrea, a strong-minded professional, would disobey Santa Anna's order and refuse to execute the prisoners. He had been profoundly disappointed to discover that Urrea, evidently anticipating such an order, had left Goliad and its prisoners in charge of Colonel Portilla.

Portilla pulled out a handkerchief, and despite the coolness of the morning, he wiped his forehead, which was suddenly covered with perspiration. "But I cannot do this."

"I do not think you should, Colonel," Mateo said.

"But . . . but this is Santa Anna's signature. He is the overall commander. How can I refuse to honor it?"

"Is it possible to find General Urrea and let him make the decision?"

Portilla shook his head, his face gray from the burden of responsibility that bore down on him. He read again the words, this time aloud. "Immediate execution of every perfidious foreigner." He looked up, and his voice was unsteady. "But doesn't General Santa Anna understand what this will mean?"

"I told him myself, Colonel. I think if he had time," Mateo said quickly, "he would see the wisdom of allowing the prisoners to live." Actually, Mateo had no such hope, but he was thinking quickly. "At least postpone the execution until General Urrea can be reached."

"When General Urrea left," Portilla said, "he commanded me to treat the prisoners with consideration and protect them in every way."

"I think that was very wise."

"But I cannot disobey my orders." Portilla knew that to disobey the Emperor of Mexico would ensure his own death. Torment etched deep lines across his face, and

Portilla whispered, "God knows what will happen when we do this terrible thing."

"I know what will happen. The Texans will gather and fight with a vengeance never seen before. We will pay for this with the blood of thousands, Colonel."

Portilla folded the message, his hands shaking, and stuck it in his pocket. "That is all, Sergeant."

At that moment Mateo knew there was no hope for the prisoners. His heart sank, and after saluting, he turned and left the headquarters. He walked outside into the morning air and asked, "Where are the prisoners being kept?"

The private he had asked waved his hand languidly. "Over there in that building."

Mateo looked at a large unpainted white building ringed with guards and walked toward it slowly. He did not know what prompted him, but when he reached the building, he walked completely around it. The prisoners were all inside, and he asked the guard, "Do they stay inside all the time?"

"No, they're let out after breakfast for exercise. They should be coming out now," the guard said.

A fatal attraction seemed to form itself in

Mateo's mind. He lingered around until the door opened and the prisoners came pouring out. He was standing not twenty yards away from where the guards ringed the prisoners, bayonets held high, so that there was no chance of an escape. He stared at the faces of the men, and most of them, he noted with shock, seemed happy. *They've been told that they'll be set free*, was his thought. He was about to turn and go away, sickened at what was going to happen, when he heard his name called loudly.

"Mateo—Mateo!"

Mateo turned and was shocked to see Brodie Hardin, who had approached the ring of guards.

Mateo's heart sank, and as he went forward, he saw Clay Taliferro standing beside Brodie along with Tim Beringer and Clyde Biddle. The horror of what was to happen became fully real to Mateo. These were his friends, especially Brodie Hardin. He approached and saw that Brodie was grinning.

"Mateo, it's good to see you."

"Hello, Brodie. Señor Clay," he said woodenly and spoke also to Tim and Clyde.

"Well, we got ourselves snapped up,"

Brodie said, "but I guess we'll be gettin' out of here pretty soon."

"I trust so," Mateo said, hating himself for lying.

Mateo saw anger and even hatred in the eyes of Tim and Clyde. He knew they despised him for what they felt was his traitorous conduct. For the life of him, he could not think of a word to say, and then Brodie spoke up.

"I saw your mother and your sister just before we left. They're doing fine."

"That is good to hear." The news of his family made Mateo feel even worse. He saw the guards were listening but doubted that many of them could speak English. He knew he had only a few moments, and stepping closer, he knew he had only one choice. "Brodie," he whispered, "listen to me."

"Sure, Mateo."

"Don't let anything show in your face when I speak. You hear me, Señor Clay, you too?"

Clay grew alert. "You hear him, boys. Whatever he says, don't let a thing show in your face. Now what is it, Mateo?"

"General Santa Anna has sent an order

that all of you are to be executed." Mateo watched and saw that the four of them contained their shock well. Quickly he said, "All of you smile and don't let the guards see anything. But I'm going to do my best to save you."

"How can you do that?" Brodie asked hoarsely. He was trying to smile, but fear was in his eyes.

"I don't know, but whenever they come to take you out, I'll be with them. You four stay with me whatever happens. You understand?"

"Sure, Mateo," Clay said quickly. "You're a good lad."

Mateo shook his head and said loudly, "God be with you all. I will see you later."

As Mateo walked away, the four turned from the guards and moved toward the center of the others. "Don't say a word about this to anybody," Clay said. "It's pretty bad, but Mateo will help us if he can. We just have to be ready."

Palm Sunday, March the twenty-seventh, was a fine day. The sun was bright and shiny, and Colonel Portilla, dressed in his finest uniform, was, nevertheless, pale of face as he faced his junior officers. He read the order from Santa Anna and saw shock run through their faces. "We have no choice. We must shoot them all."

One of the officers protested. "But, Colonel, we can't do that!"

"If you do not, you yourself will be shot!" The threat was enough to sober all of the men. They knew Santa Anna's temper well and listened as Portilla said, "We will tell them we're taking them to the boats, and they are being freed to go home. Now, go."

"They're coming for us," Clay said. "Remember. We stay right together, and we stick to Mateo like glue."

Brodie nodded, and the four moved outside with the rest of the prisoners. There were approximately four hundred of them, and a captain stopped them outside and said, "You're all being freed. You will march to the boats, where you will be sent home again." A rousing cheer went up from the men, and Clay exchanged glances with

Brodie. Neither of them spoke, but Brodie walked closer to Clay.

The men moved outside of the town, marching and talking and filled with excitement. Colonel Fannin was at the head of them, and he obeyed the orders of their captors to form three separate columns. The men moved on, and the mood was almost like a picnic.

Suddenly, Mateo appeared riding a bay stallion. He took his place along one side of the column, and Clay whispered, "There he is. Move over to the side." The four men made their way until they were marching right beside Mateo. He looked at them one time, nodded slightly and then looked straight ahead.

The route took the men through a wooded area, and Clay, who was watching Mateo closely, saw him turn and nod again.

Suddenly, a group of horsemen appeared armed with rifles and pistols. They moved to surround the group, and Mateo quickly turned his head to Brodie and whispered, "Come on."

Shots began to ring out, and screams of the wounded filled the air. Brodie heard Tim scream, "Clyde!" He turned around and saw that Clyde had fallen, the back of his shirt a mass of crimson blood.

Tim was bent over him, and even as he was, a bullet struck him in the neck, severing the artery. He fell to the ground, the crimson flow spurting out. He tried to get up, and his eyes locked on Brodie as the life flowed out of him.

Brodie started toward him, but Clay seized him with an iron grip. "Come on!" he shouted. "It's too late for them!"

Brodie tore his eyes from his two dying friends, and he and Clay ran to get beside Mateo's horse. Mateo said, "Here, hang on to the saddle."

Brodie grabbed the back of the saddle skirt, and Clay took a grip. Mateo moved his horse toward a group of scrub timber. The air was filled with the crackling of explosions as Portilla's soldiers shot as quickly as they could reload. Men were running everywhere, trying to take cover. When Clay and Brodie reached the timber, Mateo yelled, "Run quick! Go to the river!"

Brodie ducked his head and ran with Clay at his side. They had just entered the thickness of the woods when Clay suddenly grunted and fell.

"Clay, are you hit?"

"I reckon I am."

Brodie turned to examine him. "Where is it?"

"Way in the back. High up. I don't think it's a killin' shot," Clay said, wincing from the pain.

Brodie turned Clay over and saw that he had been shot very high on the left shoulder in the back.

"Missed a lung," Clay said as he slowly struggled to his feet.

"You'll bleed to death," Brodie said. He took off his shirt, tore it into bits. Part of it he used to make a pad and put it over the welling flood of blood. The rest of it he tore into strips to hold the bandage in place.

"That'll have to do," Clay panted. "We've got to get out of here."

The two moved quickly through the underbrush. They could hear the screams of the dying men, and the crackling of rifles seemed to go on a long time.

CHAPTER
THIRTY-SIX

Clay was lying on his back staring up through the trees. Overhead, a pair of gray squirrels were frolicking. Seeing the man below them, they chattered angrily, then scampered over to the next tree on overhanging branches. Clay moved painfully, and then suddenly he heard the sound of horses approaching. He struggled to a sitting position and then gave a sigh of relief when he saw Brodie coming mounted on a horse and leading another one.

"Where'd you get them horses?"

"I stole them from a farm. They ain't much, but maybe they'll get us home."

Brodie slid off the horse, tied them up, and came over to where Clay was sitting. "You're plumb white. You done lost too much blood, Clay."

"I'll make it. I got some good news."

"Well, I can use it. What is it?"

Clay reached up and touched his chest. "Feel this right here."

Brodie reached out and touched Clay's chest high on the left side. "It's a lump. What is it?"

"It's the musket ball. It didn't make it all the way through. But it's close enough. You'll have to cut it out, Brodie."

"Cut it out?" Brodie exclaimed.

"Here. Take this knife. It won't take much. Do it now."

Brodie swallowed hard and took Clay's razor-sharp bowie knife. He poised the tip of it and looked at Clay.

"Do it hard and quick," Clay said.

Brodie felt the tip of the bullet, and taking a deep breath, he sliced the skin. The blood began to flow, but the knife point struck the ball. Using the tip of the knife, he pried it out and then quickly tore off a bit of Clay's shirt and put it over the wound.

"Maybe you'll be better now that that's

out of there," Brodie said as he put pressure on the bandage.

"Neither one of us will be better if we don't get away from here. Help me get on that horse."

Brodie reached down and helped Clay to his feet. He locked his fingers together and said, "Step in here, and I'll pull you right up." He waited until Clay put his left foot in his hand, then he lifted him, and Clay straddled the horse. Brodie handed him the lines and then quickly swung on the back of the other horse.

"Come on. You'll have to do all the navigatin'," Clay said. "I'm not goin' to be much help, Brodie. Feel quite light-headed."

Brodie looked up when a large drop of rain hit his face. It was the rainy season, and he shook his head. "The rivers are going to be hard to get across if this keeps up."

All that day they rode as fast as they could, stopping only a few times to rest and water the horses. Clay never complained once and clung doggedly to the pommel of the saddle and kept his seat. Brodie could tell Clay was in pain from the strained look on his face whenever he looked back. When it was almost dark, Brodie spotted a house up ahead. "You wait here. I'm gonna see what's up there."

"Don't get yourself shot," Clay whispered.

Brodie disappeared into the darkness. The rain was falling steadily now, and Clay could barely sit upright in the saddle. It had been a long day, and all his strength seemed to have drained away. He bowed his head, shut his eyes, and clung to the mane of the horse. *You're some kind of a baby, Clay Taliferro. Now set up there like a man.*

He waited until Brodie returned a few minutes later. "We're in luck, Clay. I guess whoever lives there has run off. They must have been afraid the soldiers are comin'. Let's get you inside. We can make a fire and fix you up. Make some good bandages. And they left a wagon here. We'll hitch these horses to it, and I'll pull you all the way home. I can fix you a bed and everything in the back."

"You're right thoughtful, Brodie. You always was," Clay whispered. It was all he could do to stay on the horse, but thirty minutes later he was lying before a fireplace on a bed made of rough quilts. The fire was crackling, and Brodie had found enough food to make a stew. He held Clay up, and Clay put a spoonful of it in his mouth. He looked up and tried to grin. "We're going to make it, Brodie."

"Sure we are, Clay. You and me, we'll get home fine."

The table was crowded, and as Jerusalem moved around putting plates of vegetables on the table, her eyes went over the group. Fergus was there, and Zane had come along. She sat down beside Moriah, Clinton, and Mary Aidan and waited until Rhys Morgan asked the blessing.

No one spoke much, except Zane, who was doing most of the talking. "I heard Santa Anna broke up his army into different pieces. That'll be good news for Sam Houston. At least now he won't have to fight the whole bunch at once."

Fergus was wearing a fine white shirt and a gray flannel coat. He always dressed as if he were going to Buckingham Palace to dine with the queen, and now he nodded. "That's a stupid sort of thing to do, but good for Houston. If this army we hear he's collecting has a chance to win, it'll have to be against a part of Santa Anna's army."

"Well, the word is that he's divided them into five divisions, and he's given one division the order to burn every town and plantation in their way."

"I think he intends to start a panic to drive the colonists across the U.S. frontier," Rhys said.

"Well, he'd be pretty successful, the way our neighbors have been running for cover." Zane looked over at Jerusalem and seemed to hesitate, then he said, "Maybe we ought to go too."

"I'm not leaving this place, Zane," Jerusalem said quietly. Ever since the news had come of the Goliad massacre, she had been very quiet.

The whole countryside had hummed with the grim news of the atrocity. And the effect of it had been exactly what Mateo had warned Santa Anna about. The fury of the Texans was ignited like a wildfire. As the news of the massacre spread across the entire country, the same fury and anger grew equally white hot. General Antonio López de Santa Anna had done the one thing he least suspected. He had unified the

Texans by his merciless slaughter at the Alamo. Now with the massacre of innocent men at Goliad, the Texans and their friends and relatives in the United Sates reached a boiling point.

Moriah looked at her mother. She had eaten very little, which was unusual. "I'm grieving over Pa."

The news of the Alamo had laid a pall on Clinton and Moriah. Both of them were usually noisy and talkative, but they had said almost nothing the last few days.

Jerusalem reached out and put her hand on Moriah's back. "Always think well of your pa, daughter. He died to help us."

"Everybody is saying some of the prisoners got away from Goliad," Moriah said. Her face was pale, and she stared at her mother, her eyes pleading for hope. "Do you think Brodie will be all right?"

"God can do anything," Jerusalem said calmly.

"That's exactly right," Rhys said. He was sitting next to Julie, who turned to watch him as he spoke. "I've been praying for their safety ever since we got the news."

Jerusalem looked up and said, "I asked

God to bring Brodie and Clay back to us...and He told me that He would."

Everyone's head swiveled to stare at Jerusalem. But it was the foreigner, Fergus Nightingale, who asked in an interested tone, "God really spoke to you? I wish He'd speak to me."

Jerusalem turned to face Fergus. "He spoke to me in a dream," she said quietly.

"A dream? What kind of a dream, Ma?" Clinton asked.

"I dreamed that Brodie and Clay were in some kind of a forest or woods. They were trying to get across the river, but the river was too high because of rain. They were in a wagon, but the horses couldn't get across. I was watching them, and I was crying, and I wanted to help them." Jerusalem's voice was soft, her eyes dreamy. "I was weeping with all my heart, and the Lord said to me, 'Ask what you want.' So I did."

"What did you ask, Ma?" Moriah asked, her eyes wide.

"Why, I said, 'Lord, I want you to get them across that river and bring them home safe.' And then the dream seemed to grow fuzzy, but after a while I dreamed again, and I saw

Brodie and Clay coming out of that river on the far side. They made it across the river."

"I don't know much about the meaning of dreams, but I like that one," Rhys said. "And I'm going to keep on believing."

Julie was watching Rhys, and he turned to face her. He reached over and took her hand and squeezed it. "You can believe too."

"God wouldn't hear a sinner like me," Julie said.

"Don't be foolish. God always hears sinners if they ask the right thing, and this would be a right thing."

Julie stared at him and then shook her head. "If we know what's good for us, we'd better get out of here while we still can. Santa Anna's coming."

"Might be best," Zane said quickly.

Jerusalem sat there looking at the others. She felt the same peace as she had the night in Red Wolf's camp. There was no doubt at all in her that God had given her an assurance, and she said, "Anyone who wants to leave is free to go. There are horses, wagons, buggies, but I'm going to be here when Brodie and Clay come home."

A silence fell around the table, and no one

got up to leave. Finally, Clinton nodded. "Well, it looks like we'll all stay then."

"That's right, Clinton," Julie said, her eyes meeting those of Jerusalem. Her own faith was small, but she had great faith in this sister of hers. "We'll all stay—no matter what happens."

For two days nothing happened, and late afternoon of the third day, Jerusalem was sitting on the bench Clay had made her. She had placed it out beside the three graves, and it became a place where she would go when she wanted solitude to think and pray. It reminded her of the place she had had back in Arkansas, which seemed a thousand years ago and a million miles away. As she sat there, twilight was closing about the place. The bats were beginning to flutter, when suddenly she heard a wagon coming, which was not unusual, for many had fled down this road to escape Santa Anna's approaching army. She did not get up to look, but she sat there almost forgetful of it as she prayed for her son and for Clay. She was shocked when she heard a voice,

"Ma!" Jumping to her feet, she saw Brodie leap out of the wagon and run toward her. "Brodie!" she cried and ran as fast as she could.

Brodie caught her, lifted her clear off the ground, and squeezed her so tight she could not breathe or speak.

"You're home, son, you're safe!"

"We are, but Clay's been shot. He's in bad shape."

By this time the others had heard the wagon and had come running out of the house. Everyone was babbling at the same time, asking Brodie what had happened.

Brodie shook his head. "I'll talk later. Help me get Clay out of the wagon. He's been shot, and he's had a fever for three days. I thought he was dying this morning."

"He's not going to die," Jerusalem said. "Zane, you and Rhys take him and put him on the bed in my room. I'll be right there." Jerusalem watched as the men picked Clay up. When she saw him unconscious and helpless, her heart seemed to stop. He had always been so strong and so filled with the joy of living, and now his face was pale as paper.

"What happened, son?" she asked.

Brodie shook his head. "It was Mateo. He got us away when the Mexicans started to execute everyone that had surrended at Goliad. Tim and Clyde got killed, though. But me and Clay made it. He took a bullet as we were running away. I got this wagon and made a bed for him, but the rivers were up. We forded all of them except the Colorado. We just couldn't get across."

The details of Jerusalem's dream became very plain to her then.

"Tell me all about it," she said.

"Well, Ma, I never saw nothin' like it," Brodie said. His face was filled with wonder. "I tried to get the horses across, but they just wouldn't go. It was too risky. The strong current would have swept us down. So I didn't know what to do. Clay was gettin' sicker all the time. Finally it just seemed the right thing to do was to head South, and I did. And, Ma, we got to a place that was a cutoff, and I just knew that we were gonna get across. And we did. The river was broader there, and it wasn't as deep as upstream. We just come right across, Ma. I drove across with no trouble."

Jerusalem's eyes filled with tears, and

she grabbed Brodie and hugged him. "It was the Lord doing a miracle."

"I reckon it was, Ma. But it's gonna take another miracle to get Clay well."

"God's not going to let him die. He wouldn't do a thing like that."

When Clay woke up it was not all at once. He opened his eyes, started, and for a moment had trouble focusing. Then the features of the woman above him swam into focus, and he croaked in a voice not much like his own. "Well, hello, Jerusalem Ann."

"Clay, you're better now."

Clay felt her hand on his forehead and saw the relief in her face.

"Your fever is all gone. Your eyes are clear. How do you feel?"

"Like I was dragged through a knothole and hit in the face with a wet squirrel."

"You've got to eat something to get your strength back."

"Reckon I could."

"You lie right here. Don't go back to sleep. I'm going to bring you some food."

Clay lay on the bed and looked around

after Jerusalem disappeared. He realized he was in her bed. Most of what had happened since the massacre at Goliad was blotted out of his memory. He could remember bits and pieces of Brodie talking to him and begging him not to die, and he remembered crossing a river. But after that, nothing.

Jerusalem came back soon with a bowl of soup. She said, "You're going to have to sit up. It may hurt."

To his astonishment Clay found he was too weak to do very much. Jerusalem simply reached down, pulled him up, and put pillows behind him. "Makes me feel like a baby," he murmured.

"You be quiet and eat."

Clay accepted the spoon and swallowed a spoonful of the soup. As he began to eat, he found he was as hungry as a bear coming out of hibernation in the spring. He ate all of the soup, and when Jerusalem gave him a glass of water, he held it with both hands and gulped it down. When he gave her the glass back, he said, "I'm right sorry about Jake, Jerusalem Ann."

Jerusalem sat down beside him, took his hand, and brushed a lock of hair away from his forehead. "He was a good man in some ways," she said simply.

Somehow the words sounded like a benediction or a eulogy to Clay. It was as if Jerusalem had closed the door on that part of her life. He looked at her for a long time in silence, then said, "For a time there, I didn't think I was going to make it, but Brodie brought me back." He smiled then and shook his head. "Ain't that just like me, Jerusalem Ann? I go out to save somebody, and he has to pull me out of the fire."

Jerusalem put her hand on his chest, and leaning forward, she whispered, "Sleep, Clay. You're worn out. You need your rest to get your strength back."

"Guess I am. Don't reckon I'll ever—"

Clay did not finish his speech, and Jerusalem took his hand and held it to her cheek. She stayed there for a long time, watching his breathing, which was slow and even, and she saw the fresh color in his cheeks, which the food had brought. "Thank you, Lord, for bringing them both home."

★ ★ ★

Serena opened the door and gasped. "Brodie!" she screamed and then threw her arms around him. She cried out, "Mama, Brodie's home!"

Brodie was shocked by the embrace. He put his arms around her and squeezed her. Serena stepped back as Lucita came into the room, her eyes bright as she cried out Brodie's name. The two hugged then, and Brodie said, "I reckon I could get used to this."

"You come and sit down and tell us everything," Serena said. "But first I'm sorry about the way I acted, Brodie. I'm not going to marry old man Watkins."

"You sure would have saved me a passel of trouble if you had told me that," Brodie said, but he was grinning. He sat down and ate the food they pressed upon him, and in between bites he told them the story of the battles. When he got to the part that Mateo played, he looked at them and said, "He saved me and Clay. Ain't no other way to look at it. Me and Clay would be dead if it wasn't for Mateo."

Lucita's eyes filled with tears. "He's a good boy. I'm sorry that you two are on different sides."

"Well, maybe that'll change," Brodie said, but he knew that it would not.

Later on, when he had to leave and go back to see how Clay was, Serena followed him out to his horse. Before he got on, she said again, "I'm real sorry that I teased you, Brodie."

He put his arms around her and kissed her awkwardly.

Serena submitted to his caress and then slapped him on the chest. "You're not much at kissing, are you, Brodie Hardin?"

Brodie suddenly grinned and felt very good indeed. "Well, I need more practice. I'll be back to see about that."

Clay came into the kitchen just as the family was eating breakfast. Jerusalem was fixing his meal to take to him, as she had since he had returned, and she said, "You get back in bed! I'm going to hide your pants!"

"No you're not. I'm gonna stay up and keep my britches on."

Rhys suddenly laughed. "I think I'll get myself shot, Clay, so I can be waited on like you."

Clay winked at the preacher and said, "I guess I've milked about all the sympathy I can out of this little scratch." Still he was pale and shaky, and as he sat down, Jerusalem fussed over him and fixed his plate.

"You're going to be among the land of the living, I see," Fergus said.

"I didn't think so for a while. Any news about the war?"

"Well, Houston is running, and everybody is screaming bloody murder," Zane said.

"He'd better run," Fergus said quickly. "He's got an army, but it's not trained—not to meet regulars."

"I'm going to go join up with them," Clinton said abruptly.

"You hush, Clinton," Julie said. "We just got Clay and Brodie home. Now you behave yourself."

"Well, you might as well start on me, Julie. I'm leavin' today to go join up with Houston."

Everyone turned to stare at Rhys, who had spoken these words quietly. They were all shocked. Nobody would have been surprised if Zane had said such a thing, but now Julie said quickly, "Why, Rhys?"

"Well," Rhys said slowly, "it comes down to this. I love Texas. I want to spend the rest of my life here." He glanced at Julie and grinned. "I'm gonna find me a woman and have me a dozen kids. But I feel I've got to earn that right."

"I feel the same way," Brodie said.

Zane at once shook his head. "You stay out of it, Brodie. You nearly got killed already."

"I can't do that, Zane. If I'm gonna make Texas my home, then I figure I better be willin' to fight for its freedom," Brodie said.

"You got a point there, son," Fergus said as he looked across the table at Julie.

The men continued to talk about the Alamo and what had happened at Goliad. Julie said nothing during the rest of the meal, but she couldn't keep her eyes off Rhys as he talked. Afterwards she went outside to find Rhys, who had gone out to brush his horse. He turned to her and saw that she was serious

"I don't want you to go, Rhys," she said.

"Well, I think it's something I have to do." He could tell she was troubled, and reaching out, he took her hand. He suddenly lifted it to his lips and kissed it. He saw the surprise in her eyes and said, "Don't worry about me. I'll be all right."

"You can't know that."

"Well, I'll have to go anyway. There are times when a man has to do some things. To back away from them would be wrong."

"Please don't go, Rhys!" she pleaded.

At that moment Rhys saw again the woman that was hidden under the hard exterior of Julie Satterfield. She was a common enough woman in many ways, a sinner, and he well knew it. But God had opened his eyes and given him discernment. He took her hand again and said, "I see in you a good and wonderful woman. God is after you, Julie, and you're going to meet face-to-face with Jesus one day. After that, all the beauty that's on the inside of you that I see, everyone will be able to see on the outside."

Julie stared at him. She could not understand how anyone could see any good in her, for she had been rebellious all of her life. Somehow his words touched her deeply, and she reached up and put her arms around him and clung to him as if she were a small child. She felt a wave of innocence that she had not known for years, and finally, when she lifted her tear-stained face to him, she pulled his head down and kissed him on the lips briefly. Then she whispered, "Oh, Rhys, be careful—oh, be careful!"

Jerusalem had seen Clay go out to her cemetery. He was sitting on her bench and had been there for the past hour. She knew he wanted to be alone, but finally curiosity got the better of her. She went out and sat down beside him. "What are you doing, Clay?"

Clay motioned toward the marker that he had made for Julie's grandfather. He read the name, "Josiah Mitchell. Born 1748," and then turned to face her. "I been thinkin' about your grandpa."

"You're going to join with Houston, aren't you, Clay?"

Clay blinked. "How'd you know that?"

"I know you pretty well, Clay Taliferro."

Clay stared at her and then shook his head. "Beats me how a woman can figure out what's goin' on in a man's mind. Well, I been thinkin' about how your grandfather fought back in the Revolution. He told me lots of times how hard it was, but once he said, 'If I hadn't done it, I would have felt less than a man.' I been thinkin' about it ever since he said that, and now it looks like it's time for me to fight too. I been kind of a wanderer doin' what I please most of my life, but now this is different. I've got to be a part of this Texas, and this is the way to do it."

Jerusalem studied his face. "I love this land, Clay, and it's going to be free soon. I can feel it. Men like you and Houston and Brodie and Rhys and others like you are going to make it that way. It'll be a good land for children to grow up in and for people to grow old in. More and more I keep singing that song of yours, especially the chorus:

> Deep in the heart!
> O deep in the heart!
> Naught can be lost
> That's deep in the heart!

"That's what this land has found...this Texas—a place deep in my heart."

Clay did not answer, and for a time they sat there listening to the sounds of the evening. Finally, Jerusalem said, "Let's walk to the river. You feel up to it?"

"Of course I do. You think I'm a baby?"

The two walked slowly along the path until they reached the river. They stood there quietly watching the river flow by, making its sibilant whisper. A kingfisher dove into the water, came up with a silver fish, and then flew off to disappear downstream.

Jerusalem suddenly turned, and Clay turned to meet her. She was wearing an odd half smile.

"What are you laughing about, Jerusalem Ann?"

"I was just thinkin'. You don't know much about women, Clay. I think you're afraid of them."

"Afraid of them! Why, shoot no! I'm just *careful* around them. They can be dangerous, you know. Kind of like a bear. Most of the time bears will leave you alone if you don't mess with 'em, but then sometimes for no reason they come chargin' in and try to tear your head off. I think women are kind of like that. You never know what a woman will do."

Jerusalem's smile broadened. "So, women are like bears."

"Well, they're a little bit better lookin', I reckon."

Jerusalem looked at Clay oddly. "You know, Clay. I haven't kissed any man except Jake for twenty years. You know what I'm wondering right now?"

"Well, no I don't. I can't read your mind like you read mine."

"I'm wondering what it would be like to kiss another man."

Clay stared at her and cleared his throat. "I reckon you'll find out when men come courtin' you now that you're a widow."

Jerusalem said huskily, "Maybe I don't want to wait that long, Clay."

Clay suddenly reached out and hugged Jerusalem. He gave her a kiss, almost missing her mouth, and then stepped back awkwardly.

"You call that a kiss!" Jerusalem exclaimed. "That was pitiful!" She reached out, put her arms around Clay, and pulled his head forward.

At that moment, as her lips were pressed against his, Clay sensed the longings for love this woman had and knew the power she had over him. He was not a man to think of such things a great deal, but now he knew she had a way of stirring deep feelings in him he had not known he possessed. He held her tight until finally she released him.

She stared at him, waiting for him to speak. When he did not say anything, she said, "Well?" in a demanding tone. "What do you think of that?"

"I reckon I don't know. You get a man all confused. I'm a little bit out of practice for that sort of thing."

Jerusalem suddenly laughed. It was a deep laugh and full of joy. "Maybe you'll get a little bit bolder after a while." She saw his expression change and laughed again, then took his arm in hers and said, "Let's go back to the house." As they walked back up the path, she said, "I want you to pay me a compliment, Clay. Say something nice about me as we walk."

Clay thought for a moment and then said, "Well, your elbows ain't ugly like most women's are."

Jerusalem gasped and shook his arm. "You call that a compliment!"

"Why, sure. I mean most women have got ugly elbows all rough and red. The first thing I ever noticed about you, Jerusalem Ann, was your elbows were all nice and smooth and plump."

"Well, Clay Taliferro, what a beautiful compliment," laughed Jerusalem. "Tell me more about my elbows."

As the two walked back toward the house, the sound of Jerusalem's laughter echoed through the trees. Above, the huge silver disc called the Comanche Moon flooded the pathway. A large bobcat with tufted ears and green eyes watched them pass. Then deciding they were harmless, he licked his forepaw and then leaped to the ground and padded away into the warm silence of the Texas night.

THE LONE STAR LEGACY
CONTINUES WITH BOOK 2
THE YELLOW ROSE

The State of Texas and Jerusalem Ann Hardin are in the thick of battle—the battle to leave a legacy. Sam Houston and the Texas army can finally see a glimpse of freedom as the bloody battle of San Jacinto loosens the hold Mexico has on Texas lands. And in honor of Jake Hardin's sacrifice in the fight for Texas' freedom at the Alamo, Jerusalem Ann decides to leave her own legacy in Texas by establishing a cattle ranch.

Both Sam Houston and the Hardin family struggle to make freedom and prosperity a secure reality. Texas fights for statehood in the Union, and Jerusalem Ann battles cattle thieves, raiding parties and her feelings for Clay Taliffero. Her real test comes when her daughter is kidnapped by the worst of Comanches—Gray Wolf.

In the end, Jerusalem Ann and her family are rewarded for their faith, as are all Texans as they secure their freedom and home as part of the Union.

The Yellow Rose is a moving follow-up to *Deep in the Heart.* As The Lone Star Legacy continues, readers will feel the pull of the Wild West as its stories and rich characters tug on their heart strings.